Praise

"One of the premier _____ ___!"
Gena Showalter deli_____
—Kresley Cole, #_____ ___hor

"Gena Showalter never fails to dazzle."
—Jeaniene Frost, *New York Times* bestselling author

"Showalter...rocks me every time!"
—Sylvia Day, #1 *New York Times* bestselling author

"Showalter writes fun, sexy characters you fall in love with!"
—Lori Foster, *New York Times* bestselling author

"Showalter makes romance sizzle on every page!"
—Jill Shalvis, *New York Times* bestselling author

"A fascinating premise, a sexy hero and non-stop action, *The Darkest Night* is Showalter at her finest."
—Karen Marie Moning,
New York Times bestselling author

"[A] spell-binding love story that will stop the heart of every reader."
—*Redbook* on *The Darkest Promise*

"The Showalter name on a book means guaranteed entertainment."
—*RT Book Reviews*

"Gena Showalter is a romantic genius."
—*San Francisco Book Review*

GENA SHOWALTER

The Darkest
PROMISE

HQN™

HQN™

ISBN-13: 978-1-335-05093-9

The Darkest Promise

Copyright © 2017 by Gena Showalter

Recycling programs
for this product may
not exist in your area.

CONTENTS

To Jill Monroe—Best friend, confidante,
idea bouncer-offer!

To Naomi at French n Bookish—A treasure!

To Denise Thompson—A sister of the heart!
Thank you for being you!

To Shane Tolbert, Shonna Hurt and Michelle Quine—
My biggest cheerleaders!

To Crystal Lepinski, Penny Beerling,
Sananda Davalillo, Sarah Hutchinson,
Sarah McAdorey and Jennifer Forist—For helping me
name a character (in this book and perhaps books
to come).

The Darkest
PROMISE

Underworld Abridged Dictionary, 6th Edition

Misery. Mis·er·y. MIZ(ə)rē/.

Definition: The demon High Lord of Misery ensures his immortal host remains in a constant state of mental, emotional and physical anguish; through his host, he is able to harm others.

Example: The demon flooded Cameo with sorrow, and when she cried out, her misery-soaked voice broke the heart of everyone around her.

Symptoms: Angst, anxiety, chronic RBF—resting bitch face—dejection, depression, desolation, despair, despondency, distress, gloom, grief, heartache, heartbreak, melancholy, pain, sadness, sorrow, stress, suffering, torment, unhappiness, woe, wretchedness.

Cure: Death (not currently doctor recommended).

1

"Don't try to stay ten moves ahead of your opponent. Stay behind him with a knife."
— Excerpted from *Becoming the King You Are Meant to Be*, a work in progress by Lazarus the Cruel and Unusual

Like Alice on her way to Wonderland, Cameo, host to the demon of Misery, tumbled end over end down a long, dark cavern. When the bottom finally appeared, she braced for impact...only to slip through a glistening portal. A second later, the cavern walls vanished, and she spilled from a midnight sky—straight into a new realm.

Never should have touched the Paring Rod. But noooo. She just had to ignore common sense and brush her fingertips against the pretty glass bulb that tipped its handle. The ancient artifact had then opened a door between the physical and spirit world, and voilà! In a blink, her descent had begun.

Now she plunged toward a flat clearing, and this time, there would be no reprieve...

Like a missile that had finally reached its target, Cameo slammed into the ground, her insides exploding. A scream split her lips, her brain banging against her skull, her lungs emptying and multiple bones shattering all at once.

Agony seared her, black dots weaving through her vision. Warmth drained from her hands and feet, collecting in her torso. Her body was in shock.

Hours—days?—passed before she gained the strength to roll to her side. Her wrecked heart tap-danced a wild rhythm against broken ribs, and her head swam. Gradually, her pain ebbed. Able to breathe again, she noted the sweet scent of ambrosia hung heavy in the air. She almost laughed. Ambrosia was the drug of choice for immortals, the only substance capable of causing true intoxication. For once, lady luck had been on Cameo's side. If you had to crash-land, what better place than this?

She drifted in and out of consciousness, the passage of time evidenced by the healing of her injuries and the shift from dark to light. At some point, she became aware of a laser beam of heat blistering her pale skin, and finally woke for good.

Her nose crinkled as she inhaled. The scent of ambrosia had been replaced by burnt foliage. Where had she landed? Hell? The sun blazed so hot it had scorched sections of land.

Cameo crawled into a shadowed haven, exhaling with relief when her skin cooled. She scanned the lavender sky with its pale green clouds, then looked over an unfamiliar forest filled with towering pink trees and plots of azure grass.

Oookay. This is new. A forest fit for a storybook princess. Too bad Cameo was the villain of the tale. *Browniebitch and the Twelve Immortals.* For her and her family of demon-possessed warriors, nothing had ever been *just right*.

Cold fingers of dread crept down her spine as a butterfly the size of her fist fluttered past her. Over the centuries, the wretched insects had become an omen. *Death and destruction await...*

The heavy weight of depression settled on her shoulders, and she wallowed about the travesty of her life.

Lost so much already. All because she'd made one teeny tiny mistake when she'd lived in Mount Olympus.

That mistake? Helping her friends steal and open Pandora's box. An appropriate punishment would have been a hand amputation or two. Maybe a few hundred years in the slammer. Instead, she was forced to play host to the demon of Misery for eternity, free will a thing of the past.

To commemorate the occasion, a butterfly tattoo had appeared on her lower back.

The beginning of the end.

Misery had quickly peeled away the layers of her humanity, hope and happiness. Again and again he'd wiped her mind of any joyous memories.

The bastard *still* wiped her mind of any joyous memories. Every day he breathed his poison into her thoughts, hurt others through her voice and ruined whatever relationships she managed to forge. He'd reduced her life to one horror after another.

If only she could control him. But Misery was a separate entity with his own motivations and goals. A dark presence she'd never been able to drown out. A prison she had never been able to escape.

Right now, he's not my biggest problem. The butterfly...

Disaster was imminent.

Cameo searched for a way out of the forest. At one side, a breathtaking river with rainbow-colored water trickled into a rocky crag. Some type of fish broke the surface. A water unicorn? A long, ivory horn stretched from between his eyes and—

She gasped. Another water unicorn had jumped up and thrust his horn into the belly of the first. Blood spurted, creating a crimson waterfall. Countless other fish converged on the injured one, sharp teeth ripping into scales and organs until not even bones remained.

Mental note: *no baths in the wild, ever.*

At her other side, a field of ambrosia flourished, unaffected by the over-hot sun. Thick emerald stalks dripped with countless violet flowers, the petals drawn together to avoid the worst of the heat.

The field might be her only viable—

A thorny limb snatched the jumbo-size butterfly from the air. Her ears twitched, the soft breeze carrying the faint sounds of screaming.

Viable path or not, it was time to go.

Cameo lumbered to shaky legs, wincing as twigs sliced her heel. Her brow wrinkled. Her feet were bare, her combat boots gone.

Someone had stolen her shoes?

A quick scan proved her tank top and battle leathers were torn and stained with dried blood, but still in place. However, the daggers she'd made over two hundred years ago were missing.

Someone had robbed her while she'd drifted out of consciousness.

Someone would pay!

This villain had come here to find a formidable immortal named Lazarus the Cruel and Unusual, and she would destroy *anyone* who hindered her.

According to her friends, she had interacted with Lazarus twice before. Thanks to Misery, she remembered nothing about either encounter. Or did she? On the fringe of her mind was a suggestive montage of images that might or might not have happened.

Flicker: Cameo performed a striptease for a faceless, muscled man, a sultry half smile playing at the corners of her mouth, her silvery eyes smoky with desire.

Flicker: Cameo crawled toward the same faceless, muscled man, clearly intent on his seduction.

Flicker: Cameo sprawled beneath the faceless, muscled man, one of his big, callused hands on her breast, the other between her legs as he drove her closer and closer to orgasm. Her spine was arched, her head thrown back, her expression taut with a sublime mix of agony and pleasure.

Was the faceless man Lazarus? How had he tempted her into his bed?

She wanted so badly to remember.

Sex wasn't something she enjoyed or usually even risked. Not anymore. She had a Sexually Transmitted Demon, and almost everyone she dated ended up depressed at some point.

Guilt flared, adding to her all-consuming misery. And yet...

Every time she imagined her faceless lover, languid heat wrapped loving arms around her. Blood rushed through her veins with new purpose, molten shivers cascading through her, every inch of her tingling.

Did he miss her? Or did he rejoice, thinking he would never see her again?

Her heart seemed to crack open and seep acid. Memories were as necessary for survival as oxygen or water; without hers, she was incomplete. Weakened, even.

Would Lazarus tell her what had happened between them? If there was even a chance, she had to find him.

Problem was, she and the rest of the world knew very little about him. His past was shrouded in mystery. What she had managed to glean: her friend Strider, the keeper of Defeat, had beheaded him not too long ago. Lazarus's spirit had traveled through the Paring Rod and entered one of thousands of realms in the afterlife. Perhaps *this* one, a strange and predatory world.

Soon after Lazarus's death, her semi-friend Viola, the keeper of Narcissism, had accidentally followed him through—while still alive. Also alive, Cameo had followed *her*, intent on rescuing her.

Cue her adventures with the mysterious warrior.

If her brothers-by-circumstance hadn't launched a rescue mission of their own, would she have chosen to stay with Lazarus?

Going by the tidbits she'd revealed before Misery had cleaned her mind with mental Windex, she and Lazarus had partnered up to find Viola and Pandora's box—aka dimOuniak—both supposedly hidden inside one of the realms.

Why he'd agreed to partner with her when he had no stake in the outcome, she wasn't sure.

Unless he wanted the box? DimOuniak was just as powerful as the Paring Rod—no, more so—and could be used to instantly kill anyone, everyone, who was demon possessed. Or so rumors claimed.

Had Lazarus planned to harm her all along?

See? Loss of memory left her vulnerable in the worst of ways.

So. She would find Lazarus. Hopefully he liked her and wanted only to help her. After he filled in her mental blanks, maybe they could renew their quest for the box and he could make her happy? At least for a little while. What good was a life without happiness?

Going to forget him again. Why bother?

Because…just because! A girl without hope might as well curl up and die.

Maybe he was her faceless lover. Maybe he would help her find Viola as well as the box. The goddess of the Afterlife had been rescued, yes, but she'd purposely used the Paring Rod a second time. No one knew why, and no one had heard from her since.

Resolute, Cameo motored forward. Twigs sliced her feet, but she maintained a steady pace, maneuvering through the thicket of trees. At least the temperature had cooled.

Seventy-two percent of men have cheated on their significant other. The demon's voice whispered through her mind in an attempt to immobilize her. *Twenty-four percent are actively cheating right this second. Forty-eight percent are smug rather than remorseful. How long do you think you'll intrigue Lazarus? If you ever intrigued him at all.*

Horrid demon! Always lobbing H-bombs of gloom. Was Lazarus her faceless lover or not?

Misery smoothly added, *If he is, you should run. Considering what happened with Alex...*

"Shut up," she muttered, but the damage was done. He'd hit his target, reopening internal wounds.

Alex, a human who had lived in ancient Greece, had been her first and only love.

At the age of eight, a terrible sickness had rendered him deaf and, apparently, unworthy of his wealthy family's love. He was cast out of the only home he'd ever known. After months of starvation, a "protector" saved him from the slums. A blacksmith with a sickening taste for children.

Apprentice by day, slave by night. A heartbreaking existence.

When Alex reached his teens, the blacksmith dubbed him too old and kicked him out. Alex snapped, introducing the blacksmith's heart to his handmade dagger. Then he claimed the business as his due.

He poured his time and energy into metalwork, his talent indisputable. He'd been the only person Cameo trusted to make her weapons. The only male unaffected by the sorrow in her voice.

They fell in love, and for just a little while, she had verged on the edge of happiness. She'd craved more... but all the while, a shadow of foreboding had cloaked her like a second skin.

With every new dawn, she'd wondered why she remembered him. Why the demon hadn't yet stolen her memory of him.

The answer had proved more atrocious than she'd ever dreamed.

In a vulnerable moment, she'd told Alex about her demonic companion. He'd decided she was worse than the blacksmith and arranged for Hunters, a cult of self-appointed slayers of immortals, to capture and torture her in the worst of ways.

Razor-winged butterflies took flight in her stomach. Did Lazarus know the truth about her? Did he care?

He must know. He was an immortal living among other immortal spirits. And he shouldn't care. He was called *cruel* and *unusual*. He had a dark side of his own. *Very* dark. Pitch-black without any hint of light.

A sequence of high-pitched squawks rang out as a flock of birds leaped from treetops and scattered across the skyline, soon vanishing behind a wall of clouds.

Whoosh! Thud!

The ground shook. Cameo tumbled to her knees. Wheezing, fighting for oxygen, she reached for her daggers. Her *missing* daggers.

Cursing, she darted behind one of the bigger pink trees, shadows enveloping her. Adrenaline surged, strong and sure, but it couldn't mask the sting of bark scraping through her shirt.

Another *whoosh*. Another *thud*. The shaking only worsened, trees toppling, the surrounding shrubs falling like dominoes.

Across the distance, a path cleared, and two flying beasts appeared. Some sort of dragon hybrid, maybe? They had red eyes, elongated snouts and teeth better qualified as short swords. Their bodies were long and coiled, but without arms or legs while their tails were thrice barbed. Resplendent scales reflected in the sunlight.

So...the two were flying snakes? *Dragon* snakes?

They soared above the remaining canopy of trees, their multipointed wings clipping branches and slicing through bark as if it were butter. One creature pursued the other. When he caught his prey, the two wrestled... playfully?

"Does the pretty miss require aid?"

The unfamiliar voice somehow turned the innocent question into a sexual promise. She glanced up—and had to swallow a yelp. A two-hundred-plus pound leopard perched on the limb directly above her, his neon-green eyes steady on her. His mangled tail wagged back and forth. One of his ears looked as if it had been chewed off, and his matted fur sported several bald patches.

Misery took an instant dislike to the animal and snarled.

The cat offered her a slow, toothy grin and batted a meaty paw at a fly. He actually speared the insect on the end of a claw. "I'm Rathbone, and I'm at your service... for a small fee."

He could talk. He was a cat, and he could talk. And with that voice, he could make millions as a phone sex operator.

Had the Paring Rod transported her into a fairy tale, after all? The porn version? *Browniebitch Does Twelve Immortals*.

Was Rathbone a shape-shifter? No, impossible. Shape-shifters didn't retain the ability to speak while in animal form. Although there were exceptions to every rule, right?

"I can save myself, but thanks for the offer." Having lived over four millennia, she'd waged world wars, fought countless battles against immortal predators, humans with a grudge and monsters of myth and legend. Sometimes she'd lost, but mostly she'd won.

The leopard flinched. Hardly a surprise. Everyone always flinched. Some even cried.

She could have used sign language. She'd had to learn in order to communicate with her friend Amun, who hosted the demon of Secrets. But the majority of immortals—and uh, animals—she encountered could not understand ASL. Besides, she had a voice, and deep down she wanted to be heard.

The dragon-snakes resumed their chase, nearly causing a full-blown earthquake this time, and she grabbed a branch to steady herself. Nope, not a branch, but Rathbone's tail.

He wiggled his brows. "I've got something *firmer* you can hold on to."

Surely he wasn't referring to his…

He contorted to lick a massive set of balls.

You've got to be kidding me.

She released him and peeked around the trunk. The creatures approached at breakneck speed…only to pass her. She began to relax. A mistake. Of course. When had anything ever gone her way? Both dragon-snakes came to an abrupt stop before slowly pivoting.

Two sets of red eyes locked on her. Long, thin tongues swiped over saber-teeth, and drool dripped from the corners of their mouths. Drool…or accelerant? The pungent stench of something akin to gasoline stung her nostrils.

Well. She'd just been placed on the day's menu.

In unison, the "chefs" hissed and bowed their spines, the scales around their necks flaring.

You have an eighty-seven percent chance of being deep-fried, never seeing your friends again and never finding Lazarus or the box.

No. She would fight, and she would win. If she died, Misery would be loosed upon an unsuspecting world; he would find new prey, devour sweet dreams, beloved hopes and any glimmer of happiness. He—

Had merely distracted her, the bastard.

Dual streams of fire spewed in her direction. Attuned to battle now, Cameo dived out of the way. Upon landing, she rolled and swiped up two petrified branches. As she stood, she swung at the nearer beast.

"I wouldn't do that if I were you," Rathbone began, reminding her of his presence. The pointed tips moved across her opponent's chest, and the cat sighed. "Congrats. You just made everything worse."

Argh! The branches hadn't penetrated a single scale. In fact, the branches hadn't *scratched* a single scale.

Enraged now, the dragon-snake roared.

All right. Their scales were impenetrable. Got it. Only two other options remained. Go for the eyes or go for the mouth. Easy, not a problem, if she could hop aboard the dragon-snake express and hitch a ride.

"Ssss."

"Ssss."

Two new streams of fire spewed in her direction, the heat level jacked to instant BBQ with a side of ash. Again she scrambled out of the way, but really, she had nowhere to go. The beasts circled her, working in tandem to trap her inside a ringed inferno. Smoke thickened the air.

A tickle irritated the back of her throat, making her cough—at the same time, a wing arced in her direction. She managed to jump backward, barely avoiding being sliced in two.

"Want my help now?" Rathbone remained secure on

his perch, his smile as innocuous as a fistful of daisies. "I'll give you a discounted rate."

Ignoring him, she sprinted across the white-hot path of soot and char. As another wing swung at her, she used the branches she still held to bat it out of the way. Momentum spun her around, and she dodged another stream of fire. Next, a barbed tail lashed at her, but she jumped over it and motored on, increasing her pace. Almost within range…

There's no way you'll succeed, the demon told her, his sadness seeping into her. *You're going to die.*

No! She would win, and she would live. She would!

The moment of truth arrived.

Her heartbeat a wild thing her ribs might not be able to cage, she vaulted up, up. One dragon-snake vaulted with her—or rather, *at* her—clearly intending to snag her midair. The closer he came, the more he snapped his teeth at her. *His* mistake. She shoved a branch into his mouth.

The limb—as thick as her biceps, the length of her forearm and harder than stone—remained vertical, one end digging into the roof of his mouth, the other pinning his tongue to the bottom. Meanwhile, Cameo tightened her grip on the branch's center, swung around and straddled his neck.

He thrashed, the jerky movements impeding the glide of his wings, sending him plummeting back to earth.

Yee-haw!

Just before her second crash landing of the day, she jabbed the second branch into his eye. He screeched as thick black blood splattered over her hand and blistered her skin.

Boom!

The dragon-snake absorbed the worst of the impact, Cameo bouncing off him. As he screeched and thrashed, she lumbered to her feet, intending to run. Sharp agony seared her ankle when a hard yank dropped her flat on her face and wrenched her backward.

Her nails left grooves in the dirt. Trying not to panic, she glanced over her shoulder. Nooo! The other dragon-snake had snagged her foot between his teeth.

He began to *chew*, saliva penetrating her wound. A scream burst from her as her entire leg burned and blistered. She curled into a ball to make herself less of a target. At the same time, she swung a branch at him.

Argh! She'd dropped the branches, and hit him with nothing but air.

He dragged her over rocks and gargantuan roots, ripping her shirt. Her flesh, too. Her head swam again, oblivion beckoning. She reached for another branch, any branch. There!

He straightened, lifting her off the ground foot-first. Dangling upside down only magnified her pain.

Remember, pain is weakness leaving the body.

She could do this. No, she *would* do this.

Cameo contorted and strained her body in order to swing forward…back…forward again, faster and faster, coming closer and closer to her enemy's torso.

He flapped his wings as he soared higher into the sky—and provided a new lesson about pain.

Not sure how much more I can take.

Sweat drenched her and nausea boiled in her stomach, but still she continued swinging. Finally, blessedly, she was able to thrust the branch through the underside of his jaw, where no scales protected him, the end slamming into the back of his throat.

He jerked and roared, releasing her. Down, down she fell. She braced—her lungs emptied once again, the chambers in her bursting like a balloon.

Her pain was so strong, so shrill she could almost understand a man's suffering when he had a cold.

She remained sprawled across the ground, praying for a quick recovery. Or death. Yeah, probably death. Her mutilated ankle throbbed in time to her distorted heartbeat as the organ regenerated. From her kneecap to her toes, she felt as if her skin had been baked like cheese on a pizza.

Though the dragon-snake tried, he failed to remove the branch; his wings refused to bend as needed. In the end, he could only return to his companion, drill his fangs into the beast's chest and fly them both away.

She'd...done it? She'd won?

You'll probably never walk again, Misery told her.

Wah, wah, wah.

"I'll walk again," she grated. Over the centuries, she'd had limbs severed and her tongue cut out. Her ankle would heal...eventually. The demon only sought to depress her.

Rathbone prowled from the tree and sashayed toward her. "Ask nicely, and I'll let you ride me free of charge."

"No, thanks." Too fatigued to care if he hoped to lure her into a false state of calm simply to attack her, she said, "Where are we?"

His flinch was more pronounced this time. "We're in the Realm of Grimm and Fantica, ruled by King Lazarus the Cruel and Unusual, the only son of the Monster."

Lazarus. *Her* Lazarus. He was here. And he was king.

Go ahead. Find him. I want *you to spend time with the male known as the Cruel and Unusual.* Misery laughed his most vindictive laugh. *I bet he hurts you in ways I've never managed.*

The demon lied. Or maybe he'd spoken true. With him, she never knew what to believe.

Maybe she should return to Budapest.

Did Lazarus even miss her? she wondered again. What if they'd parted as adversaries?

Well, so what if they had? Everyone deserved a second chance. Besides, she had no idea *how* to return. And really, what did his "Cruel and Unusual" moniker matter? Many immortals referred to her as the Mother of Melancholy. Names were just that—names.

"Where is the king?" she asked, her bland tone maybe, hopefully, masking her eagerness. Reveal nothing, hide everything.

The leopard traced his tongue over his lips, as if he'd just spotted breakfast. "Do I detect *excitement*?"

Ugh. Was he planning to charge her for info if he did? "You'd be the first to do so." How true. And how sad.

"Now I detect desolation." A calculated glint appeared in his neon eyes. "The plot thickens."

"Why do my emotions matter to you, anyway?"

"Mysteries and puzzles intrigue me. Come. I'll escort you to Lazarus. However, I'm no longer willing to help for free."

Knew it.

"You will pay me a small escort fee," he said. "But be warned, my pretty. People enter his territory…and they never leave."

2

"Life is a game, and everyone you meet is an opponent."

—Becoming the King You Are Meant to Be
—The Fine Art of Decapitation

Between one second and the next, a sense of disconcertment enveloped Lazarus the Cruel and Unusual. He frowned. He wasn't unfamiliar with the sensation, but he wasn't well versed, either.

Bottom line, it could mean nothing...or everything.

With a weary sigh, he detangled from two sleeping, clinging forest nymphs and rose from the bed and fastened the pants he'd refused to remove. His legs were not for public viewing. Ever.

Anyone who had the misfortune to glimpse him bare, well, he turned the culprit into stone.

No matter where Lazarus had resided in his life or in death, he'd created a Garden of Perpetual Horror. His own personal stone army. A little like the terra-cotta armies of Qin Shi Huang, the first Emperor of China.

The newest garden currently had twenty-three statues, and they were a truly magnificent sight to behold. Each conveyed a different level of pain and panic.

His favorite? The king he'd defeated when he'd seized the Realm of Grimm and Fantica. The male was forever frozen in a position known as the blood-eagle, his body prone, his ribs cut from his spine and snapped backward to resemble wings.

Cruel and unusual. *My specialty.* Stand in the way of what Lazarus wanted, and suffer.

Cool air stroked him as he donned his shirt. He strapped on the weapons he'd discarded only an hour before. The daggers clinked together, reminding him of the day he allowed a demon-possessed warrior to behead him. The day he escaped the shackles of the sadistic Harpy who'd enslaved him.

The day his life with the dead began.

To be honest, the physical and spirit worlds remained indistinguishable to him. He still breathed, still thirsted and hungered. Still craved the touch of a woman. He could do everything he'd done before…except return to the human world. The same was true for everyone else in the realm.

In fact, there was only one difference between Lazarus and the other dead: a heart still beat inside his chest. He wasn't sure why he was the sole exception.

On the bed, the nymphs stretched and sat up. Plump breasts bounced, and tousled hair tumbled into place, sunny smiles blooming.

"If you can walk, we obviously need another go at you," the blonde said with a silky purr.

The redhead beckoned him with a crook of her finger. "How about I pretend you're a lollipop? I've got a sweet tooth…"

They had no idea he'd found nothing but disappointment in their arms.

"I have duties," he replied. Lately, no one could satisfy him. Climaxing had become a frustrating impossibility, even on his own.

At least he never had to wonder why.

He'd found his μονομανία. His obsession. Or, to be more literal, his own personal kink. Long ago his father, Typhon, had warned him about her, whoever she was.

Somewhere out there is a female capable of weakening you. You will crave her with the whole of your being…but every second in her presence will lead you closer to destruction. Kill her. Do not make my mistake and allow your μονομανία *to live. Save yourself.*

Young Lazarus had listened, rapt, for Typhon had once been the most feared immortal on Earth. With good reason. He'd murdered anyone who'd opposed, offended or questioned him.

He murdered a lot of people.

Typhon's μονομανία had been Echidna, a Gorgon. The match had most likely shocked him. Gorgons were a vicious race known for the venomous snakes that grew from their scalps and an ability to turn anyone into stone with a simple meeting of eyes. An ability Lazarus had inherited…somewhat. He created his statues through touch.

Echidna was Lazarus's mother.

For years, he believed a Harpy named Juliette had killed her. Only after his death had he realized the truth. Juliette had manipulated his memory. She could not make him love her, so she made him hate her instead.

A man did not leave the woman he longed to kill. He stuck around, determined to mete vengeance.

He ran his tongue over his teeth. He'd loved his mother. She had been Sovereign of the Sky Serpents, a clan appropriately dubbed "Sss," the sound an opponent heard just before he died bloodily. More than that, she'd been an aberration among her tribe. Kind, sweet and endearingly shy—with everyone except Typhon. She'd hated him with every fiber of her being. He'd abducted her, continually raped her and kept her from her only child.

Typhon had hated her right back, but he'd refused to let her go, his sick desire for her overpowering all else.

He'd gotten his in the end, though. Every time he'd neared her, a small portion of his flesh had crystallized. Eventually the crystallization spread to muscles and joints, limiting his range of motion, slowing and weakening him.

Hera the Cuckoldress, queen of the Greeks, had despised Typhon for reasons Lazarus had never learned. The two warred for centuries. When she'd discovered Typhon's poor condition, she'd struck at him through his wife, hacking Echidna to pieces as a helpless Typhon watched.

Hera was the one deserving of Lazarus's vengeance. Well, Hera *and* Juliette.

Hera hadn't cared that young Lazarus had witnessed the murder. That she had scarred him forevermore, destroying the one good thing in his life.

Afterward, Hera had vanished with Typhon and the warrior hadn't been seen since.

Lazarus curled his fingers around the hilt of the kris. The only dagger he refused to sheathe with leather, preferring to cover the blade with the blood of his enemies. Small barbs lined both sides; after piercing a body, they expanded into hooks, making it impossible to extract the weapon without removing a few organs, too.

One day, Hera would become intimately acquainted with the kris.

Soon after her crimes, she'd been locked inside Tartarus, the immortal prison. One day she would be free, and she would be killed, and she would end up in a spirit realm.

I will find her. His father, too. No longer a child awed by a parent, Lazarus reviled the male. Typhon had committed many crimes against his mother, but rape was a line no one should ever cross.

The pair would join the Garden of Perpetual Horror.

One of the forest nymphs leaned forward to rake her nails down Lazarus's chest. "Word has spread throughout the kingdom you seek a bride. Is this true?"

"Very." He'd found his μονομανία, yes, but soon afterward he'd lost her. Desire for her still boiled in his blood and blistered his bones, and yet he'd made no effort to find her. The last time they were together…

His chest tightened with something akin to fear. The last time they were together, she'd begun to weaken him.

He rubbed a hand against his thigh, caught the motion and inwardly cursed. Along the surface of his skin branched thin, crystallized rivers. Poisoned veins. The beginning of his downfall.

He'd collected ancient texts to research the legends about his father's familial line, hoping to find a way to save himself. A fruitless task. Anyone who'd ever developed crystal veins—if anyone ever had—had kept quiet, just like Lazarus and Typhon.

Broadcast your weaknesses today, lose your life tomorrow.

So. He would fortify his defenses, instead. He would wed a bloodthirsty woman with a large army at her disposal. She would strengthen him, never weaken him. And he would ignore his burning desire for his μονομανία all his days, lest he track her down and attempt to convince her to return to his kingdom.

His μονομανία would spell the end of him.

"Come back to bed, and I'll show you why I'm your best choice," the nymph offered with a coy smile.

Mind reading was another ability Lazarus possessed, thanks to his mother. His head filled with the other nymph's thoughts as she considered ways to kill her friend and hide the body.

"I'll show you *better*," she rasped, batting her lashes at him. "Pick me."

The females tended the roses in the Garden of Perpetual Horror. They were lovers, not fighters, and lacked the necessary malice to be his wife.

He had to be ready for war. One day Hera and his father *would* end up in the afterlife. Everyone did. So would Juliette. He would have all of his enemies in one place.

Fighting a surge of rage, he gnashed his teeth until he tasted blood. Juliette the Eradicator. A bitch without equal. She'd settled for his hate, just to keep him around—and hate her he did. Still.

"Return to your duties," he said, and the nymphs pouted.

His stride long and sure, miraculously unimpeded

by the damage his μονομανία had done, he opened his mind to search for any hidden dangers that might be awaiting him in the hall as he exited the room.

Two of his soldiers leaped from their posts to follow him.

Lazarus hadn't learned their names. He preferred to maintain emotional distance and considered affection another form of weakness.

The moment you decide to trust another being, you lose the battle.

He turned the corner and said, "Have any disturbances been reported in the village?" The sense of disconcertment remained. If someone had hurt a person under his care...

No. Wouldn't happen. No one would dare to raise a hand against one of his people. The consequences were too great. There was no trial, only punishment.

"No, sir."

"And the sky serpents?" Upon his arrival to the spirit realms, the creatures scented him, abandoned their homes and entered what was—at the time—enemy territory, determined to serve him as they'd once served his mother.

Like him, they dreamed of killing his father.

Rumors claimed Typhon slept the sleep of the dead, but the truth was more complicated. He was entombed by the same crystals now growing inside Lazarus. He wasn't dead or asleep, but immobile and aware.

"Two of your sky serpents were spotted in the forest a few miles away," a guard said. "They were playing chase."

"I wish to speak with them. I want a contingent of soldiers mounted and ready to leave in ten minutes."

Whatever the problem, he would find it. And he would end it.

"Yes, sir. Of course, sir." The speaker rushed off.

Lazarus soared inside his private bedchamber, leaving the second soldier in the hall. He stripped, showered off the scent of frustration and sex and dressed for war, donning a shirt made of thin, lightweight metal links and black leather pants. The weapons he returned to their rightful places, anchoring semiautomatics under his arms, short swords at his back and daggers at his waist and ankles.

Every piece, including the kris, bore his personal seal—a sky serpent eating its own tail, forming a never-ending circle. An outward sign of his possession and, he supposed, a sign of his station.

A king by force. A drug dealer by choice. A lover by necessity.

Ambrosia grew in the realm, and he used it to his advantage. Since the purple flowers were the only substance capable of intoxicating an immortal, he oh, so generously gifted the rulers of surrounding kingdoms with a weekly shipment, ensuring their dependence—on him.

The women he bedded kept his mind off everything he didn't have. Revenge, life…his μονομανία.

Lazarus opened a dresser drawer and traced his fingertips over the diamond knuckles and dagger pendant he'd procured for her. A wasted effort, considering he would never see her again.

He remembered the first time he'd seen her. *An immortal walks into a bar…*

Long raven hair had tumbled down an elegant back, curling at her hips. Eyes of liquid silver had peered at the world with innate sadness, and delicate features had appeared as breakable as glass.

There'd been no lightning bolt to proclaim, *Her, she's the one.* Instead, she'd intrigued and interested him. But at only five foot seven, she was too little and delicate for him. He was over seven feet and weighted down with solid muscle.

He'd thought, *With a single touch, I can damage her irreparably.*

He'd left without saying a word to her.

The second sighting occurred at the Harpy Games, a type of Olympics for the bloodthirstiest women on the planet. His μονομανία had been a spectator, perched in the stands, cheering for a friend. Once again sadness had clung to her like a second skin.

A spark of longing had heated his chest, and he'd thought, *I'd like to see her smile. No, I'd like to* make *her smile.*

A strange desire to entertain. Other people had cringed and cried anytime she'd spoken. Why had he come alive? Why had compassion roused inside him for the very first time?

Again he'd walked away without saying a word, and in the ensuing weeks his obsession with her had grown, until the mere thought of her awoke every cell in his body with lust. Even now, he hardened painfully, savage need clawing at his insides.

The third and final sighting occurred when she'd used the Paring Rod to enter the spirit realms. Then. That moment. He experienced the lightning strike of primal aggression and possession.

He'd thought, *I will have her, whatever the cost.*

Her name was Cameo, and she was the keeper of

Misery. She was an infamous Lord of the Underworld. One of thirteen warriors who'd stolen Pandora's box. Or rather, she was a glorious *Lady* of the Underworld.

A memory teased him, and he couldn't resist seeing her, even in the fabric of his mind.

"Do you ever laugh?" he'd asked her as they'd headed to his kingdom…where he'd planned to taste every inch of her…feel her wrapped around him, hear her moaning his name.

He'd burned for her. He'd ached.

"I've been told I have," she'd replied, her tragic voice as addictive as any drug.

"You don't remember?"

"No. Joy isn't something that sticks."

He'd wanted to stoke her joy as much as her passions. At the time, he hadn't cared about the tiny shards of crystal growing over his thighs. Nothing had mattered more than toppling her defenses, getting her inside his home—and him inside her.

Now he cared.

Lazarus's mind jumped to another conversation they'd had, when he'd begun to make progress with her at long last.

"Have you ever had a boyfriend?" he'd asked.

Those liquid silver eyes had filled with wry humor. The first sign of amusement she'd ever displayed, and he'd rejoiced. *I'm getting to her.* "I'm thousands of years old," she'd replied. "What do you think?"

He'd decided to tease her, knowing the expansion of her good humor would displace more of the sorrow. "I think you're a spinster virgin starving for a little man-meat."

She'd gone from wry to angry in a split second, *all*

hint of sorrow gone. "I've had several boyfriends, and I'm no virgin. And if you call me a slut, I will cut out your tongue."

"No, you won't. You want my tongue where it is. Trust me." *Please.* A woman's trust had never been so important to him. "But I'm curious. How many boyfriends?" How many men would he turn to stone for daring to touch what belonged to him?

She'd stiffened. "None of your business."

Craving another outburst of anger, hoping it would lead to passion of a different sort, he'd said, "Too many to count. Noted. What are you like in bed?"

She'd scowled, revealing her perfect white teeth, and he'd actually trembled as if he were a young lad with his first female. "You will never know."

He'd never stopped burning for Cameo. Never stopped aching. But now that they were separated by life, death and a thousand different realms, he had new perspective. He'd been a fool, allowing sexual desire to dictate his actions. Nothing mattered more than strength.

A harried knock sounded at the door, breaking into his thoughts. His mind beat him to the exit, ensuring he wasn't walking into an ambush.

The guard wrung his hands, unwilling to meet Lazarus's gaze. "The sky serpents... Majesty, we just received word. Someone..." Gulp. "Someone not only injured the two...but came close to killing..."

Rage exploded inside him, but when next he spoke, his voice conveyed only calm. "Where are they?"

"The garden, Majesty. The healer has been summoned."

Lazarus could have flashed to the garden—moving

from one place to another with only a thought—but he *liked* walking. Liked his ability to move about unimpeded by crystals.

He stalked through the palace, the opulence of stolen treasures and the luxury of hand-carved furnishings whizzing past him. The ceiling was high and tiered, embellished with a frieze that arced across two marble fireplaces. Colorful stained glass glinted in the windows, and elaborate mosaics decorated the floor.

Outside, waning sunlight cast golden rays over a hilly terrain that overflowed with flowers.

What would Cameo think of such lush beauty? Would she smile at last?

Desire joined his rage, seething inside him.

"Majesty." One of his advisers raced to his side, short legs working overtime to keep up with Lazarus's swift pace. "Lucifer sent another emissary, demanding an answer to his query."

Lucifer the Destroyer, known for deriving pleasure from the torment of others, was one of the nine kings of the underworld. He ruled over demons and Greek gods, and he was currently at war with his father, Hades, another king of the underworld.

Weeks ago, Lucifer invited Lazarus to join his alliance. In exchange, he'd vowed to return Cameo to the Realm of Grimm and Fantica.

Lazarus had toyed with the idea of accepting. Cameo…once again within reach…driving him insane with desire…

Weakening me. "Have the emissary escorted to the dungeon. I'll slay him at my earliest convenience." Tempt him and suffer.

"Yes, Majesty. Of course." The adviser raced away.

A family of butterflies joined Lazarus, fluttering overhead. Along with the sky serpents, butterflies had come to the realm in droves, as drawn to him in death as they'd always been in life. He'd never known why.

An older woman—the healer—joined him, as well. She carried a basket of salves and bandages.

Together they topped the hill, the injured sky serpents coming into view at last. One was splayed on the ground, black blood streaming from his left eye. The other writhed in pain, a petrified branch holding open his jaw.

The rage inside Lazarus darkened. Sky serpents were extremely loyal but equally predatory, with the instincts of a sociopath. But they were *his* sociopaths, the equivalent of a cowboy's prized horse. They fought for him without hesitation.

He worked the branch free and, alongside the healer, patched up both creatures. Within a few days, the two would be as good as new. In the meantime, they would suffer as torn muscle and flesh wove back together.

"Whoever did this will pay. You have my word." Finding the culprit would be easy. Sky serpent blood always left blisters behind.

The pair mewled in thanks.

Determined, Lazarus left them in the hands of the healer and headed to the stables to join the contingent of soldiers he'd instructed to arm up.

The hunt was on.

3

"The opponent you allow to live is the opponent who will stab you in the back."

—*The Fine Art of Decapitation*

Cameo limped through a crowded village fair as the vendors hawked different wares, a gaggle of voices producing a jumbled soundtrack. The scent of spicy meats and candied sweets filled the air.

She stopped abruptly. There, on a table shaded by an azure fruit tree, rested her boots. And her weapons!

With an angry huff, she approached the seller, a tall man with a long, gray beard. The pain in her ankle flared, and the blisters on her hands stung.

He spotted her and proudly waved his hand over her belongings. "See something you want?"

"Yes. Your heart on a platter."

Tears welled in his eyes. And thanks to Misery, the influx of sorrow blinded him to her threat. "Today only, I'm offering each item for the bargain price of…of…"

He quieted, his body suddenly vibrating with eagerness. "You live. You are living. Your body is alive!"

Surprise danced hand in hand with her own ever-present sorrow. How did he know she'd passed through the Paring Rod without experiencing death?

He attempted to mask his excitement with a faux aura of boredom. "I'll buy the body from you. What would you like in exchange? The daggers? You'll never find a better made pair."

"I know. Because I made them," she grated.

He flinched, the tears coming faster. "You want them, you have to buy them. I must recoup my losses, considering your friend charged me an arm and a leg. My servant won't regrow the limbs for another month, which means I have to do all the heavy lifting myself."

Her friend? The only person she'd spoken to was— She hissed at Rathbone. "*You* stole my stuff?"

The mangy feline who'd escorted her into town prowled around her ankles. "Meow?"

Cameo bent down to grab him by the scruff, but he darted out of range. "You left me defenseless, you miserable excuse for a cat. I had to fight with sticks. Sticks! I will *not* pay your escort fee." Wait. That sounded wrong. "I owe you nothing for your aid." Not that the prick had aided her.

"What can I say? Even I have to pay to play."

As a woman who'd been created fully formed by a king who'd demanded her service—*Kill for me or be killed by me*—she'd encountered many perverted immortals. Rathbone had to be the worst.

"You." Staring at the blisters now marring her hands, the vendor stumbled backward. "You're the one. You harmed the sky serpents."

Gasps of dismay erupted from the crowd, buyers and other vendors moving to form a wall around her.

As she scanned the masses, confused, Misery cackled with glee. *Eleven out of ten people agree. You're a horrible person, and the world will be a better place without you.*

Depression oozed over her like boiling tar, adhering to her soul. A sensation manufactured by the demon. He wanted to control her.

Calm. Steady.

The *click-clack* of horse hooves hit her awareness, a welcome distraction. The crowd parted down the center, revealing an army of scowling soldiers.

Everyone knelt and pointed at her. Accusing voices rang out.

"Her!"

"She did it!"

"She's the one you seek!"

Cameo lifted her chin and squared her shoulders. "You don't want to fight me. I'm a highly respected friend of your king." At least, she hoped they'd parted as friends. "Also, if you attack me, I *will* kill you."

Finding Lazarus had become her reason for breathing. Basically, he was the equivalent of an organ donor. If he shed light on specific memories Misery had stolen, he would give her a new heart.

The warriors flinched as if they'd been punched. Scowls gave way to tear-glazed eyes and trembling lips. From the crowd, a chorus of sobs rang out.

Only one soldier rode closer to her. Fading sunlight shone at his back and bathed his face in shadows.

When he stopped to dismount a rare Pegasus—a

winged warhorse—those shadows vanished, and bolts of electricity arced through her.

He was utterly magnificent, the most beautiful male she'd ever seen. He radiated raw masculinity and sexual arrogance.

His mass of jet-black hair spiked in windblown tangles. His eyes were dark, fathomless, with tiny pinpricks of light. Like stars. His features could have been chiseled from stone. He had a proud, blade-sharp nose, prominent cheekbones and a strong jaw darkened by stubble. His unnatural but oh, so delicious height was perfectly balanced by an abundance of muscle and sinew.

Tattoos peeked out underneath the collar of his shirt. Black birds. A pyramid? Oh, yes. A pyramid with an eye in the center. Roses with bloody thorns, a snake eating its own tail, a skull—several skulls and butterflies. On one hand, he had the word LOVE branded over his knuckles. On the other hand, the word HATE.

Unease prickled at her as his gaze raked over her, slowly, almost brutally, *devouring* her. As if she were a last meal and his only means of salvation. She shivered even as her blood heated.

Misery hissed and kicked at her skull. *Run! Run now!*

Afraid, demon? What an interesting development.

Did the man possess power over evil? Or over Cameo specifically? Could he be the one she sought?

Better question: Did she want him to be?

"At last." Ferocious tension and undiluted aggression radiated from him, making the most feminine parts of her soften. "We meet again."

Another shiver, courtesy of his voice. The husky

timbre was as carnal as the rest of him. She licked her lips. "Again?"

Unlike the leopard, the vendor and everyone around them, the brute merely arched a brow at the sound of her voice. "Are you going to pretend we're strangers?"

"I *wish* I were pretending." Her heart fluttered, and her knees trembled. "Who are you?"

His study of her intensified, his dark eyes mesmerizing her so thoroughly she almost missed the phantom fingers brushing across her mind. Almost. She recognized the sensation and frowned. Was he attempting to read her thoughts?

Anger sparked. *Must protect my secrets.*

The few times she'd encountered an immortal with such an intrusive and dangerous ability, she'd slayed first and asked questions later.

With a concentrated effort, she gave a mental push. The second he was out, she erected a mental shield.

"You truly don't remember me." Steps clipped, he closed the distance...and oh, wow, he smelled good. Like expensive champagne and honey-glazed chocolate.

She grew light-headed. When he cupped her face with big, callused hands and forced her gaze upon his, the sensation worsened, the simple touch searing her.

"I am the one you seek," he rasped. "I am Lazarus."

Confirmation shook her to the bone. She waited for a spark of recognition, prayed for it, but her mind remained a dark abyss of sadness, sorrow and...arousal? Her nipples puckered, her belly quavered and warmth pooled between her legs.

Misery killed the wanton feelings in a hurry, leaving her bereft.

Satisfaction teased Lazarus's features…and Cameo. "Your body remembers me, at least," he said.

Electric currents charged through her, sizzling in her marrow.

This time Misery flooded her with a boiling ooze of depression, and her shoulders slumped.

"Well." Lazarus sneered. "You're still a bitter crone, I see."

A crone? Her hands fisted. The need to find Lazarus had plagued her, a sickness…a fever…and all along he'd thought the worst of her. "You're a bastard, I see."

Gasps and wails rose from the crowd.

He smiled slowly, wickedly. "That's right. But I'm *your* bastard, sunshine."

Sunshine? Her? She nearly choked. "I'm only using you for your brain. Tell me about our time together." *Please!*

"Answer a question for me first."

She gave a clipped nod.

"What would you do if a man kissed you? Asking for a friend."

He dared to tease her, and she dared to like it. Desire suddenly overshadowed her curiosity. *Does he want to kiss me?*

Before Cameo had returned to this realm in search of Lazarus, her friend Anya had said, "We don't chase men, we erase. Fine, you can make this one the exception. Just remember to hide your beef. Why buy the cow when you can steal it and eat for free?"

Cameo had replied, "You mean, why buy the pig when you're only going to get a little sausage?"

"Your hands," Lazarus said, drawing her back into the present. Eyes narrowed, body stiff as a board, he clasped her wrists and lifted her hands into the light to study her multitude of blisters. "You fought the sky serpents."

She jerked from his grip. "I protected myself from becoming an all-you-can-eat dinner buffet, if that's what you mean."

Those dark eyes narrowed further. "I vowed to make the person who injured my pets pay a terrible price."

His *pets*? "You may try." He would soon learn she could take a licking and keep on ticking.

A new chorus of gasps and wails rose from the crowd.

"I don't try, sunshine, I do, and I always keep my word. I said the culprit would pay...but I didn't say *how* the culprit would pay." He toyed with the ends of her hair. "Since you are my *friend*, I'll have to think of an appropriate punishment."

She sputtered. "You lay a hand on me, and I'll—"

"*Come*. I know."

What!

Misery gave her skull another kick. A sharp pain lanced her temple.

Lazarus angled his body, his muscles bunching under his shirt. His eyelids hooded over irises blazing with savage heat, his ferocity sharpening into a double-edged sword. He was almost...intimidating. Scratch that. He was intimidating. Only a true warrior could pull off mesh and leather.

"Sunshine, I know what you sound like, look and feel like when you're experiencing the ultimate pleasure."

Her breath caught, steaming up in her lungs. Her bones softened, and her knees wobbled. Not just pleasure—he'd said *ultimate* pleasure.

He was lying. He had to be lying. No one had ever given her the slightest bit of pleasure. Unless…

Misery had wiped her memory of the first orgasm she hadn't faked.

The thought *destroyed* her. Such a loss would be a violation, a rape of her mind.

Lazarus's angry countenance returned in a blink. "What are you doing here, Cameo? Why did you return to the land of the dead?"

Whatever had transpired between them, whatever pleasure she had experienced, the end had clearly been tumultuous.

Should have stayed in Budapest with my friends.

As she backed away from him, Misery lapped up her dismay and whispered conversations drifted from the crowd.

"I bet he kills her…with pleasure."

"How do I sign up for *that* death?"

Gaze remaining on Cameo, Lazarus said, "Leave us. Now."

It was a softly spoken command, and yet the crowd dispersed in seconds, tables and wares abandoned without question. Soldiers and horses trotted away.

Lazarus was king, his word law and his power unquestioned. He was a god among men. Did he know about Misery? she wondered again. He must, considering he'd read a portion of her mind. Did he want her dead, the way Alex had?

She'd never blamed Alex for his betrayal of her. No, she'd blamed fear.

When she'd escaped the Hunters, she'd gone back to Alex and, while on her knees in supplication, her body bloody and broken, she'd told him about the box.

He'd dropped his sword, joined her on the floor, and wrapped his arms around her. She thought he'd begun to understand.

Evil such as yours has to be extinguished, he'd said. Then he'd shouted for the Hunters again. Only then had she accepted the truth. Misery had infected him, and Cameo was to blame.

As she'd fought her way free a second time, a Hunter had stepped forward and said, *Come with us willingly or Alexander dies.*

Alex had died.

Even now, guilt prodded her, her sense of misery no longer manufactured by the demon. *I am no man's prize.*

No, you are every man's downfall, Misery said.

She took another step back, her bruised heel landing on a sharp rock. She winced.

Lazarus's gaze dropped to her feet, a scowl pulling at the corners of his mouth. "Your feet. Your feet are bloody. You've been hurt."

The word *hurt* on his lips was a vile curse. A promise of violence.

"The doing of sky serpents?" he demanded.

Would he punish his pets if it were? "Blame the trek here, and the POS shape-shifter who stole my shoes."

He ran his tongue over his teeth. Planning to harm Rathbone?

Why did he care who did what to her when he clearly hated her?

"Harsh words, darling. Harsh." Rathbone appeared in the distance, prowling around a table. "And after I saved you from a tragic end."

Liar! "I saved myself." She waved a fist at him.

The leopard tsk-tsked, as if she were too stupid to know the difference between salvation and danger.

Lazarus curled a hand around the hilt of a dagger.

Rathbone began to backtrack. "You're clearly in the middle of your lady time. Both of you. I'll return later." In a blink, he was gone.

Cameo envied the ability to flash. *Get what you want, and go.* "You asked me a question," she said to Lazarus. "Now I'll answer. I'm here because I want answers. I want to know everything that happened between us."

Silent, he bent at the knees and gently but firmly pushed his shoulder into her stomach.

"What—" she began.

He straightened, lifting her, ensuring she remained draped over him.

She was too stunned to protest. The fearsome keeper of Misery was being carted like a sack of potatoes? This was happening? Truly?

"We'll continue our conversation," he said. "Later."

"What are we doing *now*?" she asked, curious but not frightened.

A pause. Then, "We're picking up where we left off."

As he spoke, a butterfly with wings of scarlet landed on the table with her daggers, and she groaned. Here was another sign of impending doom.

Her relationship with Lazarus wasn't going to end well, was it?

4

"How to win a war in six easy steps. One: Taunt."
—~~The Fine Art of Decapitation~~
—How to Achieve Victory

Lazarus marched through the towering front doors opened by the guards he'd stationed there, a shockingly docile Cameo hanging over his shoulder. The last time she'd entered the spirit realms, he'd sensed her and caught her as she'd hurtled to the ground. Why hadn't he sensed her today?

"Did you fall through a portal?" he asked. "Or did you enter the realm another way?"

"The portal," she grumbled. "Landing sucked."

Had he somehow blocked her from his mind, the way she'd blocked him from hers? Or had she blocked him from the start?

Well, he wasn't blocking her now. He could think of nothing and no one but Cameo.

In the spacious entryway, servants stopped cleaning to bow to him…and watch him with wonder. He'd never handled a female so publicly before.

Cameo was more beautiful than he remembered. Silken ebony locks, sterling-silver eyes, ruby red lips. Her eyes said *come closer* while her demon said *that's close enough.* She was his own personal temptress. She enchanted him, and she had no right!

Even now, his legs tingled and burned, the first sign the crystals were expanding.

Did she know how terribly she affected him? Or how greatly she could weaken him, making him easy prey for his enemies? Did she care?

He opened his mind to hers only to bump against her shield. His questions remained unanswered, a familiar frustration seething inside him. Frustration, rage and that ever-present desire.

His hunger for this woman was insatiable, but he couldn't have her. Unless, of course, he abandoned his vengeance against those who had viciously wronged him and accepted an eternity entombed in indestructible crystal.

Never! Why not kill her, here and now? Removing her head would be an act of self-defense.

With the thought, Lazarus physically recoiled.

"Whoa, big guy." Cameo patted his ass, calm when she should have been hysterical. "Is one hundred and fifteen pounds too much for you?"

Smart-mouthed female.

Was there any better kind?

Patch her up and send her home without *ravishing her beautiful body.* "Someone is suffering from another convenient bout of memory loss, isn't she?" The words left him with more force than he'd intended. Perhaps he was a wee bit bitter? "She's forgetting about an extra five pounds."

The little she-devil beat her fists into his lower back. "You might or might not have intimate knowledge of my body. You definitely know things I've said and done. The good, bad and ugly. You know if we parted as friends or foes. You know *where we left off.* I don't. That isn't a convenience for me but a nightmare."

Her fury doused his own, the need to comfort her rising. Memories offered a form of protection; they told you whom to trust and whom to revile, saved you from repeated mistakes, and created a clear path for your future.

Compassion bloomed, and he cursed. Another weakness, thanks to this woman.

Beyond them, servants sobbed. He glared at the sorry bunch. He might have to invest in earplugs for his entire staff—or slay them all.

"Back to work," he snapped.

A flurry of motion erupted as everyone obeyed.

He pounded up a flight of stairs, his hand flush against Cameo's ass as he maneuvered through different hallways. He couldn't wait to see her surrounded by his things, knew he would enjoy having her luscious scent—a mix of bergamot, rose and neroli—infuse his sheets… He would take great pleasure in presenting her with the gifts he'd collected for her. Would her face light up with delight? Or would she frown at him, all the world's sadness in her gaze?

Did it matter? After she departed, he had to do everything in his power to end his body's obsession with her. That meant erasing every trace of her from his home.

Can't share my bedroom with her. Not now, not ever.

He entered the room beside his. One he'd saved for—
A guest. Any guest.

With a swift kick, he shut the door behind him. He tossed his beautiful bundle onto the bed. *Look away!* The sight of Cameo splayed atop a mattress, any mattress, would only damage his defenses against her.

Lazarus focused on the bed itself. Each of the four posters had been uprooted from the forest and potted. Lush red leaves thrived, forming a canopy above. The comforter was made from flower petals imbued with summer Fae dust; those petals were softer than silk yet far more durable.

Cameo scrambled to an upright position and scanned the room.

He knew she'd cataloged every exit as well as everything she could use as a weapon, and he did the same. There was only one exit—the one he'd shut. At the hearth, a marble sky serpent stood sentry at each side, heat wafting from their open mouths. Weapons the pokers balanced between their claws.

The dresser had been cut from an amethyst geode. Pieces could be chipped off and used to cut through vulnerable flesh.

The vanity had a solid gold top, too heavy for her to lift. The legs had been hand-carved to resemble sky serpents. Rubies lent an unnatural life to their eyes, while their tails curled into glimmering diamond points. The jewels could be removed with little effort.

The gilt mirror had once belonged to Siobhan, the goddess of Many Futures and supposedly the most vicious of the Erinyes. Lazarus had been told simply peering into the glass would reveal the different paths to finding true love. So far he'd seen nothing but his reflection.

If Cameo desired weapons, she would have weapons. He would never interfere with her efforts to protect herself.

When her gaze landed on Lazarus, a flush painted her cheeks. He knew just how hot her flawless skin could burn, and his fingers itched to touch.

Resist! "You want a memory, sunshine. Here you go. Last time we were together, we kissed."

No, *kissed* was too mild a word. She'd been fire in his arms, with no hint of sadness or sorrow. She'd sucked on his tongue as if it were her favorite candy, had breathed his breath as if she'd needed him to survive, as if she would *always* need him. She'd been a live wire of passion.

She'd forgotten him so easily while his remembrance of her had the power to scorch him.

She stared at his lips and whispered, "We kissed. Nothing more?"

That voice! A burst of sorrow accompanied every word.

He comprehended the reason other people flinched and cried. They'd never experienced such a fervent punch of undiluted sadness. Lazarus had. Many times. First, after the brutal loss of Echidna. Then his inability to find and kill his father for the crimes committed against his mother. Then his centuries-long enslavement. Cameo's voice simply couldn't compare.

"We stripped and rolled around like two teenagers in an empty house." He hid the intensity of his desire for her behind a glib tone. "You writhed against me, begging for more, but I stopped before penetration." He'd had to work, trick and cajole to get her that far, and the wait was torturous…but the agony was worth every second of ecstasy.

He'd stopped because two of his men had burst into his room. And because she'd learned the truth—she hadn't been captured by an enemy intent on selling her goods and services, as he'd led her to believe; she had been tucked safely inside Lazarus's very own kingdom.

Breath hitched in her throat as her pulse raced. *She desires me still…* Lust threatened to raze his good intentions…until the tingling in his legs magnified.

Leave! Now!

Concern for her rooted him in place. Her wounds needed tending. Would his control snap when he got his hands on her?

"Why did you stop?" she rasped.

"We were—are—enemies," he croaked. *Kick me out.*

Her eyes widened. "Enemies. Because you hate me… hate what I am?"

"I don't hate you." He feared her and the power she wielded over him. He hungered for her like a man who'd been denied proper sustenance for years. "But I don't like you, either."

He expected her to recoil with hurt. Instead, she exuded acceptance.

His black heart shattered. How many times had this woman faced rejection?

My μονομανία will be respected at all times!

He cursed his growing sense of possession. This woman would never belong to him. He would always choose strength over weakness.

"Why are we enemies?" she insisted.

"I want you too much," he admitted with a snarl.

She gaped at him. Then she pressed her lips together.

A habit he'd noticed before. And he got it, he really did. People despised her voice, and she despised their reaction to it.

"Use your words like a big girl," he said, purposely taunting her. He believed in the law of displacement. Like a glass set underneath a dripping faucet. Eventually it would fill up, and the liquid would spill out, leaving the container empty…and ready for something new. It had worked in the past, allowing him to manipulate her mood. Misery for anger, anger for passion. "Little girls get spanked."

She reached for a dagger no longer in her possession, then shook her empty fist at him. "Try and lose a hand."

"Only one?" He tsk-tsked. "Someone is practically *begging* to get spanked."

"*Someone* is wondering why she thought it would be a good idea to spend time with you."

"That's easy. You are addicted to my massive…"

She bowed up, preparing to attack.

"Wit," he finished, trying not to smile. Teasing her had *always* been a source of delight. For him.

With calculated grace, she flipped her hair over her shoulder. "No worries, warrior. I can get *wit* anywhere."

An-n-nd he lost the desire to smile. Any male who dared *wit* her would be met by Lazarus's—

Handshake and hero's send-off. *I* will *let her go.*

Determined, he focused on the worst of her injuries. "You have multiple wounds, but I'll ensure you heal before you go. You'll have no scars, or what I like to call *love buttons*." There would be nothing to remind her of their newest interaction. If the demon decided to wipe her memory clean once again.

Now hurt twisted her expression, and the sight was nearly his undoing. Did she *want* to stay with him?

She rebounded quickly and buffed her nails. "Don't bother with patch work. I refer to bandages as sissy support."

"I'll bother. Otherwise you *won't* heal." He strode into the en suite, where he found the salve made with winter Fae ice.

He hadn't saved it for Cameo. Of course he hadn't. Helping the only female capable of hurting him? No! Such an action would have been foolish.

What are you doing now?

Ensuring she lived long enough to travel home. Nothing more.

He swallowed a growl and returned to the room to crouch before the dark-haired beauty. Her intoxicating scent enveloped him, his mouth watering for a taste. Perhaps he'd steal a kiss, a single kiss, before he began his "patch work." He'd promised to pick up where they'd left off, and he always kept his promises...

The rest of the world faded as he leaned into her...

Her breath hitched, maddening him further, but also returning him to reality.

Her appeal meant nothing. Her affect on him, less than nothing.

With his attention fixed anywhere but her too lovely face...and perfectly rounded hips...and the long, lean legs she'd once wrapped around his waist...he cleaned her wounds and applied the salve.

"Must get you home," he grated.

"When we part," she said softly, "I'm not going home. Not until I find the goddess of the Afterlife and—" She pressed her lips together.

And…what? Or who? If she sought another man, Lazarus would—

Nothing.

"Your moods change lightning fast," she said. "Are you manstruating?"

He suppressed a laugh. Then he probed the outer recesses of her mind a final time, nearly grunting with relief and triumph when he realized she had inadvertently lowered the shield.

She also searched for Pandora's box.

He experienced a flare of guilt. Should he admit she'd come close to finding it? The last time they were together, the artifact had been inches away.

He'd stopped her from making a play for it, and in the process stopped its guardian from awakening, and Cameo from dying, her spirit forever stuck in the phantom realms.

Lazarus would have been stuck with the key to his downfall.

So he'd led her away from the box, knowing he could return for it at any time. He'd even played with the idea once or twice. But why mess with a working system?

He ignored the guilt, remained silent and dug deeper into her mind. Well, well. She had secrets of her own. The little minx hadn't mentioned the box because she didn't trust him and she didn't know how he would react to Misery. She actually believed he would seek her destruction.

Deeper still. She—

Screeched with fury and horror and shoved him out of her thoughts. Then she erected the shield.

She raised her fist, as if to hit him. Their gazes collided as he clasped her wrist. The delicacy of her bones, so different from his, the warmth and softness of her skin. The feel of her wild pulse hammering against him...

"I know you're demon possessed," he told her. "I've always known, and I don't care. I'm not a human with limited views. I'm the Cruel and Unusual."

The tension drained from her, leaving a gale-force of surprise.

Surprise would taste delicious on her lips.

The tingling in his legs worsened, grounding him. With this woman, pleasure and doom would forever walk hand in hand.

He released her and stood. "Stay here. I'll send a servant to help you." Every time she moved, the rips in her shirt gaped, coming dangerously close to revealing her breasts.

I want her breasts in my hands. Her nipples in my mouth...

"I'll gather your daggers and boots and take you to your friend." His voice was a silken rasp.

"She's here?"

"She is." *Get out while you can.* He exited in a hurry, slamming the door behind him.

Two males stood sentry. "No one enters the room, and no one touches the girl. If she leaves, one of you will follow her, the other will summon me."

"Yes, sire."

He continued on. The first female servant he happened upon, he sent to Cameo's room, with explicit instructions. He wanted her wounds tended, and specific scents placed in her bath.

As he turned a corner, he opened his mind, sending

his awareness through the entire palace...finally bumping against the object of his search. Rathbone the Only.

The bastard waited in the throne room.

Once inside, he dismissed every guard with a wave of his hand. Booted footsteps rang out. The doors shut, one after the other, sealing him inside. He saw no hint of the leopard who'd stolen Cameo's belongings, but the dark presence remained, a thorn inside his mind.

Like Cameo, Rathbone had erected a shield, hiding his thoughts.

"Show yourself. I know who and what you are." He'd realized the truth at first glance.

The leopard appeared in a puff of smoke, a wide grin revealing razor-sharp teeth. He approached Lazarus slowly but methodically, his form shifting into a very tall, very muscled man with long black hair, eyes like diamonds and skin as dark and red as blood.

He wore no shirt, but black leather pants sheathed his legs. He had thousands of tattoos, even more than Lazarus, who was covered. While Lazarus had thorny roses to represent the ones found in the Garden of Perpetual Horror, skulls to represent the enemies he'd slain—and would slay—as well as butterflies and sky serpents to represent his followers, every image on Rathbone was the same. A closed human eye.

An odd choice. A *distinctive* choice. Lazarus had guessed correctly. This was Rathbone the Only, one of nine kings of the underworld. He'd earned his moniker by being the last man standing in every battle he'd ever fought. He could shape-shift into any form, no matter how big or small. Animal, human and even inanimate objects.

Lazarus had heard the male once shifted into another

man's wrist cuff, forcing him to beat his entire family before beating *himself.*

"You have much to answer for, warrior." He crossed his arms over his chest.

"That's Majesty to you." A careless shrug. "I *always* have much to answer for."

"Cameo's weapons and boots. Give them to me. Now."

"And cheat the vendor who bought them from me? For shame."

"You'd rather cheat my woman?"

When the words escaped, he cursed. *My woman.* He'd just struck a powerful verbal claim and offered sufficient ammunition for any enemy intent on overseeing his destruction. He'd also proved he'd done a deplorable job of resisting Cameo's carnal appeal.

Perhaps the bastard wouldn't notice.

Rathbone's smile widened. Oh, he'd noticed. He wisely chose to remain quiet on the subject.

"I know why you're in my realm." Lazarus traced his fingertips over the hilt of the kris.

"Do tell."

"The war between Hades and Lucifer brews hotter."

The very reason Lucifer continued to send emissaries. Every leader of every immortal army had to pick a side. "Who do you fight for?"

"With. I fight with Hades. And so do the Lords of the Underworld."

Meaning *Cameo* fought for Hades. Meaning, siding with Lucifer would make his μονομανία his enemy.

Isn't she already?

Lazarus stalked a circle around Rathbone, a predator deciding the fate of his prey. The male remained in place, never turning. But then, he had no need to turn. Those eyes were tattooed all over his back as well, and as Lazarus moved behind him, the lids flipped open, the irises following his every movement.

A stab of envy. Such a singular power…

"Let Hades know I'll render my decision by the end of the week." All personal feelings aside, only one question mattered. Who would get him closer to his vengeance?

Rathbone inclined his head in agreement. "Very well."

"And now that that's settled." Lazarus tossed the kris without any warning. The blade cut through the male's torso and came out the other side—with his liver. "I vowed to Cameo I would punish the one who hurt her. Now my vow is complete."

Rathbone winced before a new smile bloomed. "The first organ is free. The next one will cost you. Dearly."

"So you understand there will be a next. Excellent. We're on the same page."

A bark of laughter echoed from the walls. Used to intimidating his foes, Lazarus had no idea how to proceed with this one.

"I think I like you," Rathbone said. "I think we'll be great friends."

"I have no need of friends." Though he did sometimes yearn for someone to trust, to guard his back and back his cause. "I don't dislike you, but I'll remove the rest of your organs, one at a time, if you steal from Cameo again."

"I now *know* I like you. If ever you need me—"

"I need no one." The statement rushed from him.

A reassurance for himself as well as the underworld's shape-shifter king.

"But if ever you do—"

"I won't."

"—say my name." A second later, Rathbone vanished.

Lazarus stood in place, his hands curled into fists. Breathing became a little more difficult as he struggled to rein in his temper...and his lust.

With the king gone, he had no distraction from Cameo's magnetic allure. She was here. In his home. The woman against whom he would forever measure all others. The fever in his flesh, the ache in his bones.

The weakness he had to excise, one way or another.

5

"Step two: Threaten...and follow through."
—*How to Achieve Victory*
Subtitle: Except with Lovers

Cameo remained seated on the bed as an unfamiliar female bustled about in the bathroom. Rejection still rattled inside her brain like a barbed metal ball.

I don't hate you. But I don't like you, either.

Lazarus had told her what had transpired between them, but instead of setting her free of Misery's shackles, he'd wrapped a new chain around her neck. The man had kissed and touched her...had given her pleasure. To her knowledge, he was the first. Also, he had no issues with Misery. And yet he couldn't get rid of Cameo fast enough.

Destined to be alone with me. Misery's poison dripped from every word, searing hidden corners of her mind.

Fate would not be so cruel. Fate—

Could be far crueler. Her shoulders rolled in, her

head bowing. A small flame of hope snuffed out, and a drop of wax seemed to splash onto her heart, burning a hole in the center. No matter how horrid her life, things could always get worse.

At least her wounds had stopped stinging when Lazarus applied salve. Torn flesh had even woven together. He was right; no love buttons for Cameo.

Of course, when he applied the salve, her pride had *started* stinging. His touch had been impersonal and rough, his expression twisted with repugnance.

A sniffle wafted from the bathroom. Cameo stiffened. *Never fails.* Not a single word had left her mouth, and yet Misery had managed to infect the other woman.

Poor servant girl, the demon said, his voice deceptively soft and sad. *Your presence is torture for her.*

Wah, wah, wah. Cameo would not accept guilt for this. She wouldn't! She wasn't responsible for anyone else's feelings.

Aren't you, though? You brought me—Misery—into this realm.

So what. Other people had brought sadness, sorrows, violence and a thousand other dark, terrible things. People were responsible for their own reactions and feelings. But…

Maybe she should go. There was no reason to await Lazarus's return. She could find Viola without his help, thanks.

No, she needed to stay. Her clothes were hanging on by a thread and a prayer, and the dirt caking her shirt itched.

A new plan formed. *Bath, change into clean clothes. Won't let the door hit me on the way out.*

Most important, she would stay away from Lazarus.

He knew so much about Cameo while she knew so little about him, and the imbalance chafed.

What kind of ruler was he? Harsh? Or fair? How did he treat his people? Like chattel? Or prizes? Did he currently have a girlfriend? Or maybe *girlfriends*?

Her nails dug into the mattress. Did he enjoy monogamy or have a fear of commitment?

The pale-haired servant appeared in front of her. "The water is ready, miss. If you wish to bathe…please, this way."

First, Cameo gathered a handful of objects she could use as weapons.

Weapons were a girl's best friend.

She selected a fire poker, and plucked the diamond tails—or rather, the perfect daggers—from the hand-carved sky serpents. For her troubles, she awarded herself both sets of ruby eyes.

Ready for anything, she entered a spacious bathroom that was bigger than her bedroom at home. The walls of the shower stall were made of glistening crystals. Pillars braced the entrance of a large alcove, where a small, winding staircase led to a bubbling hot spring. Steam curled from the water's surface, fragrant with the scents of rose, bergamot and neroli—

Cameo blinked with surprise. Rose, bergamot and neroli. The essential oils used in her favorite soap. Coincidence?

Had to be. No way Lazarus had noticed her preferred scents. *Really* no way he had purposely re-created the mix.

I don't hate you. But I don't like you, either.

Her nails scraped the fire poker as she continued her study of the bathroom. *Find your exits long before it's time to leave.* A crystal chandelier hung above the hot spring. Grab, swing, drop. In a second crystal stall, she found a 24 karat gold toilet and bidet.

Blondie attempted to remove Cameo's shirt. With a snarl, Cameo leaped out of reach. No offense, but enough was enough. Until she wanted to be stabbed in the back or decapitated, she would not allow a stranger to stand behind her.

Take me unawares once, my bad. Take me unawares twice, you die.

Correction. *Take me unawares once, you die.*

Cameo motioned for Blondie to leave. Unfortunately the servant missed the action, remaining in place, her head bowed.

Rather than speak, Cameo gave Blondie a gentle push…she stumbled but quickly dug in her heels.

Had Lazarus ordered her to spy? Fear of his wrath must be great.

Fine. Whatever. Keeping Blondie within sight, Cameo stripped. A miraculous feat, considering she retained her hold on the weapons. After walking up the stairs backward, she entered the welcoming water and placed the weapons around the rim of the tub.

With a sigh akin to contentment, she eased onto a waiting bench, where multiple jets massaged sore muscles.

Blondie sniffled again, ruining the moment.

Misery kicked against Cameo's skull, a flash of memory consuming her mind.

"Maybe I'll kill you and gift her with your head," Cameo had said. She sat in the thick of a forest, glaring up at the warrior.

She'd *threatened* him? Why? Unless the demon

hoped to taint her feelings for Lazarus. It was possible, even probable.

And what had she meant? Gift *her*. Her who?

Juliette, Misery said. *The Harpy who once enslaved him*.

The demon loved to parse out the details he'd stolen from her, giving just enough info to send her imagination into a tailspin.

"Maybe I'll cut out your tongue and do the world a favor," Lazarus had replied. He sat at her side, a tower of menace and strength, sexy beyond imagining.

Whoa. *He* had dared to threaten *Cameo*?

Obviously. At least she'd gritted her teeth in irritation instead of fear and said, "Maybe I'll gut you just for giggles."

"Maybe I'll stab the life out of you and do *myself* a favor."

Oh, yes. He'd dared. But he'd been amused rather than enraged.

Cameo had jumped to her feet and motioned him closer. "You want to do this, warrior? Because I'm ready. Anytime. Anyplace."

His big body had unfolded as he'd stood, the movement graceful, his strength on display…and fascinating. "You don't want to take me on, little girl. You'll lose."

Little girl? She would hack him into a thousand pieces.

"I think differently," she'd said, surprising her present self. *Stop baiting him and start attacking!* Maybe take him on the worst date of his life…to a karaoke bar. "On both counts."

She hadn't attacked. She'd pressed her chest against his and reveled in his hardness.

Well. Attraction had clearly addled her brain. Despite everything, she'd wanted his strong arms wrapped around her, his warm breath on her nape.

"Do your worst, then," he had said. "But have no doubts, I'll then do mine."

The memory began to dwindle. Nooo! Cameo scrambled to keep the playback front and center. She had to know more! What was his worst? What had followed his newest threat? Had they apologized to each other? Or had they split up?

Her mind blanked. With a frustrated shriek, she slammed her fist into the rim of the tub.

Blondie heaved a great sob.

Fighting the crush of defeat, Cameo slunk deeper into the water. Not knowing the minute details of her life *killed* her. Especially because the tricky demon only ever unveiled bits and pieces of her past, and always completely out of context, forcing her to speculate about why, what and how.

Cameo washed from head to toe, and wondered about Lazarus. He claimed she'd writhed in his arms and begged for more. If anyone could rock her world, it was that male. Beauty and strength wrapped in smoldering sensuality, sprinkled with ferocity.

Finished, she gathered her weapons and descended the stairs. Blondie rushed over to dry her, but she snatched the towel to dry herself. The material wasn't cotton or silk, but something a thousand times softer.

Blondie gathered clean clothing, and Cameo dressed without complaint while cringing inside. A diamond-encrusted bra and blink-and-you'll-miss-them bottoms? Really?

Brow arched, she pointed to the gossamer cloth.

"Shorts," Blondie said and hid a chuckle behind her hand.

Silly me for not knowing. Call her old-fashioned, but Cameo believed her shorts should be longer than her butt crack.

Whatever. She secured the weapons and headed for the door. Blondie raced in front of her to motion to the vanity. Wanted to brush and style her hair, did she? Deep down, Cameo wanted to say yes, despite the foolishness of the act. She wanted Lazarus to take one look at her and basically crap himself. *Don't like me? Fine. But you'll wish I liked you!*

Problem: Blondie would have to stand at Cameo's back to—

Oh, who cared? What kind of warrior couldn't protect herself from a single person?

Cameo placed a dagger on the vanity—in plain sight—and eased onto the chair.

Blondie trembled as she lifted a brush. One minute bled into another, zero attacks launched, and Cameo began to relax...until the mirror in front of her *moved*.

With a yelp, she jumped to her feet. Blondie stumbled back, confused.

Cameo pointed to the liquefied glass, and waves rippled over the surface.

"The mirror once belonged to the goddess of Many Futures," Blondie said softly. "Its power fuels legends... and nightmares."

Siobhan, the goddess of Many Futures. The youngest of the Erinyes, or Furies.

As a Greek, she'd fallen under the leadership of Zeus. Rumors claimed the goddess had been cursed soon after her sixteenth birthday, forced to spend the rest of her days trapped inside a glass prison.

Cameo had encountered the teenage girl only once before her curse. Siobhan had been a beauty with hair as white as snow and skin as dark as night. She'd looked Cameo up and down, and said, "Must you always frown? Laughter is the best medicine. Unless you have diarrhea."

A wave of trepidation swept through Cameo as she returned to the chair—from the demon, or from her own sense of self-preservation, she wasn't sure. Either way, she refrained from peering into the glass a second time.

Glass prison…mirror…if the goddess *were* trapped inside…

I don't want to know what fresh misery awaits me.

Over the next half hour, Cameo's hair was brushed, dried and fashioned in a complicated half braid she would never be able to replicate. Her face was sprinkled with something sparkly.

"This is stardust," Blondie said. "It is *very* expensive."

Who, exactly, had Lazarus spent his big bucks on? A favorite mistress? Was Cameo receiving her leftovers?

A tendril of jealousy surprised her. She had no future with the man, so there was no need to waste emotion on him.

"A witch sells the dust in town," Blondie continued. Babbling to distract herself from the sadness Cameo exuded? "She's a crazy one. Does nothing but compliment herself. And she has a devil for a pet. The creature—"

Cameo grabbed the edge of the vanity. Nothing but compliment herself…devil for a pet… No help for it, she had to speak. "Do you know where I can find Viola, keeper of Narcissism, and Princess Fluffikans?"

Blondie burst into tears.

Cameo jumped up and took the woman by the shoulders, shaking her. "Concentrate. Look past the despondency and tell me what I want to know."

An-n-nd Blondie hunched over, sobbing and dry-heaving. When she calmed, she rattled off coordinates beyond the forest.

"Is there another part to this outfit?" she asked, not waiting for an answer but rushing to the dresser.

Blondie burst into a fresh round of sobs.

"Go." Exasperated, Cameo waved toward the door. "Leave me."

The woman didn't have to be told twice. She beat feet, gone in a blink.

Story of my life. Always better off alone.

She searched through every drawer, at last finding a wraparound skirt that tied at the waist. If someone mistook her for a lady of the evening, well, someone would die.

She exited the room, stunned to find Blondie hadn't locked her in. Not that a locked door would have mattered. Cameo could pick any lock anytime. A skill she'd honed as a better-safe-than-sorry measure against Hunters.

The reason Blondie hadn't felt the need to engage the lock became very clear a second later. Two armed males stood sentry in the hallway.

Both males gazed up at the ceiling, as if afraid to look at her.

"Milady—" the tallest said.

"Cameo," she corrected without thought. Titles had never been her bag.

Both males flinched. One teared up. She gnashed her back teeth.

"If you won't return to your room," Crier began.

"I won't," she interjected.

Fat teardrops slid down his cheeks. "Then I will be your shadow."

The tall one sprinted away, as if he couldn't bear her presence a minute more.

Misery cackled with glee, and a familiar wrath boiled inside Cameo. *Hate the demon!*

"What if I don't want a shadow?" she demanded.

Crier gulped. "The king's orders."

What, did Lazarus think she would steal the silver? Run away? And did he really think a single guard could stop her if she decided to go?

Why not make use of him?

"I'm to protect you with my life," he added.

Oh. Well. "Take me to the exit. Also, I need a map of the forest. I'm visiting my friend. The woman with the pet Tasmanian devil." Cameo wasn't looking forward to seeing Fluffy again. The rat-like beast was the size of a small dog, had sharp teeth, spiked black fur and a hair-trigger temper. He emitted a noxious odor when he was stressed.

The guard tried to hide a second flinch. What sweet progress, she thought drily.

"I know of whom you speak. Horrid pair. Are you sure—never mind. There's no need to respond. I'll take you to her abode." He strode in front of her, careful not to brush against her, and led her downstairs and out the back door.

The backyard took her breath away. Moonlight blended with multiple rows of torchlight, illuminating the rainbow-colored river winding through a spectacular rose garden.

Between the bushes were life-size statues, both male and female, each depicting different degrees of terror and regret. Some of the statues were missing limbs. Others were posed in defensive positions.

The artist had done a remarkable job, ensuring every creation captured the full range of human expression. From the crinkle at the corner of an eye to the shadow of every individual lash. The statues even had fingerprints, and on one of the females, Cameo noticed a chip.

Never, in all her days, had she seen such detailed work. Had Lazarus inherited the garden from the former king? Or had he collected the pieces for his own enjoyment?

When she noticed countless butterflies swooping down to land on one of the statues, she froze. Her heart sped up, slamming against her ribs.

I get it. Danger is coming. Leave me alone!

"So many," the guard said, his awe unmistakable. "So beautiful."

In an effort to distract herself, she said, "A group of butterflies is called a kaleidoscope." *A group of men is called a migraine.*

He cringed, making her feel worse. She rushed ahead to escape the area—again she froze. This time, her stomach churned.

Up ahead, two pikes waved proudly in the wind. Atop each pike rested a severed head. Not stone, but flesh. *Rotting* flesh.

Lazarus's doing?

Of course! Who else would have dared?

What had the victims done to earn such a gruesome punishment?

Although, Lazarus could have done a lot worse. She and her demon-possessed brothers-by-circumstance *had* done worse.

Their motto: *the enemy who fears you is less likely to attack you.*

What would Lazarus do to *her* if she inadvertently harmed someone in his kingdom?

She wanted to ask the guard about his king's motives, but remained silent. Whether she intended it or not, the question was an admission Lazarus hadn't trusted her with his reasons. Also, the question disrespected Lazarus, reducing his choices to fodder for gossip.

Over the centuries she'd learned a warrior's pride needed care and tending. Males spooked easily, so it was always best to handle one in private.

Not that she would be seeing Lazarus again.

"If you want to reach the witch by nightfall, we had best continue on," Crier said, and motored forward.

She followed, soon reaching a gaggle of females who were pruning the rosebushes and wearing the same bra and butt-crack shorts as Cameo. When they spotted the guard, they accidentally on purpose dropped their tools and bent over to retrieve the items, revealing a hidden slit in the center.

Well. The Bend-Over Babes certainly gave new meaning to the term *come and get it*. Were they here in porno land for Lazarus's personal enjoyment? Did he sample their pleasures regularly?

The guard couldn't hide his new pant-tent.

"Chop, chop. Night is coming," Cameo said, and his

tent instantly collapsed. "Free lesson of the day. Distractions can get you killed."

He leaped into action, desperate to escape her. They cleared the garden a mile or so later, only then slowing. They reached a golden wall. He opened the only gate, stepped through and unsheathed his sword.

Sensing a threat, Cameo palmed the diamond daggers.

Too late. An arrow sliced through the guard's temple.

Her first thought: *see! Distraction kills.* Her second: *stupid butterflies!*

As he crumpled onto the twig-laden ground, she ducked.

A war cry sounded. A tribe of Amazon warriors stepped from behind the trees—their narrowed gazes locked on Cameo.

6

"Step three: Prove your strength. The more vicious the act the better."

—*How to Achieve Victory*
Subtitle: Except with Lovers

Lazarus raced through the Garden of Perpetual Horror, a contingent of soldiers close on his heels. Butterflies led the charge. His own personal yellow brick road.

He was grateful for their unsolicited aid. The sense of disconcertment had returned with a vengeance.

One of the guards he'd left with Cameo had sent word of her departure and her intent to begin her search for Viola, the bane of his realm. *Leaving without saying goodbye? No!*

For weeks the demon-possessed goddess had plowed through his territories, stealing armor, artifacts and anything else she fancied. Not once had he retaliated. He hadn't even attempted to stop her, too afraid he would inadvertently harm her and devastate Cameo.

She owed him, and she *would* pay. *Then* they would part.

His ears twitched as a war cry pierced the air. With the kris firm in his grip, Lazarus quickened his pace. Tree limbs shrank backward, afraid to touch him. Carnivorous insects hid.

Feminine wails rang out as he soared through the gate.

He lowered his mental guards to gauge the situation ahead. Amazon warriors had launched a sneak attack, killing his soldier. Cameo remained unharmed.

Relief poured through him.

He reached the group—and halted. Though the Amazons surrounded Cameo, they were on their knees, their hands pressed over their ears as sorrow washed over them, *drowned* them. His woman walked from female to female, disarming them completely while chatting about everything and nothing.

Every muscle in Lazarus's body tensed. Cameo looked good enough to eat, her beauty unnatural, ethereal. Her raven braid added a new level of delicacy to her features.

A tiny crop top paired with the world's smallest shorts and a transparent wrap paid proper homage to pert breasts, a nipped waist and gloriously long, toned legs.

The massive butterfly tattoo on her back made his hands itch to touch. Jagged wings the color of onyx complemented the paleness of her skin.

He opened his mouth, ready to announce his presence, when a beam of moonlight stroked her, revealing flecks of red within the lines of onyx. Like lava bubbling beneath the image.

Magnificent.

She was a sex dream come to startling life.

"—a seventy-nine percent chance you'll be stabbed at some point in your life. Or your death. Whatever," she said. Sorrow wafted from her, creating a cloying perfume. Though she clutched two diamond daggers, she looked depressed enough to kill her opponents…or herself. "Except when you challenge me, of course. Then the odds increase to one hundred and one percent."

"You are correct," Lazarus said.

Cameo whipped around to face him. "Lazarus."

Her liquid silver irises held him captive more surely than Juliette's forced bond, and even her lie.

Staggering desire and savage hunger began to gnaw at him. *Give me.*

Now isn't the time. He attempted to read Cameo's mind, only to curse when her shield held firm.

"Live by the sword, die by the sword," she said.

The Amazons wailed with more gusto, not yet realizing Lazarus's soldiers had taken up posts around them—until the soldiers moaned and groaned just as loudly.

"The Amazons will die," Lazarus added. "Badly."

Not only had they killed a male under his protection, they'd threatened his woman. If he failed to deliver a proper punishment—

Who was he kidding? He always delivered a proper punishment. That way, no one else considered breaking his rules a good idea.

"I have things under control," Cameo said.

I'll have you under my control. Just like that, his hunger sharpened. He would have her, here, now. If the earth began to crumble, so be it. He would die with a smile.

The veins in his legs tingled and warmed.

Fool! He needed to hate this woman. If he failed to let her go, she would destroy him the way his mother had destroyed his father.

Typhon made the mistake of ignoring his weakness, and look where he'd ended up. Bested by his worst enemy, now a cautionary tale.

"At least you remember me this time." Oops. His bitterness was showing again. Better moderate his tone. "We're making progress."

Her eyelids narrowed to tiny slits, the thick fan of her lashes making her appear coy and innocent rather than perturbed. "You can leave. The situation is h-handled."

Her eyes watered, and her chin trembled.

Was she about to…cry?

Will murder *that demon.*

Can't. He couldn't kill the demon without killing Cameo.

He should act, anyway. No Cameo, no weakness.

His fingers twitched on the hilt of the kris.

Never again experience the bliss of her scent, her kiss? Never again delight in her touch? The prospect horrified him.

He tore his gaze from her and focused on the Amazons. "Why are you here, inciting my wrath?"

A black beauty calmed enough to reply, "Queen Nethandra…your marriage proposal…"

His rage sparked anew.

"Hold up." Cameo approached him, her hips swaying. A mating dance. While his men and the Amazons cried out, the sweet muskiness of his woman's scent enveloped him, testing the bounds of his control. "You proposed to this woman's queen? When? Tell me! If you got freaky with me while you were engaged to someone else…"

Was his little ray of sunshine jealous?

Primal possessiveness nearly burned his control to ash. "I have no betrothed. I merely sent an envoy to inquire of Nethandra's willingness to join her house to mine."

For a split second, relief stamped out her ever-present sorrow, and he had to fight the urge to pound his chest in triumph.

"Good," she said with a faux-casual air. "If you'd made me a cheater, I would have had to disembowel you."

Adorable. "You think you can defeat me?"

Her shoulders lifted in a casual shrug. "My usual method clearly wouldn't work on you," she said, quiet so no one else would hear her, "but there are more ways to take down a man."

"True." He spoke just as quietly. "Strip, and I'll willingly drop to my knees."

He expected her to balk, curse, something. Instead, she whispered, "Thanks to you, I'm practically naked already. Go ahead and drop." The words were a dare.

His lips twitched at the corners. "*Practically* isn't the same as *definitely*, now, is it?"

"True. You're definitely a pain in the ass."

He took a step toward her. "You like me this way."

Both the guards and Amazons watched him. Hands fisted, he forced his attention on the female warriors. "If your queen truly wished to create a union with me, she would have protected my people. Would have seen my forces as an extension of her own."

She bowed her head in shame. "The mistake is mine."

"If *you* wish a union," Cameo muttered to him, "you'll see her forces as an extension of your own and forgive her emissary's oversight."

What, she *wanted* him to wed the queen now?

Lazarus ran his tongue over his teeth and snapped his fingers. Limbs shook and leaves clapped as his men restrained the women and discarded their weapons. The Amazons remained subdued, putting up zero fight. Odd.

Lazarus opened his mind...and snorted. Because they'd failed to override his forces, they planned to topple his household from within, using poison they'd acquired from Viola.

Good luck with that.

"They swallowed bags of poison," he said. "Strings are attached to their teeth."

The Amazons gave a collective gasp of shock and horror.

"Remove the bags as urgently as possible," he added. "Take the Amazons to my dungeon. All but the leader." To her, he said, "Tell Nethandra what transpired today. If her apology pleases me, I'll allow her to live. If not..."

He let his words trail off, knowing the imagination could be more frightening than a threat.

"This is where we part." Cameo took a step backward, widening the distance between them.

Denial roared through his head. *Not ready to lose her. Not yet.*

Tense, he motioned Cameo onward. "I'll take you to the goddess...and the portal home."

Lazarus had passed through the portal only once. After Cameo returned home the first time and his desire for her had overridden his common sense. He'd spent weeks trapped inside a dark, endless void. He'd had to fight his way free and ended up in a fiery spirit realm.

"Thank you, but I'll be fine on my own," she said. "No need to spend time with someone you dislike."

Still smarting about that, was she? "To open the portal, blood must be spilled, a sacrifice made. Do you know what kind of sacrifice?" He shook his head. "No, sunshine. You won't be fine on your own."

Her thoughts blasted into his awareness. No, no, had to be the *demon's* thoughts.

He never considered asking you to be his bride. You are no one's prize.

Cameo agreed with the fiend, and a muscle jumped beneath Lazarus's eye. How dare anyone think poorly of his woman—even the woman herself! He'd seen her fight. Girl had skills. Enemies had best beware. And she was smart. No one got the upper hand with her. Not even Lazarus. She was beautiful. Exceptionally so. No one compared.

Why would the demon push such a depressing conversation past Cameo's mental shield?

The answer came easily. To incite sorrow in *Lazarus*.

Misery was worse than he'd realized, and this was just another reason to despise the fiend. *Could kill him in seconds...*

The notion calmed Lazarus, even as it disconcerted him. He could kill *Cameo* in seconds, too. She wasn't safe. He wanted her safe.

Fool!

Her head canted to the side. "Why are you looking at me like that?"

"Like what?" *Like you are the reason I breathe?*

"Like I'm hungry, and you are a smorgasbord of desserts?"

"Yes," she hissed.

"Because you *are* a smorgasbord of desserts." He chucked her under the chin. "You are a prize worthy of *any* man."

She shook a fist in his face, an action he adored. Her anger always thrilled him. "Stop reading my mind."

"Stop projecting." He stalked down the cobblestone path, calling over his shoulder, "This way."

Cameo raced to catch up with him. They walked side by side, the close proximity an agony and a pleasure. Torches lined the path, soft golden lights painting her with irresistible radiance.

Her eyes were molten, a sea of silvery fire. The night's warmth brushed her cheeks with an exquisite pink flush. Her bloodred lips were lush and lickable, a temptation like no other and a special kind of torture. *One kiss*, they said. *Satisfaction awaits.*

"Just so you know," she grated, "I might have desired you before, but I resent you now."

"Might?" He laughed with smug assurance. "Your passion nearly burned me alive."

She sputtered, her memory loss making her unable to refute his claim.

Hoping to encourage her irritation and displace what remained of the misery, he took the lead and pushed a flowering branch out of the way only to release the branch before she passed by. The soft flower petals slapped her in the chest.

She glared at him. "You did that on purpose."

"No need to punish me. Your voice is punishment enough."

"That's it!" She hooked her hands around his neck and jerked, using the full force of her body. A body she then coiled around him, as deft as a sky serpent. Her weight and momentum toppled him.

The action was unexpected. The only reason it worked—of course.

Upon impact, she maintained her hold and rolled, forcing him to his back. He had no time to react. She straddled his chest, unsheathed one of her diamond daggers and pressed the tip into his carotid.

Instant hard-on. No one else had ever taken him to ground.

Proof she would only ever weaken him?

Instant soft-on.

One of her midnight brows arched, her usual misery edged with smug satisfaction. "You were saying?"

Such confidence. Such cunning. Was there any woman more beautiful?

With her hands otherwise occupied, she wouldn't be able to stop what he did with his own...

He should resist. A man didn't play with temptation; temptation played with *him*. Their association could not end well.

In that moment, he simply didn't care.

Lazarus gripped her by the waist, grunting as skin met heated skin. "So soft," he intoned. "So perfect."

A tremor rocked her against him. His hard-on returned with a vengeance.

With a hiss, she pressed the tip of her dagger deeper, drawing a bead of blood. Her jaw dropped. "You're bleeding. And your heart...I can feel its beat against my thigh. I don't understand. You're dead. You died. Didn't you?"

"I did. I'm not sure what sets me apart. I only know I'm not considered one of the living." Otherwise he would have returned to the mortal world when he'd passed through the portal.

As a child, he remembered his father telling him, "We are the last remaining descendants of Hydra. Our kind is not supposed to die. Not by fair means, and certainly not by foul."

Hydra was the first nine-headed water she-beast ever born, with venom so toxic her breath often proved lethal. She could regrow decapitated limbs, even her heads, in seconds.

Why didn't I?

Lazarus caressed his thumbs up and down Cameo's quivering belly and circled her navel. "I still bleed, yes," he said. His voice dipped. "I'm capable of spilling another fluid, too."

"Stop," she demanded, breathless.

"Stop giving you pleasure?" He traced his fingertips up, up, and met the undersides of her breasts.

Beneath the fabric of her bra, her nipples hardened into tight little buds.

"Yes. No." She covered her breasts with her free arm. "Stop screwing with my mind."

"How about I just screw you?"

One night. He wanted one night with her. His father had spent five years with his mother before the crystals slowed him in battle. Granted, Typhon had visited his μονομανία only when his body's needs overpowered him. One night would cause little damage to Lazarus. Surely.

In the morning, he would say goodbye.

"No?" Cameo replied, a question when she'd probably intended to make a statement.

Up...up... He slid his hands underneath her arms and cupped her breasts. "Exquisite." His mind steamed with lust. "Look how responsive you are to me." *Only to me.*

Goose bumps broke out over her arms, and the flush in her cheeks deepened. The pressure of the blade eased. "Did you know twenty-one percent of women are unable to achieve an orgasm?"

"Must be the twenty-one percent I haven't slept with. I'm an orgasm donor."

"You admit to being a he-slut?"

"I admit to a misspent youth, when anyone in a skirt... or pants...or shorts...or bare skin...would do the trick."

She licked her lips, the epitome of wanton. "And you pleased them all?"

"Multiple times."

"You're sure? Every single woman could have faked it."

"You forget, it's impossible to hide the truth from me. I can read minds." He arched his back, causing the blade to slice into his skin again. But he didn't care, the motion causing her to slide down and straddle his hips. "Want to test me out, sunshine?"

"I want..." She leaned down, and her breasts smashed against his chest, her nipples still hard little buds. Her heartbeat drummed against his in a too-fast rhythm.

Life. She's life.

She's my life.

No! They would have one night. No more.

Her lips hovered over his, and their breath mingled. He inhaled her essence as though she was his last hit of oxygen.

"Lazarus," she whispered.

Molten desire blistered him. "I want Lazarus. That's what you said. I'll allow no take backs."

She shivered and then she stiffened. Even as her pupils spilled over her irises, reminding him of a storm being chased away by the sun, she said, "Take backs. I will never sleep with a man who dislikes me. I don't need another reason to hate myself."

"Don't sleep with me, then." Not yet. "I can get you off with my fingers or my mouth. Lady's choice." He *had* to touch her impossibly soft skin, the need as necessary as breathing.

Her expression pinched, and he didn't have to read her mind to know why. The demon had protested. Loudly.

"Focus on me," Lazarus commanded softly. When her gaze met his once again, he framed her face and brushed his thumbs over the rise of her cheekbones. "Your circumstances will never be good enough for Misery. If you want to be happy, you have to purposely fight him. Victory won't happen by accident."

She dropped the dagger and circled her fingers around his wrists. "You think I don't know that? You think I haven't fought him every hour of every day for centuries?"

"Want a different outcome, do something different." So easy to say, so difficult to do.

"What? What can I do?" she snapped.

He...wasn't sure.

Fury crackled in her eyes, but it soon gave way to utter heartbreak. "If I sleep with you, I'll forget you. Once again, you'll know what I look, sound and feel like in the throes of a passion I've always longed to experience, while I'll know nothing about you. I'll lose another piece of myself. I'll lose the kind of memory others take for granted. Thoughts to keep me warm on cold winter nights when I'm alone. Always alone."

A pang slicked through his heart. "Cameo—"

In the distance, a twig snapped. Someone approached.

Protective instincts surged, overriding his desire. He rolled his woman underneath him and prepared to attack and defend.

7

"Step four: Study the enemy. i.e., Study everyone."
—*How to Achieve Victory*
Subtitle: Except with Lovers and Their Family

Cameo burned. Every inch of her ached. Oh, how she ached! A delicious buzz vibrated in her cells.

This was…arousal? True arousal, with no hint of Misery's taint?

Yes. Had to be. A true miracle, and a first for her. *Need more of this.* She had to have more. Now!

Lazarus wanted to sleep with her. He'd cupped her breasts and thumbed her nipples. He'd looked at her with aggression, possession and brutal longing. But saying *yes* to the warrior was saying *yes* to Misery. After sex, Lazarus would send Cameo away, guaranteed.

Discarded like trash.

He'd made no promises about the future and hadn't apologized for his "I dislike you" comment. The demon would wipe her memory once again, and she would lose another piece of herself.

No, thanks.

The heat and aches faded at last, leaving her cold and hollow.

Lazarus's desire must have died, as well. He'd rolled her over, his muscled body pinning her softer one to the moss-covered ground, his erection no longer prodding the notch between her legs.

Do not cling to him. Fight the urge.

"I need you to quiet down, sunshine." Whispered words, but fierce with command.

Confusion delivered a well-placed punch to her frontal lobe. He'd just told her to *quiet down*, even though she hadn't spoken a word.

"You're thinking out loud," he said, exasperation thick in his tone. "Now hush."

Ugh. How could she have forgotten his ability to read her mind?

With a growl, she erected a mental block.

In the distance, new twigs snapped. Her ears twitched while the rest of her stiffened.

Feminine mumbles penetrated her awareness. Cameo swiped up the diamond dagger at the same time Lazarus palmed a spiked blade. His motion was barely perceptible. Had he not been on top of her, she would have missed the action.

The mumbling grew louder, until Cameo could make out the words. "—so much trouble! I mean it. Auntie Vie has a good thing going here. Babysitting duty will screw everything up."

The familiar voice almost incited excitement. Almost.

"Viola." Cameo experienced a single beat of relief

before Misery poured an all too familiar sorrow into her heart.

Lazarus's rigid posture softened. Sighing, he pushed to his feet and, with his fingers twined around hers, drew Cameo to a stand. The calluses on his palm created an undeniable zing of friction, a lance of pleasure shooting straight to her core. The heat returned. The aches reignited, and she trembled.

Look away from him! A difficult feat, but one she managed to accomplish. Barely.

Branches rattled and parted, revealing a five-foot-three pixie with long blond hair and cinnamon-colored eyes. As sexy as ever, she wore a black sequined dress. The center veed to a pierced navel and revealed the perfect swell of cleavage. The hem reached her knees, while a split on one side showcased a Kentucky bucket-load of thigh.

Though Viola was the keeper of Narcissism, she'd had nothing to do with Pandora's box. However, there'd been more demons than thieves who'd released them, and those demons had required containment.

What better recipients for the leftovers than the immortals trapped in Tartarus? They couldn't run, couldn't hide.

Why Viola was imprisoned, she hadn't yet shared.

The goddess spotted Cameo and stopped. Surprise never registered on her delicate features, only irritation. "A girl spends quality time building the perfect stay-away-from-me rep so losers will stop trying to steal her body, and this is her reward?" In each well-manicured hand, she clutched a dirt-caked child. "Look who dared show up at my door!"

Cameo jolted as if she'd been punched. Those dirt-caked kids were Urban and Ever. Her twin godchildren. Their father was Maddox, the keeper of Violence. Their mother was Ashlyn, a newly minted immortal, thanks to her marriage bond to Maddox.

Urban had his daddy's black hair and startling violet eyes while Ever had her mother's curling honey-colored hair and twinkling gaze to match. Both children possessed extraordinary powers, with some abilities yet to be tapped.

Cameo rushed over and pulled the kids against her, hugging both. She opened her mouth to demand answers. What were they doing here? How had they gotten here? Last time she'd seen them, they'd been in Budapest with their parents. But she snapped her mouth closed and remained quiet. Sadly, even little ones cried at the sound of her voice.

Frustration ate at her, making her miss Lazarus's indifference.

An unexpected savior, he sidled up to her to ask the questions she couldn't. When neither child responded, Viola gave them both a little shake.

"Start talking or I start spanking," Viola said.

"Do you know how many toy soldiers will fit into a toilet before it clogs?" Urban asked with attitude. "Twelve. The number is twelve."

Ever's chin quavered as she peered down at her feet and kicked a pebble. "Mom and Dad are super worried about you, Aunt Cam. While they dealt with the great toilet crisis, we used the Paring Rod to check on you."

Touched, Cameo pressed a hand over her heart.

Astonishment pulsed from Lazarus. "You're children. Who taught you to use the Paring Rod?"

Urban crossed his arms over his chest, looking far

older than his years and just as stubborn as his mother. "I don't know you, so I don't have to tell you anything but *get lost*."

Viola pinched the bridge of her nose, as if she'd been pushed past the limits of her tolerance. "For disgusting little urchins, they're extremely intelligent. They watched their aunts and uncles use the Paring Rod and *ta-da*. Here they are."

Well. The kids needed to learn a hard lesson, and if Cameo had to make them sob in the process, so be it. "Coming here was irresponsible. Your parents are probably worried sick. And what if they followed you through the Paring Rod? What if they ended up in a different realm? They could be injured. Or worse!"

Ever hunched over and vomited the contents of her stomach.

Instant guilt. Puking was a little too harsh of a lesson.

Tears poured down Urban's cheeks as he wrapped an arm around his sister's shoulders.

"Ouch," Lazarus muttered, his lips twitching at the corners. "Aunt Cam is a hard-ass."

She ignored the guilt…and the urge to lean against him, to bury her head in the hollow of his neck.

Viola fluffed her hair, her eyes dry. Like Lazarus, she didn't react to Cameo. Either overwhelming sorrow already brewed inside her or she hid her sadness behind a veil of self-love. Either way, Cameo made a quality decision. *She's my new best friend.*

"Mom and Dad don't know we used the Paring Rod," Urban said through his sniffles. "I hid our actions, even from Uncle Torin."

Torin, keeper of Disease and one of Cameo's old

boyfriends, monitored the comings and goings of the entire fortress in Buda. Hiding *anything* from him required skill.

"You can't know—" she began.

"I do know. Besides," the little boy added, "you're being a hypocrite. *You* came here. *You* worried my parents."

Oookay. She couldn't ignore the guilt any longer. She'd known her friends would worry, but she'd sought out Lazarus, anyway, desperate to regain her memory… secretly hoping to create new ones.

All for nothing! He dislikes *me.*

Great! Bitterness frothed alongside the guilt.

"I told the little monsters they're fools," Viola said. "Because I'm smart. The smartest one here, no question."

Urban flipped her off.

"Oh, how sweet. You're my number one fan." The goddess patted the top of his head. "That's not exactly a shocker, kid. I'm *everyone's* favorite."

The self-love sprang from the demon, so Cameo wouldn't castigate her.

She motioned for the children to cover their ears. As soon as they obeyed, she said, "Where have you been? One day you were safe at home, the next you were gone, a note on your pillow. *Don't wait up.*" She notched a fist on her hip. "Why did you return to the spirit realms?"

"Maybe I get better cell service here." Viola gave her hair another fluff, a silver ring glinting on her finger. "Maybe my real friends are here."

"I decided we're besties. Deal with it."

Viola waved a hand in front of Cameo's face. "You really know how to bring down the vibe, don't you?"

She nodded. Truth was truth.

Lazarus stepped between them, a muscle jumping beneath his eye. "A ball gag would make an excellent lip gloss for you, goddess." Fury crackled in his tone.

Uh, what had gotten him so worked up?

Viola wiggled her perfectly plucked brows. "Is that an invitation, warrior? Because I accept."

Oh, no she didn't.

A dark, gnarled limb sprouted through the chambers inside Cameo's heart, growing from a root of envy. Despite the presence of Narcissism, Viola exuded a normal woman's sensuality. She could flirt and charm with abandon and happiness was hers for the taking—and the giving! She could give a fierce man like Lazarus what Cameo could not—untainted pleasure.

Rethinking our friendship...

Ever heaved a disgruntled sigh. "Earmuffing is getting old."

Urban tapped his foot, impatient.

Cameo held up her index finger, requesting another minute. Glaring at Lazarus, she asked, "Is Viola in the running for your wife?"

Viola said, "Yes. Of course. I'm in everyone's running."

He snorted. "Say the word, and I'll gladly introduce her to the end of my sword. And before your raging jealousy decides I'm bluffing in an effort to hide my desire for her, know that I burn for one woman, only one, and she is a black-haired, silver-eyed vixen."

The limb in Cameo's heart shrank, the root catching flame. Her knees trembled. Lazarus might not like her, but he desired her. No, he *burned* for her.

Breathless, she said, "We need to get the children to

the portal." The sooner the better. Maddox and Ashlyn
had to be agonized by the loss of their children. "How
far must we travel?"

"Three days in the opposite direction. We'll return
to the palace and head out at first light."

"But—"

"You don't want the munchkins in the forest at
night," Viola interjected. "Trust me. I'm surprised the
plants haven't tried to eat us already."

Lazarus's chest puffed up with pride. "The plants
fear me. With good reason."

Gorgeous warrior. His strength tantalized and
tempted her. *I burn for him right back.*

I'm doomed, remember? He's not for me.

As their group motored forward, Lazarus said to
Viola, "Where's your pet?" His gaze slid to Cameo.
"Princess Fluffy— whatever gnawed off my hand at
our first encounter."

"Did you retaliate?" she asked.

Urban and Ever burst into tears, again, and Cameo
withered. Right. The two were no longer covering their
ears. Better zip her lips.

Lazarus flicked the children an irritated glance. As
if he were protective of Cameo's feelings. Had to be a
misinterpretation on her part.

"I *could have* retaliated," he said. "Quite easily. Instead, I chose to forgive the slight."

Her brow knit with confusion. "Why?" Forgiveness
clearly wasn't his thing.

"My reasons are my own."

"And probably manillogical. Meaning ridiculous,"
Viola said. "As for Fluffy, he's chasing a hideous beast

who's been following me for weeks. A fun game of hide-and-seek."

The children decided to play a game themselves, throwing and catching a small rock. Urban threw it first, flames erupting from the ends of his fingers.

Ever possessed the opposite ability. She sprouted ice, dousing the flames. Though Urban used to wield ice and Ever used to wield fire.

They were opposites in many ways, but they were also two halves of a whole, complete only with each other. They could switch abilities at will.

Oh, to have a devoted partner in crime.

Cameo's gaze slid to Lazarus, and lingered on the bulge of his biceps. One small vein glinted silvery white in the moonlight. The desire to touch registered a split second after she'd already reached out.

Without turning in her direction, he captured her wrist, his long, strong fingers forming a hot brand and unbreakable shackle. As electricity arched between them, her heart galloped, a racehorse headed for an invisible finish line.

A low growl rose from his chest, echoing through the trees. Birds took flight, squawking in protest, and leaves wrinkled as they drew back.

"No touching in public." Lazarus released her.

"Why?" Minutes ago, he'd said he wanted her. Now she wasn't allowed to caress him in front of other people?

He's embarrassed of you. Misery cast a dark shadow over her thoughts and wrapped her in sorrow.

The tears she'd so often caused in others welled in her eyes, but she blinked them back.

His spine rigid and his stride long, Lazarus moved

ahead to claim the lead. Cameo and the others followed him through the rose garden, past the statues she'd admired earlier and into the palace. The children stopped playing, stopped laughing.

Her misery was already spreading, affecting those around her. The knowledge only added to her sorrows.

Viola threw open her arms and shouted, "I'm here at last. Drink me in."

Lazarus escorted her and the children to a spacious room. "Rest," he said. "Food will be brought to you."

He shut the door before the trio could protest. As two guards raced from the shadows to stand sentry at the door, he strode down the hall, turned a corner and stopped at Cameo's door.

Tension radiated from him and thickened the air, air sweet with his scent and sultry with his delicious heat. Breathing became more difficult, as if she were trying to inhale molasses.

"Invite me in," he rasped.

The change in him devastated her senses. She licked suddenly dry lips. "Why? Minutes ago, you couldn't stand my touch."

"Untrue. We were in public, and you were about to touch a...wound."

He's not embarrassed of me. "I'm sorry, Lazarus. I didn't know."

He took a step toward her, invading her personal space. "I want a night with you, sunshine. From sundown to sunrise, I want to make you scream with pleasure."

The blatant sexuality of his claim nearly knocked her off her feet. He'd meant what he said and would do as he'd promised; she had zero doubts about that. His dark eyes sizzled with lust and challenge.

Must decline. But why?

His dislike. Her memory loss.

Um, surely she had more than two reasons?

Only need one. "No," she croaked.

Without missing a beat, Lazarus took her by the hips, swung her around and pressed her against the door. "Have dinner with me, then. Give me a chance to sway you."

Misery hissed.

Cameo chewed on her bottom lip. "Why do you want me?" Why not go for Viola, the surer thing?

"Desire is a beast more insidious than your demon."

In other words, he didn't want to want her. And she couldn't blame him!

She should lock herself in her room, end the madness. Problem was, she would only buy herself an hour, maybe two. He was a warrior, and walking away from him would incite him to battle. He would only come after her with greater fervor.

What harm could food, conversation and a little innocent flirting do? He would never breach her resolve. She, too, was a warrior. Yes?

"Yes," she whispered. "I'll have dinner with you."

8

"Step five: Plan an attack. Trash it and plan another. Trash that one, and act without planning. If you surprise yourself, you'll surprise your enemy."

—*How to Achieve Victory*
Subtitle: Except with Lovers and Their Family

Cameo's heart thundered against her ribs as Lazarus led her into the bedroom. She stopped short, dumbfounded.

He'd planned ahead.

Servants were lighting candles here, there, everywhere. A small, round table had been brought into the room and covered with dishes. The scent of sweetmeats and candied treats teased her, and her mouth watered.

Misery had curtailed her appetite for years, and yet her stomach rumbled, a sign of hunger she wasn't used to feeling. Usually, when she spent time away from her friends, she had to set an alert on her phone to let her know mealtime had arrived.

Never breach my resolve? I'm an idiot.

"You are not an—" Lazarus began.

Erecting a mental shield, she pressed a finger against his lips. "If you respond to my thoughts one more time, I'll insist on eating alone."

He nipped at her fingertip, his straight white teeth sinking into her tender flesh. She barely noticed the sting...but gasped as he licked the same spot, her cells buzzing. Languid heat consumed her.

"Out," he barked, never looking away from her.

The servants dashed from the room. The males wore T-shirts and jeans while the females wore cashmere sweaters and lightweight pants. *I call foul!* Lazarus only dressed his pretties scantily while everyone else got to wear whatever the hell they wanted?

"You are no longer in charge of my wardrobe," Cameo informed him. "Sexable women aren't your personal Barbie dolls. Some of us prefer to wear something other than sequined bandages."

"A simple *thank you* would suffice. And I like the word *sexable*. You offering?"

"What! No!" Right?

Right.

With a smirk, Lazarus snaked an arm around her waist and led her to the table. He pulled out her chair, ever the gentleman. "Please, have a seat on the quitter bench."

Muscles contracted at both corners of her mouth as if...as if... Nope. The sensation eased, and disappointment flared. Sighing, she sat down.

He eased into the chair across from hers, light and shadows flickering over his rugged features. Taking turns caressing him? Lucky lights. Lucky shadows.

He smiled as he filled her plate with flaky crabmeat in a butter cream sauce, mixed vegetables steamed to perfection, and a casserole that smelled suspiciously like…

"Doritos?" she asked.

"At the Harpy Games, you ate a bag of the cheese-flavored chips while cheering for your friend, so I had a special dish prepared." He hiked a shoulder in a casual shrug. "One of the newly deceased members of my staff had a recipe." His dark eyes twinkled at her. "Are you impressed?"

She sooo did not want to admit the truth, but unlike Gideon, the keeper of Lies, deceit wasn't her thing and it would only fuel Misery's power over her. "Yes," she grumbled. "I am."

He'd noticed her before she'd even met him. How sweet was that?

She toasted him with a glass of red wine and added, "Here's hoping you disappoint me the rest of the evening."

"Alas. Your hopes are for naught. Disappointment is a feat I've never managed."

"I'm sure," she grumbled.

"You sound jealous. Are you jealous?"

"You sound hopeful. Are you hopeful?"

His husky chuckle proved headier than the cabernet. "For dessert, we're having chocolate cake. I'm told mortals think this one is better than sex."

Hmm, chocolate. Despite her lack of appetite, she sometimes craved chocolate as if it were the only path to happiness. "Well. Meet your competition. I'm tempted to spend the night with *the cake*."

"In that case…" He lifted a round lid, revealing the chocolate cake in question. With his free hand, he stabbed his knife into the center. "Unfortunately, this cake has been murdered."

She snickered—no, Misery swallowed the sound before it had a chance to escape, leaving her deflated.

"When first I arrived in your realm," she said, jumping from pleasure to business for the sake of her sanity, "a man noticed I'm living rather than dead. How?"

He rolled with the punches, not missing a beat. "When a living being passes through the Paring Rod, their body becomes a type of suit. It's there, the dead can see it, but the spirit shimmers through it."

Interesting. "How many living—"

"Nope. My turn to ask a question." He leaned back in his seat and regarded her intently. "You've mentioned your desire to find Pandora's box. What are your plans for it?"

"I'm...undecided," she admitted. No option struck her as "the one."

She could destroy the box and sentence herself to an eternity with Misery and without hope. She could open the box and remove Misery, but she would kill herself and all of her friends.

Rumors stated anyone demon possessed would die when the box was opened, the demons sucked out of their bodies. Because evil had become an organ over the centuries. A cancerous but necessary organ. Without it, a gaping wound remained. She and the others would hemorrhage.

Kane, the former keeper of Disaster, had proved the demon possessed *could* survive the wound...if love replaced the evil. A transplant, of sorts.

Love conquered all.

But who could love a woman like Cameo?

"I'm surprised you haven't worked up a disposal plan." Lazarus glared at her. "The box can be used as a weapon against you and everyone you love."

How to explain her selfish desire to be rid of Misery without coming across as, well, selfish? "Keeley, the girlfriend of Torin—"

"The keeper of Disease, whom you used to date. Yes." He gave a clipped nod. "I know of them both."

Was he jealous? No, no. He couldn't be. No man had ever envied another's affiliation with her. Especially a man who only wanted one night in her bed, planning to bail in the morning.

Only because he can't tolerate another minute in your presence...

Only. Stupid demon!

"Continue," Lazarus said through gritted teeth.

"Yes," she said. "I dated him. We didn't last long, and he's now with the love of his life. Anyway. She's the most powerful immortal I've ever known. More powerful than you, I'd bet."

"I wouldn't put money on that. You haven't seen me in action."

Shivers as delicious as his touch, heat burning through her veins. In battle, he would be a magnificent sight, his sword in hand, the blood of his enemies splattered over his skin.

"Anyway," she said with a sigh, "Keeley told me there's another being inside the box."

Lazarus drained his wine and nodded. "Yes. The Morning Star."

Eyes widening, she dropped her fork. "What do you know?" Keeley claimed the Morning Star could provide a lifeline for every Lord. A type of Hail Mary.

Lazarus buffed his nails, doing a poor job of hiding his smug grin. "Would you like to *buy* the information from me?"

With her body? "You think I'll be okay with whoring for you?"

"Of course," he said, unrepentant. "Role-playing is fun."

Dirty-minded bastard. Why was he *sexier* right now? "No? I mean, no." If he knew about the Morning Star, others knew. Cameo could ask around. "Now it's my turn. Why do you plan to marry a woman you may not love?"

He pretended to stab himself in the heart. "Way to kill the mood."

Exactly!

"I plan to marry a woman I do not love because her army will merge with mine, and together we will mete out vengeance when my enemies enter the realm of the dead."

"Vengeance matters more than pleasure?"

He could have insisted on taking his turn but, over the candlelight, he reflected her somberness back at her. "For me, vengeance *is* the ultimate pleasure." The hardness of his tone transformed the words into a vow.

One she had best heed.

Her shoulders rolled in, pushed by the heaviness of disappointment. Perhaps she'd begun to hope. Perhaps she'd thought he would be the one to help her, maybe even save her. He could tolerate her voice, after all, and he found her attractive. *Lazarus for the win!*

But he would never choose her, would he? She would always be a conquest, unimportant, easily forgotten. As if she had any right to judge. But. He wouldn't fight for her if—when—*she* forgot *him*.

Who would? Misery asked.

"You're not going to score tonight," she told him softly. "In fact, you need to leave." Before she started to cry.

Viola, goddess of the Afterlife, secret love child of parents she refused to name, and an all-round badass, crossed her arms over her chest and stared down at Urban and Ever. The pair had seriously interfered with her plans to hide from the monster on her tail, steal powerful artifacts lost throughout the ages, and unite the different spirit realms. Her birthright!

What good was a queen without a queendom?

"Stop looking at us like that," Ever snapped.

"Like what? Like you're nasty little creatures? Well, news flash. You *are* nasty little creatures." Viola shuddered. Despite her lack of experience with the care and feeding of anyone under the age of two hundred, she was certain she had this babysitting gig nailed.

Children were drawn to her, whether they appeared to be drawn to her or not. They couldn't help themselves. No one could. Why, she could have bagged and tagged the deliciously gorgeous Lazarus if she'd wanted him. But what woman in her right mind wanted a man who peered at another female as if she were the only portal to heaven?

Not me.

Been there, done that, suffered for it.

Ever, the little snot, said, "You're a horrible person. I hate you and want my momma!"

Beneath the armor of self-love Narcissism had

erected, Viola screamed, *I know I'm horrible! Run from me. Run now. Run far. Never look back. I'm your worst nightmare, sweetheart.*

"Go—" she pursed her lips and waved her fingers "—see how many toy soldiers are needed to clog the toilets here. Auntie Vie has important duties to attend to. And yes, there's a hidden message in my words. You aren't important to me." *You can't be.*

As soon as she cared about people, animals, places or things, she lost them. Princess Fluffikans was the sole exception, and only because a piece of her heart beat inside his chest. Literally! Loving him was the equivalent of loving herself.

Ever, the grubby little urchin, anchored her hands on her hips. "We're more important than anything. Momma always says so."

Narcissism kicked against Viola's skull, a sure sign she approached the danger zone. Measures had to be taken immediately.

She bent to Ever's level and braced her palms on her knees. "I'm not comfortable speaking for all mothers everywhere, but I'm absolutely certain all mothers everywhere *have* to tell their kids they're important. It's a law. But—and this might be hard for you to accept—those mothers are lying. Until you're able to protect Auntie Vie from her legion of admirers, you are merely a nuisance."

Urban tilted his head to the side, as calm as a summer morning and as serious as a heart attack. "I can burn you to death."

"Wrong. All you can do is set me on fire." She wagged a finger in his face. "Unfortunately for you, all I'd do is thank you for helping me warm up on a chilly day."

"You aren't impervious to my flames. No one is."

She patted the top of his head. "Look who's using his big boy words."

He snapped his teeth at her, his ferocity a rival to his father's.

"Careful," she told him. "Break my finger, and you buy it."

"What does that even mean?" Ever stomped her foot, the ice in her veins rising to the surface of her skin. "You speak nonsense."

Why do you even try to relate to inferior beings? Narcissism offered the thought with a hum of displeasure.

Even closer to the danger zone... "You know what's nonsense? This conversation," Viola said. "Now. Are you two going to go destroy something or not?"

The little girl tossed her arms up, exasperated. "Of course we are."

Urban peered at Viola with...affection? "You enjoy destruction?"

And another one falls for my awesome awesomeness.

"Doesn't everyone?" Viola gently chucked him under the chin.

"No," he replied. "I like you."

"Of course you do. You and everyone else I've ever met. Probably people I've never met, too."

"You can't like her." Ever scowled at her brother. "You don't like anyone but me, and sometimes Momma and Daddy."

"Well, now I like her." He faced Viola and said, "You will like me, too."

"No, thanks, kid." She didn't just lose the people, animals, places and things she liked; she witnessed their destruction. Narcissism insisted she cater to him and no other, and punished anyone he deemed competition. So. To save the boy's life, she added breezily, "You're an infant. I'm into men."

Ever punched her brother in the shoulder, leaving ice crystals on his shirt. Viola hid a smile behind her hand. The little rug rat had a temper.

She almost pitied the man Ever fell in love with. He'd not only have to survive the girl's brother, father, uncles and aunts, but also Ever herself.

No doubt the man would consider the opportunity an honor. Ever would grow up to be an incomparable beauty, desired by all who gazed upon her.

With a roar of displeasure, Narcissism kicked at Viola's skull. *I am incomparable. Me! No one else.*

The heat drained from her cheeks. "If you're going to hang with me, you're going to have to get used to being stuck in the shadows of my astonishing allure," she said to Ever. "I'm irresistible, darling. Always have been, always will be. Age doesn't matter."

The demon purred his approval, and she breathed a sigh of relief.

"Now." She tapped the razor-sharp tips of her nails against her chin. "What was I saying before you so rudely interrupted me?"

"That you're the most wonderful person in the history of ever," Ever replied, her derision clear.

Right. "I am." She paused to admire the bejeweled ring on her thumb. The previous owner had put up quite a fight when Viola had stolen it from him. Until Fluffy had snacked on his internal organs.

The ring had the power to transport her from one spirit realm to another, *without* the Paring Rod. The perfect getaway tool.

A gasp of shock and horror ripped Viola from her thoughts. Both Ever and Urban were staring at a window, their tiny bodies exuding great strain. She threw herself in front of them, facing the threat, whatever it happened to be, and mentally calculated the reward she would demand from Maddox and Ashlyn for such a deed.

A gasp of shock and horror escaped *her*.

The massive glass panes had been opened, and between them loomed a man. A winged man. A grotesque and yet somehow exquisite winged man. His facial features were too sharp but strong and rugged and framed by long black hair that billowed in a wind she couldn't feel. His eyes were pale blue, almost white. His muscles were so big, so well-defined, they bulged. His skin was a darker blue than his eyes but still pale, like that of an ice demon, and she wavered between disliking… and liking.

His wings appeared infected by evil. The ends were stained black, the thick veins snaking from top to bottom as hard as stone.

He pointed a curling black nail in her direction and spoke a single word. "Forsaken." His voice was rough and sharp, just like his features.

Her heart sped into a faster rhythm. Narcissism remained shockingly quiet. From awe? Or disgust? Perhaps fear?

The intruder wore a loincloth, nothing more, his sculpted body on perfect display. His feet were bare, his toenails as black as the tips of his feathers.

"Um, I'm going to pass," Viola told him. "In other words, thanks but no thanks."

"Forsaken," he repeated. A second later, he launched into the air and vanished in the darkened skyline.

Fluffy dived through the window, his teeth bared as he unleashed an otherworldly snarl. He'd intended to bite the...fallen Sent One? Sent Ones were demon assassins. Perhaps he'd come here to murder Viola? Instead, Fluffy skidded across the floor and slammed into the wall.

"My baby!" She rushed over and gathered him close. Throughout the centuries, he'd become her best friend. The only living being she trusted. "You chased the bad guy as he chased me. Then you saved the day!"

"What," Urban said, punctuating the word as he pointed to the window, "was that?"

As she nuzzled Fluffy's fur, she waved a dismissive hand. "Only another admirer, I'm sure." But even as she spoke, a tidal wave of foreboding overtook her.

As the goddess of the Afterlife, she sometimes had premonitions about other people's pain and death. She had one now—about herself! That man...whoever he was, whatever he was, he was part of her future, and he would hurt her worse than anyone ever had.

Siobhan, goddess of Many Futures, watched Cameo through the glass prison that had served as her home for far too long. The magic mirror, some called it. Many had slaughtered entire villages for a chance to gaze upon it.

And *she* was considered the evil one? Because she'd caused twelve little wars? Hypocrites!

Well, the past was the past, and the future awaited.

Another war brewed in the immortal realms. The underrealms, to be exact. Hades versus Lucifer. Even Siobhan would have to pick a side.

Who was she kidding? She'd *already* picked a side. As a young child, she'd taken one look at the beautiful but reviled Hades, fallen in love, certain he was simply misunderstood and she could save him, and asked him for his hand in marriage. He'd been a big, bad warrior, even then, but he'd said, "Sure thing, kid. We'll set the date for four thousand years from now."

Over the next decade, her love for him had only magnified. He was such a strong, capable male and, if she were being honest, his dark side had thrilled a secret part of her.

Finally she could wait no longer. As a teenager, she'd returned to him, certain she was old enough to be with him. Just as certain he would accept her.

Instead, he and his current lover had laughed at her pathetic attempt at seduction. Humiliated and angry, Siobhan had kinda sorta ripped out the woman's heart.

Oops. My bad. Accidents happened.

At Hades's command, a powerful witch then cursed her to live inside the mirror.

Siobhan had spent the last four millennia trapped behind the glass, growing from teenager to woman alone, denied the touch of another.

Only by manipulating those who'd gazed upon her glass had she managed to escape the underworld. But as the centuries passed, she'd dreamed of returning, of ruining Hades's life.

Once again she'd had to scheme and manipulate, until she'd finally ended up in the Realm of Grimm and Fantica, a land ruled by a known associate of Hades's.

Would the king of the underworld visit? Would he remember her? Perhaps sense her behind the glass?

She didn't blame the witch for her predicament; the woman had simply followed her master's orders. It was Hades who deserved to know the pain of imprisonment and the horror of watching the world live on without him.

He deserved to switch places with Siobhan.

Vengeance, she knew, corrupted in the worst of ways. In fact, one of the ends she foresaw for Lazarus and his quest to destroy Hera and Juliette was the destruction of everyone and thing he loved. Only poisonous fruit could grow from a poisonous tree, and in all honesty, there were no greater poisons than bitterness, hatred and sorrow.

Deprived of contact, comfort or camaraderie, those tainted fruits had grown inside Siobhan, anyway.

Her motto? *Strategize. Lead. Strike.*

I'm ready to strike!

Problem: she could foresee the paths others could, should and would take, and the ultimate results of their choices…but she couldn't foresee her own possibilities.

However, she didn't require a magical gift to know she needed to gain her freedom. To do so, she had to help other people fall in love. Every time she succeeded, a hundred years was subtracted from her sentence. But every time she tried and failed, a hundred years was *added* to her sentence.

You think you understand matters of the heart, Hades had said. *Prove it.*

Should she attempt to help Lazarus the Cruel and Unusual? As stubborn as he was, Siobhan had crossed him off the list of potentials the first time she met him. With Cameo here, she reconsidered.

Cameo had many choices and many possible outcomes.

Death…so much death. Betrayal. Sadness. Rage.

Happiness…a glimpse, only a glimpse. Quickly stolen away.

Victory, defeat.

Darkness, light. Tears. Laughter. A field of vibrant butterflies.

Everything jumbled together. Siobhan's head ached, and she forced her mind to blank, the images to clear.

Would Cameo ultimately choose to be with Lazarus? Would she do whatever proved necessary to save their relationship?

Siobhan focused on the warrior woman who hurried around her bedroom, readying tools she'd demanded the guards bring her after Lazarus had exited—two chisels, anvils, a rasp and a file. She loved her friends, would die to protect them; she sought joy.

Reminds me of the girl I used to be.

Once Siobhan would have done absolutely anything to win Hades. If she and Cameo *were* alike…

Decision made. New plans forged. *Yes, I will aid her.*

9

"Step six: Slaughter your enemy, as well as everyone he loves—then celebrate your triumph."

—*How to Achieve Victory*
Subtitle: Except with Lovers and Their Family

Lazarus endured a torturous night. Perhaps the worst of his life. Definitely worse than the time a female had fed him a poisoned kiss, weakening him. She'd restrained him while he couldn't fight back and gloatingly hacked off all his limbs.

Look at the mighty Lazarus now.

Turned out, she was an assassin sent by one of his father's old enemies.

She would have succeeded in killing the Monster's son, if not for two fatal mistakes. The *A*s and *B*s of defeat. (A) she'd believed him helpless without his arms and legs, and (B) she'd taunted him with a second kiss. A goodbye.

Pride—believing lies about oneself to inflate self-worth—often heralded a nasty fall.

As the female had lifted her head, ending the kiss with a smirk, Lazarus had ripped out her trachea with his teeth. *She* had bled to death, and he had lived. Afterward, he'd poisoned himself over and over again until he'd developed an immunity.

Why had Cameo kicked Lazarus out of her room? How could she be so blind to the truth? He could enjoy a night with her *and* achieve his vengeance against Hera and Juliette. One did not negate the other.

With a curse, he stalked from bed. A fly buzzed around him, but no matter how swiftly he swatted, the pesky insect eluded him. Irritated, he escaped into the bathroom, where he showered and dressed in a long-sleeved shirt and battle leathers. As usual, he would be sleeping fully clothed.

The pants covered the crystals that wound through his legs from thigh to calf. The shirtsleeves hid the crystals now intersecting his biceps.

The weakness had spread.

Fury burned through him. He strode into the bedroom, crossing over the unicorn-skin rug that had been prized by the former king. His pace was slower than usual. Did he have a limp? He better not have a limp!

His metamorphosis hadn't just spread, it had sped up. He was changing faster than his father.

Lazarus pounded his fists into the punching bag hanging in the corner. His knuckles cracked and blood welled, but he continued to whale on the bag until it exploded, sand spilling everywhere.

Did he want Cameo more than his father had wanted his mother? Was that the problem?

He couldn't be sure. His mind refused to analyze anything but the woman's bra size—perfect. His every thought revolved around a single question. *How do I get her into bed?* Ragged hunger gnawed and clawed at his insides, insatiable. Obsession ruled him.

He had to have her. Once, only once. *Then* he could let her go, his body safe from further harm.

He stuffed the diamond knuckles and dagger pendant in his pocket and moved to the window to peer down at the Garden of Perpetual Horror. Dawn approached.

A three-day journey loomed, each day a compendium of minutes and seconds he had to use to his advantage. Surely he could win his prize. After all, he'd started and ended wars in less time.

The fly returned, buzzing around him. He remained still, listening, his ear twitching— *Whack!*

Screw this. He'd missed.

Lazarus combed a hand through his hair, the muscles in his shoulders knotted and strained. She had two objections to him. One, he put vengeance before pleasure, and two, she would forget him.

The first he could easily assuage. For their night together, he would concern himself *only* with her pleasure. The second was the problem.

Lazarus had done his research. He knew two of her brothers-by-circumstance had survived the loss of their demons. Kane, once the keeper of Disaster, and Aeron, once the keeper of Wrath.

Kane… Lazarus wasn't sure how he'd recovered. Aeron was given a new body—a new house for his spirit—by the One True Deity, leader of the Sent Ones and angels. But then, Aeron had wed a Sent One, so the gift made sense. Cameo was single, and if Lazarus had anything to say about it, she would remain that way for the rest of eternity.

My possessiveness matters more than her happiness?
Going to let her go.

Little growls rose from deep in his chest as he started
pacing. He needed to see her. Was she asleep? Did she
dream of him?

He opened his mind, saw her puttering around her
bedroom, and hardened. Tools were strewed across the
table where they'd dined; she hammered, chiseled and
filed a small dagger. Already she'd made two helmets
and two breastplates, size small. For the children, he
realized. She feared an attack on the journey to the portal, and this was a preemptive strike.

Had she stayed up all night?

Such a wickedly smart woman, his μονομανία. And
talented. The magnificence of the craftsmanship stunned
him.

Before they parted, he would have a sword made by
her, a blade to cherish throughout an eternity spent alone.

By the time morning arrived, Cameo's eyes burned
and her limbs trembled with fatigue. At least she'd finished the armor for the children, using skills she'd acquired under Alex's tutelage.

Alex… A familiar tide of sorrow battered her.

Ignore it. Protecting Urban and Ever—even without
her customary embellishments—trumped any discom-
fort on her part.

She bathed and dressed in a clean tank, another pair
of butt-crack shorts and a sarong. Her combat boots
and daggers rested atop the bureau, surprising her. The
guards must have brought the items during one of their
many deliveries, which meant Lazarus had kept his
promise to return her personal belongings.

Dangerous warmth cascaded through her veins.

Ignore it! She anchored the boots in place and sheathed the daggers at her ankles. Along with armor, she'd made a vial for the—very expensive—salve Lazarus had used on her wounds. A vial she hung around her neck with a leather cord. Sky serpents bore her no love. If they decided to attack her, she had best be prepared.

She brushed and braided her hair—well, *attempted* to braid her hair. She failed royally and opted for a messy ponytail. Her usual. Noting her pale cheeks, she pinched here and there to add color. Not that she cared about her appearance. She'd never cared before. After all, the very second she opened her mouth, most men fled as if she were toxic waste.

But Lazarus was different. He placed vengeance above everything else, even pleasure, as if it was forgettable. Bastard! She would do *anything* to experience and remember pleasure. So. Let him look at Cameo and want what he couldn't have. Let him stew in his desire and find no succor.

Let him know the trials she endured on a daily basis!

Or prove he's better off without you…

She inhaled sharply, the demon's words hitting her where it hurt the most. Her hope.

A knock sounded at the door, and she jolted, her heart skipping a beat. Lazarus, come to fetch her? "Enter."

Blondie stepped into the room, and Cameo deflated.

"Breakfast, courtesy of the king." She placed the tray on the table, pushing aside Cameo's tools, and uncovered multiple dishes of food. Chocolate cake, cupcakes and pudding, with a steaming pot of hot chocolate to wash everything down.

Her cheeks warmed with *pleasure*. Lazarus was lethal to her resolve.

How was she supposed to resist him?

Cameo waved the servant away, wishing she could act like a normal person and say, "Thank you."

Alone, she gobbled up the food, an addict finally getting a hit. But the delicious sweetness only added to the turmoil inside her head. What had caused Lazarus to make vengeance his number one priority?

Before using the Paring Rod the second time, Cameo had asked around. Hera the Cuckoldress, the dethroned queen of the Greeks and once a lover of William the Ever Randy—one of Cameo's allies—had warred with Typhon, Lazarus's father. Terrible deeds were committed by both. Ultimately Hera killed Lazarus's mother before hiding and imprisoning his father. Hating her was understandable.

Ever since the Titans had taken control of the third heaven, Hera had been locked in Tartarus, utterly helpless, starved and beaten by other imprisoned immortals. Had she paid for her crimes? Had she suffered enough?

When would the cycle of evil end?

Juliette the Eradicator had enslaved Lazarus for centuries. Cameo remembered seeing the couple together on two separate occasions. When Juliette's temper had threatened to detonate, he'd patted her hand to calm her. He'd been the only one *capable* of calming her.

When she had gripped him by the nape and yanked him close for a kiss, he hadn't denied her. No, he'd kissed her back with equal fervor.

Jealousy simmered, scalding Cameo. At one time, Lazarus *had* desired the Harpy. Perhaps he would have offered Juliette forever if she hadn't forced the issue, perhaps not. Now he yearned to punish her.

How quickly a man's feelings could change. But then, feelings were unreliable and unpredictable, and if left unchecked, they would lead to disaster. Misery had proved it again and again.

Lust was unreliable and unpredictable. And yet, as Lazarus's arms wrapped around her, Cameo wanted her lips on his.

He'd offered a night in his bed. Maybe she should accept.

Maybe he would rock her socks off. Maybe she would have to fake a good time. Either way, she would forget him afterward. For whatever reason, Misery despised the male and, judging by past behavior, would allow no reminders of him.

Maybe the loss of Cameo's memory could be a good thing this time?

Once a "boyfriend" had told her, "You have no poker face. You're miserable, and you want me to stop." It hadn't been a question.

She'd nodded, hating herself as much as the demon.

Funny thing, though. The boyfriend had stopped without any effort. He hadn't been overcome with passion, or so close to coming that he'd been driven to the brink of sanity. He'd simply dressed and stalked away, silent, never even casting her a second glance.

She would *love* to forget the humiliation of that night.

What if the warrior gives you what you've always wanted? Misery stroked her mind, as if he was petting her. *I might allow you to keep your memory of him...if you kill him after you sleep with him.*

She choked on her tongue. Kill Lazarus? Murder a

lover in cold blood simply to retain her memories of an orgasm?

An *orgasm? As in,* only one. *Silly Cameo. That male will never stop with one.*

With a screech, she punched her fists into her temples. "You're *that* desperate to end my association with him?"

She'd killed before, yes. She'd killed *many times* before, but always in the heat of battle. Never would she consider the demon's offer. Besides, Misery had no honor. If she kept her end of the bargain, he could wipe her memory, anyway. How would she know?

"Foolish demon." She tsk-tsked. "You've made a grave mistake. You've shown your cards. You're scared of him. Because he can make me happy."

Misery hissed in denial, but the truth was suddenly crystal clear.

Lazarus can *make me happy.*

Dazed, she eased onto the chair in front of the vanity. Ripples appeared in the glass, distorting her reflection. She gasped.

As an image began to take shape in the center, Cameo gasped. The goddess of Many Futures *was* trapped inside.

Hope ignited. What if a bright future awaited Cameo?

"Show me," she whispered. "Please."

The screen split, revealing *two* images. In both, Lazarus was cut and bruised and standing in front of two towering trees, holding Cameo's hand and watching as Viola and the children entered the glittering space between and vanished.

The portal home, she realized.

On one side, vision Cameo—VC—remained by Lazarus's side. He led her away from the trees…and escorted her back to the palace. Time blazed by, as if on fast-forward. They spent days—weeks—talking, getting to know each other, *pleasuring* each other.

He introduced her body to bliss. Despite the many times they made love, he never removed his clothes. Why?

"This way or no way," he told her.

This way, *any* way, she thought. Maybe they didn't want such different things, after all.

In the vision, Cameo smiled. Smiled! She whistled a merry tune and skipped through the halls. However, her dream come true was somehow a nightmare for Lazarus. The happier she became, the *angrier* he grew. Eventually, he glared at her with hatred.

Real-Life Cameo—RLC—battled horror as Lazarus returned VC to the portal and placed a piece of black heart in her hand. When she stepped forward, her back to him, he raised a sword, as if he meant to strike her down.

VC remained unaware of his malicious intention. In the present, Cameo's horror intensified. *He becomes my enemy?*

When he spun on a booted heel and stalked away *without* harming VC, RLC breathed a sigh of relief. Then VC tossed the black heart into the portal.

The air shimmered, a countdown clock ticking; the portal would stay open for a minute, maybe two. She entered, and the light in her eyes began to fade. Because Misery allowed her to keep her memory of Lazarus… of his abandonment. Of happiness she'd been unable to sustain.

Cameo's stomach threatened to rebel.

On the other side of the mirror, a different fate played

out. Lazarus insisted Cameo spend a night with him and return home in the morning. She said no. They argued, and he kissed her with such intensity her knees weakened—in the future and in the present. Then she backed away from him, entered the portal and—

The mirror blackened, not telling her if she kept her memory or not.

No, no, no. Cameo gripped the sides of the gilt frame and shook. "What happens next? Show me!"

A minute passed. Then another. Still nothing. She cursed.

How reliable were these visions? Did she have no other options?

If she left soon after Viola and the children, would she later return to Lazarus? Would he come after her?

Smug again, Misery said, *The dead cannot pass through the portal, remember. And even if he could, would he choose to be with you...or finally end you?*

Light-headed, Cameo massaged her temples. She knew so little about the man on whom she'd pinned her hopes. Knew nothing about his wants and motivations. What would happen if they parted at the portal? Something better than loving and losing him? Or something far worse?

I must *see the rest of the second vision!*

Cameo considered her options. There was no way to sneak the mirror out of the palace. Maybe a piece of it? Yes! She grabbed a pillow and punched the glass with all her might, again and again.

Nothing happened. Not a single crack appeared. Frustration mixed with anger and helplessness.

Guess I'm on my own. As always.

10

> "Cowardice is a disease. Kill it before it kills you."
> <s>—How to Achieve Victory</s>
> <s>Subtitle: Except with Lovers and Their Family</s>
> —Living on Your Own Terms, Always

"Rathbone." Lazarus sat upon his throne, his fingers drumming against the armrests. He should be on the road. Morning had come, and the children had already clogged two sets of pipes. But the presence of his unwanted visitor had kept him home. "Show yourself."

Buzz, buzz.

Another fly? Oh, no. Not *another*. *The.* In the center of the room, the fly morphed into a fully dressed man. Irritation clawed up Lazarus's spine.

Should have known.

A grinning Rathbone spread his arms wide. "You called?"

Lazarus gnashed his teeth. "Why have you remained here?"

The warrior's grin widened. "Perhaps I wanted to

tell the world I spent a night in bed with Lazarus the Cruel and Unusual."

"No one will believe you, considering you're still able to walk."

"An enthusiastic lover, are you?"

"Very." Lazarus gripped the arms of his throne. "You've been spying on me."

"Obviously. I am not only the Only. I am the Spy Master." Amusement rather than shame peered at him through those diamond eyes. "Should you really cast stones, mind reader?"

Until Lazarus declared his allegiance to a king of the underworld, this type of nuisance would be happening over and over again. "Tell me. Will our entire conversation take place in question form?"

"Would it please you if it did?" Rathbone asked, one brow arched.

Is this how I come across to Cameo?

Of course not! I'm charming.

This had to end. He held Rathbone's gaze as he opened his mind to the other man's—

Roaring, Lazarus broke the connection.

Rathbone remained stoic. "I gave you a glimpse of horrors I've suffered in my lifetime. Attempt to read my mind again, and I'll give you full access."

Before today, Lazarus had thought he understood torture. He'd endured and received his fair share of it. Truth was, he hadn't understood until this moment. What the warrior had experienced... New respect for him bloomed.

"Take care of the woman," Rathbone said, no longer amused. "She is Hades's ally, and therefore my ally. We want her protected."

She—is—mine.

No. No! Denial screamed through his mind. He would not claim the woman who would herald his downfall. "You want her protected. Nothing more?" Did Rathbone desire Cameo in his bed?

"And help you spit on your one chance for true love?" Rathbone tsk-tsked. "No."

"True love?" He scoffed. "I mentioned nothing of love, true or otherwise. Love weakens."

"*Fear* weakens. Love strengthens." Rathbone held his stare, unblinking. "One day your woman will tire of your rejection and seek the comfort of another man. I hope to be a fly on the wall when you discover the great blessing you've lost, but I'll settle for being the one she accepts into her bed when you're gone."

He does *want my woman in his bed.* A growl reverberated in Lazarus's chest, so rough he suspected he was bleeding internally.

Calm. Control. When "one day" came, Lazarus would have already let Cameo go. No ties, no crystals, no vulnerabilities.

"We share the same hope, then," he replied. "Flies get swatted."

Rathbone laughed, but sobered quickly. "Your woman hates Misery, wants so badly to be free of him. You can aid her."

Bastard couldn't know about the box. "Let's pretend I care," he said. "Tell me, O Great One, how I can aid her."

"When did I become your life coach? Find the answer on your own." With a wink, Rathbone vanished.

Lazarus remained atop the throne, certain the bastard had lied. There wasn't a way to remove Cameo's demon and keep her alive. So. He would not change his plan. He would have a night with her.

One and done. Not by choice, but by necessity.

Afterward, he would let her go with a warning. *Never return.*

And he would not feel guilty. He would move on.

The first day of the journey passed without incident. No one attacked, and there were no grasping, hungry limbs or swarms of killer insects. Cameo was almost disappointed. She itched for a fight.

As their ragtag group had ridden away from Lazarus's palace, the Bend-Over Babes had given chase. As suspected, they'd once enjoyed quality time in bed with their king, and they'd felt entitled to a goodbye kiss.

To his credit, Lazarus had appeared flustered by the attention and had sent the Bend-Over Babes away *without* a kiss. Shockingly enough, Cameo had wanted to *murder* the women. She'd thought, *Mine! I will not share.*

No doubt the mirror's vision had screwed with her head. She'd seen herself make love to him, again and again, screaming with pleasure she'd never before known, so *of course* she'd grown a wee bit possessive of him.

Also saw him contemplate whether or not he should kill me. Where's my righteous anger over that?

Well, everyone had flaws. And wanting to kill her was actually a common occurrence among immortals and even humans.

Viola had spent several hours shamelessly flirting with the soldiers, and Urban had spent those same hours *burning* the soldiers. Apparently no other man was allowed to speak to, smile at or encourage the goddess. Ever had quickly doused the flames with her ice.

The few times Urban had remembered to be a little boy rather than a jealous stalker, he'd complained incessantly about the helmet Cameo had made.

"My hair aches," he said for the thousandth time.

"I'm sure we'll be setting up camp soon, and you can remove it." The sun had been falling steadily for the past hour.

Her voice had a ripple effect, shudders sweeping through the crowd.

During one of their many bathroom breaks, Lazarus had looked over the weapons and armor Cameo had made. "Amazing," he'd said. "Your skill is unsurpassed."

She'd almost blushed.

"Where did you learn?" he'd asked.

"A forge in the Middle Ages." Alex had—

She'd stopped the thought, unwilling to give Misery an open-door invitation to flood her with sorrow. Or Lazarus a chance to read her mind.

"There's a story there," he had remarked.

"Yes, but it's one for another day."

"Our time together grows short." He'd stared straight ahead, and a pang had cut through her chest.

When would a man want to *keep* her?

"I think you should have made the armor out of magnesium infused with dense silicon carbide nanoparticles," Ever said, breaking into her thoughts. "It's as light as aluminum, but as strong as titanium."

Cameo gaped at her.

Viola beamed as Fluffy raced around her horse. "You, little monster, are a girl after my own heart. Magnesium infused with dense silicon carbide nanoparticles has the highest strength-to-weight ratio."

As the two chatted—intelligently—about metals, Cameo's gaze sought Lazarus. He sat atop his massive winged steed, his head high, his shoulders squared, his spine rigid. What an awe-inspiring sight. Over a hundred soldiers rode with him, creating a shield for the women and children.

A horde of sky serpents flew overhead. Their numbers were fluid, beasts coming and going as they pleased. One thing remained constant minute by minute—the death glares Cameo received.

On more than one occasion, a drop of accelerant had splashed onto her face. And not by accident. The burns were too well-placed.

"Ow!" Another droplet hit her, this one burning the end of her nose. "All right. Enough. Do something about your pets. Before I pick up a branch," she shouted to the sky.

Heart-wrenching sobs rang through the crowd. She pressed her lips together.

Misery cackled with glee. *Wonder how many suicides there'll be tonight...*

Doing her best to ignore him, she smoothed salve on the newest wound.

Lazarus glared at the sky as he bellowed a string of words she didn't understand. The sky serpents understood, though. Multiple beasts roared in response, wings frenzied as they flapped.

His gaze lowered to Cameo. "They want you dead and themselves splattered in your blood."

"Trust me," she whispered, hoping no one else heard

her. If she made one more person cry… "The feeling is mutual."

Pensive, he rubbed two fingers against the stubble on his jaw. "Perhaps the sky serpents would be satisfied if I…spanked you."

A spanking? Really? "Don't you—"

He wrapped an arm around her waist, wringing a gasp from her.

"What—"

He lifted her from her horse, his biceps flexing. Such incredible strength…and yet, he began to tremble. Fearing he would drop her, she clung to him. Then he settled her in front of him, his scent and heat enveloping her, and she shivered.

Misery clawed at her skull, sending sharp pains through her temporal lobe. So much for enjoying the ride.

Or maybe not. Lazarus rubbed his cheek against hers, distracting and *delighting* her.

He chuckled softly.

She shivered harder. *Shields up!*

"Well?" she demanded. "Are you going to spank me or not?"

"Do you *want* to be spanked?"

"Do you *want* to lose a hand?"

"As if you'd remove one of the only means capable of giving you pleasure."

Air punched from her lungs. "Let me guess. The others are your other hand, your mouth and…?"

"And everything else about me. My voice…my scent… even my mind. Face it, sunshine. You crave the total package."

I do. I really do. "What about your cock…iness?"

Oookay. They were bantering, which meant they were headed down a dangerous path. Time to change the subject. "Never mind. What language did you speak to the sky serpents?"

He allowed the change without protest, surprising her. "Typhonish, the language used by my father." Warm breath fanned her cheek. "You, sunshine, are exquisite. Resisting the urge to touch you has been hard. Very, very hard."

Tendrils of desire slipped down her spine. "You're touching me now. You *didn't* resist."

"And I have yet to hear your thanks."

Part of her wanted to laugh. Most of her wanted to cry. All of her wanted him.

Okay, it was time for another subject change. "How'd you acquire the goddess of Many Futures' mirror?"

Again, he allowed the change without protest. "Inherited it with the palace. Why?"

Act casual. "Have you seen your futures?"

His posture grew more rigid. "Have *you*?"

Why not tell him? *Give and you shall receive.* "Yes. Two possibilities. In the first, we returned to the palace and had sex. Congrats! It was good. Then you escorted me to the portal, briefly considered killing me, but ultimately walked away without saying goodbye."

He flattened his hands on her thighs, and she sucked in a breath. "So we have sex, and it's good," he breathed into her ear. "You're *very* welcome."

Anticipation held her at the edge of a cliff, her insides buzzing and heating. What else would he do? "Why would you want to kill me?" she asked, a tremor in her tone. "You aren't like others. You don't react to my voice."

He stiffened, but said silkily, "I'm sure you gave me reason. But I walked away, yes? Reward me?"

As he spoke, his fingers played with her knee. The anticipation began to agonize her. But one minute bled into two. He did nothing more, the bastard.

"No reward for you," she grated.

"Very well. No reward for *you*. So what was the second vision?" he asked. "Tell me about it."

"I returned home the same day as the others."

"And?"

"And nothing. The mirror blanked."

"Little wonder I'm leaning toward vision one. The things I can do to you before you go…" He gently pressed his knees against the flanks of the Pegasus. Those feathered wings lifted, hiding her and Lazarus from the rest of the world as he nuzzled her cheek. "Or maybe we should ignore the mirror and create a new path, spend the entire night together as I've wanted from the beginning. Would you like a taste of the pleasure I'll give you?"

Yes! No. Absolutely not. Maybe? She licked her lips, tempted, so wildly tempted. But why enjoy an appetizer when she couldn't have the full meal? Why forge precious memories the demon would turn around and steal? Or even hold hostage. Life was torturous enough already.

"Fair warning," she grated. If she couldn't resist Lazarus's appeal, she would do everything in her power to ensure *he* resisted *hers*. "Misery told me I could keep my memories of you if I killed you. He hates you."

The demon hissed, which she interpreted as: *How dare you tattle!*

"He wants me *dead* dead?" Lazarus shrugged, unconcerned. "He'll have to get in line."

A flare of hope. "You aren't upset or surprised?"

"Demons hate people and love destruction. I'd be surprised if he liked me."

"But he could hurt you," she admitted quietly. "Over the centuries, he's encouraged people to kill themselves. And he's…" She licked her lips. "He convinced me to end my life once. Or six times. Maybe twelve."

He stiffened, as rigid as steel. "You tried to kill yourself a dozen times?"

She gulped, nodded. "The sorrow had become too much to bear." Each time, her friends had found her broken and bloody, and their disappointment and hurt had only added to her problems, breaking an already splintered heart.

Can't ever win.

Lazarus tightened his hold on her, as if he feared she would float away like a balloon. "I don't need the mirror to tell me what's in your immediate future. You're going to *come*."

He traced a path of fire up, up… She stopped breathing, her belly quivering, an ache blooming between her legs, but he merely played with the waist of her shorts.

"Do you *want* to come?" he whispered into her ear. "Give me one night."

Goose bumps broke out over her skin. "You don't want weeks of sexual bliss as predicted by the mirror?"

He tightened his hold, almost bruising her. "One night is all I can offer. Nothing more, nothing less."

Had the mirror lied about the different paths her future could take?

"Why only one night?" she asked softly. "Make me understand."

His sigh ruffled the hairs on her crown. "You want to remember me, sunshine. I want to remember you *well*."

Meaning…what? Misery would taint his thoughts if Cameo stuck around?

Ouch! The knowledge cut, and yet it shouldn't have been a blip on her radar. Truth was truth. But… shouldn't the man of her dreams consider her worth *any* hardship?

"I can walk into a room and ruin a party," she snapped. "You can open your mouth and do the same."

Not missing a beat—when did he ever?—he traced his white-hot tongue around the shell of her ear, nibbled on the lobe. "Speaking of a party, I'm inviting myself to the one in your pants."

The blistering heat of arousal quickly melted her anger. Which made her angry all over again. "Stop. There isn't—"

"But there *will* be." His hands inched up, up to cup her breasts, and her nipples puckered for him. As a reward, he strummed the aching crests. A stream of passion-fire shot straight to her core.

She groaned. Her hips undulated, her bottom meeting the long, hard length of his erection. Oh, mercy, the pleasure such a simple touch elicited was incredible and…the demon inundated her with sorrow, causing the sensations to cool, just as they always cooled.

Lazarus kneaded her breasts and, mentally, physically, she knew his actions felt just as good as before. Really, really good. Maybe even better. But emotionally, she couldn't be reached. Which made everything worse. A lot worse. For Cameo, emotion mattered most.

Now, no matter what Lazarus did, pleasure would remain at bay.

"You might as well stop," she told him. "I could fake my enjoyment, but I wouldn't be doing either one of us a favor."

Far from disappointed, he uttered a husky chuckle. "I'm going to need you to promise me something, sunshine."

That didn't bode well. "What?"

"You'll be very, very quiet the next time I move my hands. All right?"

Oh, no, no, no. He'd fallen into the alpha-male trap. He believed he could make all women lose their minds with pleasure. Fool! He thought he could bring home the gold despite Cameo's warning.

Actually, he thought he could bring home the gold *because of* her warning. She would have to teach him better.

Class is in session, and Miss Lord is a bitch.

"Listen up," she said. "Hear me when I say —"

"Promise me," he insisted.

He wasn't going to drop this, was he? He'd have to learn the blue-balls way. With a sigh, she twisted to look him in the eyes. "Very well. I promise."

Her wry tone continued speaking long after she'd quieted. *You're going to regret this.*

She thought…maybe, there was a chance… The corners of his mouth were lifting in a grin. Before she could be sure, he forced her to turn, traced the lobe of her ear with his teeth and slid his hands down…down…once again stopping on the waist of her sarong.

"You're not fighting a moan, are you?" he asked.

He sounded amused. "Not even a little," she said.

"Tsk. Tsk. I told you to be quiet."

"You asked me a question!"

"What about now?" He moved a fingertip along the sarong's band, brushing against her navel. "Are you fighting a moan now?"

She tingled and ached and thought, *Yes, this is it, this is actually going to happen*... But once again the glorious sensations faded.

"No," she grated.

"Still talking," he said on a sigh. "My sunshine is so terribly unresponsive. I'm disheartened." And yet he still sounded amused.

He truly believed he'd stoked a fire inside her.

Teeth gnashing, she said, "A few moans and groans mean nothing. I haven't climaxed, *darkpit*." He compared her to sunshine; she would compare him to an abyss.

"A *few* moans and groans? You're adorable."

"And your little experiment is finished."

"Temper, temper." He tsk-tsked. "Someone—and I won't mention any names—*needs* to climax."

For centuries she'd been desperate to experience something millions of women enjoyed on a daily basis. And now he thought teasing her was a good idea? *After* he'd failed to deliver what he'd promised?

A bomb of anger detonated inside her. "Your prowess is far overrated. And so is your opinion of yourself!"

"There she is, the vixen I've been waiting for," he said, and then he pushed his hand between her legs, under her shorts—and thrust a finger deep inside her.

A surge of bliss exploded inside her, and she gasped.

"Your anger weakens the demon," he purred, "giving me an opportunity to act." As he spoke, he moved his thick, beautiful, amazing finger in and out of her. His erection pressed insistently between the cheeks of her ass, adding to the delicious sensations.

"More." She leaned back, resting her head on his shoulder and offering him easier access. "I want more." *Neeeeded* more. "Please." Here, now, she wasn't too proud to beg.

He withdrew his hand, despite the nails she dug into his wrists in an effort to hold him in place. "Someone just broke her promise."

"What are you doing? You were finally getting somewhere. Keep going!"

Eyes like pools of sizzling obsidian, he licked his finger. "Isn't it obvious, sunshine? I'm punishing you, leaving you in a state of torment. You're going to remember the feel of my finger inside you and soon you're going to beg me for its return."

Teasing a woman into a snit had never been one of Lazarus's life goals. Until Cameo.

After giving him her version of the finger, she returned to her horse. He hid a grin. Let her desire for him grow and fester. Soon she would become a boiling pot of lust. The steam would, hopefully, create a barrier against the demon.

Besides, Lazarus wanted revenge. The little vixen had kept him shielded from her mind all day.

The next time he glanced at her, exhaustion had completely overshadowed her anger. She was slumped in her saddle. Her adrenaline had crashed, and crashed hard.

"Let's stop for the night," he called.

The entire procession stopped. Lazarus dismounted and patted his mighty steed on the rump for a job well done.

Within minutes, tents were erected. Viola and the children were ushered inside the biggest—the goddess insisted. When Cameo attempted to follow the trio inside, Lazarus clasped her hand and led her toward *his* tent.

At any other time, she probably would have protested. Tonight she leaned against him, using him as a crutch. Her feet dragged, leaving deep grooves in the dirt.

"Up you go, sunshine." Lazarus swept her into his arms and carried her inside. The significance of the action wasn't lost on him and it—

Nothing.

When he set her on her feet, she stumbled to a thick mound of furs and collapsed. Eyes already closing, she muttered, "Whatever you plan to ask me, the answer is no."

Sleep claimed her in the next instant, her beautiful body going lax.

"Here's a question," he muttered. "Should I keep my hands to myself tonight?"

He eased beside her, careful not to touch her. He would personally oversee her protection. All night long.

Her roses, bergamot and neroli scent enveloped him. His mind opened, seeking a connection with her. She'd never been more vulnerable, and he hated himself, but *closing* his mind proved impossible.

Must learn more about her.

The images he saw disturbed him. Misery plagued her, even in her dreams, filling her head with memories she probably despised. The times she'd been hurt physically. When people had called her terrible names.

When friends had died. When those she trusted had betrayed her.

She tossed and turned, unable to settle. Poor Cameo. Poor Lazarus. Desire for her plagued *him*. Only a few minutes before, her breasts had overflowed in his hands, her nipples flush against his flesh. His finger had been inside her, her inner walls nearly burning him alive. The little sounds she'd made in the back of her throat were auditory porn.

What he wouldn't give to strip her, to feed his aching length into her, to have her nails digging into his back and her legs wrapped around his waist...

Already addicted to her.

For whatever reason, fate had decided she was his μονομανία. Or perhaps something as simple as body chemistry had made the call. Either way, the choice... pleased Lazarus. Somehow Cameo had found a direct line to compassion he'd never felt for another. Her sharp tongue and quick wit amused him. The love she had for her friends and family roused envy.

He wanted to be the one, the only one, she turned to for comfort.

What you want isn't what you need.

He flashed outside the bounds of camp, not wanting anyone to know he'd left the tent, and slammed his fists into the trunk of a tree while cursing the moon, again and again. The vines shrank back in fear. Cool wind blustered around him.

When the bones in his hands shattered, he flashed back to the pallet. Cameo slept on, unaware of his turmoil.

When the time came, he would let her go. As planned.

No matter what the cursed mirror had shown her. Because...

The crystals in his arms and legs had thickened yet again. Now hundreds of glittering rivers branched from the hardening veins.

Like a weakling, he'd nearly dropped her when he'd hefted her onto his lap—nearly dropped a woman who weighed less than his sword. It was laughable. But he wasn't amused.

Cameo was far more dangerous than he'd ever suspected. *Because* she pleased him. Because she weakened more than his body—she weakened his resolve.

If he wasn't careful, she would do the very thing his enemies had been unable to accomplish. She would utterly destroy him.

11

"Everyone is allowed to betray you once. Mistakes happen. Just kidding. No one is allowed to betray you ever. Always keep an executioner on staff."

—*Living on Your Own Terms, Always*

"Wake up, sunshine. Eat."

Cameo blinked open dry eyes. Her body ached as if she'd just been in a car accident. A common occurrence. The demon had infiltrated her dreams, making her toss and turn and tense up hour after hour.

As she studied her surroundings, she arched her back and stretched her arms over her head. The first thing she noticed—a tent made from an unfamiliar animal skin. The only furnishings? The soft white furs beneath her. A few feet away, a small fire pit crackled, smoke wafting up and out an opening in the roof.

The scent of buttered eggs saturated the air, and her mouth watered.

A fully dressed Lazarus pulled her to an upright position. He released her as soon as possible, as if she'd burned him. A scowl marred his rugged features, the gorgeous alpha male clearly riled up about something.

Had Misery sunk his claws inside the warrior?

Lazarus handed her a linen napkin and a plate with scrambled eggs. Scrambled *green* eggs.

"What, no ham?" she asked.

"We have no pigs here. Give me half an hour and I'll acquire a nice Griffin flank steak for you."

Griffin. A γρύφων in ancient Greece. Half lion and half eagle. "No, thanks." She took a tentative bite and moaned with delight. "I guess I shouldn't have pegged you for a Dr. Seuss fan."

"Who is Dr. Seuss? A past boyfriend?" He spat the word.

The corners of her mouth twisted. *My, my, how suddenly his mood changed.* "Perhaps he is. He *does* have a special way with words."

Lazarus snapped his teeth at her.

"What kind of egg is this?" she asked.

"Sky serpent."

Whoa! The nastiest creature in the realm had the sweetest, most succulent eggs? How was that fair?

She swallowed another bite and asked, "Is it going to cause my intestines to explode?"

"Only your loins. It's an aphrodisiac."

"Well, here's to exploding loins." Cameo dug in as if she hadn't eaten in years. After licking the plate clean, she wiped her mouth with the napkin.

Lazarus watched with savage intensity, making her shiver.

"Ask me anything." He sat in front of her. "I'll answer truthfully, without fail."

Did he need a distraction from his own loins?

What would he do if she crawled into his lap?

Resist the urge! One, he'd just offered her a gift. Learn more about him? Yes, please! And two, she needed a toothbrush stat. No reason to scare him away with her morning breath.

What to ask, what to ask? Oh! "Why are you so determined to mete vengeance against Juliette? There were times you seemed to like her. *Despite* the fact that she enslaved you."

His eyes glittered. "She did more than enslave me. She manipulated my memory." His tone lashed. "Before you, she owned the Paring Rod. It does more than open portals into other realms—it cleaves spirit from soul. She used it to cleave free will from me, making me *think* I wanted her. But the effects were only temporary. I would read her mind and come to my senses…and she would remove my hands to stop me from killing her, buying enough time to cleave my free will once again. Eventually, she realized hate was a better motivator for me. I would stop trying to escape and willingly stay by her side if I wanted to kill her, so she made me believe she murdered my mother."

Horror thundered through Cameo, bringing Misery to the forefront of her mind. He attacked with lightning flashes of sorrow. Tears filled her eyes, obscuring her vision.

Stiff as a statue, Lazarus reached out to capture a single droplet, pinched and sifted the moisture with his fingertips. "Courtesy of you or the demon?"

"Both." She used the linen napkin to blow her nose.

"You are too sweet and tenderhearted for your own good."

"I so am not." She sniffled. "It's just…you *suffered*.

No wonder you were willing to let Strider behead you. You realized the best punishment for Juliette was what she feared most: leaving her." To be tricked into believing you loved someone you hated...someone who was abusing you in terrible ways...to have your memory manipulated for someone else's gain...

Cameo sprang at Lazarus, enfolding him within the circle of her arms and burying her head in the hollow of his neck. As he relaxed into her embrace, *his* arms wound around *her*.

"I'm sorry," she said. When she returned to the mortal world, she would find Juliette. She would punish the Harpy on Lazarus's behalf.

Payback's gonna hurt, bitch.

"Do not challenge her," he commanded, his hold tightening. "You could be hurt. Or worse."

He'd read her mind again, but for once, she couldn't bring herself to care. "She won't best me." The Mother of Melancholy had *skills*.

"Cameo—"

She eased to her haunches, regretfully severing contact, and turned his attention in a different direction. "If the Paring Rod can cleave spirit from soul, can it also cleave spirit from demon?"

Misery screamed obscenities. He had no desire to escape her. Not really. Ruining her life was too much fun.

Gripping her shoulders, Lazarus shook her with enough force to shut up the demon. A total alpha move, his strength and fervor oddly arousing.

This time, she recognized the arc of electricity shooting through her, not to mention the warmth and awareness throbbing in different parts of her body.

"Don't you dare try," he snarled. "If the Paring Rod

succeeded, you would die. You cannot live without the demon."

"No, I can't. Not at this time." Her head canted to the side, her scrutiny of him deepening. Her blood sang with what she assumed was happiness.

My first taste, and it's glorious!

"But don't you worry, darkpit. I won't allow myself to die until I've found Pandora's box and ensured the eternal safety of my family."

He began to relax.

"Why does the thought of my demise bother you?" she asked, and he stiffened all over again. "I'm nothing but a possible one-night stand, right?"

"No. Yes." He leaped to his feet and paced directly in front of her. A hand tangled in his hair. "I'm going to a lot of trouble to save your life, sunshine. The least you can do is live it."

Excuse me? "How? How are you saving my life?"

"In this realm, the living are fair game. Had I not granted my protection, the sky serpents could have killed you a thousand times over. For that matter, the citizens could have killed you in order to claim rights to your body. They want to possess it and pass through the portal."

She bristled at his lack of confidence. "You under-estimate me if you think I'm anyone's easy mark. For that matter," she added, mimicking him, "even Viola and the children managed to survive without your aid."

His dark gaze crackled with flames of fury. "You misunderstand. Juliette got the better of me. *Me*. What makes you believe you can— *Umph*."

With no outward tells, Cameo had palmed and tossed

one of the diamond daggers. The tip had embedded in his shoulder.

A thick river of blood trickled from the wound. She'd known he had a heartbeat, despite his death, but the stark reminder startled her.

Had he somehow come back to life? Could he walk through the portal with her? Excitement bloomed.

"No," he said, reading her mind. "I can't."

Excitement died a tragic death. "I'm not you. I could defeat Juliette with a blindfold and both hands tied behind my back."

Lips pursed, he plucked the crimson-soaked weapon free. "A tigress roars beneath the kitten's facade. I'm glad."

Urban whisked into the tent without any advanced notice, interrupting her next "roar." He spotted Lazarus and heaved a relieved breath. "I want to present the goddess Viola with a token of my affection. What are men supposed to give to their women?"

How adorable. "Urban, honey. You're too young to court a woman. You can't—"

The little boy flinched, and Cameo pressed her lips together.

"The head of an enemy is always a nice touch," Lazarus interjected.

What! She gave an adamant shake of her head.

"Is that what you're going to do for her?" Urban hiked his thumb in Cameo's direction. "Give her the head of an enemy?"

"No." Lazarus shook of his head. "I'm going to give her the heart of an automaton."

Um, thanks? Automaton, sometimes called Colossi, were half man or animal, half metal.

"In fact, I'll be gone the rest of the day." He strapped two short swords to his back. "In order to pass through the portal, a sacrifice must be made. In order for four people to pass through, a *large* sacrifice must be made. Automatons are big enough for an army."

"I'm going with you," she said. No way could she remain quiet.

Why? You cannot help him, Misery whispered. *You're a woman. The weaker sex. You'll only hinder him.*

Lies, only lies. She'd trained. She'd toppled kingdoms. She'd survived seemingly endless rounds of torture. She'd been knocked down, but had always gotten back up. And that—*that* was true strength.

"No," Lazarus said, his tone intractable. "I go alone."

She met his narrowed gaze and raised her chin, knowing she portrayed the very picture of stubbornness.

She wasn't the only one.

He considered himself strong enough to defeat an automaton without aid, and he probably was. But she wouldn't let him risk his life—or death—without risking her own.

Viola stomped into the tent, Fluffy directly behind her. "All right, I'm tired of listening at the door. I can get us into automaton territory *and* to the portal by the end of the day."

Heart hammering against her ribs, Cameo jumped to her feet. Part with Lazarus *today*?

Too soon!

A muscle ticked beneath Lazarus's eye, and she wondered if he'd had the same thought about her. "No."

"Hello, Viola." Urban waved at her before executing a graceful bow. "How are you?"

The goddess gave him an odd look but waved back. "Isn't it obvious? I'm as awesome as always."

"How can you get us to the portal?" Cameo asked her, ignoring Lazarus. The more time she spent in his presence, the faster her resistance crumbled. The sooner they parted the better.

"Uh, hello. I'm the goddess of the Afterlife. Perhaps I know shortcuts through the spirit realms." She waved her fingers at Lazarus, the ring on her thumb glinting in the light. "Perhaps *this* allows me to leap between the realms, put us in automaton territory, then directly in front of the portal home. Who's to say, really?"

Lazarus took a step toward her, a tower of menacing aggression. "I want the ring. Give it to me. Now."

Viola shrank back, even as Princess Fluffikans and Urban jumped in front of her to block his path.

"The ring is mine," the goddess said. "I stole it fair and square."

"Don't make me take your head," the little boy told Lazarus. He popped his knuckles. "I'll do it. Won't even hesitate."

The Tasmanian devil screeched. He was a nocturnal creature. Mornings were not his friends.

"No one is taking anyone's head, and no one is stealing anyone else's jewelry. And everyone is going to knock before entering Aunt Cam's dwelling, wherever or whatever it happens to be. Starting today. Understand?" She crossed her arms over her chest. "Viola, concentrate on me and not your reflection in the ring. Good girl. Now answer a few questions for me. You've had the ring all along? Why not mention it before? Can you use it to take us home?"

"Yep. Had it all along. And I didn't mention it because I knew Lazarus the Selfish and Greedy would attempt to claim it." She toyed with the ends of her pale braids. "And no. I can only use it to take us into other spiritual realms."

"Give me the ring. Of your own free will," he added. "Consider it payment for the slaying of the automaton."

Viola fluffed her hair. "I'll be slaying him on my own, thanks. I've got mad skills. And I can always use him as a shield." She hiked her thumb in Urban's direction. "I'll survive and return home. You can explain to Mr. and Mrs. Maddox why their son is dead."

"Hey!" Ever stomped into the tent, the color in her cheeks high. "I'm the only one who can use my brother as a shield."

"Here's the thing," Viola said to Lazarus, ignoring the girl. "If I give you the ring, you'll leave me behind. That's a problem. I want to see the automaton's home."

Lazarus spread his arms, acting like the last sane man in the universe. "You want to die, then."

Okay, this had gotten out of hand. "If you give him the ring, Viola, you can go with us. You'll soon be leaving the spirit realms, anyway, so you won't *need* the ring. Correct? Urban, Ever. Stop crying. You're staying here with the guards. The adults are going out to do some adulting."

She steeled herself for a slap of lust and met Lazarus's gaze. "You. Help us get what we need and I'll kiss you goodbye."

Cameo brushed her teeth with a brush and paste Lazarus gave her, and bathed in a basin he filled with ice-cold water. Refreshed, she changed into a T-shirt and jeans provided by the goddess.

Apparently Viola had used her portal-opening ring last night, fetching hundreds of T-shirts she'd had made weeks before, planning to give the too-small garments to everyone in the realm. Every shirt had a different message, but every message meant the exact same thing.

I Heart Viola.

Team Viola.

If I Can't Have Viola I'd Rather Have Death.

I Hung Out with the Goddess of the Afterlife & All I Got Was This Amazing T-shirt.

Lazarus used the time to pet his new ring and sulk about…Cameo wasn't sure. Did he wish she'd donned the *I Dream of Jeannie* outfit? Was he pouting about having company on his automaton-heart mission?

Did he not want Cameo to leave him?

The thought electrified her, and for once, nothing Misery did to counteract the sensation affected her. Her blood continued to simmer, her bones to vibrate.

Slay an automaton, kiss Lazarus goodbye.

Cameo joined the warrior, Viola and Princess Fluffikans outside the tent. Sunlight glared from an unforgiving sky. Thankfully sky serpent wings spanned a great distance and cast the perfect amount of shade.

Guards rushed around the campsite, searching for the children, who'd decided to play hide-and-burn-the-one-who-seeks. She would have worried, but gleeful giggles drifted on the wind, reassuring her all was well.

Besides, Viola had told Urban to watch his sister, stay by the tents and not kill anyone. He'd agreed, saying, "For you, my sweet, anything."

Maddox would flip his lid when he found out about his son's crush.

"—will remain here," Lazarus was saying to a group of his men. "You will protect my cargo with your lives."

Cargo. Well. The children had been called worse.

A butterfly chose that moment to fly into the camp and land on Lazarus's shoulder, and a sudden sense of dread choked Cameo.

Something terrible was going to happen today.

"Do as he says and protect the children with your lives," she called, "or I'll remove your spines through your mouths—while singing."

A chorus of agonized wails broke out.

Lazarus faced her, admiration flickering in the depths of his dark eyes. Admiration...and just a little anger. He stalked toward her, the butterfly taking flight. "Ordering my men now?"

She held her ground. *I was created for war. I will not surrender to him or any man.* Even when this one's chocolate and champagne scent teased her senses.

"Now and always," she said.

"Sure you want to go with me?" He traced a fingertip along her jaw, sending shivers skittering through her. "If you're harmed, I'll be very displeased."

"Don't worry. I won't miss our kiss goodbye."

He leaned down, his nose brushing hers, his warm breath fanning her chin. "You know I'm a vengeful man, and still you taunt me. You're either brave or foolish. I'm not sure which. I do know I want more than a kiss. I want my night."

"I'm going home." For now. She would return to the spirit realms a third time to search for Pandora's box.

Would her search lead her back to Lazarus's kingdom?

"The others can go through the portal today. You can go through tomorrow."

Spend a single night with him? It's what he'd offered. A new path... "Sorry, but I—"

"Don't say no. And don't make me wait for my kiss. I want it now." The look he gave her...it was as if she were the only woman ever born. The only woman he could see. The only woman he had ever wanted. "Give it to me."

Just like that, he stripped her of inhibition and apprehension, and exposed the rawness of her desire. Denying him wasn't an option, but helping him wasn't wise.

"You want it?" she croaked. "Take it."

He cupped her nape and yanked her against the solid line of his body. As she gasped, he pressed his mouth against hers and thrust his tongue deep. Just like his scent, his taste devastated her senses; it was as dark and rich and sweet as a fine wine, and more intoxicating than ambrosia.

In his arms, she came alive.

The simmer in her blood heated to a rolling boil and burned her from the inside out, branding her, and she moaned. Her bones dissolved. To remain upright, all she could do was cling to him.

He kissed her without reservation, as if he wanted to savor her. He kissed her as if he wanted to *devour* her. As if she were a treasure he'd sought his entire life—as if he planned to enjoy her forever.

When passion and pleasure collided with the demon's sadness—passion and pleasure won! Cameo careened from shock, her nails sinking into Lazarus's wide shoulders. So strong. So *male*.

How can I ever let him go?

A growl reverberated in his chest as the tone of the kiss changed. From a molten exploration to an unstop-

pable consumption. Their thirst for each other was un-
quenchable. He rubbed against her, the feel of his shaft
incredible. It was hard and long and thick.

Cameo's breath mingled with his, until they were
inhaling the same air. Until she—

Heard a feminine sigh of annoyance?

Lazarus released her and stepped back, no part of
him touching her. A travesty. Cameo panted, her knees
quaking, her limbs fighting to return to their solid state.

Fury darkened his features, and he spat, "Distraction kills."

Wait. He blamed her for the kiss?

"—can't ever get enough of me," Viola was saying.
"The same isn't true of you two. Can we go now? I'm
late for a very important date."

Lazarus wiped his mouth with the back of his hand.
As if the taste of Cameo were suddenly repellent to
him. He focused on his men. "If any harm comes to
the children, you had best run. Not that it will do you
any good. I'll give chase."

Misery snickered, and Cameo wither—

No! *Not this time.* She lifted her chin and squared her
shoulders. Lazarus had given her undeniable pleasure,
muting the effects of the demon. She would forgive his
brutish behavior, whatever the reason for it.

But will I forget?

She flattened a hand on her stomach. His rejection
had stung, yes, but it had come as a result of their kiss.
The single greatest experience of her life. She would
rather lose a limb than her memory.

To Viola, he said, "Tell me how to use the ring."

"Sorry." The goddess held out her hand, palm up. "I
need to *show* you."

He opened and closed his mouth. With a blistering curse, he relinquished control of the band. "If this is a trick…"

"Why would she trick you?" Cameo demanded. "Right now, we all have the same goal."

He ignored her, wouldn't even glance in her direction.

Viola blew her pet a kiss. "There's no reason to worry. Mommy will return." She waved the ring through the air, and a rift sliced into the landscape. An opening between one realm and another, wide enough for the seven-foot-tall Lazarus to step through with ease.

Cameo followed on his heels, and the goddess followed on hers. The rift closed with an audible *snap*.

A barren wasteland surrounded them, the heat nearly unbearable. Sweat beaded over Cameo's skin. The ground had been scorched, the dirt black and layered with char, while tendrils of smoke curled from red-veined cracks. The sky fared no better, thick clouds leaking an oily black substance.

Viola skipped to a boulder and sat down to file her nails. "I've decided to bench myself. Go on without me."

What! She'd insisted on coming, only to skip the action?

Lazarus marched over, unceremoniously removed the ring from her finger and stalked onward, all without speaking a word. And *she* was the one referred to as the Mother of Melancholy. He should be the Father of Pity Parties.

Cameo raced to catch up, then kept pace at his side. Charred earth soon gave way to a cobbled path.

"Have you ever fought an automaton?" she asked.

"When I was a child, my father dropped me in the

middle of a horde. Literally. He told me not to come home without a piece of metal and pushed me off the back of a sky serpent."

"That's horrible, Lazarus!"

"No. That's life. My past forged me into the man I am today. Strong and fearless."

"And humble?"

He nodded. "My humbleness is one of my favorite things about myself."

A smile attempted to bloom on her face. "Would you do something so coldhearted to your own son?"

"I'll never have children," he replied easily.

"Because you can't or because you don't want any?"

"Don't want?"

He wasn't sure?

"Do *you* want children?" he asked.

She imagined herself as a mother, and Lazarus as the father. He would be protective of his brood. He would tease his little boys and girls when they cried, turning tears to laughter.

Her heart squeezed with longing.

"I do," she admitted. "One day. But only if I'm demon-free."

They reached a bank of gnarled trees. With Lazarus's aid, the limbs softly slapped her cheeks. His own personal joke? Or a means of keeping her on edge rather than saddened?

He helps me, doesn't he?

If only she could keep him. Thanks to the mirror, she knew she would lose him if she stayed here.

But what would happen after she left him?

Would she return, as planned? Would he find a way to pass through the portal? *Could* he?

She wished the mirror had shown her the outcome of the second option.

As she trudged forward, she made sure to step only where Lazarus stepped, but his tread was so light she often had trouble detecting his footprint.

At the end of the path, they stopped. Lazarus kept one hand in his pocket, rattling *something*, and used the other to hold her at his side. She shivered as she studied the terrain—a mountain with a yawning mouth, the opening of a cavern.

"I sense only one presence inside the cave," he whispered, "but a whole lot of power." A pause. A wicked smile to drive her mad. "Mine is stronger."

"Since I'm more powerful than you, the metal beast doesn't stand a chance against me."

He snorted.

"You saying you're more powerful than me?" she demanded.

"No, I'm not *not* saying you're more powerful than me. There's a difference."

Funny man.

He marched inside the cavern, a dagger in hand, and once again she followed. As they moved through the darkness, the fetid stench of rot clung to the air. Severed limbs in different stages of decay tripped her.

You won't survive the coming battle, Misery taunted. *I'm going to miss you when you're dead.*

Ignore him, she told herself. *Carry on.*

Lazarus pressed against a rocky wall before inching around the corner, and Cameo did the same. As they moved down an incline and around another corner, odd sounds began to penetrate her awareness. Slurping? Scraping?

A light flickered at the end of the corridor. A glowing torch, she realized. They turned another corner, and discovered the walls were lined with rows of torches leading to a massive room filled with sheets and shards of what looked to be steel, titanium, tungsten and Inconel, and yet the metals possessed a light glow, as if mystical.

Like called to like.

A mighty roar blasted through the enclosure, and an enormous beast dropped from the ceiling to perch on a pile of metal. A femur dangled from the side of his mouth like a cigarette. A *human* femur. Eyes of crackling red flame searched...searched...

Her heart rate jacked up. An automaton of a griffin with the body, tail and back legs of a lion, but the head, front talons and wings of an eagle.

When he opened his beak to squawk, she spotted *teeth*. Metal spikes extended from the top of his head, jaw and underneath his chin, even flaring along the entire length of his spine. What flesh he possessed was a mix of feathers and fur. His wings could have spanned an entire football field; they glinted in the torchlight and looked as if a thousand swords had been welded together.

With a single swipe, he could sever *anything* in two.

"Surprise!" a voice bellowed behind them. "I'm here to help...myself to the metals."

Cameo spun to find a grinning Viola in the cavern. "Shh."

The griffin unleashed a bloodcurdling roar and flew toward them.

Lazarus grabbed both Cameo and Viola and flung them to the side with a single flick of his wrist. They smacked into one of the piles, knocking it down. The cold metal rained over them, and Cameo yelped.

No wonder Lazarus hadn't complained about her company. He'd planned to incapacitate her all along.

Another roar echoed, one of excitement. A whoosh of air, the flap of wings. A grunt.

Lazarus was fighting the griffin on his own. Any other day, he might have won. Today, a butterfly had landed on him.

She had to help him.

"Wow. This is the thanks I get?" Viola muttered. "I prefer flowers."

Cameo fought her way free of the weight. Daggers still in hand, she stood. Where were— There! Lazarus had climbed atop one of the piles. Or he'd been dropped there. The griffin hovered above him, spitting poison. Lazarus dived out of the way while tossing the spiked dagger he so often stroked. That dagger cut through the griffin's throat and came out the other side—with a trachea caught in one of the hooks.

The loss would have killed any other creature. This one shook his head, injured but alive—and angrier. He chomped at Lazarus, trapping his wrist. As Lazarus had done to her and Viola, the dragon did to him, tossing him across the room.

My cue. Hurt my man and suffer. Cameo threw herself into the fray.

12

"Fear isn't your friend and it won't keep you safe.
Fear is the first stage of self-destruction."
—*Living on Your Own Terms, Always*
—*Eternal Truths for Every Man*

Lazarus had made several tactical errors, each of them
critical.

Oh, he'd done everything he'd set out to do. He'd hidden the females under a pile of steel. He'd forced the
griffin to focus solely on him while opening his mind
to the beast's thoughts—erratic, dark, vile—in order
to predict every move against him. But he'd underes-
timated Cameo's resolve, and his own growing weakness. He'd thought the fight would end swiftly, so he
hadn't given her the gifts currently burning a hole in
his pocket. He'd expected her to stay down and safe-
guard the weaker Viola.

Instead, Cameo attacked the griffin, moving too
quickly for Lazarus and his crystallized veins to block her.

She soared past the griffin and slashed at his ankles. The second she hit the ground, she rolled and stood.

Thump. The beast's foot detached. A high-pitched squawk nearly busted Lazarus's eardrums. At the same time, rage consumed him; through his connection with the beast, he felt the white-hot burn of the emotion in every cell.

To the griffin, Cameo had just been marked for a bloody death.

As Lazarus shouted, "No," leaping at her with every intention of sheltering her body with his, the griffin flared his wings. One wing swiped at Lazarus and nearly tore him in two. The other swiped at Cameo. She jumped out of the way and—yes! She reached the safety zone. Or she would have, if other blades hadn't unfolded from the tip of the wing, drawn to her as if she were a magnet.

Lazarus watched in horror, helpless, as the blades cut through her midsection.

Her eyes widened, and she grunted with shock and pain. Trembling, she dropped her weapons and clutched at the gaping wounds.

Blood and organs spilled to the floor as her knees collapsed.

No. No!

The griffin loved the sight and smell of her injury. He clicked his teeth together and inhaled deeply.

That. Very. Second. The tether to Lazarus's control snapped, his own rage overtaking him. He became the stuff of nightmares.

For the first time in his life or death, fangs sprouted from his gums, more lethal than any sword. Claws grew from his fingertips, sharper than any weapon. His veins burned as if molten lava rushed through them, even where the crystals had grown.

A thousand times as a child, he'd witnessed this transformation overtake his father, making him strong. Invincible. In all his years with Juliette, he'd *prayed* for this to happen.

Lazarus was every inch the Monster's son.

As he raced forward, the griffin chomped at Cameo's neck. She shouldn't have the strength to move, but by some miracle she managed to roll over, the creature's teeth sinking into her shoulder. Her back bowed, and she screamed.

Lazarus grabbed hold of matted fur, his claws slicing all the way to bone. He swung himself around—a move he'd watched Cameo execute against his sky serpents when he'd first invaded her mind and witnessed her memories of the battle—and dropped down in front of her, at the same time using his momentum to snap the griffin's spine in two.

Hurt…more.

The creature's head hung at an odd angle. However, the lack of muscle control didn't stop him from flinging his weight at Lazarus.

Expecting the action, Lazarus blocked, buried sharp claws in the griffin's chest and tossed him across the cavern.

Lazarus flashed, greeting the griffin when he landed by punching fangs into his vulnerable neck. He shook his head and ripped out the bastard's regrown trachea, black oil spraying from the wound.

More!

Lazarus used his claws to slice those metal wings into ribbons…to cut through scales as easily as butter.

A flicker of rational thought. *Careful, need the heart.*

He flung the dead, withered organ aside. Then he railed, overcome by madness once again. There went the face. The shoulders. The entire chest cavity, what remained of the organs ripped into so many pieces they were unrecognizable.

At first, the griffin fought, desperate to fend off Lazarus's relentless brutality. As black oil continued to spray, the source of his afterlife drained, along with his strength. Bones snapped and shattered, until the griffin *couldn't* move.

"I'm keeping this!" Viola called. "And this. And this. This, this and this. Oh! Cameo, did you see this? We've hit the mother lode of metals. Am I weeping? I think I'm weeping. I can build armor…the home of my dreams. I can protect myself and my Fluffikans from *everyone*."

Panting, Lazarus scanned the cavern until he found Cameo. She'd managed to stuff her internal organs back inside her torso, her flesh in the process of weaving back together.

A cool tide of relief swept over him. She would heal. And now she would forever know the truth. He could defend her from any danger.

Despite my weakness, I am stronger than ever.

The realization bolstered him. Did this mean… Could he dare to keep her?

"Over here, Lazarus," Viola called. "Come help me. It's the least you can do since I'm letting you borrow my ring, right? You kind of owe me one. A big one. And this small one. Oh! And this one. And by *kind of* I mean *definitely*."

"*My* ring." Lazarus pushed to his feet.

He couldn't go to Cameo like this, not while she was

in such a fragile state. He breathed in and out with purpose, focusing on a single thought in an effort to calm himself. He would be kissing his woman at some point today. Would finish what they'd started...

His veins sizzled as rage bowed to arousal. He grew rock hard, his erection straining against his leathers, throbbing, desperate for the clasp of her hand, her mouth. Her beautiful red mouth, with lips so plump and soft. Her hot, wet inner walls. How tightly she had squeezed his finger.

The woman had been made for him. She came to life within the circle of his arms. He and he alone could bring her to climax.

He just had to prove it to her.

The red waned from his vision. The bitter taste of griffin dulled, and his fangs and claws retracted.

I'll give her pleasure every day, every hour, every—

Between one heartbeat and the next, his weakness returned. His veins constricted, the rivers of crystal spreading.

His hands balled into fists.

No, he couldn't keep Cameo.

"Lazarus?" Her raspy voice beseeched him.

He picked up the kris and closed in on her. She hadn't moved from her spot on the floor. He thrust his arms under her and gently lifted her, cradling her against his chest.

Going to part soon. Must enjoy her while I can.

With a sigh, she relaxed against him. "Did you know you have griffin meat under your fingernails?"

He scoffed at her. "You mean the *must have* accessory of the spirit realms?"

She snorted, then she sniffled. "I'm sorry. I meant

to help, not hinder. I thought you were doomed, and I didn't want… I'm sorry."

Doomed? He probed her thoughts.

She stiffened, only to release another sigh. "Fine. Do your thing." The shield fell, her mind opening up to him, filling him with satisfaction and possessiveness.

A clip of her life played inside his head. Earlier, a butterfly had flown through camp and landed on Lazarus. She'd panicked. Over the centuries, butterflies had become a sign of impending catastrophe to her.

Made sense in a warped way, he supposed. Upon her demon-possession—an action forced upon her—a butterfly had been branded into her flesh. The mark he'd so admired.

Lazarus had seen the mark on her fellow warriors, as well, and hadn't cared one way or another for it. But the sight of it on Cameo always revved him up.

Will trace my tongue over every inch—make it my mark instead of Misery's.

"Butterflies are drawn to me," he told her. "Always have been. They've aided me, never doomed me."

Her brow furrowed. "But why are they drawn to you?"

"Must be female."

She barked out a laugh. Then her eyes widened with surprise.

He wanted to pound his chest with pride. *I amused her.* Now to soothe her fears. "Butterflies are signs of impending success, sunshine. If one leaves her chrysalis too easily, her wings are weakened. She must struggle to exit or she will never have the strength to fly. But because she flies, she brings her strength to you."

"You think so?"

"I know so."

In a rare show of affection, she petted his chest. The simple action nearly drove him to his knees.

He'd wanted her for so long, and now he had her. In his arms. In his realm. *Take her!*

Not here, not now.

He carried her to Viola, who was so weighed down by pieces of metal she couldn't straighten her spine. "You'll never be able to walk through a portal."

"Then I'll run. And I'll create a portal right here, thank you very much." She waved her hand, the ring she'd given him, then taken back, then ceded to him once more on her finger yet again. When a rift failed to form, she sputtered. "It's not working."

He eased Cameo to her feet and removed the ring from Viola's finger, saying, "We should return to the spot we entered. The seams holding the realm together are more malleable there."

"Carry me?" the goddess asked, batting her lashes.

"I will not—"

Cameo gazed up at him with beseeching eyes— sparkling eyes? "She's letting you borrow her most favorite ring. Shouldn't you help her?"

A grinning Viola placed a hand over her heart. "The pearls of wisdom you're dropping right now are lovely, Cameo, my dear. Though not as lovely as my new titanium. Look!" She petted a sheet of metal.

He should stand firm and at least *pretend* to have defenses against his warrior woman. "The ring is mine forever." A weapon he could use in his favor. "But I will carry the goddess because you oh, so sweetly asked. I will only expect one boon in return."

Cameo smiled, a quick up and down quirk of her

mouth, but a smile was a smile, and his chest puffed with pride a second time. He was addicted to her amusement and wanted more. Wanted a full-blown smile next time. Or an unstoppable laugh.

"Let me guess," she said. "I have to spend the night with you?"

He traced the line of her jaw, luxuriating in the feel of her silken skin. Then he leaned down to whisper in her ear, "Don't be ridiculous, sunshine. I would never leave room for interpretation. I would demand you spend the night with me...naked and eager for my touch."

As he lifted his head to peer into her eyes—no longer sparkling but *burning*—lovely color darkened her cheeks.

"If I say no?" she asked, her tone ragged.

"The goddess walks."

Little panting breaths left her. Such a telling reaction pleased him. Her desire for him had grown, his ability to bypass the demon's sorrow getting easier. She *wanted* to spend the night with him.

"I—" she began.

Dust rained from the rafters. A thousand roars suddenly echoed through the cavern, silencing her.

"Uh-oh. More automatons," Viola said.

A *lot* more. Their thoughts slammed into Lazarus's awareness all at once, a terrible blast of hate, malice and rage. They had sensed the forever-death of their kinsman and hungered for revenge.

"Hurry!" Cameo grabbed his hand and stumbled forward. "We're in no condition to fight another battle."

"I can fight anyone, anytime, and emerge victorious." But even as he snapped the rebuke, determined to mask his own weakened condition, he knew another battle would put his woman at greater risk, and *that* he wouldn't allow.

She comes first.

Today. Only today.

She'd chosen to fight for him. Had willingly placed herself in danger on his behalf. Not because he'd commanded it, or because she would be rewarded. Her only objective had been his protection.

Loyalty wasn't a gift he'd ever received. Until now. Until her.

Juliette, who had claimed to love him, had never put his needs before her own. His men fought beside him because they feared his wrath, not for any other reason.

Astonishment blazed through him. Would she choose him over her brothers-by-circumstance? Would she trust him to keep her safe…trust him to take care of Pandora's box?

I want her to choose me. Always, only me.

The two sides of him—self-protective versus possessive—engaged in a violent tug-of-war. Be with her for a day…be with her forever…a week…forever.

How could he ever give her up?

Focus!

He kissed her knuckles before pulling from her grip. He picked up the griffin heart. More roars sounded. More dust rained. The griffins drew closer.

Lazarus twined his free hand with Cameo's and raced from the cavern. Once they cleared the mountain, Viola picked up speed and claimed the lead, encumbered by the metals but no longer affected by their bulky weight. Her will to survive on her own terms must be stronger than any physical limitations she incurred.

The goddess wasn't the weak link he'd considered her.

"Faster," he commanded, pulling ahead of Viola. In the jungle, the slowest gazelle got eaten.

Despite Cameo's injury, she ran with innate elegance.

As they raced around burnt trees and maneuvered around sharp, gnarled limbs, Viola decided to belt out a song she couldn't remember. "'Running something something something. Holding something something. Trying something something something.'"

He expected her to spread her arms wide and twirl. As deceived by Narcissism as she was, she must believe no one and nothing would ever attempt to harm her—must consider herself too valuable to harm.

One day, someone would prove her wrong, and she would suffer greatly for it.

By the time their group reached the mound of boulders where they'd first arrived, sweat drenched him. His lungs burned.

Behind them, a dark cloud of smoke moved through the skyline, heading straight toward them.

Lazarus waved his hand while rubbing his thumb over the ring, creating friction, exactly as Viola had done earlier. Having read her mind, he knew to picture the realm he wished to enter.

Electric pulses cut through the landscape, creating a rift. Dust motes shimmered, dancing in a sudden burst of wind through the portal. He tugged Cameo through, and the goddess followed. The portal closed behind them.

Relief abounded. They'd done it. They'd escaped.

They stopped to take a breather.

"Wow," Viola said. "That was—"

Another portal opened, the griffins zooming through.

Cameo grated a curse.

Well, hell. Lazarus tightened his hold on her, sprinted forward and whistled. A second later, the hiss of his sky serpents drifted across the land. A few seconds after that, the horde found him, hovering overhead, awaiting his command.

"Attack!" he shouted.

"Can your pets win?" Cameo asked between panting breaths. "They're outnumbered three to one."

"They can. They will. Poor griffins."

13

"There are no second chances to kill at first sight."
—*Eternal Truths for Every Man*

Cameo sensed a change in Lazarus as soon as his soldiers came into view. Any hint of softer emotion evaporated. He became a man without a hint of vulnerability. A man determined to kill anyone who might detect one.

What she'd learned from his fight with the griffin: if he decided to strike, his opponent wouldn't survive.

Never, in all her days, had she seen more aggression, darker rage or twisted brutality. And she'd lived with eleven demon-possessed immortals!

Did Lazarus realize he'd smiled while he'd ripped the griffin to ribbons?

She'd been mesmerized by the beauty of him. His array of tattoos—the ones she could see on his arms, anyway—had glowed with life and vitality, and she'd longed to see the rest of him stripped bare. He'd moved swiftly, so expertly and with such fluid grace he'd appeared to glide on water.

If he could mete such violence without a corporeal form, what feats could he perform if ever he rejoined the land of the living?

At his shout, his men loaded up the tents in record time.

"Mount up." He stored the griffin heart in a satchel hanging from his winged horse and leaped upon the saddle.

Cameo offered her hand, and he yanked her in front of him.

The wounds in her shoulder and midsection throbbed, but she swallowed her wince. No reason to make him feel bad—the way Misery always did to her—when he only wanted to help her.

"Where are the children?" Viola spun in a circle, her delicate features contorted with worry.

"Your future husband is here, goddess." Urban trotted his horse to her side.

Ever rode behind him. "Your crush is officially creepy, brother."

"Agreed," Viola said, even as she exhaled with relief. "I don't want to brag, but I would only ever agree to marry…myself."

"I'll change your mind," the boy insisted.

Lord help the ladies when he became an adult.

Since their birth, Urban and Ever had been sheltered from the rest of the world. With their abilities, they'd had to be. Plus, whenever they were angered, horns sprouted from their heads and claws extended from their fingers. Bronzed skin morphed into colored scales, and their eyes turned neon red. As young as they were, they had little control of the transformation.

"You've got the ring. You can use it to take everyone to the portal. I'm going to meet you there." Viola waved them on. "Go. Now!" Then she vanished before anyone could protest.

"Viola can flash." Lazarus snapped the stallion's reins. "Good to know."

He collected information about others, just in case ally ever became enemy, she would guess.

I'm learning him, Cameo realized.

"I don't want to use the ring while the griffins are so close," he said.

"Agreed."

As he led the charge away from camp, and the creatures out for their blood, she decided to monitor the battle and threw a leg over the horse's head, careful not to impede his wings. Then she kicked her other leg around Lazarus's waist, straddling him. Palming her semiautomatic, she scanned the sky and gasped.

Sky serpents and griffins collided with so much force a blast of heated air exploded, shaking even the ground. Fangs slashed. Claws cut. Griffins utilized their metal-tipped wings. Sky serpents used their tails like whips, sometimes lashing, sometimes wrapping around snouts, necks and limbs to wrench and break.

Before, the threat level had propelled her into survival mode, drowning out the demon. Now Misery demanded what he considered his due.

Sky serpents hate you, and yet they fight to protect you, simply because Lazarus demanded it. Many will die today. The survivors will blame you. And rightly so! How long will Lazarus's desire for you last then, hmm? One day you'll look back and comprehend this is the moment you traded his affections for safety.

A pang of sorrow nearly sliced her in two. *They protect him, too*, she retorted.

Misery flashed an image inside her head. The last scene Cameo had spied in the mirror: Lazarus walking away, never looking back.

The sorrow redoubled.

"Are you *literally* watching my back?" Dark amusement layered Lazarus's voice.

"Sir, yes, sir. Sergeant Cameo has reported for duty."

"Duty…or desire?" He was hard, long and thick between her legs, his erection rubbing against her heating core as the horse galloped.

She moaned, unable to escape the delicious friction, the constant pressure.

"You are too precious, sunshine." He bit into her earlobe, igniting a wave of shivers inside her.

Her? Precious? Not a description anyone had ever used for her. She softened against him. His beard stubble abraded her cheek. Her breasts swelled for him, and her nipples beaded. Shocking heat stole through her, languid and sultry.

So easily seduced. He wants his night, nothing more…

Her hands clenched on her daggers. Demons ruined everything!

"Tell me," Lazarus commanded softly. "How did Misery cock-block me this time?"

"Why don't you read my mind like usual?"

"Because I suspect you've got a bomb in there."

Hooves thundered, faster and faster. She caught sight of a man who appeared in the midst of the sky serpents. Sky serpents he ignored. He arrowed through the griffins, using his wings to slice and dice limbs from those in his path.

He wore a loincloth. His muscles were bigger than Lazarus's and the top half of him sapphire, the bottom half of him emerald.

He spread long feathered wings, only to retract them and arrow through the beasts. In each hand he clutched a small hatchet.

"Who is *he*?" she asked.

Lazarus cast a glance over his shoulder and frowned. "Don't know. But I will allow him to live since he isn't harming my pets."

True. Even though both griffins and sky serpents treated the newcomer as an enemy, biting and slashing at him.

"I wonder why he's helping you," she said.

"Or you. Perhaps he's another of Hades's emissaries."

"Another?"

He disregarded her question, saying, "Perhaps he's lulling the sky serpents into a false sense of safety. No matter. They'll defeat him, too."

"How can you be so sure?"

"My father trained them just as he trained me."

So…they had been dropped into dangerous situations and left to fend for themselves? "I know Queen Hera—"

"Former queen," he snapped. "Her title has been stripped."

"Right. The *former* queen hid your father, yes?"

His expression twisted with a flash of rage. "Yes."

"Tell me." She rubbed her cheek against his. "Please."

"He…lost mobility. He could walk, barely, but he couldn't swing a sword. She swooped in and killed my mother while he and I watched. He was unable to do anything about it, and my efforts were ineffective. Then she flashed him away."

Telling him *You were only a child* wouldn't alleviate his guilt. Guilt always found a way to poke and prod at a heart that sought absolution.

"You're no longer a boy," she said. "You're a man. The strongest one I know."

A heavy pause. Then, with clenched teeth, he said, "I'm just like my father."

"How?"

"I am—I don't wish to speak of this any longer." He adjusted her more firmly against him, his thumbs brushing against the undersides of her breasts.

A distraction? Too bad. She ignored the resurgence of heat in her body. "The queen I remember loathed the male species. Why would she keep your father?"

Oh, Cameo had heard the rumors. Zeus had locked Hera in his tower, enslaving and impregnating her. Then, when he'd broken her at long last, wedding and releasing her. Over the ensuing years, Hera had proved unbroken, sleeping with any man the king of the Greeks considered an enemy—or friend. She'd made secret deals with other powerful queens to ensure the most powerful males of myth and legend lost everything they held dear.

Had the formidable Typhon and his wife gotten caught in her crosshairs?

"A trophy, perhaps," Lazarus finally replied.

She rested her head on his shoulder and wrapped her arms around him, offering comfort. "I'm sorry."

"Typhon's relationship with my mother weakened him."

Cameo heard bitterness…and accusation? Did he think *she* weakened *him*?

A perceived weakness could be the reason he demanded a single night and eschewed anything more. To win him, she'd have to prove she strengthened him.

Did she? Could she?

He added, "Hera had no desire to hurt a child, or so she claimed, but she knew I would grow into a man. She used the Paring Rod to clip off a sliver of my spirit. Meaning, the owner of the artifact had the power to control me. When I was older, she gave the Paring Rod to Juliette. Gave the Harpy a piece of me, as if I were property."

Her grip on him tightened. "I'm sorry," she repeated, tears welling in her eyes.

"I will punish both females. I must." Hatred laced his words, giving his tone frightening ferocity. "I, too, will keep a trophy."

The demon purred with delight, sensing what Cameo hadn't. The "need" for revenge was just another form of misery. As long as Lazarus remained focused on the wrongs done to him, he would never see what was right.

Poor Cameo. Never the priority. Always the consolation.

I'm not his consolation!

But…wasn't she? Lazarus would never put her needs above his desire for retribution. With him, she would always come in second place. If she ranked at all. And wasn't *that* a depressing thought.

For once, Lazarus didn't try to tease her out of her bad mood, and it worried her.

Buck up! His view of me doesn't matter. Thanks to

Viola's ring, we'll be parting soon. In fact, we might never see each other again.

The pep talk failed to cheer her up.

As their group motored on, the only sound to be heard was the thunder of horse hooves and panting breaths. Eventually they were far enough away from the action—and the griffins, who would surely try to follow—to open a new portal. One that led directly to the portal home.

Lazarus had to open the portal again and again to allow the entire contingent of soldiers to walk through. He and Cameo entered last.

"We're here," he said, his voice flat.

Already?

To his men, he called, "Halt." He dismounted and helped Cameo and Ever do the same before draping the satchel that contained the griffin heart over his shoulder.

Viola appeared as promised, the stolen metals nowhere to be found, her arms cradling Princess Fluffikans.

Urban refused Lazarus's aid and hopped down on his own to bow. "My most beautiful majesty."

"Laying it on a little thick, kid." Viola gently tapped him on the chin.

"I'm not a kid, I'm a warrior."

Fetid air wafted to Cameo, and she wrinkled her nose. A dreary, gray landscape surrounded their group. Bare trees stooped over, as if they had been defeated by life and had just given up. At least fifteen different animals were scattered across a bloodstained ground, each in a different stage of decomposition. Insects crawled through empty eye sockets and hollowed torsos. Small, misshapen creatures chewed on the bones.

Viola's brows knit with…confusion? "Something's off. Well, no matter. I've braved through worse."

Ever clapped and rushed forward, her arms outstretched. "Look! A puppy! Can he come with us? Please?"

"Ever," Cameo called. "Stop!"

Lazarus linked their fingers and squeezed. His other hand remained in his pocket, jiggling whatever he'd stored in there. "The girl is fine, I promise you. At least physically. Anyone else would have run in the opposite direction."

He led her forward and…the terrain changed in a blink. Cameo gasped. Here, the sun shone from a gloriously blue sky. Trees stood tall, leaves lush and amber. The color of happiness, just like Lazarus's eyes. She inhaled deeply. The air smelled clean and fresh.

The carcasses were gone. So were the insects and the creep-fest of animals.

Ever stomped her foot. "No fair. I want my puppy."

"Aunt Katarina will find the perfect dog for you," Urban told her. "She vowed it, remember?"

"How is this possible?" Cameo demanded of Lazarus. He was responsible, guaranteed.

"You know of my ability to read minds. I'm also able to…affect minds. I can create illusions. Usually those illusions work," he added drily.

Was there nothing this man couldn't do? "So you created the rotten terrain?"

"Yes."

Of course. Because who in their right mind would want to continue on?

"Where is the portal?" she asked. *Don't tell me. I don't want to go.*

He motioned to two towering trees, the air between their trunks shimmering like a diamond-dusted cloth.

The moisture in her mouth dried. The vision had come to life.

"Let's send your friends home." Lazarus strode to the portal. He peered into the distance, one minute bleeding into another.

Thinking of keeping me?

He must be. His words implied she was to remain in the realm. Her pulse points raced.

He removed the griffin heart from the satchel and a blade from the sheath at his waist. With a single flick of his wrist, he sliced the organ in two. Black goo dripped from the chambers.

Glimmering hands shot out from the portal and snatched one half of the heart. The diamond-dusted air undulated with more force, ripples rolling from top to bottom. He stored the other half in the satchel. For Cameo to use tomorrow?

"All right, you little terrors." Viola placed Princess Fluffikans on the ground and clapped. "Are you ready to go home?"

Ever pouted. "I guess."

Urban shrugged. "If we must."

"You must," Cameo said. "Your parents have probably burned Budapest to the ground in an effort to find you."

Both children flinched.

Viola linked an arm with Urban and an arm with Ever and glanced at Cameo over her shoulder. "Give Lazarus a kiss goodbye for me…and use tongue. I would." She winked, then marched forward with her charges in tow.

They passed through the portal, Fluffy at their heels, and vanished.

Tremors racked Cameo as Lazarus spun on a booted heel and pinned her in place with his hot gaze. "Stay. One more night."

"I…" *Want to.* So badly.

She longed for pleasure-filled nights, erotic mornings and blissful days. The consequences be damned. Thanks to the mirror, she knew exactly what would happen if she traveled that path.

When she and Lazarus parted—and they *would* part—Misery might allow her to keep her memory, as he'd done in the first vision…or he might erase her memory, hoping she'd make the same mistake again. Curious about an immortal named Lazarus who might or might not be the key to her happiness, who might or might not have contemplated killing her before she left him.

And then there was a completely unknown path. Spending a single night with him. What would happen then?

She had no idea if humiliation, rejection and danger awaited her…

Without great risk, there was no reward.

I'm going to roll the dice. I'm going to take a chance on the second vision.

There were things she wanted to do in the mortal world. Things for Lazarus…

"No," she croaked, then shook her head for emphasis. "I won't stay the night."

Sunlight stroked his features as he cupped her cheeks. He was just so beautiful, with those sardonic dark eyes, eyes so black they suddenly appeared blue.

With that thick fan of lashes. Those sharp cheekbones. That blade of a nose. Those soft lips that were made for kissing. Correction: made for kissing *her*. The dark stubble on his jaw.

His Adam's apple bobbed, a sign that her scrutiny pleased him—which in turn pleased her. "I can force you to stay," he said. "Can hold you here until the portal closes."

Oh, no, no, no. Her friends often acted like dictators, and it ticked her off. Her fantasy man would treat her as an equal. "And I can use your heart to reopen it."

A small smile, quickly gone. "We aren't done, sunshine. One way or another, I will see you again. I will find you. I will always find you." The words were thrown at her, but she loved them, anyway. Loved them as much as Misery hated them.

She reached up to toy with the ends of Lazarus's dark hair. "I might return…for the box."

He gave a jerky shake of his head. "The box isn't here."

"You can't know—"

"I do. It's not hidden here, I swear it."

"Rumors—"

He cut her off with another shake of his head. "Rumors claim the box is in a spirit realm. There are thousands of spirit realms."

She gulped. This was it, then. The end. "Will you miss me?"

"I will," he grated.

Satisfaction flared…died. This *couldn't* be the end. "I'll make a pact with you. If you find a way through the portal, I'll reward you. I'll kiss you—" She traced a fingertip down the center of his chest. "Anywhere you desire."

His pupils expanded, pinpricks of light blazing deep, deep in their depths. "Kiss me."

Yes. She rose to her tiptoes and pressed her lips against his. He opened without hesitation, rolling his tongue against hers, tasting her as if she were a fine wine but also claiming control—claiming her. He sucked and nibbled, slid hands down her arms, around her hips, and cupped her bottom.

With a forceful yank, he tumbled her against him. Mmm. He was hard and strong and he held nothing back. Each glide of his tongue offered a hint of the satisfaction to come, and teased her with a glimpse of contentment.

And…and…happiness glimmered inside her, pure and incandescent, the only flame in a world of darkness. The light she had forever craved, but had always been denied. The sweetness she had never known, not even with Alex.

Lazarus had no illusions about who or what she was. He knew her, and he liked her, anyway. For that alone, she lo—*liked* him right back.

Misery fought her, deluging her with sorrow, drowning her lust.

Crying out, Cameo broke the kiss and stepped back. Lazarus reached for her, but she stepped back. "I'm sorry."

"Cameo." The growl had returned to his voice. "You're mine, and I want what's mine."

So possessive. Shivers cascaded through her, sweeping away the sorrow. *Welcome back, lust.*

No more kisses to fuel her dreams and drive her wild,

maybe even mad. She forced herself to walk backward, widening the distance between them, and closed in on the twin trees.

"I think your kiss got me pregnant," he said. "You had better stay until we know for sure."

"If you want me, darkpit, you'll have to come get me." *Anything is possible.*

"Stay."

Tempted, oh, she was tempted. If she stayed, either long or short term, they had a present but maybe not a future. *I want a future. This is my only hope.*

Another step backward. "Remember your reward."

Expression agonized, he followed after her. "I won't be forgetting. Will you?"

Ugh. What if she *did* forget him? "It's a risk we have to take."

"Why? Why do we have to take it?"

"Because I want more than one night."

"You can't have it." His hands fisted at his sides. "Stay here," he insisted. "Your nipples are hard. I bet your panties are drenched. Let me ease us both before you leave."

Lust tangled inside her, and her knees nearly buckled. Required all her might, but she shook her head, grabbed the other half of the heart from his satchel, blew him a kiss and raced through the portal.

14

"Never ask. Always demand."
—*Eternal Truths for Every Man*

Lazarus stood in place for a long while, unseen by his men. Lust sizzling inside him, playing havoc with the turmoil in his mind.

He hadn't given Cameo her gifts. The giving and receiving would have been too final. Then she had left him, anyway. But not before she'd teased him.

You want me, darkpit, you'll have to come get me.

An impossibility. And yet, he still wanted his night with her. He *deserved* a night with her. Had earned it inside that cavern, when he slayed the griffin. But he wouldn't get it.

Now all he had were memories of her.

Soon she would have nothing of him.

He punched a tree, leaving a fist-size hole in the trunk.

He could have killed Cameo at any time; he *should have* killed her, his one and only weakness. Instead, he'd helped her and those she loved. He'd saved her from griffins. He'd teased her and kissed her, giving her a taste of pleasure. Her first. Her only.

Possessiveness clasped him by the throat and squeezed.

He should have stripped her, should have tongued her nipples and laved the sweetness between her legs. She would have moaned and tugged his hair, would have begged him for more.

They would have consumed each other.

Cursed demon. Lazarus stroked the hilt of the kris.

He knew where Pandora's box was hidden. He hadn't told her.

If he retrieved the box, Cameo would be forced to return to the Realm of Grimm and Fantica. He would see her again. Perhaps threaten the demon. *Let her keep her memory, or die.*

A threat Lazarus would never be able to see through.

On the flip side, Cameo could use the box to harm herself.

I'll keep her safe—even from herself.

Every muscle in his body clenched onto bone. The plan was sound. He would draw her back. Cameo would be…upset when she discovered his deceit, of course. No, not deceit. He'd withheld the truth. Hardly the same. He would pleasure her out of her pique.

One day, she would thank him.

Caution tempered his eagerness. He wasn't at his best. Just the thought of seeing Cameo caused his veins to burn white-hot and throb. The crystals had stretched through his arms, legs and…chest? Oh, yes. Heat seared the spot above his heart. Had to be the crystals. Not, say, guilt for failing to tell Cameo about the box.

He tested his range of motion, noticed a slight resistance and scowled. Not great, but not terrible, either.

Waving the ring through the air, rubbing his thumb over the metal, he pictured the Realm of Skulls. A space guarded by Hilda the Deadly One.

Hilda was a Sphinx, a cousin of griffins. She had a human face, the body of a lion and the wings of an eagle.

Lazarus knew Hilda well, the immortal world as small as it was large. Their fathers—both equally atrocious—had once been friends, so they'd spent many years together. They'd shared a mutual acrimony.

The ring vibrated, electrical currents arcing through the air like lightning, creating a new rift. Beyond the forest, an office came into view. Lazarus entered, the portal closing behind him.

Such an ordinary setting. Plain beige walls, with a few impersonal pictures. A file cabinet, a desk and a glass display case. A small white box rested on one of the shelves, and appeared to be made of phalanges and metacarpals.

Familiar power pulsed from that shelf, stroking over him. His blood fizzed.

His gaze shifted to the human skull beside the box. He frowned. The teeth had been sharpened into razor points. Something about it...

Didn't matter. "Show yourself, Manhilda." He opened his mind to hers, but she'd erected a block. "Or do you prefer the name Hildabeast?"

The space in front of the bookshelf shimmered before she appeared. A monster in more ways than one. She'd spread up and out, and developed muscles on top of her muscles. A thick, black mustache led to a thicker beard and exaggerated jowls. Veins bulged in her neck.

A spiked metal collar circled her neck.

Collaring a Sphinx was the same as enslaving a Sphinx. The master could force the beast to do *anything*. But who had collared her? Very few immortals were strong enough to defeat a Sphinx.

Lazarus didn't have to wonder about why she'd been collared. Her unknown master was forcing her to guard Pandora's box.

A breastplate covered her ample chest, and leather cuffs wrapped around both of her wrists. Her only adornments. With four legs, she had the option to walk as an animal or a human. Lady's choice.

When most people looked at her, they saw a skinny man with red eyes. An illusion.

Few immortals could defeat her, yes, but even fewer could sustain an ongoing illusion. The small list of potential masters decreased even more so.

"Hello, Hi-lazarus." Rising to the top of her back legs, she was at least seven and a half feet tall. "We meet again."

The last time he'd been here, Cameo had been at his side. He'd told his μονομανία only that the "beast" had beaten him in a fight—and he'd taken great delight referring to the beast in the masculine form. Lazarus had left out a critical detail. His age. He'd been four.

"Good news," he said. "This is the last time we'll ever meet. Today you die. Unless you want to hand over Pandora's box?"

"To you, the one who prevented others from finding and freeing me? Not even if I were ordered."

Lazarus had been here twice before. The first time,

with Cameo. The second, he'd returned to cast an illusion of his own, hiding the box from all who searched. Even then he'd known the box could be used against Cameo. Not that her friends would ever purposely hurt her. But why take chances?

The very reason he had to keep his sunshine away from the item she desired most, even denying her the opportunity to fight for it.

Necessary. The demon depressed her. One day, she might try to end her life. Again! With the box, she could kill herself in seconds, before anyone had the opportunity to stop her.

If she dies, she'll join me in the afterlife...forever...

Forget the fact that she would ruin him. He wanted her to live the life of her dreams.

"Are you upset because you had no one to kill and eat?" He rubbed his fists under his eyes, mimicking tears. "Poor Hildabeast."

She ran her tongue over blood-stained fangs. "I'm going to enjoy eating *you*. I remember how sweet your organs taste."

Only once had she managed to chain him and cut into his torso. Unlike other immortal children, who would have died after losing every vital organ, Lazarus had regenerated and rebounded.

Can never die. His father's words echoed in his head.

Lazarus popped the bones in his neck and briefly considered wearing the diamond knuckles he'd stolen for Cameo, only to decide he didn't want them splattered with blood and...other things.

"Who managed to collar you?" he asked conversationally.

Hilda sharpened one set of her front claws against the other. "Some questions cannot be answered."

Her master had commanded her silence on the subject, then. He—or she—would come for the box. *Bring it.* Lazarus would kill the master just as easily as he killed the slave.

He pulled his short swords from the sheaths anchored to his back, metal whistling, and took a step forward—

An invisible wall stopped him. Scowling, he stabbed repeatedly, attempting to create a fissure. The weapons bent while the wall remained unharmed.

Hildabeast smiled a smug smile. "You wish to pass? Answer me this. The man who makes it has no need of it. The man who purchases it will not use it. The man who uses it will not know he's doing so. What is it?"

Her stupid riddles. In his haste to ensure Cameo's return, Lazarus had forgotten the way of the Sphinx. No man could approach without first answering a riddle. One of the reasons the creatures made such excellent guard dogs.

Last time, whenever Lazarus or Cameo had neared the wall, they'd experienced vertigo before being flashed to the far corner of the room.

This time, Lazarus wasn't newly dead. He was stronger, despite the crystals, and he was far more determined.

He rolled Hilda's riddle through his mind, and decided she'd gone easy on him. She *wanted* to fight him.

The man who makes "it" had no need of it…because he lived. The man who purchased "it" wouldn't use it… because he lived. The man who used "it" wouldn't know he was doing so…because he was dead.

"The answer is *coffin*," Lazarus said. "What you will need today."

A loud whoosh sounded, hot air gusting over him. The wall had just come down.

Glee darkened her eyes. "Do you truly believe you can best me?"

"I do." Smiling his own smug smile, he tossed his damaged swords to the floor and stalked toward his opponent. They'd do this hand to hand. Or rather, hand to paw.

Without warning, she swiped her claws at him. He dodged, only to put himself in the path of another hand. Pain tore through his midsection, momentarily rendering him immobile. Like any predator, she used his paralysis to her advantage, latching onto the back of his thighs and yanking.

He hit the ground with a heavy thud. Stars flashed through his line of sight.

Rather than launch her next attack, as any sane person would, she peered down at him. Gaze locked with his, she raised her fingers to her mouth. Out came her tongue, lapping up his blood.

"Delicious," she said.

Fury blazed through him. Perhaps humiliation. "You're a fool. You should have taken me out while you had the chance. You won't get another."

"Ready for more so soon? I know I am."

Lazarus jumped up. This time, when she swiped at him, he dropped to his stomach, palming two daggers on the way down. She missed, and he stabbed both of her feet.

Her roar echoed off the walls, shaking the entire room. Claws ripped across his back. Ignoring the newest onslaught of pain, he rolled to the side. When she took another swipe at him, he caught her wrists, kicked up his legs and crossed his ankles at her nape.

He rolled to his back this time, flipping her over his head. The daggers fell from her feet. He ended up on top of her, his knees pinning her shoulders. Anger contorted her features into a whole lot of ugly.

Not so smug now, are we?

Grinning, he punched the underside of her jaw. His knuckles cracked, but so did her jaw. She bucked, but the action failed to dislodge him. Then her wings swept up and knocked him across the room. Fueled by adrenaline, impact barely registered. He leaped up and spit out a feather. She climbed to all fours.

They circled each other, every step she took leaving a bloody paw print.

"There's something different about you." Her gaze slid over him. "But what?"

If she noticed the crystals, his weakness, he would—

Not care. Hilda died today.

He blew her a kiss. "I'm no longer a child, but a man. Not quite the man you are, of course, but everyone has a cross to bear."

The sneer in his tone did exactly as he'd hoped. Provoked beyond reason, she dived at him, fangs bared, claws ready. He swiped up the fallen daggers and ducked. As Hilda soared overhead, missing him by only a few inches, he used one hand to punch up and cut through her breastplate—through her body, from sternum to pubis. The other hand sliced through her wing.

Blood and organs rained. A pained shriek blended with his satisfied grunt as she flopped to the floor. Dark stains spread over the carpet. Acting quickly, knowing she would regenerate everything she'd lost in mere seconds, he threw himself atop her and framed her face with his hands. Skin on skin.

Her eyes widened when she realized his ultimate purpose. "No!" She erupted, fighting him with all her might.

He cursed. Too slippery. Soaked with her blood, he soon lost his grip on her, allowing her to kick him off. But he returned in a blink, knocking her down as she tried to sit up. She punched his face, kneed his balls. Air gushed from his lungs. Her elbow collided with his cheek, and he staggered to the side.

When she attempted to stand, he punted her in the jaw. No mercy. Down she tumbled. He jumped on top of her yet again, determined to hold on this time. His claws dug into her temples. If she tried to remove his hands, she'd lose hunks of skin and muscle.

"This is happening," he told her, embarrassed to be panting. "Take it like a man."

"If I took it like a man," she snarled, "I'd be crying like a baby." She batted his hands away. And yes, she lost hunks of skin and muscle. Her cheek resembled raw hamburger meat.

Even as she grunted with pain, she rolled to her side and booted his chest. But her strength had waned, and the action only knocked him *halfway* across the room.

By the time she made it to her feet, he'd pushed his way back. Remaining prone, he kicked her ankles together. She flailed as she fell. The second she landed, he rolled on top of her. She fought for dominance. Punching. Biting. Clawing.

Blood dripped into his eyes. His own? Or hers? She bit into his shoulder and tore out a hunk of flesh and bone. Pain seared him. He roared to the rafters, pin-pricks of light winking behind his eyes.

Overcome by his rage, Lazarus lifted his head, sank his teeth into her vulnerable neck and tore out her trachea. She gasped, the gaping wound sucking raggedly at whatever air it could steal. He rolled a final time, ending up on top, shoving his knees into her torso and cupping her cheeks.

With the flip of a mental switch, heat flowed out of him and into her, such intense heat. Sweat suddenly drenched her. Her flesh began to turn to stone...

At first, she flailed. As her skin and fur hardened, beiges and browns darkening to gray, her motions slowed...

Bastard, she mouthed as the last of her petrified.

To his knowledge, the process could not be undone. Which meant he'd won.

Relieved, he collapsed beside her. The process always drained him, the reason he only ever used the ability when he lacked an audience.

"Told you," he rasped.

He studied his newest statue. Her agonized features were forever frozen, her eyes gazing upward, pleading for mercy, her mouth open, revealing fangs. Her arms were extended, her hands balled into fists. Both sets of legs were extended as well, now pushing at oxygen. Her broken wing lay at an odd angle, while the other wrapped inward in an attempt to protect her. Her chest cavity was split open, not yet having healed.

She would have a place of honor in his garden.

One last thing to do...

He lumbered to a stand and stalked across the room, stopping directly in front of the display case. The power he'd encountered earlier brushed over him, his blood beginning to fizz all over again.

He pulled off the remains of his T-shirt, wrapped the material around his fist and punched through the panel that protected the box.

The glass shattered and slashed through the cotton. Sharp stings zinged over his fingers, and crimson beaded from a thousand tiny wounds.

Steeling himself, he reached for the box…only to still. The pulse of power wasn't coming from it. He frowned and focused on the skull, the true source. Why had its teeth been filed into razor points…if not to guard something of importance?

Acting on instinct, he reached inside its open mouth. Those teeth clamped down on his wrist, and he hissed, but he didn't yank out his hand. His fingers bumped against a small object anchored inside, and the power arced through him, pure and undiluted. The scratches in his stomach and back healed. The cuts on his knuckles closed up.

This was the same power he'd experienced the few times he'd encountered Kadence, the goddess of Oppression. Upon her death, her bones were used to make the box.

Satisfaction bubbled inside him. He latched onto the item, whatever it was, and yanked. The skull's teeth remained embedded in his skin. Poison leaked from the incisors, but it was no deterrent to him. One by one, he tossed the bits of enamel to the floor. Then he examined the small trinket he'd liberated.

Definitely made from bones, just like the box. Fingers and knuckles. And yes, they belonged to Kadence.

The bones had been shattered, the pieces welded together and stained red to resemble an apple.

An apple. The original temptation. But…

This was the infamous Pandora's box?

Problem: the other Lords remembered a literal box, like the one he'd first reached for.

Possibility: whoever made the box could have *remade* the box after it was opened. A good strategy. How better to hide it? But who had made the first box? And why?

The Lords believed a living being was still trapped inside. The Morning Star. Not a demon, but a creature able to destroy Lucifer and his evil with a single touch. Able to free the Lords of their demons, too, while ensuring the warriors lived on.

Lazarus had done his research. Some said the Morning Star was a Sent One, the best demon slayer ever to live. Others claimed the Morning Star was a literal descendant of celestial beings known as Starlights, so bright the sun would weep with envy. Still others suggested the being was a jinni, a granter of wishes.

The next problem, or maybe the biggest paradox: Lazarus would love to use the Morning Star, but to do so, he would have to open the box. Cameo could die before he had the chance to use the Star, saving her.

Could she be saved?

Speaking of his μονομανία, how was he to get word to her? He had what she craved.

She expected him to show up at her door, all *Remember you said you'd reward me if I escaped the spirit realm?*

He knew what he would request. Her mouth on his shaft.

Lazarus hung the pendant from a chain around his neck and tugged the ruined remains of his shirt overhead, hiding the artifact under the material. Using the ring, he created a portal to the Realm of Grimm and Fantica. He dragged Hilda through and ended up in front of the *other* portal. The one leading to the mortal world. To Cameo.

He glared daggers at the shimmery air. *You took my woman from me.*

A strange tugging sensation drew him closer. His mind whirled as he dug in his heels. Pandora's box, attempting to reach the demons?

No, couldn't be. The sensation originated in his veins. In the crystal. He didn't understand, but he expected the worst and backed away.

His men were just as he'd left them. His sky serpents, too. Trees had been felled, but so had griffins. Their bodies lay in pieces throughout the forest.

"Good boys and girls," he praised. To his soldiers, he called, "Rope."

One of the men rushed forward to offer the desired item. Lazarus anchored one end to Hilda and the other to his stallion's saddle, ensuring the braided length wouldn't tangle in the steed's wings. He mounted.

"You, you and you." He pointed to his strongest men. "Camp here. When the dark-haired woman returns, protect her with your lives and escort her to the palace. The rest of you…let's go home."

Lazarus positioned Hilda in the Garden of Perpetual Horror. Only the best for his newest addition. Her broken body lay underneath a squatting troll who'd raided a nearby village and slaughtered the males in order to steal the females.

Satisfied with his selection, Lazarus marched into the palace. No servants rushed to greet him. In fact, the halls remained eerily quiet. He withdrew two daggers even as he opened his mind to gauge the situation.

Mental chatter from the soldiers who'd returned with him. They wondered about Cameo, what she meant to their king. The only other occupants were...dreaming? Nothing else explained the image of a dancing elephant with a tutu, a talking car and a horny robot.

He turned the corner, entering the dining hall, and found the bodies of soldiers and servants slumped over furniture and splayed on the floor.

Finally—an answer from the Amazons he'd imprisoned. The bags of poison had been decoys. They'd already turned their blood to poison—for others.

He'd been tricked, distracted by one ploy while another brewed. What he'd done, they'd wanted him to do.

And now, he sensed another presence. Someone he'd warned away.

"Rathbone," he shouted. He stormed through the Great Room and past the exquisitely painted arched doors that led into his throne room.

The dark-haired male reclined on the throne, one leg crossed over the other in a lazy, relaxed pose. There was only one outward sign of his impatience—he drummed his fingers against the chair's arms.

"Look at you," Rathbone said. "Alive and well. And practically shirtless. Determined to set maiden hearts aflutter, are we?"

"What are you doing here?" Lazarus demanded.

"Protecting your people in your absence. You're welcome." The king of the underworld waved to the far wall. "Behold."

He turned to see the Amazons suspended in the air.

"They escaped and attempted a coup." Rathbone grinned without humor. "Their queen has plans for you. An enslavement masked as a wedding."

His grip on the daggers tightened. *She thinks to enslave me? She dies!*

"They'll receive prime spots in my Garden of Perpetual Horror by the end of the day." He would not thank Rathbone. The words would be an admission he'd needed help. He hadn't. He could have reclaimed the palace on his own, no problem.

Amazonian fear left an acrid scent in the air. The females collectively fought Rathbone's hold...and failed.

"Excellent. I'll be going, then." Rathbone stood. "But I'm afraid I must hear your decision. The war no longer brews. The first battle between father and son has been waged. A sneak attack. One of Hades's homes was destroyed, everyone inside it captured or killed."

A loss always stung, but a loss at the start of a war *devastated*. Motivation among the troops plummeted.

Begin the way you hope to end. Words his mother had once spoken to him. She'd referred to his romantic relationships, offering her only child a bit of advice to help him in the years to come.

Never align with the losing side. Their losses become yours. Words his father had spoken.

Then and there, Lucifer should have earned Lazarus's support. But...

"Very well," he said. "I'll fight for Hades." For Cameo. *Only parted from her a few hours, and I yearn for her as I would a missing limb.* "My time frame hasn't changed, however. I'll use my month to get my own house in order." To get his woman back. Until he had his night with her, he would be useless.

"You are needed now."

"So? The war might have started, but it won't be ending anytime soon. Put your best player in at the end to ensure victory."

The male pursed his lips, but nodded. "I should probably warn you. Hera escaped Tartarus. The Greek queen is now free."

Every muscle in his body tensed. Outside Tartarus, Hera was fair game. *Vengeance…finally within reach…*

Reveal nothing. "Former queen," he said with a shockingly even tone.

"Will you hunt her?" Rathbone asked.

"You know I cannot leave the spirit realms." The words were grated. *The bastard taunts me!*

Rathbone's head canted to the side. "You are Lazarus, only son of the Monster, yes?"

"Yes," Lazarus snapped.

"Then I know no such thing." Smiling, Rathbone vanished.

People suffered tragedies every day. They cried, sobbed and one day, they woke up and their hurt had mysteriously diminished. Cameo had suffered for centuries, her pain constant. But now, without Lazarus, she suffered *worse.*

She'd been home only two days, and already she missed him as she would miss a limb. And she should know! During her incarceration, the Hunters hacked off her hands and feet to stop her from fighting back.

Half of the day she longed to forget Lazarus—and

hated herself for it. She'd lamented the horror of losing her memory for so long, she'd lost sight of the peace she could gain without it.

The only reason Misery had allowed her to keep her precious…hated…beloved…really hated memories— was to ensure she never, ever felt any peace at all.

Did it matter, though? The other half of the day Cameo longed to return to the warrior, anyway.

For a night. Only a night.

One night with him had to be better than a thousand nights without him, right?

Every time she considered going back, the demon threatened to take her memory, despite the vision she'd had.

Can't lose my memory of Lazarus. The way he'd smiled at her had warmed her…the way he'd teased her had soothed her…both were precious to her. And their goodbye kiss…it had set her ablaze, changing the very fabric of her being.

I'm Lazarus's woman.

She needed a distraction and, remembering Lazarus's treatment at Juliette the Eradicator's hands, she knew just what to do.

She texted her friend Gwen, the Harpy consort of Sabin, keeper of Doubt. When the reply came in, a tendril of anticipation swept through her. She packed a bag and strapped on her favorite weapons.

As she strode into the hall, cheers and laughter drifted from the dining room downstairs.

Once Urban and Ever had been reunited with their frantic parents—and worries and tempers had calmed— everyone who wasn't in the underworld helping Hades had celebrated. There'd been feasts, bad karaoke and far too much drinking. Ambrosia wine for adults, juice boxes for kids.

Like every celebration in the past, Cameo had watched from a distance, not wanting to ruin everyone's happy buzz.

Now she headed for Viola's room. Every great warrior should have a sidekick, someone to guard her back, and the goddess would be hers.

"Pandora's box is in play. I repeat. Pandora's box is in play." Torin's voice boomed from strategically placed speakers in the ceiling. "This is not a drill. Danika painted a new scene, and Keeley was finally able to use the artifacts to get inside the office, where the box was being kept. Key word. *Was*."

The cheers from downstairs ceased abruptly. Cameo froze, her mind spinning.

Danika was the All-Seeing Eye, able to peer into the heavens and hell, as well as the past and the future. She painted the things she saw.

Keeley treated Danika's paintings like maps and used them in conjunction with three other artifacts. The Cage of Compulsion, the Cloak of Invisibility, and of course, the Paring Rod.

Questions shouted from different areas of the house. "Do *we* have the box?"

"Where is the box now?"

"Is the Morning Star still inside?"

"The box is not in our possession, no," Torin said, and his words were met with groans. "It's been moved or taken. The women are searching, and they will find it. Do not come knocking on my door to repeat your questions. My answers won't change. I've told you everything I know."

As murmurs rose from the kitchen, Cameo's heart thundered. Who had the box? Would it be opened? Were she and her loved ones destined to die?

A sense of urgency assailed her, her biggest regret suddenly clear. If her days were numbered, she wanted her night with Lazarus, wanted the pleasure he'd promised her.

Pleasure she couldn't experience if she were killed.

When immortals possessed by Pandora's demons passed away, their spirits ended up inside a prison realm. Baden, former keeper of Distrust, and Pandora, former owner of the box, had escaped the place only by becoming enslaved to Hades. No, thank you.

Wondering what could have been...fantasizing about but never feeling Lazarus against her...inside her...*that* would be the true misery.

Cameo had rolled the dice on her future and left Lazarus behind, hoping he would find a way into the mortal world. A mistake, she realized now. A mistake she could rectify.

New plan. *Find and fight Juliette, return to Lazarus.*

She launched into motion, skirting past a chamber filled with prowling, growling hellhounds. Baden had wed a woman who trained the horse-size hounds.

Trained, not tamed.

Each of the hounds bared razor-sharp fangs while giving Cameo the stink eye. Did she look like a grab-and-go snack? Oookay. Moving on. She picked up the pace, turned the corner—

And smacked into William the Ever Randy, Hades's son.

Ever since the object of William's affections had

wed another man, he'd been crazed. A madman with a short—cough nonexistent cough—fuse.

According to the ladies of the house, William was the reason Hades had lost the first battle with Lucifer.

He glared at her with eyes bluer than any ocean. "Watch where you're going, Misery."

"Sure thing. But you had better watch your tone," she snapped. "Why are you man-pouting, anyway? Why aren't you out fighting for your girl? Time is short and—"

He flinched, and she pressed her lips together. Right. Lazarus could tolerate her voice, but few others had the fortitude. While here, she had to watch her mouth.

"Her coward of a husband has hidden her from me." William raised a half-empty bottle of whiskey to his lips.

The demon snickered. *Don't consider it half-*full? *Does it matter? The bottle is refillable.*

Gulp, gulp, gulp. With his free hand, William wiped his mouth. "Anyone ever mention you sound like death?"

"Only everyone," she muttered.

"Well, you do," he grated, perhaps not realizing she'd agreed with him. "Now get out of my way before I'm forced to cut through you." Despite the threat, he stumbled around her when she remained in place.

His shoulders brushed against hers, his sorrow pulsing over her skin. Misery purred with delight.

A hot tear slid down Cameo's cheek. "William," she called.

He shuddered but ignored her, and then he was gone.

With a sigh, she continued forward—and nearly smacked into another warrior.

Sabin, keeper of Doubt, glared down at her. "I know what you're planning, and I'm not on board. I forbid you to leave! We need you with us, searching for the box."

"You forbid me?" She sputtered with indignation. "Tell me you're joking."

The big, black-haired warrior with battle-hardened features flinched, just like William, irritating her. "You know I have no sense of humor, Cam. Come on." He forced her down the hall and pushed her inside his bedroom. "Let's talk about this in semiprivacy."

The beautiful Gwen stood in front of a rumpled bed, chewing on her bottom lip. Her strawberry blond locks were piled in a messy bun on top of her head, and her petite body was packed inside a tiny tank and shorts shorter than anything Lazarus had given Cameo.

Sabin pointed an accusing finger at her. "We just got you back. We—"

Cameo punched him in the face.

As his head whipped to the side and blood dripped from his lip, Gwen cheered. The Harpy loved her husband, but she loved girl power, too.

In the heavens, Sabin had been appointed general of Zeus's army. Lucien, too. They had called the shots, two big, bad Papa Smurfs to Cameo's Smurfette. They'd continued to call the shots here in the mortal world. Well, no longer! She was taking charge of her life.

"Nice right hook. You've improved, and I'm impressed." He rubbed two fingers into the knot she'd left behind. "But Juliette is trouble. We don't need more trouble right now."

"She hurt my friend, and she will pay." Knowing Sabin would freak if she mentioned her plan to return to Lazarus, even for a single night, she offered no more.

"Your friend. You mean Lazarus, the man our brother beheaded." He peered up at the ceiling and muttered, "Please tell me the woman I trained isn't so foolish."

Whispers of uncertainty drifted through her mind. *What if Lazarus only wants to be with you to punish Strider? What if he's sleeping with someone else? What if—*

She threw her arms into the air. "Put a muzzle on your demon. Now."

"Sorry," he mumbled.

"Look, I know you're worried about me, but I'm a big girl. I've got this." She patted his cheek. "I love you even though you're an asshole, and I *will* return." After she'd spent a night with Lazarus, lost in a sea of passion.

"Yes, but will you return in one piece?" Sabin quipped.

"No promises."

"If you attack Juliette," Gwen said, "the entire Eagleshield family will come after you."

"I know the risks. I don't care." Lazarus had told Urban the best gift to give your date was the severed head of an enemy. Cameo would present him with something even better—Juliette's hands.

He lived for vengeance, and she would give it to him.

Trying to buy his affections? Misery tsk-tsked. *For shame!*

"Cameo—"

"I'm going, and that's final." She stomped from the room.

To her surprise, Viola waited in the hall, dressed in a leather catsuit, ready for battle. Princess Fluffikans danced between her ankles.

"Is the mission to fight Juliette Eagleshield still a go?" Viola asked.

How had she known?

Well, it didn't take a mind reader to learn the answer. Torin. His mics and security cameras were everywhere. Plus, he knew Cameo better than most. He'd seen her at her lowest and even helped her pick up the pieces. Despite their failed romantic relationship, he loved her, wanted the best for her. Wanted her protected. Whether he'd known Cameo's plan to speak with Viola or not, he'd acted accordingly.

"It—" Cameo jolted. A butterfly had just fluttered down the hall to land on the goddess's shoulder. A sign of impending doom.

Or coming success, according to Lazarus.

Deep breath in, out. The sign—good or bad—didn't matter, she decided. Her goals were too important. She couldn't back down.

She nodded. "It's absolutely a go."

15

"Be the monster other monsters fear."
—*Eternal Truths for Every Man*

Lazarus returned to the portal. He dismissed his soldiers, preferring to be alone with his crazy.

The mortal world was only five steps away. His enemies were there. *Cameo* was there.

He'd gone three days without her. Far too long. A fact that baffled him. The last time they'd parted, the separation had grated but he'd managed. This time, he wasn't managing. His mood grew darker by the second.

His conversation with Rathbone continued to play through his mind, torturing him.

"Will you hunt her?"

"You know I cannot leave the spirit realms."

"You are Lazarus, only son of the Monster, yes?"

"Yes."

"Then I know no such thing."

The warrior believed Lazarus could pass through

the portal *without* ending up in the void? Why? How? Nothing had changed. He—

Not true. Many things had changed. His alliance with Hades. Had it strengthened him? The pull the portal now had on him. Why? The apple hanging from his neck…a living being might or might not be trapped inside it. Another means of strength? The magic mirror. Since it had revealed possible futures to Cameo, he'd brought it with him. Maybe it had the power to reunite him with his woman, maybe not.

Desperate enough to try anything.

But. More of his veins had filled with crystals. Soon he wouldn't be able to hide the transformation from others. A certain weakness.

If he ended up in the void, he would lose precious time. Another immortal could take over his realm, steal his army. When he returned, he would have to waste even more time fighting the new king.

If he ended up in the mortal world, he would have to give up his army, anyway.

He bit his tongue until he tasted the metallic tang of blood. He would have to wed a queen sooner rather than later. There would be no faster way to regain the power he would lose.

Was a chance at vengeance worth the risk? No. He could wait, as he'd always planned to wait, for Hera and Juliette to die and end up in the spirit realms.

Powerful immortals died every day. He was proof.

Was Cameo worth the risk, considering he couldn't keep her?

No need to ponder the answer. Yes. Cameo was worth *any* risk, and the irony wasn't lost on him. She hosted Misery, but only she could make him happy.

With one hand, Lazarus picked up the mirror. With the other, he reached into his satchel, and withdrew a freshly squeezed Amazon heart.

Cameo and Viola strode into the Downfall side by side. The immortal nightclub was located in the third level of the heavens, where evil and good often collided. It was owned by three Sent Ones. The walls and floor looked to be made of thin, white clouds, allowing the occupants to peer at the black sky and bright stars both beyond and underneath the building. An astonishing phenomenon, since those clouds were solid to the touch.

The scent of liquor, sex and clashing perfumes hung heavy in the air. The heat had been jacked up, either to encourage drinking or stripping. Probably both.

Cameo spotted the mirrors on the ceiling and groaned. Every demon came with an array of flaws, and mirrors were one of Narcissism's. Anytime Viola caught sight of her reflection, she became entranced. Anyone could attack her, and she would never see it coming, wouldn't even react until far too late.

"Don't look up," Cameo told her. "Please."

"Why?" Of course, Viola attempted to look up.

Cameo pinched her chin and held her gaze. "Trust me."

"There's a mirror, isn't there?" The goddess chewed on her lower lip. "Surely I can afford a single glance… I'm so pretty."

"Sure. Take a glance. Make yourself vulnerable to everyone in the club. You could become an immortal piñata. Every girl's dream!"

A shudder rocked Viola on her hooker heels. "Right.

No glances. We're here to find a delicious beefcake and—"

"No! To find the Harpy. Juliette. No beefcake." Wasn't like anyone would tempt her. As long as Cameo remembered Lazarus, he would be her standard of measure. No one could hope to compare.

Viola wiggled her brows at a bear shifter. "Maybe a *slice* of beefcake?" Fluffy sat at her feet, snarling at any male who passed. "I'm hungry for a distraction."

"Well, consider today low-cal, gluten-free and one hundred percent vegan."

A man she'd never met looked at her, looked away, then lurched and *stared* at her. He ran his tongue over his lips as if he could already taste her kiss.

He didn't want her, not really. Yesterday, after she'd made the decision to spend a night with Lazarus, desire had begun to simmer inside her. Desire she now radiated, right along with sadness. The men she'd come across had responded...enthusiastically.

When this one walked toward her, his graceful glide suggesting he was a vampire, she held up a dagger in warning. He grinned with relish, revealing fangs, and kept coming.

She said, "Want to have a discussion about deep and meaningful things?"

As her voice drifted over the music, he cringed and backed away.

"Yeah, that's what I thought," she muttered, hiding her hurt behind a blank mask. *I'm man repellent.*

Misery laughed with his customary glee. *Lazarus is glad to be rid of you.*

She swallowed a cry of distress. The demon loved

peppering her with statements she couldn't currently dispute. An insidious weapon in his arsenal of evil.

Would Lazarus be happy to see her? Or had he realized he was better off without her?

"Friendly tip," Viola said from behind her hand. "When the cute man wants to flirt with us and pay for our drinks and appetizers— Hey, do you want to split cheese fries?"

"No. What's your friendly tip? I shouldn't talk?"

"Don't be ridiculous." The goddess waved a dismissive hand. "I was going to suggest you steal his wallet before you talk."

Not exactly bad advice.

Cameo did her best to block Misery from her thoughts as she scanned the club. A live band played atop a dais in the corner, women's underwear strewn around their feet. On the dance floor, males and females of every immortal race writhed together in wicked harmony. Multiple bartenders manned an overly crowded bar.

One of the bartenders—a handsome man with pink hair—spotted Viola and dropped a glass. The color drained from his face, leaving him pallid.

"Do you know him?" Cameo asked, pointing. He had a very distinctive look. Tears of blood were inked into the corners of his eyes, and a steel ring protruded from his lower lip.

"I wouldn't say I know him. I'd say I once destroyed him," Viola replied, her tone breezy but her eyes tortured. "I'm sure he bears me no hard feelings."

A list of things Cameo trusted more than Viola's assurance: gum on the bottom of the tables, an armed enemy at her back and a dinner buffet hosted by Lucifer the Destroyer.

The bartender hurried through a door in back, vanishing from sight. Within seconds, another male appeared. White and gold wings arched over his shoulders. He was a Sent One. Cameo had never met him, but judging by the telltale white hair, scarred alabaster skin and red eyes that proclaimed his identity, this was Xerxes. One of the club's owners.

His gaze landed on Viola and narrowed.

"Do you know *him*?" Cameo pointed. If the demon assassin had a beef with Narcissism, he'd have a beef with Misery, too.

"Definitely not." Viola bent down to pet Fluffy behind his ears. "Now. What was I saying? I'm sure you were hanging on every word."

Cameo watched with dread as Xerxes moved his gaze through the club and gave an almost imperceptible nod to—

Another Sent One, who plowed through the crowd, heading straight for Viola. Cameo stared at him, amazed. He looked…he couldn't be…but his image never changed. Wavy black hair, vibrant blue eyes and chiseled features usually only found in feminine fantasies— or in the reflection of William the Ever Randy.

They couldn't be twins. This guy appeared younger and less hardened by life. Well, that, and he had magnificent white-gold wings.

No way William was related to a Sent One. No way, no how. Right?

The male stopped in front of Viola and grinned a sinner's grin. *Exactly like William.* "Hello, ladies. I'm Axel, the man of your dreams."

Something William would have said.

Cameo nodded a greeting, wanting to deluge him with questions. No reason to ruin his night.

"Actually," Viola said, "I'm the woman of my dreams, and I'm in a committed relationship with my-self."

"I'm intrigued." He offered his arm, and the goddess accepted without hesitation, as if his admiration were her due. "Tell me more."

"Prepare to be riveted."

The two wandered off, their conversation soon drowned out by music. Some sidekick.

"Viola," she called. "Stranger danger is real. You shouldn't—"

Without looking back, the goddess gave her a thumbs-up. The people around her began to sob.

Cameo's shoulders rolled in. She wouldn't go chasing after her friend, treating Viola the way Sabin had treated her. As if she were an invalid incapable of protecting herself. She would trust Viola to see to her own safety.

Cameo turned her attention to hunt for her prey. Thanks to Gwen, she knew Juliette Eagleshield would be—there!

Oh, wow, Cameo had forgotten how beautiful she was. Tall and toned with dark hair and lavender eyes. A man could get drunk looking into those eyes.

The Harpy tossed back a shot, lifted her arms and shouted, "Woo-hoo." She wore a purple tank top and a miniskirt, the wealth of tattoos on her legs perfectly displayed. In several places, different symbols wove together, creating an optical illusion, making her skin look as delicate as lace.

When Juliette threw back her head and laughed, a blade of envy cut through Cameo.

Why would Lazarus want you, a pity party waiting to happen, and not her, a pleasure party?

Cameo raised her chin. The answer didn't matter. Juliette had removed Lazarus's hands. More than once! Today Cameo removed hers.

Determined, she closed the distance.

Xerxes stepped into her path, stopping her. "Fights aren't allowed inside the club." His red eyes glowed, as ominous as they were unusual. Up close, his scars stood out in stark contrast to his pale skin, and it became obvious they were claw marks.

No help for it. She had to speak. "How do you know I plan to fight?"

He flinched ever so slightly before motioning to her hand. "You are clutching a dagger."

Was she? Oops. She couldn't recall palming one.

Cameo sheathed the weapon. "Happy now?"

"No." Moving with a speed she couldn't match, he claimed the dagger and its twin.

Whatever. From head to toe, *she* was a weapon.

"I'll keep these until you're ready to leave," he said. "No reason to play with temptation."

"Fine. But just so we're clear, I'll shove those daggers in your eyes if you or your friends harm Viola."

Surprise registered, softening his features. "No harm will come to her."

She believed him. Sent Ones were incapable of lying.

"Nor will any come to you," he added. "Unless you cause trouble here." He strode away, disappearing in the crowd despite his size and unique appearance, a feat that required talent.

Well. Time to cause trouble.

Finally Cameo reached the Harpies. Voice nothing but heartache and despair, she said, "Juliette the Eradicator."

Juliette cringed, but quickly covered the action by arching a dark brow. "Cameo, Mother of Melancholy. I suggest you move along. Your friend killed my consort."

She ran her tongue over her teeth. "He wasn't your consort. He was your slave. And why would I move along? I'm going to wipe the floor with your face."

The Harpy tensed, even as tears filled her eyes. Actually, every Harpy at the table tensed. Six in total. Meaning, six pairs of watery eyes focused on Cameo and flickered with rage. *We're off to a good start, then.*

"Look who decided to steal a pair of balls." Juliette flicked her tongue over the sharpened edge of an incisor, mimicking Cameo. "Too bad for you, we know the balls belong to Hades. We're on different sides of the war, and you think he can protect you. News flash. He can't. Make no mistake, I'll rip off your limbs and mail them to your family."

The crowd of immortals caught wind of the argument and formed a circle around Cameo and the Harpies. The music came to a screeching halt and silence reigned. Then mutters began to rise from the throng.

"Are you filming this?"

"Is that Cameo, keeper of Misery? Five bucks says we're about to find out if blood is her best color."

"I once watched Juliette pull out a man's spine—through his mouth. Cameo's going down."

Everyone assumed the Harpy would beat her? Wow. That stung.

Your loss will be humiliating, Misery said, and cackled.

Sadness threatened to drown her. No! Not here. Not now. *I can do this. I* will *do this.* If she could control her thoughts, she could control her emotions. She *could.*

Three Sent Ones pushed their way to the front of the circle—Xerxes and the other owners, Bjorn and Thane—hurling people out of their way.

No fighting in the club? "Hypocrite," she muttered.

Bjorn had dark hair, bronzed skin and the most spectacular pair of rainbow-colored eyes. Thane had innocent blond curls but hardened blue eyes. All three males radiated malice as they crossed their arms over their massive chests, daring Cameo and Juliette to deliver the first strike.

Cameo stood her ground. "You hurt Lazarus," she spat at Juliette. "Now I hurt you."

Lavender eyes narrowed to tiny slits. "Lazarus is my consort, now and forever, in life and in death. Mine! He is nothing to you."

Borrowing a page from Viola's playbook, Cameo fluffed her hair as if she hadn't a care. "Are you sure? I just spent the weekend with him."

Tremors swept through the Harpy. "You found him in the spirit realms?"

"Found him…kissed him."

"Kissed—" With a shriek, Juliette launched at her.

Just before contact, a streak of black slammed into the Harpy, knocking her backward. Fluffy, Cameo realized, shocked to her core. He clawed at Juliette's face, a bundle of rage, and the Harpy screamed in pain.

The crowd gasped collectively and backed away. Someone must have tripped over someone else, because a fight erupted. The Sent Ones leaped into action, doing their best to stop the worst of the violence.

One of Juliette's friends pulled a thin, silver rod from the leather cuff around her wrist. A rod she swung at Cameo.

Reflexes well honed, Cameo caught the end and threw a punch. Contact! Her knuckles shattered the Harpy's cheekbone.

Viola appeared in a puff of crimson smoke. No longer angelic, she looked like the demon living inside her. Two horns extended from her scalp. Red scales had replaced her skin, and her eyes flared like radioactive rubies. Sharp, deadly fangs had grown from her gums, and her nails had lengthened into claws. The scent of sulfur wafted from her.

The goddess slashed the neck of Cameo's opponent— as if it were a stick of butter. Blood sprayed, the Harpy grasping at newly torn tissue, desperate to breathe but unable.

The Sent Ones focused their efforts on Viola, but failed to stop her. She was simply too strong. As she worked her way through the Harpies, slashing at anyone within reach, the table fell over and glasses fragmented.

Cameo seized the opportunity to attack Juliette, who hadn't yet fended off the Tasmanian devil. She kicked the bitch in the stomach…then kicked again as the Harpy hunched over, gagging.

Fluffy released her—but he took a piece of her ear with him.

Cameo backhanded her across a bloody cheek, sending the Harpy stumbling into the riotous crowd.

The huffing, puffing Juliette shoved another woman at Cameo—a siren—driving them both backward. As she struggled for purchase, the Harpy grabbed a piece of broken glass and leaped.

Impact drove Cameo farther back. When she slammed into a table, Juliette slashed at her twice. Cameo dodged both times, tripped over a chair, but somehow maintained a tight grip on the Harpy's wrist, saving herself from dismemberment.

A muscled arm suddenly wrapped around Juliette's waist, yanking her off Cameo.

"Let me go," the Harpy screeched, struggling for freedom.

Without a word, Thane carted her to the balcony, flared his wings and launched into the sky.

Cameo jumped up, intending to race to…she wasn't sure. She couldn't follow. A muscled arm wrapped around *her*. A scarred arm. Xerxes. Bjorn, she noted, had finally gotten hold of Viola while a snarling Fluffy attacked his ankles.

"Break our rules," Xerxes said through gritted teeth, "and face our wrath."

"Harm her," a rough, masculine voice announced, "and die."

Cameo's heart tripped against her ribs. The rest of her stilled, vibrating with…anticipation?

Oh, yes. The crowd parted, and a glowering Lazarus came into view.

16

"If you make something easy for yourself, you make it easy for your enemy. Therefore, make it difficult. Better yet, make it hard. Very hard."
—*Eternal Truths for Every Man*

The man holding Viola handed her to a fallen Sent One named McCadden as if she were a bag of panties. The tattooed bartender with pink hair clutched her close and, in an effort to escape the chaos that had erupted at the appearance of Lazarus, sprinted from the room.

Without wings, he couldn't leave the building. He would need help. Unless he possessed the ability to flash?

Just before McCadden rounded the corner leading into a hallway of offices, Viola's gaze caught on Cameo's. The beautiful wench had stopped staring at her man with awe in order to search for Viola. Surely a feat of unimaginable strength, considering the gorgeous Lazarus had been beheaded and now walked among the living. Did the dark-haired beauty intend to launch a rescue for her? How sweet.

I've made a true friend?

Viola shook her head, silently telling Cameo to back down. She would be fine. She owed McCadden, and for once, she would pay her debt. She would face his wrath rather than use her ability to vanish in a blink. Because…just because!

Cameo nodded in understanding.

Fluffy nipped at McCadden's heels, refusing to allow his momma out of his sight.

The fallen Sent One whisked her into a luxurious office with enough space between every piece of furniture to welcome the easy glide of wings. He kicked the door shut, sealing her inside with him. Alone. A soft snick echoed between them, an ominous warning.

Viola wrenched from his embrace, found her feet and turned her back on him, something she normally wouldn't have done. *Trust no one but myself.* Well, and Fluffy. But this man wouldn't hurt her; she knew it with every fiber of her being.

Besides, Fluffy stood guard over her. He perched at her feet, his fangs bared in warning.

"Do you know who I am, goddess?" McCadden asked softly.

"I…" Narcissism used to wipe her memory the way Misery so often wiped Cameo's. Only, he hadn't wiped away the good times in an effort to keep her mired in regret. He'd only erased the things she'd done to ruin her high opinion of herself, all in an effort to keep her prideful. A condition she'd once lauded. *I'm wonderful. Why fight it?*

Sooner or later, pride always led to a very hard fall.

One day, Narcissism had realized Viola's happiness tainted his own. He strengthened only when he tore others down. Including his host. He enjoyed his power only when he purposely weakened others. Again, including his host. He felt in control only when he caused others to lose theirs. Yep, including his host.

That was the nature of a demon. Of *all* demons. The fiends weren't something you could accept and placate. They weren't cuddly teddy bears who just needed the love of a good woman. They weren't an evil that could be used to your advantage. They destroyed. Always. They ravaged, plain and simple. And they only ever craved *more* destruction, *more* ravaging.

Sometimes, when the last of Viola's pride burned to ash, Narcissism weakened and retired to the back of her mind, his presence barely discernible. She would remember the things she'd done and said and her heart would shatter. She would fall to her knees and sob, forced to acknowledge that, by yielding to evil, she had *become* evil.

But the demon always rebounded, and the cycle always began all over again. Build her up, tear others down. Tear her down. Heartache to rival Cameo's. A resurgence of pride.

This was a time she wanted to fall to her knees and sob. Not that she would ever do so in front of an audience, especially an audience that included McCadden. The foolish male would do everything in his power to comfort her.

She deserved no comforting.

"Yes," she said. "I do."

"I'm glad."

"Don't be." She wrapped her arms around her middle

to mask her trembling. She had picked up the pieces of her shattered heart countless times, and she could do it again. "I've already proved I'm your downfall."

When he offered no response, she padded through the office. The spacious enclosure had a high, domed ceiling, bookshelves framed in gold and columns carved to resemble specific immortals. She recognized Thane, Bjorn and Xerxes, but not the female who appeared to be engulfed by flames.

Obviously a Phoenix... Thane's wife? Yes, yes, of course. According to gossip, the most angelic-looking of the Sent Ones was utterly besotted with his fiery Elin. Why *wouldn't* he erect a statue in her image?

Oh, to be loved in such a way.

I love you, the demon said.

Liar!

"You were already my downfall," McCadden said, his voice soft.

The words ripped her from her momentary reprieve.

He'd meant what he'd said literally. He'd given up his place among the Sent Ones, allowing his wings to be cut from his back, his position in the armies to be stripped, and his home to be given to another, simply for the *chance* to be with her.

Narcissism had fed off his adoration. Sent Ones were his favorite snack, after all. Maybe because Sent Ones carried a piece of Love in their hearts, a gift of their exalted bloodline. They were children of the One True Deity, who was more powerful than the Greeks, the Titans and any other race of immortals. Demons despised the One True Deity and his followers, and took great glee in meting their destruction.

Narcissism used Viola to do his dirty work.

As the goddess of the Afterlife, she could siphon someone's—anyone's—life force. She simply needed permission, whether that permission came wittingly or unwittingly.

The night she'd met McCadden, she'd sensed an easy target. Rejected by his family for…a reason she'd chosen not to hear, he'd been desperate for affection. She'd smiled and turned on the charm, and in only a few weeks he'd handed over his life force on a silver platter, allowing her to feed Fluffy, keeping her beloved pet alive another century or two.

I won't feel guilty. I won't!

Afterward she'd walked away from McCadden, leaving him to his doomed fate, certain she would never speak to him again.

How can he look at me with such kindness?

She wanted him to rail and scream at her.

"I love you still," he said.

She shook her head, adamant. "You can't. I sentenced you to hell."

He pounded a fist against his chest, unyielding. "I know what I feel."

Burning behind her eyes. *No crying. Not here.* "Feelings change," she whispered. "Besides, look where yours got you."

A thousand screams erupted inside her head—and they were all her own. She wanted to shout at him, *You're a fool! Protect yourself from further harm!* She would only ever do what proved best for herself and her pet, and therefore the demon.

She'd catered to the fiend so long, he'd gained a stronghold inside her. Had shackled her with invisible chains. Now he owned her.

But that was how evil worked, wasn't it.

At first, the demon's darkness had been nothing but a tiny seed. The more attention she'd paid it, the more she'd watered it, the bigger and stronger it had grown. Until its roots had anchored deep, deep inside her, its branches and leaves shielding her from any hint of light.

"My brother has vowed to find you and take back what you stole from me," he said.

"There's nothing left to reclaim." It was the truth. Soon the mortal Fluffy would need another infusion of power, and Viola would hunt for another Sent One. Any immortal would do, but hey, why not kill two birds with one stone? Save Fluffy, placate Narcissism.

Besides, Sent Ones had the purest life forces. "Hate to be the bearer of bad news, but if your brother picks a fight with me, I will do to him what I did to you."

Cannot lose my baby. Just can't. He'd become her best friend, her only source of comfort…her family. Her fanged, rage-happy, overprotective family.

She would hate herself for hurting another immortal, and probably cry, but she would do what needed doing without hesitation.

McCadden clenched his fists, and she noted the small claws protruding from his nail beds. He'd begun his transformation, then. So often fallen Sent Ones became look-alikes for the demons they had once hunted.

"My brother's name is Brochan," he continued as if she hadn't spoken. "He is—was—the best demon slayer ever born. He's cut through hordes like butter."

"His name is Broken? Seriously?" Poor guy had been shafted from day one.

McCadden continued. "Spelled B-R-O-C-H-A-N. Perhaps you've heard of him? He's fallen but still winged.

He escaped to the skies before the appendages could be removed." Envy now layered his tone. He missed his wings, then, and she wouldn't feel guilty—she couldn't let herself. "Evil has infected him, twisted him…made him into a monster."

Fallen…winged…twisted…

Monster.

Had to be her shadow. The one who'd called her "forsaken."

For several seconds, her heart forgot how to beat. Now, at least, she knew what the blue-skinned, silvery-eyed beast had planned for her.

He planned to destroy her. To punish her for her crimes against his brother.

But why hadn't he struck already? He'd had multiple opportunities, and yet he'd only ever warned her.

Perhaps he sought to lure her into a false sense of trust? Perhaps he planned to do to her what she'd done to his brother, willingly ceding her heart to him, leaving her with nothing?

She should have dreaded the coming battle, but it was anticipation she experienced.

"If you stay here," McCadden said, "I'll protect you from my brother. The others will protect you, too. They've vowed it."

Break him once and for all. Finish him off, so he'll stop looking out for me and start looking out for himself.

"The others are fools," she told him. At last she met his gaze, allowing her features to harden right before his eyes. "But you are worse. You seek to protect the one who harmed you—the one who will harm you again—and you've asked your friends to do the same."

Cruel to be kind. A motto as deceptive as the demon, but one she clung to, lest she finally break down.

Devastation darkened his eyes annnnd yes, fangs extended from his gums. Becoming the demons he'd once slain.

"You don't mean those words." For the first time, he'd slurred.

Cruel. To. Be. Kind. She twirled a lock of pale hair around her finger and offered her most self-loving smile. "You aren't the first male to fall for me, and you won't be the last. At least the others had the balls to hate me afterward. I suggest you do the same before I take more than your manhood."

His body trembled…or vibrated with growing rage. As he took an aggressive step toward her, the doors burst open and the beast—Brochan—swooped into the room. He landed between Viola and McCadden, his gaze on Viola.

Fluffy snarled, his little body vibrating with fury.

She'd never been this close to her stalker, had only ever seen him from a distance, at different heights. On level ground, he towered over her, a fortress of muscle and hostility. His wings flared, stretching from wall to wall, the black tips reeking of blood and ash. His face… before she'd thought he somehow straddled the line between grotesque and exquisite. Now she knew. He was magnificent. He had lashes so long they curled at the ends. And freckles! He had three freckles underneath his left eye. His chin had an adorable cleft, basically a sign that said *Lick here.*

Narcissism began to wonder if making such a powerful creature fall in love with her would prove to be his greatest accomplishment. The first sparks of panic bloomed in Viola's chest.

Brochan extended a clawed finger, pointing at her. "Forsaken."

McCadden grabbed his brother by the shoulder, but Brochan easily shook him off and moved toward her.

Heart hammering against her ribs, Viola scooped Fluffy into her arms and flashed away. Retreating. Something she'd told herself she wouldn't do.

But she needed time. Time to plan her next move.

Lazarus struggled to control blistering rage, staggering shock and searing arousal.

Cameo was here, finally within reach, and yet another man had dared to put his arms around her. Possessiveness consumed him, and Lazarus's veins burned as new crystals formed.

He decided to deal with the shock first, wanting no obstacles to his prize. His woman, and the death of the Sent One holding her.

He'd done it. He'd actually entered the mortal world.

Upon stepping into the portal, he'd experienced total sensory deprivation. He'd thought he'd taken a gamble and lost. The knowledge had awakened his inner monster, his fangs and claws returning, the crystals in his veins throbbing. But as they'd throbbed, lights had begun to pulse and blur. Seconds later, he'd fallen down, down, down, landing in an open field of wildflowers. No one had been around. Not spirit, not human, not immortal.

Cautious, uncertain but not daring to hope, he'd flashed to a home he'd built and hidden centuries ago. It resided in one of the lands that formed an archipelago of New Zealand Subantarctic Islands. A place he'd been unable to reach inside the spirit realms.

Seeing his cabin had driven him to his knees. Yes, the wood had rotted, and yes, weather and wildlife had left their mark, but what did that matter? Lazarus lived. Lived! *After* being beheaded.

His father was right. He would live forever. He wasn't sure how or why, exactly, but he now suspected the crystals were the catalyst. The way they'd throbbed...

Impossible. The crystals were his downfall. They didn't strengthen him; they weakened him, and a feeble man survived nothing. Lazarus's movements were already slower than usual, his range of motion more limited.

He'd thought, *Find and seduce Cameo. Kill Juliette and Hera before it's too late.*

He'd cloaked himself in an illusion of invisibility and flashed to Budapest. He'd swept through Cameo's home, a veritable fortress, remaining unseen to the occupants. After reading a mind or twelve, he discovered she'd left earlier that morning. He'd hidden the magic mirror in her bedroom, happy the glass had survived the journey, and set off on a hunt of his own.

Murmurs filled his head, yanking him into the present.

"Is that Lazarus the Cruel and Unusual?"

"Dude! Didn't I hear he'd gotten his neck trimmed?"

Lazarus breathed deep, the scents stronger here than in the spirit realm. He detected notes of alcohol and ambrosia, a cloying mix of immortal perfumes, the wood, steel and mortar used to build the club, and a deluge of too many other things to pinpoint. No, not too many others—three stood out above all the rest. Roses, bergamot and neroli.

He hardened, his erection straining against the fly of his leathers.

His gaze met Cameo's, and the rest of the world disappeared. There she stood, the μονομανία responsible for his pain…and his pleasure. Only days had passed, but her beauty struck him anew, as if he were seeing it for the first time. Her raven locks were anchored in a high ponytail swinging back and forth. Her liquid silver eyes smoldered with sorrow, yes, but also heat.

She drew him, but he drew her, as well. At least they were in this mess together.

Her ruby red lips softened, as if preparing for his kiss. *Rest assured, I'll be kissing you as soon as we're alone, sunshine. And then I'll be collecting my reward…*

As his body thrummed with need, he opened his mind to her, barring everyone else. Too many thoughts at once could incapacitate him. Her shield was in place.

Had Misery wiped her memory?

Ready for war, Lazarus stepped forward. Two bear shifters reacted to the aggression he radiated, stepped into his path and growled. Lazarus grabbed one by the wrist and yanked before the punch could land, turning the brute so that his back pressed against Lazarus's chest, creating a shield. The other twin ended up punching his brother.

As the one in his arms fell, unconscious, Lazarus hammered at the brother's jaw. When he fell, Lazarus stepped over him, once again on a path toward his woman.

The Sent One released Cameo. Without hesitation,

she raced through the part in the crowd—and a group of Harpies—to stand before him.

She remembered. Relief showered over him.

"You're here, and you're alive," she whispered. She reached out with a trembling hand to brush her fingertips across his jaw.

The simple touch threatened to unman him, the sensations far more intense now that he had a physical body. The heat of her skin, the incomparable softness, the friction caused by the small callus on her palm...

Can't ever let her go.

Must!

"You're tangible to me in the mortal realm and—" With a gasp, she jumped away from him. "Filled with electricity? You are literally sending tingles through every inch of me."

Electricity? "Animal magnetism is strong in this one." He forcibly disregarded the urge to shout, *Touch me again. Never stop.* "Did anyone hurt you?"

"No, I was doing the hurting until the Get Bent Ones stopped the festivities."

She spoke so quietly, he had to strain to hear. Someone—probably multiple someones—had made her feel bad about her voice. Did no one have balls anymore?

He clasped her hand, all but shuddering with pleasure. The rightness of their connection...

Once again she jumped away from him. Frowning, she rubbed her palm, as if he'd burned her.

The tingles *pained* her?

What the hell would—

Pandora's box. Pandora's box hung around his neck, hidden by his shirt and pressed against his skin. How could he have forgotten? Did the box's power use him as a conduit?

Guilt slithered through him. This woman—*his* woman—had searched for Pandora's box for centuries. He'd planned to use it to draw her to his realm, but he'd never intended to give it to her. Too many risks involved.

Her friends wanted it destroyed. Part of Cameo probably wanted it destroyed, too. What would happen when—if—the Morning Star escaped? Would someone else harness the being's power, perhaps even use that power against Cameo? What if the Lords decided to hide the box, and Misery later convinced Cameo to end her life as well as the lives of her loved ones?

Oh, yes. Too many risks. And too many unknowns. Lazarus would not be mentioning the box to her. Would not gamble on her reaction.

He should have left it with the mirror, and would have if he hadn't feared the Lords would sense its presence in the fortress, fail to realize what it was and open it.

Must protect her. He created an illusion. Anyone looking his way would see a man and woman standing a few inches apart, their heads bent together as they talked. In reality, he ripped the hem off Cameo's shirt.

"Uh, what are you doing?" she asked.

"I'll explain later." Some watered-down version of the truth, anyway. He pulled an apple pendant from beneath his shirt and tied the strip of material around it before hiding it once again, preventing any contact with his skin.

"Pretty," she said. "I would never have pegged you for an apple guy."

"Why? It's the forbidden fruit. The original sin." He steeled himself and offered his hand to her. A slight hesitation before she accepted. An-n-nd she breathed a sigh of relief.

"Better," she said with a nod.

A sigh of relief escaped *him*. He dropped the illusion and led her right back to the Sent One. The male needed to understand the error of his ways—and the consequences he would face. "You do not touch her. Ever. Understood?"

The red-eyed, white-haired male looked him up and down and smiled without humor. "Careful, warrior. My dance card is currently full, but I don't mind penciling in your name."

Cameo moved between them to act as a buffer. "I appreciate the macho-man routine, darkpit, but you need to know something. Juliette was here." The people within hearing distance flinched, and yet she continued. "Thane flew away with her. If we hurry, we can follow."

Juliette. Nearby. Vengeance at last. Sooner rather than later. Red dots winked through his gaze, his fury resurfacing. Time to create a new Garden of Perpetual Horror. Juliette Eagleshield could have the honor of the first spot. *Follow. Now!*

No. First things first. He'd come here for Cameo, defying time, space and death to be with her. Vengeance had once been his number one priority, but here, now, his woman's pleasure mattered more than anything else.

He would stick to his original plan. He would have his night with her, *then* hunt Juliette.

First, he needed a room. He blasted through the Sent One's mental blocks. The name Xerxes hit him before countless images of the abuse and torture he'd endured in his too-long life. Lazarus gritted his teeth and pushed on until he found the schematics of the club.

The bastard sensed his intrusion and shoved him out with a strength rivaled only by Rathbone.

"Do not *ever*—" Xerxes grated.

"Consider the sixth guest room in the west wing occupied for the rest of the night." Lazarus squeezed Cameo's hand and led her away from the crowd.

When they exited the public areas, it became clear the entire building was designed to confuse intruders. Armed guards paced in certain hallways and in front of specific doors, but no one made a move against him. Sent Ones could communicate telepathically, and Xerxes must have voiced his blessing. Probably because they were allies with Hades and therefore each other.

When Lazarus reached his destination, he opened the door and waved Cameo inside. She passed him, leaving a sweet-scented cloud in her wake, and he followed her in, his mouth watering.

The door closed with an ominous *click*.

He took in their surroundings with a swift scan. The room was small but elaborate, every piece of furniture finely made…and intended for lovers. Mirrors decorated the ceiling, and the covers on the bed were scattered with fresh rose petals.

"Hold up." Cameo stretched out her arm to hold him at bay. "What about Juliette?"

"She can wait. You and I cannot." He gently pushed her hand aside, consumed her personal space…and kissed her.

She welcomed him eagerly, returned his embrace passionately, with no hint of sorrow. She wasn't just sweet; she was his favorite candy. She wasn't just intoxicating; she was all-consuming. She wasn't merely his μονομανία; just then, she was his everything.

He cupped her nape, locks of silken hair weaving through his fingers. Little mewling sounds drifted from her, and he growled in approval. His senses were heightened as her breath mingled with his, becoming necessary for his survival. His lifeline.

Arousal blistered his insides. Need clawed at him. Waves of sensation pulsed over and through him. The crystals ached, perhaps even spread, but he didn't care.

He devoured her with abandon, afraid he would never get his fill, terrified his thirst would never be quenched, and he would only ever want more. *Need* more.

In so many ways, she owned him. He was more a slave to her than he'd ever been to Juliette.

The thought should have panicked him. *Did* panic him. And yet he stayed put, unwilling to let her go. *Mine!*

Panting, she lifted her head and traced a fingertip over her sexy red lips. "You found me," she rasped.

He almost roared a denial, almost grabbed her and pulled her back for another blistering kiss. *Can't push for too much too fast.* Misery would use the opportunity to strike.

"I will always find you, sunshine."

"Because you want to have sex with me." A trace of bitterness…a wealth of arousal.

"I do. So let's get to it, shall we?"

17

"Always err on the side of killing."
—*Eternal Truths for Every Man*
—*Eternal Truths for Men Without a Woman*

Shivers racked Cameo, and warm honey seemed to flow over her from head to toe. In an instant, the yearning she had fought so diligently to impede resurged with undeniable force. She trembled. Her blood heated to the boiling point. Her belly clenched. Between her legs, she ached.

Misery hissed, acting like a petulant child. He kicked at her skull again and again, causing a strange tingle to tease the corners of her mind.

I'm going to do this. I'm going to roll the dice. Going to sleep with Lazarus, and pray I retain my memory. Pray he wants me afterward.

If she lost a single memory of him…the way he'd looked at her during their reunion, as if she were everything right in a world gone wrong, the feel of his hands on her sensitive flesh, tangled in her hair, the way his lips had forced hers to mold to his…no, she would rather die.

"Take off your shirt," she croaked. *Let me see what I'm risking my sanity—my life—for.*

A muscle clenched and unclenched in his jaw. "My clothes stay on. Yours come off."

Was he kidding? He had to be kidding. But…

The mirror predicted this. As many times as they'd made love within the vision, he'd remained fully clothed.

"No way," she said. "Strip."

"Ladies first…gentlemen never." He reached for the shirt he'd ripped, but she batted his hands away.

"Tit for tat," she insisted.

"I prefer tit."

"Too bad." She held her ground. "You want to see mine, you've got to show me yours."

"Fine." He yanked his shirt over his head and stood perfectly still as she examined him, not even daring to breathe.

Why such resistance? He was magnificent. Row after row of muscles and sinew that mesmerized and tempted her, fueling a craving to touch, taste and explore. From the neck down, a cornucopia of gorgeous tattoos covered every inch of skin. More than she'd realized. Those thorny roses, butterflies and skulls were paired masterfully with creepy insects and black birds. In the center of his chest was the eye within the pyramid. From navel to pecs, a gnarled tree consumed his flesh. A single red apple hung from one of the branches.

Both of his nipples were pierced. A dark trail of hair traveled under his navel and ended below the waist of his leathers.

Pure masculine perfection.

Her brain melted. Her ovaries exploded.

Beneath the tattoos, shimmery lines crept over and around his biceps. Wounds, he'd once called them. They were thicker now, longer, too.

As she considered them, he reached up to cover the lines with his hand. He was *that* self-conscious? Or did he fear being hurt worse?

"I'll be careful with your wounds," she assured him quietly. But, as an act of mercy, she turned her attention to the necklaces hanging between his pecs. Viola's ring and the apple pendant Lazarus had covered with the strip of material from her shirt.

Cameo reached out…another strange pulse of power brushed over her skin, and her heart rate increased, going from sixty to six hundred in a blink.

Whatever the sensation was, it antagonized Misery. His hisses became curses.

"Why did you cover the pendant?" she asked.

His gaze veered away from hers. "It's an ancient artifact. Dangerous."

And he wanted to protect her from it? "What kind of artifact?" To her knowledge, the only mythical apple belonged to Snow White, whose story was a lot more complicated than humans realized…and a lot more true. "Is it not dangerous to *you*?"

"A life and death artifact," he said. "And yes, it is, but I happen to enjoy danger."

"Did you use it to return to the mortal world?" She licked her lips—and still tasted the essence of him. "Are you now Lazarus 2.0?"

"I'm the original. Lazarus 1.0, somehow made corporeal to all realms. Why mess with perfection?"

Why indeed? "I'm struggling to believe you're real, and that you're actually here. I mean, you were dead. And if you *are* here, should you be classified as a zombie?"

"Maybe I *am* a zombie." He stared at her chest and grunted. "Breastsssssss."

A chuckle—nope. Thanks to Misery, the chuckle died in the back of her throat. Stupid demon!

Disappointment glimmered in Lazarus's eyes, but it receded as he continued to peer at her breasts. When her nipples stood at attention for him, a predatory glint appeared.

"Don't worry." The tenor of his voice dropped to a husky rasp. "I'll get you there."

"So certain. You, Lazarus, are a lothario."

"Unrepentantly so." He brushed his knuckle against her nipple, sending ripples of pleasure straight to her core. Her *wet* core. "This lothario is done talking. Kiss me," he commanded. "Don't be gentle. Be rough. Hold nothing back."

"Your wounds…"

"Kiss. Me."

Yes… Light-headed with want, she lifted to her tiptoes and wrapped her arms around him. Their lips met in a frenzied rush, his tongue sweeping inside her mouth, tasting her, relearning her, delivering a new punch of passion…devouring her. The sweetness of him thrilled her. The chocolate she so loved mixed with a fiery heat she would forever crave.

"Don't want to stop with a kiss and a few touches this time," he rasped. "Want to do more. So much more."

The moment of truth had arrived. If she said no, he would stop. He would probably leave altogether. No one-night stand, perhaps no future, either. *Roll those dice, baby.*

"Yes," she whispered. "Please."

Triumph flared over his expression as he walked her backward. Her knees hit the edge of the bed, and she tumbled onto the mattress. She kept her nails deep in his shoulders, so he had no choice but to follow her down.

She'd never liked being pinned by a male's heavy weight; too often she felt trapped and vulnerable. But with Lazarus, the epitome of raw masculinity, savage strength and aggression, she'd never felt safer.

"Shirt. Off. Now," he commanded.

The wrapped pendant grazed her collarbone, pure energy zinging her. She jolted while Misery bellowed.

"Seriously. What *is* that thing?" she asked. He'd said "a life and death artifact," but what did that mean, exactly?

Lazarus paled. "It's—gone. See?" He removed the necklaces and stuffed them inside his pants pocket. "Now. Shirt off, sunshine. Show me what I've been missing. I'm eager for a taste."

A refusal to answer. A change of subject. Again.

A topic for another day, then. One she would not let go next time.

Today was a different story, entirely. Dedicated to rapture.

Cameo pulled off her torn shirt and ripped the center clasp of her bra, freeing her breasts. Cool air caressed her nipples, and they stood taller. Lazarus braced his weight on his knees, liberating his hands…he cupped and kneaded her, and worked the hardened buds between his fingers.

"Lazarus…"

"Such perfect little morsels," he praised.

Shock waves of pleasure left her trembling, and those tremors only intensified when he bent his head to suck on her nipples.

"I haven't forgotten my reward." He kissed and licked his way to her navel, her belly clenching. "You'll please me, but only after I've made you come. Twice."

Twice! Once would be a dream, but twice? Yes, please. *Now I'm getting greedy.*

She combed her fingers through his velvet-soft hair, scraping his scalp, urging him on or silently commanding him to taste her somewhere else, she wasn't sure. The sensations he roused in her... Too much, far too much, but she suspected she would internally combust if he walked away now.

The hot stroke of his tongue moved across the waist of her pants, leaving fire and quivers in its wake. He looked up at her through thick black lashes, his eyes twin midnight skies with a million stars on brilliant display. "I want to be with you, Cameo. All the way, nothing held back. Say yes."

Her bones liquefied. Yes! Please! The cry of her heart. And yet, she hesitated. What if he failed to please her during the act? What if Misery erased her memory before he climaxed? What if she slept with him, and he walked away afterward? More than ever, she wanted time with him, a real relationship, not just a fling.

She managed to croak, "No. No sex. We can do anything else. I want to do *everything* else."

He'd become her only life raft in a terrible storm. She couldn't let him go. Not yet.

"Why?" He plucked the button on her pants. "Still don't think you'll like it?"

"Yes." No. Maybe. What if she simply hated sex? A dead fish. An ice queen. All hope would be lost.

Okay, let's break this down. Say he did make her climax. Great. Wonderful. What if *she* couldn't make *him* climax?

As soon as her pleasure ebbed, Misery would fight to overtake her. Cameo would become nothing but a cold, dry body Lazarus rutted upon. He would be disgusted with her.

"I'm sorry," she said.

As he laved her navel, his fingers traveled down her legs, behind her knees, caressing the pulse there. Against her moist flesh, he rasped, "Don't apologize, sunshine. You want what you want, and I'll take what I can get." His hand slid up, up and squeezed the globe of her ass. "Do let me know if you become too sad to continue, all right?"

He unfastened her leather pants and drew the material down with his teeth. Teeth that grazed her soaked panties...

Her liquefied bones caught flame. "Lazario!" The nickname gasped from her, her blissful mind somehow morphing his name with lothario.

"There's nothing sweeter than my sunshine. I think you're going to like what comes next." He didn't bother removing her pants, didn't push them to her ankles or even maneuver her panties out of the way. As if he'd been drugged and needed another hit now, now, now, he licked and sucked on her *through* the flimsy lace.

Her back arched of its own accord, a moan bursting from her. Afraid she would yank out his hair in her excitement, she reached overhead and clung to the headboard. All the while he continued to lick. Suck. Liiick.

Suuuck. Unable to stop herself, she writhed against him, her hips rolling.

"Lazarus, I—"

"Lazario. Like having a special nickname. Yours alone."

"Yes. Yes!" This was all so new to her. So surreal and perfect and wondrous. It was…undiluted, unpolluted pleasure, something she'd never thought to experience. "Don't stop. Please, please, don't stop."

Of course, Lazarus, being Lazarus, ended the sweet torment before she could ride his mouth all the way to completion.

Argh! "I curse your name and the day you were born, you climax-blocking bastard!"

He smiled up at her, wicked and brutal at once, and so astonishingly sexy she suspected—prayed—this image would be forever branded into her mind, and there would be nothing, absolutely nothing, Misery could do to erase it.

"You'll thank me soon enough…Cami."

Mmm. She liked having another special nickname.

He unfastened his leathers and drew down the zipper, releasing his massive erection from its cage. Gaze white-hot on her, he stroked himself up, down. "Do you trust me?"

She licked her lips, nodded. "I do."

"Then trust me not to take more than you've offered me…no matter how much you might beg me otherwise." He bent down slowly, catching his weight with one hand—a hand he rested next to her waist. He used his other hand to…

She moaned before panting with shock and rapture. He'd wrapped his shaft around the crotch of her panties, the most intimate part of him pressing against the most intimate part of her. The rest of him was coiled around the thin—and now drenched—fabric. He hadn't entered her, and yet he'd managed to wedge himself against her aching core.

He cupped her ass to lift her…then, oh, then, he rubbed against her. A long, firm stroke. He rubbed again and again, coating his length with her arousal. Another moan burst from her, this one broken at the edges. The intensity of the pleasure! Nothing could compare.

Rub, rub…she chanted his name…he hit the spot where she ached most, stoking her need higher.

"Feels so good, sunshine. *You* feel good. Don't think I'll ever get enough of you."

She wanted to offer an intelligent reply, but couldn't quite catch her breath. Besides, her mind had fogged, her thoughts had fragmented.

"You like this?" he asked.

Incoherent words spilled from her, and she wasn't sure if she was begging him to stop…no, no, never stop…or to move faster…yes, yes, faster! The pleasure continued to build, creating pressure, scorching pressure that demanded she arch her hips and grind on him.

Inside her, a maddened frenzy escalated. A wild craze, the sensations so intense she feared passing out and missing the best part. Need pulsated from head to toe, even created a song of passion. Touch him…taste him…*devour* him.

This was…life. The life she'd always dreamed of having. As new moans rose from her, she fought the urge to do what he'd suspected and plead with him to take her. To give her more, to give her everything.

Never had she felt so empty. He had to fill her up… *please…please!*

"Lazario… I can't… I need…"

"This is what you'll have with me, my Cami. Ecstasy. Every—time."

"Every time?" Had he just offered her the relationship she desired? *Should never trust a man lost in the throes of passion.* "As in, more than once?"

"More than *many*. With me." Faster…faster… "Only ever me."

He had!

"Tonight," he said, bending down to run the lobe of her ear between his teeth, "I'll make you come a thousand times, in a thousand different ways." The veins in his arms stood out as he used more of his incredible strength to—

Whoa. *Tonight*, he'd said. The word echoed in her mind, her hopes plummeting. And yet somehow her physical bliss continued to magnify; it was great and terrible, exquisite and excruciating; she was going to explode, and only pieces of her would remain.

Desperate for relief, she cupped her breasts, pinched her nipples. *Think I'm losing my mind!*

She traced the plane of her stomach, circled her navel…and stroked his erection's wet tip. He sucked in a breath.

"Love the feel of you. Hard, hot steel."

A new growl rumbled deep in his chest. "Look at my woman as she takes what she wants. Owning her pleasure. Owning mine."

How proud he sounded.

How intoxicated.

He was just as snared by pleasure as she was, and the

knowledge felled her, destroying what little remained of her control. The pressure inside her finally burst. She screamed as satisfaction arced through each of her limbs and coalesced in her center. Aftershocks jolted her. Tremors reduced her to a limp rag doll.

That was... She... Wow.

How had she ever lived without it?

She drank in the sight of her gorgeous, lust-consumed Lazario. His features were pulled taut, his teeth bared. The corners of her lips lifted...continued to lift...until she thought she might be...smiling at him.

His gaze met hers. A second later, he threw back his head and roared at the ceiling.

Siobhan studied her new surroundings, a bedroom both feminine and masculine. The king-size bed had navy blue sheets, a brown comforter, but a single strip of cream-colored lace graced the edges. Different weapons hung on the walls, some modern, some ancient. A vanity was scattered with even more weapons rather than toiletries.

Cameo's personal chamber, Siobhan suspected.

Lazarus had deposited her here and vanished. He'd had no idea two Amazons were following him. Word of his last deed as king of Grimm and Fantica had spread throughout the tribes, among the living and the dead. He'd turned a contingent of Amazons to stone, and now he was marked for death. Again.

He would learn of the intended hit soon enough. And he had better destroy his new enemies. If the Amazons succeeded and he died before committing to Cameo, Siobhan would be forced to spend another hundred years in captivity. All because she'd decided to help the couple, and showed Cameo two possible futures. There was no going back.

The curse demanded she bring couples together, and if she failed, she suffered.

Denial screamed inside her head. How could she help Cameo?

Use her visions to convince someone to redecorate the room, make it more romantic? No one loved romance more than Siobhan. Perhaps she would convince someone to redecorate the room to *her* tastes. There would be a velvet sofa—purple! Dressers and other pieces would be made of pure ebony. The chandelier would drip with gold-set diamonds. A Gothic-style canopy bed with a separate chandelier that hung from the center would replace the sleigh monstrosity she now rested upon. The closet would overflow with the finest gowns from the finest seamstresses in the world.

Her favorite knickknacks would decorate the dresser. An hourglass held by her sister's severed hands. A case filled with poisons and an assortment of crowns.

The door suddenly burst open, and her breath caught in her throat. A visitor!

A black-haired, blue-eyed warrior stumbled inside, and heavens above, he was beautiful beyond compare, despite the hollows in his cheeks and the week's worth of stubble on his jaw. Despite, even, the disheveled clothes he wore, the material ripped and stained with dried blood.

"Cameo." He was slurring. Oops. "I came to hear your apology."

Images of the warrior's future played through her mind, teaching her much about him. He was William of the Dark, though his friends referred to him as the

Ever Randy. His conquests were legendary. He'd bedded queens and goddesses, and he'd killed kings and gods.

He was the adopted son of Hades—

She huffed with indignation. Hades adopted a son? When? Why?

Siobhan scoured the visions for information about the mother…a petite blonde whom William seemed to be meeting for the first time in…she wasn't sure when, the days, months and years blurring together.

A thousand new images poured into her mind, and she cringed. Every path led this man to the same end: death.

Like her, he bore the heavy burden of a curse. Unlike her, he owned a book written in code. He'd been told the code would free him. He had hope.

If I save him from certain death and help him fall in love, I could shave another hundred years off my sentence. Then…finally, blessedly, she would be free.

The prospect tantalized her. But…

Help Hades's beloved son? Never!

Although…for freedom, she would do much, much worse.

Fine! She would aid him. But how? Before Lazarus had left, he surrounded her with an impenetrable illusion. William couldn't see her…could he?

Peering at her, he dropped to his knees at the side of the bed. The bottle of whiskey rolled from his grip, what little liquid remained spilling across the floor. Torment and hope battled for dominance, tightening his features.

He knows what—who—I am, Siobhan realized with no small amount of surprise. Few ever did.

"There's a girl. Her name is Gillian. Gilly. Her last name changes, depending on the ID she's using. Shaw.

Bradshaw. She's—" He scrubbed a hand down his face. "She was too young for me. Was. Now she's not. She was abused by men who were supposed to protect her, has only seen the worst in the male species, and I want to show her the best. Sometimes she thinks I'm beautiful and sexy, and she wants to try. Sometimes, most times, she's afraid of me. Of sex. But. I should have handled her differently. In many ways. On many days. When she needed me most, I refused to bond with her. I didn't want to risk being made human or watching her love for me turn to hate. No other reason she would try to kill me as the curse predicts, yes? Because she hates me? Then another man came along, Puck the Undefeated. Soon to be defeated. He's the keeper of Indifference, yet he took one look at my Gilly Gum Drop and saw what I have known from the beginning. She's a treasure worth waiting for. The bastard did what I wouldn't and now he's bound to her, body and soul. I long to kill him but hurting him will hurt her. I can't hurt her. Show me my end," he croaked. "Show me who kills me. If I know…"

William assumed knowing the future would allow him to let go of Gillian at last. He also assumed Gillian was the only one for him. And she was…if he made certain choices. If he made other choices, well, there was *another* woman…

Problem: at this time, the woman was a stranger to him. She meant nothing to him. *Was* nothing—no, not true. In his mind, she would be worse than nothing; she would be an obstacle to a supposed happily-ever-after with Gillian. And what did warriors like William the Ever Randy do to obstacles? Cut them down at the first opportunity. Mercilessly. Brutally.

And he would. He would kill his fated mate. Decisions were being made even now…

What to do, what to do. If Siobhan helped him and he ruined his happily-ever-after—

No. She couldn't risk it.

When the glass remained clear, William cursed and labored to a stand.

"Hades." A softly spoken word, and yet, Siobhan reacted as if she'd been punched in the gut.

Would the king of the underworld come? Would she face her enemy at last?

Yes! He appeared in a haze of shadows, sending her heart into overdrive.

He was more beautiful than ever, and he had no right. Taller and more leanly muscled, with inky hair and matching eyes. Eyes so black they were endless pools. He wore a pin-striped suit, the perfect fit for his powerful frame, the only signs of his uncivilized nature the stars tattooed on each of his knuckles.

She beat against her prison wall—*bang, bang, bang*—desperate to reach him, to claw out his eyes.

"Like me, you have the power to see past any illusion, yes?" William asked his father.

"Oh, yes. The blow-up doll is a nice touch, though."

"Cameo is unable to cast illusions." William sniffed the air. "I scent Lazarus the Cruel and Unusual…and aren't the Lords of the Underworld going to love their girl's choice of dates."

Hades continued to stare at her. "You are correct on both counts."

"I know the mirror is what I think it is. I can *see* the power radiating from it. What I don't know is how to activate it."

"Her, not it. She decides who sees and who doesn't." Hades flashed, appearing directly in front of her, crouched atop the mattress. "The goddess of Many Futures is still trapped inside. I feel her. Angry little thing, isn't she."

She banged the glass harder. His hand shot out, touching where she touched, and she gasped. A stream of heat penetrated her ice-cold prison. As shudders racked her, the pane rippled.

Hades's pupils expanded with excitement.

Bang, bang, bang. How she would love to replace his excitement with pain.

"Are you kidding me?" William tossed his arms up. "You're getting a hard-on for a mirror? I doubt Taliyah would approve."

Taliyah the Cold-Hearted? The vicious Harpy that Siobhan could see moving in and out of Hades's past.

He doesn't deserve to date. He deserves to suffer!

"Taliyah hasn't spoken to me in weeks," Hades said, his tone cutting. "I've moved on. I always move on."

Good girl.

Once again Siobhan opened her mind to the days and years to come, but this time, no matter how intently she probed, she saw…nothing. Not a single path, and she cursed. Hades's future must be so intertwined with hers that she couldn't see *anything* that happened to him.

Well, well. Looked like her luck was finally turning. To have a future with him, she had to escape the mirror.

"How did Lazarus acquire this treasure?" William asked.

"I know not." Hades tensed, his spine snapping ramrod straight. "But I'll find out."

"She's our ally. We can't steal from her without jeopardizing her allegiance and the allegiance of the other Lords."

Hades rubbed two fingers against his clean-shaven jawline. "Perhaps we'll offer a trade."

Yes, please do. Did he know how much Siobhan hated him? Did he suspect she would only ever plot his downfall?

A sudden commotion in the hallway jolted both males. The pitter-patter of running children and the pounding footsteps of chasing parents.

"Do *not* stick another toy soldier in the toilet, Urban," a woman shouted. "I mean it!"

Hades and William shared a look of determination before flashing away, leaving Siobhan alone…but she didn't have to be the goddess of Many Futures to know she would see the father-son duo again…and very, very soon.

18

"To ensure your skills remain honed, ~~make a new kill~~ pleasure your woman every day."
—*Eternal Truths for Men Without Women*
—*The Art of Keeping Your Female Happy*

World. Rocked.

Lazarus reeled as he cleaned Cameo, then himself. He righted his pants before hooking the clasp of her bra, covering her beautiful breasts. A necessary travesty. One glance at her feminine perfection, and he would be on her again…and again…

He fastened her pants, but left both their shirts on the floor, intending to enjoy a little skin-to-skin contact.

He should leave. He'd gotten off, and he'd gotten *her* off. A miracle, she would say. His mind should be clear of the passion-fog, vengeance against Juliette his number two priority.

His number one priority? Stopping new crystal formations. Lava flowed through his veins, scorching him, and his muscles ached. Telltale signs of impending growth.

Even still, he crawled into bed with Cameo and tugged her close. Her smile had unmanned him. He would never be the same. Her entire face had lit up, and happiness had glowed through her pores. There was no sight more beautiful in any realm.

He was addicted, already wanted another one.

First, he had questions for her. Later, he would explore every inch of her beautiful body, would see and touch her butterfly tattoo…would see and touch *all* of her. Nothing held back. Then she would bless him with another smile.

In both his life and death, he'd been with a lot of women, but no one had ever meant more than his μονομανία. He shared something with her that he'd never shared with another. An emotional bond.

"I don't know how," she said, her voice raspy and tragic, her warm breath fanning his chest, "but you, Cuddles, make everything better."

"Of course I do." *For you, only ever you.*

"Correction. You make *most* things better."

"Sorry, but there are no take backs."

In his arms, she'd been Cameo, a woman without a demon. Happy and content. Never had he beheld a more magnificent sight. Her skin had flushed and glowed with health, vitality—and pleasure, so much pleasure. Her eyes had sparkled like freshly polished diamonds in a setting of platinum. Her kiss-swollen lips had glistened with his essence.

I'll be forever haunted.

"I'm surprised you were willing to lower your guard in an unfamiliar environment," she said.

"How dare you." He gave a mock growl. "I never once lowered my guard."

She arched a single black brow. "So you didn't give my body your full attention?"

He barked out a laugh, awed by her wit. "This is a first. You've backed me into a corner. If I say yes, you'll call me a liar. If I say no, you'll call me a horrible lover. Either way, I'll be in a whole lot of man-trouble."

"Well, I can't exactly accuse you of being a bad lover while I'm still twitching from my very first orgasm." As she rubbed her soft cheek against his bare chest, he wrapped an arm around her waist. "I actually climaxed. A real one, not a fake."

"Trust me, sunshine. I noticed. Also, I had no plans to stop my *expert* seduction until you erupted."

"Well, thank you." She kissed the hollow of his neck, where his pulse had yet to slow, her lips soft, sweet and giving. "But also no thank you! How am I supposed to live without at least one orgasm a day?"

He nearly choked on another laugh. "You're not?"

"Exactly!"

Something dark twisted in his chest, his good humor evaporating. What if, when Lazarus parted with her, she turned to another man?

"Hey. You stiffened." She frowned at him. "Why?"

"Maybe I'm missing your smile."

"Please. You've never even seen my smile."

Had she already forgotten? "Sunshine, you smiled after you came."

"What? Me?" The ends of her hair tickled his skin as she shook her head. "I *can't* smile."

"You can. You did." She *had* forgotten. Poor Cameo.

Poor *Lazarus*. How soon would she forget *him*? And how would he react when she did?

Self-preservation said, *You'll rejoice. No μονομανία, no weakness.*

The rest of him bellowed, *Kill the demon!*

Lazarus had known the outcome of his dalliance with Cameo from the beginning. One way or another, he would lose her. He'd thought he'd accepted their end. Now, with her cuddled against him, he only wanted to rage. Never again touch her softness? Or glide against the liquid heat only he could draw forth? Never again hear her voice change from tragic to breathy as she moaned in pleasure? Never again watch her unravel as satisfaction burned centuries of hopelessness to ash? Never again see her smile?

There would be no chance he could make her laugh.

Desperate to discover if the memory of him had already begun to fray at the edges, he opened his mind to hers…and brushed against her shield.

"You stop that right now before I remove something you don't want to lose." She traced a fingertip around his nipple and he shuddered—in a very manly way. "What is it you want to know?"

"If the demon has begun to erode your memory of me."

"No." She sighed. "I wish I had the ability to read minds. I could read yours after Misery does his thing." Her chin trembled. "I could remember through your eyes."

The guilt he'd experienced earlier returned, only sharper. He now had the means to free her of the demon. He also had the means to kill her.

Can't risk it. Lazarus did everything in his power to

turn his own heart to stone. Why bring up Pandora's box, anyway? He and Cameo would part soon enough, and he would never use the thing against her. He would keep it safe, never allowing *anyone* to use it against her. Including Cameo herself.

What if she had imprisoned Juliette and Hera, but never told him?

The question was a poison injected straight into his mind. Inescapable and without an antidote.

This—his silence about the box—was the same. If Cameo discovered his deceit, she would be hurt; she would rage and seek vengeance, and rightfully so. If she discovered how close she'd come to achieving a life-long goal, and discovered *Lazarus* was the one who'd betrayed her...

No. Absolutely not! His silence wasn't a betrayal but a kindness. He *protected* Cameo.

Ask questions, receive answers, give her another orgasm, leave. That was the way his second chance at life had to go. He had to build a new army and attack clan Eagleshield from every side. A new army took time. "You said you were afraid sex with me would be bad. Have I alleviated your concerns?"

She traced one of the crystallized veins in his biceps. "First answer a question for me. Are these...wounds the reason you refused to strip?"

Share his secret? His shame? His fear that he would end up like his father, defeated, trapped and hidden from the rest of the world?

He trusted Cameo, but he didn't trust her family. If she were to tell a friend—whether wittingly or unwittingly—and that friend told another, so on and so forth, soon the entire immortal community would know about his weakness.

While the crystals remained dormant without contact with Cameo, given life only in her presence, the damage she caused was permanent.

He would become a target for every vampire, shifter or witch hoping to earn a moniker. *Look at me. Look, look. I'm the one who took down the only son of the Monster.*

Juliette could use his weakness against him. Hera, too.

"Perhaps I think I'm fat," he finally muttered. "Do these pants make my ass look big?"

The corners of her mouth twitched, giving him hope he would see…nope, her frown returned. "Be serious. You're hiding a bad tattoo, aren't you? Maybe a past girlfriend's name scripted inside a heart? Oh! I know. A man's face on your thigh. Or a rocket that resembles a penis?"

"I'm making a mental note to get each of those tattoos. They sound world-class."

"Yeah, but what name will go inside the heart?"

"My own. I've always loved myself best."

She batted her lashes at him. "We have so much in common. I've always loved myself best, too."

Her attempt at flirting was a-dor-able. "Such a naughty little liar. I'm your favorite. Admit it."

"Darkpit, you barely crack the top ten."

Lazarus was a selfish bastard, greedy in the extreme, and so possessive he wanted to lay siege to every aspect of his woman's life—even if they wouldn't be together. "Give me names. By morning I'll be the only one left." Half tease, half unadorned promise. "You'll *have* to award me the number one spot."

She snorted. Then she fell silent. Then she stiffened. Her defenses lowered, her mind suddenly open to his, the shield gone. Her relationship with Alex and the heartache the male had caused consumed her thoughts. So had the torment the Hunters had dished.

She'd been confined to a dank, dark cell that reeked of sweat, urine and other things Lazarus couldn't bear to contemplate. She'd been chained to a wall except for the times she'd been chained to a rack, each of her limbs pulled out of its socket. Hot pokers had been pressed into her filth-caked skin, appendages removed while she screamed in pain. While her demon laughed. *Laughed.*

The bastard had no right!

Lazarus struggled to control a blistering surge of rage. *Calm. Steady.*

Galen, once a leader of a cult known as Hunters, had swooped in, demanding to know more about the other demon-possessed warriors. Cameo refused to give him a single bit of information, no matter how many beatings he delivered, or how many times he cut out her tongue.

Don't want to talk? Fine. Now you can't *talk.*

Back then, Galen claimed to be an angel—a defender of humankind. He told his followers they had a single purpose: the destruction of evil...of immortals. What his followers didn't know: he was as far from angelic as a being could be. He was demon possessed. The keeper of Jealousy and False Hope.

For some reason, the Lords had recently welcomed him back into their fold, despite centuries of war, betrayal and cold-blooded murder.

Lazarus's rage only worsened. He was not as forgiving as the Lords. In fact, he added the name "Galen" to his vengeance list. One day soon, the male would become a star attraction in a Garden of Perpetual Horror.

As for Misery, Lazarus yearned to use the box, to *laugh* as the demon was ripped out of Cameo.

He continued digging through her memories, a strange detail seizing his attention. Blurred at the edges. Why? He followed the thread and landed square in the middle of Misery's memory.

Lazarus began to dig through the demon's thoughts and sucked in a breath. The evil creature couldn't wipe Cameo's mind without her permission. And when that permission was granted? He could do more than wipe it. He could distort it, causing her to view the past through a sorrow-tinted lens.

Lazarus had uncovered a fact Misery tried desperately to hide.

Cameo hadn't loved Alex, not in the deep and romantic way she believed. She'd loved her ability to speak with him without causing an influx of tears. *My darling Cami.* For centuries she'd craved companionship, understanding and adoration.

The truth was, Alexander had been a tiny bandage placed over a massive wound in her soul. The human hadn't helped her, but he hadn't hurt her, either. At the time, she'd never experienced anything better.

And how sad was that?

Alexander had been a troubled man, searching for someone, anyone, to blame for his own wounds. Cameo had offered comfort and at first, the human had felt grateful, even indebted to her. Lazarus could *see* the gratitude in his eyes. As the days, weeks and months had passed, Cameo's personal misery had fed the human's. He'd continued to hurt, and eventually he'd come to consider her the perfect outlet for his pain.

The day Hunters approached him with tales of demons released from Pandora's box, Alex had been ripe for plucking.

"Lazarus. Stop!" Wave after wave of sadness poured from her, sweeping them up in an ocean of grief. Then her mind blanked, her shield back in place. She bolted upright, dark hair a cascading waterfall around her strong but delicate shoulders. "My head isn't your personal playground."

When she threw her legs over the side of the bed, he clasped her by the waist to hold her prisoner. "I won't apologize. I know you better now. *Like* you better. And you have nothing to be ashamed of. Alexander's actions reveal *his* weakness, not yours."

Tremors rattled her in the cage of his arms, stoking the need that always simmered in his blood. "My past is off-limits unless I choose to share it. Or maybe you'd be fine with me exploring yours without permission?"

His guilt resurfaced, an anchor dropped in the middle of her ocean. *Denying her so much already.* "You've made a valid point. I'm sorry, sunshine."

Bit by bit, she relaxed against him. "I told you a handful of people committed suicide after spending time with me, right?"

"Right." *You also told me you tried to kill yourself,* he silently added, nauseated by the thought. What if she'd succeeded?

"By the time I met Alex, I had the worst of the sorrow contained, except when I spoke. I allowed myself to hope, but I should have stayed away from him. I should have stayed away from you, too."

"No!" The denial rushed from him with more force than he'd intended. *Calm!* He might have been better off without his μονομανία, but he was certainly happier having her at his side. "You're allowing Misery to speak for you now."

Lazarus had lived for a long time, had fought many different opponents. Demons were evil, detestable and spiteful, no exceptions; they possessed not a single shred of goodness. They enjoyed corruption and destruction, feeding on the carcasses of those they successfully corrupted and destroyed. They couldn't be tamed or redeemed because they didn't *want* to be tamed or redeemed.

"How can I not?" Cameo said. "We are one."

Lazarus combed his fingers through her hair, soothing her the way his mother once soothed him, the few times they were allowed to be together. "No, you are separate. I'm attracted to you, not Misery. Him, I hate. He takes what belongs to me." Her memories of Lazarus. Her smile still haunted him. *Need another. Soon.* "To me, you are Snow White, and he is an amalgamation of all seven dwarfs, operating independently of your commands."

Some of the tension drained from her, her beautiful curves melting into him, melding to him. "Funny. I have thought about Snow White, as well. Your apple…"

He stiffened and she shook her head, adding, "But I'm not gentle and soft-spoken like she was created to be. In fact, while I was in your realm I was more comfortable comparing myself to a villain like the evil queen. And in case you haven't realized, Misery isn't

Happy, Sneezy, Dopey, Sleepy, Bashful or medically inclined. He's only grumpy. So he can't be an amalgamation of the dwarfs."

"I didn't say which dwarfs, now, did I? He's Angst, Woe, Grief, Depression, Heartache, Despair and Forlorn."

As she coyly batted her lashes at him, she wickedly scraped her nail around his nipple. "Be honest. You're really trying to convince me that *you* are Prince Charming."

"Your lips may call me by any name, sunshine, and I'll answer with a kiss."

Cameo's mouth twitched and, beneath his fly, his shaft hardened and ached.

She rolled closer and kissed his sternum—lower than he'd hoped for and yet not low enough. "I want so badly to be free of Misery. Now that I've tasted pleasure? Darkpit, I can't live with the demon much longer. I just can't."

Panic seared and branded him, overshadowing his arousal. "You will not harm yourself, Cameo. You will not allow harm to come to you." *Must remove the demon. He's the danger.*

How?

"The order of a king?" she asked, and he thought he felt a hot tear slide down the ridges of muscle in his stomach. A tear.

The order had been issued from a man. *Her* man. But he found himself saying, "I will find a way to help you destroy the demon. A way you will remain safe." *Shut your mouth. Offer no more. You can't*— But something inside him had broken. His resistance? That tear…

"Until then, I'll stay with you, guard you. Even from yourself if I must."

Her gaze snapped up, meeting his—and yes, there were tears caught in her lashes. His guts twisted.

"I'm a one-night stand, remember?" She glared at him. "I don't want you hanging around me just because you're afraid I'll put the final punch in my Lifetime Achievement card."

She'd just given him an easy out. A way to say goodbye now…or in an hour…perhaps in the morning. Maybe in a day. No more than two. He should take the out and run, never looking back. The longer he stayed with her, the faster his health would decline, the more mobility he would lose. He had to be at his best if he hoped to defeat Juliette and Hera.

Time wasn't his friend, not anymore. In the spirit realm, he'd had decades, centuries and even millennia to fortify the defenses of his palace, to grow his army and train his men to be the best of the best. Here in the mortal world, where Juliette and Hera lived, he had less than four weeks to get his life together before he had to enlist as a cog in Hades's war. A war that would require his full attention in order to survive.

"Plus," Cameo added, "I'll be busy. I have to find Pandora's box. It's now in play. Torin says someone found it."

Annnd his guilt used him as a punching bag, beating him black-and-blue. However, his resolve remained firm. He would *never* give this woman the box. If ever Misery overwhelmed her, she could use it to facilitate a swift—and certain—end.

"Any ideas about the culprit?" he asked.

"Not yet."

Not ever. He would take precautions. "What about

finding your pleasure?" He leaned down to draw her nipple through his teeth. "Shouldn't you take this opportunity to use and abuse me? By the way, I'm naming your nipples. This one is Naughty."

Moaning, she slid her hands in his hair. "What's the other one's name?"

He turned his attention to the little beauty in question. "She's Nice. And you will remember our time together…every second. Vow it."

"Just because you decree it, doesn't make it so."

"The demon needs your permission to wipe your mind."

Cameo jolted upright, dislodging Lazarus. "What? No way." She pushed him, widening the distance between them. "I would never agree to part with my memories." She opened her mouth to say more, only to bite her lower lip. "I wouldn't," she reiterated with a lot less force. "And how could you even know something like that?"

"How do you think?" He seized her shoulders, pushed her back and rolled on top of her, pinning her to the mattress. "Misery makes you so sad that you beg for a fresh start." Which meant she had willingly parted with her memory of Lazarus.

The knowledge settled, but poorly.

He nudged her legs apart, his lower half settling more comfortably against hers. Hardness to softness, need to need. Then he pinched her chin, staring at her with enough force that her gaze met his.

"Whenever the demon inundates you with sadness, think of this."

She licked her luscious red lips, leaving a glimmer of undisguised intent behind. "You on top of me?"

"No, sunshine. Think of the things I make you feel."

He rubbed the tip of his nose against hers before shifting to nuzzle her cheek with his own and then bite the lobe of her ear.

Going boneless, she said, "Give me another orgasm?"

"Are you asking or telling?"

"Asking." Though her eyelids were heavy and hooded with desire, he could see her eyes glowed with wicked challenge. "The first time could have been a fluke."

"A fluke? A fluke!" He rubbed his erection against her core. "Sunshine, I'll be giving you *three* orgasms today."

She gasped with mock horror. "No, please. Anything but that. Absolutely anything, oh great and mighty king of Grimm and Fantica."

Funny girl. "Keep talking. Dare you. You're about to earn yourself a fourth."

"I owe you a special kiss, remember?"

"As if I could forget."

She opened her mouth to reply. He swallowed the words, pressing his lips against hers and thrusting his tongue deep.

"Lazario." Moaning, she softened against him and wrapped her arms around his neck.

He nearly howled in triumph. He loved when she clung to him, her treasure of femininity his to plunder. "Going to explore every inch of you," he told her. "Will leave no part of you untouched. *Then* you can give me that special kiss."

A hard knock sounded at the door. "You'll want to get dressed now." Thane's voice blasted through the room. "Juliette the Eradicator has returned—with her entire clan."

19

"Never allow your bark to be worse than your bite.
The two should be equally terrible."
    —~~The Art of Keeping Your Female Happy~~
    —*Becoming the Monster You Were Born to Be*

Cameo jumped from the bed, her mind racing with a million different thoughts but also tingling, as if Misery were still kicking at her skull. No, not kicking—she felt no pain—but dancing over her cerebral cortex. An odd sensation, and one she'd never experienced until earlier today when Lazarus arrived at the club.

Heightened sensual awareness? Simple, wanton desire?

Fury? Juliette's arrival had interrupted Cameo's second orgasm.

Juliette would pay.

Trembling, Cameo pulled on her shirt. As Lazarus donned his, his motions were sharpened by a dark rage she'd only ever glimpsed inside the griffin's cave. He should be overjoyed. One of his dreams was about to come true.

She sheathed one of his daggers and checked the magazine of a small semiautomatic he'd stored in his boot. Excellent. Fully loaded.

"Hope you don't mind, but I'm borrowing these," she told him.

He glowered at her. "Keep them. They are yours. But stay here." Almost as an afterthought, he added, "Please."

As the only female in a group of strong, burly males, she'd heard a variation of that very command—*stay here*—so many times she'd lost count.

"Screw you, darkpit." She had to work harder than her male friends simply to be regarded as an equal. While doing so, she had to endure ridicule. What men considered strength in other men, they considered malicious in her. She had to fight to be heard after listening to repeated mansplaining. "Your former consort needs to learn I'm a formidable enemy. Apparently, so do you. Also, she needs to know your ass belongs to me."

"Camco—"

"No. No excuses about the big strong man protecting the weak little female. If you want me in your bed, you'll have to accept me at your side. No other outcome is tolerable." Okay, she'd just taken a huge gamble. Before, Lazarus had only requested a night with her. He'd just agreed to more, but not because he liked her or couldn't go on without her. Because he feared for her safety.

Oh, she knew he still desired her. He had a fully loaded AK-47 under his straining fly every time he glanced in her direction. Was desire enough to herald her happiness—and sustain it?

He'd been clear from the beginning that he wanted to wed a queen, not for love. That he wanted an alliance, an army. He didn't consider her marriage material.

The reminder stung, and Misery gloated.

His eyes narrowed as he palmed a dagger. "Your heart is too sweet."

"Are you talking about my heart, or one of the hearts I keep in a jar at home?"

He blew her a kiss. "I know what you're doing. Extolling violent escapades so I'll see you as a warrior rather than a passionate woman, but it's not going to—"

She grabbed his balls and twisted. "I *am* a warrior."

"Work," he finished on a high note. When she released him, he rubbed his precious. "Very well. You can come with me."

"Gee whiz. You're letting me come with you? You're swell. Just the best!"

He continued as if she hadn't spoken. "If you get hurt, even a single scratch—"

"You'll rage, and people will die, blah, blah, blah. We can't have your one-night stand unable to perform her duties, now, can we?"

"Oh, you'll perform your duties, all right, or people won't just die, sunshine. They'll beg to die."

How could he be so sexy and so infuriating at the same time? "Let's stop chatting and go get exhibit one of two in 'Lazarus's Quest for Vengeance.'"

His dark gaze held her captive for a blissful eternity, those ebony irises deepening and swirling, almost hypnotizing her. Then he stalked out the door. She raced after him. The hallway had been emptied of guards. Inside the club itself, Sent Ones pushed the remaining guests outside. Guests who were more than happy to leave. No one wanted to be in the path of an enraged Harpy, much less an entire clan.

There would be carnage.

Cameo moved to one of the windows in back. A beautiful garden bloomed with night roses, the macabre petals bloodred. At the edge stood the Harpies. They were well-armed, and they surrounded the building, perfectly backlit by glittering stars and the glow of a vibrant moon.

Juliette claimed the helm, the wind lifting her dark tresses and the hem of her short leather skirt.

Lazarus is going to be enslaved. Misery pretended to choke on a sob. *He's going to blame you, hate you.*

"There are more than a hundred Harpies out there and only two of us," Cameo said, doing her best to ignore the demon.

"I know. Poor Harpies." Lazarus stopped directly behind her and rested a hand on her hip.

The strange tingling started up again, but as the warmth of his breath caressed the top of her head, she shivered with delight.

Misery hissed and even lapsed into silence.

"If I unleash the demon," she said, refusing to claim him with the word *my*, "he can incapacitate the Harpy forces with sorrow. We can pick them off one by one without risking injury."

"And incapacitate you in the process, I'm sure."

"Yes," she admitted. Terribly so. Ceding the reins of control allowed Misery to fill her with so much despair she longed for death. Only with time and a miracle would she break free from his clutches.

"No." Lazarus shook his head, determined. "We fight."

Wasn't willing to achieve his vengeance the easy way? A shock!

More sexy than infuriating...

"The club has been cleared." Thane approached, the tips of his wings brushing against the floor. "The Harpies gave me an ultimatum. Kill Cameo, or start a war. I do not appreciate ultimatums, so I've decided to start a war. We'll stand with you in this battle."

Beside him stood Bjorn and a seven-foot-tall Berserker—the master of the club's guard. Bjorn nodded, and the Berserker stepped forward, saying, "As will I." Where was Xerxes?

She expected Lazarus to protest. His vengeance, his battle. He added to her shock by nodding his thanks.

Wait. Had he agreed to their help as a means of protecting her?

More infuriating than sexy.

She wasn't weak. And she would prove it!

There was no sign of Viola or the bartender who'd absconded with her. Too bad. Would have been nice to fight beside the goddess and her furry sidekick. *My new best friends.*

Who are you kidding? You have no friends. What could you possibly bring to the table?

Misery wanted to depress her before the big battle so she would be felled quickly and easily. A tactic he'd used many times before.

What do I bring to the table? she asked the demon. *Easy. The table. I built it.*

"By the way, you chose the right side," Lazarus told the others. "I've summoned my sky serpents."

He had? When?

He said, "They should arrive—"

High-pitched screeches echoed through the club.

Over a dozen sky serpents hovered in the sky, their membranous wings gliding up and down. Their huge, jewel-toned bodies radiated tension while their tails were coiled, ready to lash. Accelerant dripped from their fangs. With every exhalation, brilliant blue flames crackled inside their nostrils.

Lazarus offered a cold grin. "Now."

"You will, of course, be liable for any damage the building sustains," Thane said.

"Of course." Lazarus pointed to Juliette. "Feel free to send the bill to her next of kin."

Half of the Harpy army turned to face the sky serpents while the other half remained focused on the club. So. They were dividing their forces. A dangerous choice, placing the Harpies at a severe disadvantage right from the start. But then, it wasn't as if Lazarus had left them much choice.

Cameo liked that about him.

Xerxes appeared at Thane's side, stepping from an invisible doorway. He stretched out his arm in Cameo's direction, a dagger resting in his palm.

Lazarus caught him by the wrist, preventing him from ever making contact with her. "Keep your hands to yourself."

"My blade!" She sheathed the gun she'd "borrowed" from Lazarus and claimed the dagger.

Xerxes arched a white brow, and Lazarus released him with a huff.

Movement outside the window drew her attention. She groaned. Griffins had joined the party. *Living* griffins. They'd lined up across from the sky serpents, ready to fight for Team Harpy.

"How did she summon griffins?" Cameo demanded.

"Word of my exploits has traveled fast." Lazarus hiked his shoulders in a shrug. Reading the Harpy's mind? "The griffins found her."

Juliette smiled. "Lazarus!" Her voice echoed through the club. "I can't tell you the depths of my happiness, knowing my consort lives. Join me, my love. There's no need for a clash. We were meant to be together."

If the Harpy hadn't already signed her own death warrant, well, she would have done so then. Lazarus shouted the most obscene curse Cameo had ever heard.

"Juliette the Eradicator is mine to kill," he snapped at the Sent Ones. His gaze locked on Cameo. "And you..."

"Hey, don't worry about me." In battle, distraction killed as brutally as any sword. "I'll leave her to you. And before you command otherwise, I *will* put myself in danger, unnecessary or otherwise. But I'll also win."

A muscle jumped beneath his eye. "Have you ever fought a Harpy? Before today?"

"Hasn't everyone?"

"And you?" he asked the others.

The rainbow-eyed Bjorn released a *tell me you're joking* snort. "We've lived for thousands of years, and Harpies have no filter or boundaries. What do you think?"

"Right." Lazarus nodded. "Then you know you have to break their wings to slow or weaken them."

Harpy wings were small and usually fluttered too swiftly to grab. Cameo had never managed that particular feat, but there was a first time for everything.

"Stop worrying," she said. "We've got this in the bag."

Lazarus pressed a swift kiss into her lips. "Be careful. Or else." Then he focused on the others, his obsidian eyes crackling like the flames emitted by his sky serpents. The rest of him looked as cold as ice. "Be prepared. The second we step outside, the Harpies will fire off their arrows. Concentrate on them. My sky serpents will handle the griffins."

In union, the Sent Ones stretched out their hands. Swords of fire appeared.

"Will your sky serpents handle *me*?" Cameo muttered.

"They know of your feud with the ones in my realm, if that's what you are asking," Lazarus replied. "Shall I protect you from their wrath, or would you like to assert your independence once again?"

Jerk. "I'd like to assert my independence right up your—"

"Kill!" With that, Lazarus smashed through the door, sharp splinters flinging in every direction. The move was as unexpected to the Harpies as it was to Cameo.

She followed him, remaining close to his heels, and the Sent Ones poured out behind her. As Lazarus predicted, arrows were launched.

You can't win, Misery whispered, unwilling to give up. *You will lose, one way or another. Maybe you'll win the fight, but you'll definitely lose Lazarus. If not today, tomorrow. Like everyone else, he'll grow tired of unsuccessful attempts to cheer you.*

Cameo tuned out the lies. Only lies. Distraction killed, and sorrow debilitated. She focused on battle. The very thing she'd been created to do. The world around her slowed to a crawl, but her pace remained swift as she waved her arms and angled her wrists. The arrows pinged off her daggers, useless.

Sky serpents unleashed a storm of fire, cranking up

the heat. Smoke formed a cloud of gloom as beads of sweat ran down Cameo's temples and spine.

A fierce war cry sounded. Harpies darted forward, three eager beavers meeting Cameo halfway. She braced for impact and—

Lazarus slammed into the females, a bowling ball to their pins.

You've got to be kidding me.

Other Harpies sprang over their fallen comrades, their gazes locked on Cameo. Thankfully Lazarus was preoccupied with... She frowned. Why was he moving so slowly, allowing the women to claw him to shreds? A battle strategy? Hoping to give the Harpies a false sense of victory?

Yes or no, she couldn't help him right now. The new group reached her. She blocked a bite and then a slash. Surprise darkened their eyes.

What, they expected to take her down easily?

She wouldn't go for their wings, she decided. No doubt the move was expected. Instead, she spun, dropping into a crouch and kicking out her leg. One Harpy tripped, then another. As they toppled, she stabbed her daggers into their midsections.

At first, the women didn't realize they'd been injured. Adrenaline pumped through their systems, probably numbing the pain. But Cameo remained crouched. When the females attempted to stand, probably thinking they'd punt at her while she was down, their intestines spilled out at her feet. Howls of agony rent the air.

My cue. Determined to finish off her opponents, Cameo jumped up. With quick jabs, she stabbed one in the heart and the other in the neck. Unfortunately, they had a friend. The girl raked her claws across Cameo's cheek.

Her flesh tore, burning as if it had been doused in acid. Her knees gave out and smacked into the ground. Maddened by rage, the Harpy followed her down.

Ignoring the influx of pain, Cameo sank her dagger into her attacker's trachea. The girl jerked before slumping over.

Group one—done.

Different sounds registered, making her ears twitch. Crackling flames, grunts and groans, roars, the snap of breaking bones, other howls. Where was Lazarus? She lumbered to her feet—

A hard weight slammed into her, pitching her across the garden.

She lost her breath, pinpricks of light winking before her, momentarily blinding her. A hard fist punched her injured cheek once, twice. A *cold* fist. Brass knuckles? Her jaw snapped out of place, and her brain banged against her skull. Blood leaked from the sides of her mouth as waves of blistering pain washed over her.

Don't stop. Keep fighting. She stayed down and kicked up her legs. At the same time, the Harpy leaned down to deliver the next punch. Perfect. Cameo crisscrossed her thighs, locking onto the girl's neck. She rolled to her stomach, forcing the Harpy facedown.

Crack! The Harpy's forehead met a rock, and the rock won.

Though her opponent scratched at her legs in an attempt to rise, the blow had weakened her, allowing Cameo to stand and slam a boot into her once-pretty face.

Lights out, Harpy.

Dizzy, panting, she searched the battlefield. The sky serpents had thinned out the enemy herd while the Sent Ones had felled their fair share of Harpies—without actually killing the women. Bjorn and Xerxes were in the process of confining the injured females inside a cage camouflaged by stone.

Only Juliette remained on her feet. Well, not her feet. Not exactly. Lazarus had her by the throat, her legs flailing through the air. She clawed at him, desperate to win her freedom.

Crimson splattered him from head to toe, especially thick down the inseam of his pants. His shirt and a good portion of his skin had been shredded. Obvious strain tightened the skin around his eyes and mouth, Juliette's weight seemingly more than he could tolerate. His lips were pulled back from his teeth in a fierce scowl.

Was the Harpy's bronzed flesh...turning gray?

Juliette's wild gaze darted over her surroundings, probably seeking anything or anyone she could use against her tormentor. When she spotted Cameo, she gasped, "Box. Know...who...box."

Only one box mattered to Cameo. Pandora's. Did Juliette know who possessed it?

Heart slamming against her ribs, Cameo called, "Lazarus." With her jaw still out of place, she slurred his name.

He gave no notice of her. Was his thirst for vengeance so great he'd lost track of everything else? Or did he simply not care what she had to say?

After everything they'd done in bed, the second possibility hurt worse than the beating she'd taken.

"Lazarus," she repeated, springing forward. She tripped over a body, but remained upright and kept running. "Let her go. You have to let her go." If Juliette knew who had the box, Cameo needed her alive. At least for a little while.

Yes, the Harpy had probably lied to save herself. And if so, her death would be a thousand times worse. But better safe than sorry when the lives of Cameo's loved ones were at stake.

She crashed into Lazarus, expecting him to stumble; he toppled to the ground, instead, losing his grip on Juliette. The Harpy rolled and sprang to her feet.

Nooo! Cameo made a play for her, but even winded, Juliette managed to fake a left and then zoom right. She sprinted away, and Cameo gave chase. They neared the edge of the cloud. The Harpy would have to stop and—

Juliette dived, falling from view. Cameo skidded to a stop before she, too, plummeted to her death.

One of the griffins swooped underneath Juliette, catching the Harpy on his back, and relief showered Cameo. There would be another fight—another chance to get answers.

The remaining sky serpents hissed at her, reminding her an enemy still lurked nearby. Lazarus's pets would love to punish her…and so would Lazarus.

He roared. "Why, Cameo? Tell me why!"

She closed her eyes and rested her jaw against her shoulder. With a shove, she forced her jaw into place—and nearly doubled over with pain.

When she'd calmed, she said, "You heard her." She pointed in the direction Juliette had flown. "Your consort might know where to find Pandora's box."

"She was never mine." He reached Cameo's side, his gaze spitting fire at her. "And she doesn't know."

"How can you be sure?"

His eyes filled with guilt and anger. Why guilt? "I just am."

"Well, I want to talk to her before you kill her. Okay?"

A sky serpent landed behind him and squawked.

"No," Lazarus shouted. His gaze remained on Cameo as he grated at the creature, "She isn't to be harmed. Ever. Not by you."

Not by you. And wasn't *that* reassuring?

"I'm returning to Budapest," she said. "You can come with me, or you can stay here. Right now I don't exactly care. Actually, I do care. Stay here!" A mimic of his earlier command to her. How would a guy feel about reversed chauvinism? "When my wounds heal, I'm going to find Juliette and have a chat with her. And she had better be alive. The safety of my family is more important than your vengeance. Do you hear me?"

"I think everyone heard you," he snapped.

Cameo stormed around him, first glaring at the sky serpent, then the Sent Ones. "Someone better volunteer to give me a ride home, or I'm going to start singing a lullaby."

All three Sent Ones and their Berserker friend begged for the privilege. And, okay, wow, the sky serpent prostrated himself to allow easy access to his back.

Maybe the knock to her skull had destroyed her sense of self-preservation since she decided to go with the sky serpent. Sure, he'd like to rip her to shreds and suck the marrow from her bones, but so what? If he ate her, he ate her. If he dropped her midair, he dropped her. She'd either die or survive. Right now she wasn't sure which one she most wanted to happen.

What the creature wouldn't do? Lecture her.

Sky serpent for the win. All aboard the SS Express.

She approached him only to pause and glare at Lazarus. "Will humans see us and freak out?"

"No. He'll camouflage himself."

Camouflage? A puff of white smoke wafted from the sky serpent's nostrils, covering and hiding him.

"Well. That explains how you've gone so long without detection," she said, marching forward.

"Cameo." Lazarus shouted her name, somehow turning three syllables into a harsh command.

"Nope. Our conversation is over." She settled onto her transport.

"I will come for you," he said. "I will *always* come for you."

He'd said those words before. The first time, they'd been a promise, both sweet and reassuring. Today, they sounded like a warning.

20

"~~Never apologize~~. Always apologize, but only ever
to your woman."
    —~~Becoming the Monster You Were Born to Be~~
        —*The Art of Keeping Your Female Happy*

Three days. Three torturous days Lazarus remained
parted from his Cameo. He'd reached his limit.

He gnashed his molars, his jaw aching in protest.
He had yet to leave the guest room at Downfall. Because of Juliette, he wasn't strong enough to rejoin his
μονομανία. Toward the end of the battle, the Harpy
had gotten her claws into his groin and, with a victory
shout, removed one of his testicles. He'd been too slow
to stop her.

He'd used his time to create a leather sheath for Pandora's box, lining it with thin chain mail as an added
layer of protection. The craftsmanship was flawless,
and yet no match for Cameo's.

Surprisingly, the separation from her had agonized
him far more than the loss of his man-egg. He should

have healed by now. No Cameo, no worsening. Yet he'd begun to regenerate only this morning.

Whatever the reason, Juliette would pay for his imprisonment *and* the days apart from his woman. She would pay with her life, yes, but first she would bleed.

He missed Cameo. Missed her wit and ferocity. Craved her sweet kisses and decadent taste. Hungered for her seductive purrs of arousal. He yearned to have her nails in his back once again, her legs wrapped around his waist. Dreamed of the way she soaked her panties for him. Even the way she'd fought those Harpies...

Most of all, he *needed* to see her smile again, rare as it was. He was now a junkie in need of a fix, twitchy and trigger-happy, ready to rip to shreds anyone who dared get in his way.

He saw her for who she was—strong, intelligent, brave—all of this and more. She deserved to be his partner, not just a pretty decoration at his side.

He'd almost stepped into the shadows, his personal vendetta against Juliette and Hera forgotten, just to watch her. She'd wielded a sword as expertly as she'd made one from scrap metal, the weapon an extension of her arm. She had moved like ripples in water, so smooth she'd seemed harmless until far too late.

Yesterday he'd broken down and summoned the Sent One with rainbow-colored eyes. Bjorn. The oldest.

"Do I have your word this conversation will go no further?" Lazarus had asked.

"You do," the Sent One had replied. Unable to lie, he'd effectively bound himself to silence on the subject.

Which was the only reason Lazarus had continued. "You've been alive a long time. As long as I have. What do you know of Hera? Of...my father?"

"Very little about your father. Hera and your mother, I knew. At one time, they were friends."

Friends? The news had come as a shock. How could one friend mercilessly murder another? "When did they become enemies?"

"When your father abducted your mother."

A simple case of jealousy? Had Hera wanted Typhon? Why?

He had turned the tide of the conversation, saying, "Do you know a way to remove Cameo's demon and keep her alive?"

Bjorn had tapped his fingers to his chin. "An empty vessel withers. That's why she will die when he is removed. *If* you managed to revive her afterward, which isn't a guarantee, her spirit would have to be patched— or healed—and refilled. Love for hate. Joy for sadness."

It made sense, but it was too risky. Neither he nor Cameo knew how to love. And had he ever known joy? True joy?

Lazarus paced through the bedroom he'd shared with Cameo and grimaced as tender, regenerating flesh rubbed against his leathers. He should let her go now rather than later. He should turn his efforts to building an army. Yes, he should. But staying away from the keeper of Misery was looking less and less like an option for him.

He'd told her he would help her control the demon. He'd told her he would protect her, even from herself.

Must protect her.

Fool!

He was thousands of years old. Had experienced the best and worst life had to offer, and yet he had no defenses against Cameo. Her mere existence made her enemy one. Without her, he would live. He would be strong, a leader among men. But without her, he would not live well.

I am my father's son.

Never! He wouldn't take Cameo against her will, ever.

He *would* romance the hell out of her.

Need for her threatened to supersede his will to survive. He'd craved her before; she'd been a temptation. Now she was a necessity, essential to his existence.

Was this how his father had felt about his mother? Crazed? Had this been the beginning of the end for Typhon?

Make or break time, Lazarus realized. He had to decide. Walk away from Cameo for good, or go all in. Accept the crystals, and the end result—a life in the shadows, unable to fight—or eschew the crystals and win his personal wars.

If he chose the first, there could be no half measures. He'd made that mistake before, demanding Cameo accept a one-night stand. As many times and as many ways as she'd been hurt, she needed security from her man. She deserved to know she was adored. Only then would he win her trust. Only then would she share her body…and choose to remember her smile.

In return, she could help Lazarus achieve his vengeance. What better warrior to have at his side? He could have it all, his woman and his vengeance, before the crystals overtook him.

But. Always there was a "but." If Lazarus planned to spend what remained of his days with Cameo, he had to tell her about Pandora's box. He had to tell her before she challenged Juliette for information the Harpy did not—could not—have.

What if she used the box to hurt herself?

He could destroy the box and simply show her the remains.

She would hate him.

And what about the Morning Star? The apple hung from his neck once again. He wrapped his hand around it and squeezed. If he destroyed Pandora's box, he might destroy the Morning Star, as well. Or would the mysterious being finally go free?

Could the Morning Star save Cameo?

If there was even a chance, he couldn't destroy the box. The risk outweighed the reward. That meant he couldn't tell Cameo about it, no matter how much she deserved the truth.

Can't jeopardize her well-being. Or her future. And he wouldn't feel guilty about this anymore. He wouldn't! She meant too much to him, and what he did, he did for her.

He protected her. End of story.

New plan, next move. He would kill Juliette before Cameo had a chance to chat her up. Then he would turn his attentions to Hera, beat his father's location out of her and finally kill the woman who'd murdered his mother as well as the man who'd enslaved her. He would act fast. Then he would spend the rest of his days with Cameo, basking in the contentment only she could give him.

A sound plan.

"Hello, Lazarus."

The familiar voice drifted from the space behind

him, every muscle in his body knotting. Palming a dagger in each hand, he spun—

And came face-to-face with Hera.

Lazarus cast an illusion, hiding his fury behind a blank mask, erasing any sign of the apple underneath his shirt and the weapons strapped to his body. Let her believe he was unarmed.

The years had been kind to her, making her more beautiful than ever. Her hair resembled a fall of moss intermixed with lush pink flowers. Her eyes were, in essence, an aerial map of the Earth, blue with spots of green and brown. The perfect complement to the beautiful sienna hue of her skin.

She wore a gown made entirely of enchanted rose petals, the flowers' sweet perfume wafting from her.

A bitch like her should smell like brimstone and sulfur!

He had not expected her to come to him. Hadn't expected her to remember the little boy she'd orphaned. As Lazarus had grown into a man, he'd kept his intentions for her to himself.

"Hera. I have long dreamed of seeing you again."

"You were beheaded. I find it difficult to believe you dream at all, let alone live," she said conversationally.

"Haven't you heard? I cannot be killed."

"Makes sense, I suppose. You are, after all, your father's son." Her lips pursed. "Typhon. Such a slippery little pig who has managed to evade death...so far."

Did she realize she'd just confirmed his father's survival? "You killed my mother. Your friend," he finished with bite. "Who's the true pig in that picture?"

Rage darkened her features. Then he detected a crackle of power similar to his own—to his father's—

and her expression blanked. Did she have the ability to cast illusions, too?

"Do you know why I'm here?" she asked.

"Oh, yes. To die at my hands."

"You have Pandora's box. *My* box. You killed my slave."

His illusion masked his shock. Hera the Cuckoldress had been Hilda's master.

"I know the box is nearby," she said. "I can feel it. Don't lie to me, Lazarus. You see, before being incarcerated in Tartarus, I spent my days killing the males who proved to be any kind of threat to the fairer sex. I was very good. *Very* good." She twirled a strand of hair around her finger, playing innocent. "Hold your tongue and return the box to me now, or you shall join my list of undesirables."

"You yourself said Death can't get his grubby hands on me." He kept his tone pleasant. "I'll go with option C, and hack you to pieces."

"Good luck with that." She wandered about the bedroom with undisguised indifference, trailing one fingertip along the top of the antique dresser...the vanity... one of the posts on the massive bed, where the rumpled sheets still bore a faint trace of Cameo's scent. Lazarus owned nothing here, and yet his sense of possession flared.

Vengeance demanded he slay his foe. Act now. But he remained in place. *Never start a fight you cannot win.* Weakened as he was—as powerful as *she* was— he had to proceed carefully...stealthily.

"What a hypocrite you've become in your old age, eh." He allowed a cold smile to slip through his illusion, the truth in his bold stare an open taunt. "You, the avenger of the violated, known for punishing anyone who dared take something not freely offered—*you* stole Pandora's box and prevented the demons from being put back inside. *You* unleashed those demons upon an unsuspecting world. For centuries, they've pillaged, plundered and destroyed the innocent."

A bitter laugh filled the space between them. "You're right. I'm a hypocrite. And I'm punished every day for my choices."

Trying to turn the tables on him and earn his sympathy? Never! "I weep for you," he told her, and flicked away an imaginary tear.

"I'm sure you do." She met his stare with unflinching determination. "Where's my box?"

"Where's my father?"

She lifted a brow. "Do you wish to save him?"

"I wish to kill him."

A pause laden with tension. Then, "Where's my box, Lazarus?"

"Where's my father?" he said, stepping toward her.

"I learned my lesson well, Lazarus. Letting you live was a mistake. Tell me where you're keeping my box, or I will destroy your family, beginning with your young."

"I have no young." He cupped his groin. "But you're welcome to drink them straight from the tap."

Ashen, she performed a half pivot, always keeping him within her sights. "I saved you from becoming a copy of your father. As a child, I spared your life. You owe me."

"You enslaved me and relegated the care of my soul to a Harpy. I owe you nothing but a painful death."

"Brave words. *Foolish* words. Do not force me to

dismember your precious Cameo the way I dismembered Echidna."

Had her voice wobbled there at the end? "Force you?" The hatred he'd harbored for so long *exploded* inside him, emotional shrapnel embedding itself in every inch of his body. The wounds bled more rage, only rage.

"I've never enjoyed harming my fellow females."

"Touch Cameo, and I'll—" There was no threat great enough.

"What? Freeze up like your father, unable to move, trapped inside some sort of chrysalis?" She laughed. "I checked on him not too long ago. A tragic fate for a once-strong male."

A fate Lazarus would share.

He'd already resigned himself to it—or thought he had. If he stayed with Cameo, he would continue to weaken. Perhaps now *was* the time to attack. Perhaps he would never have more power than he had now.

Decision made.

Without forecasting his intent, Lazarus threw himself at Hera. His shoulder plowed into the softest part of her belly, and he roared with satisfaction at her sound of distress. As he followed her to the floor, she took the brunt of impact, the back of her skull shattering.

Despite the injury, she banged her forehead into his chin. Adrenaline jacked, he barely registered the hit. Never missing a beat, he drew back his elbow and jabbed his arm forward. The blow met nothing but air as she flashed away.

Hoping she would return, he jumped to his feet. He paced the room for five minutes…ten…but she never appeared.

New plan. Weakened or not, he would return to

Cameo's side. Today. Now. They would hunt and kill Hera and Juliette together. They would find and slay his father. He trusted Cameo and admired her skill.

He didn't need an army. He just needed her.

"Get your asses in gear. Our one millionth family meeting is about to kick off." Torin's voice echoed over the sound system he'd installed inside the fortress.

Great! Wonderful! Cameo knew what would be discussed. Or rather, *who* they would be discussing.

When she'd told her friends Juliette maybe, just possibly might know where to find Pandora's box, excitement and hope had bloomed. The Harpy had become the Lords' enemy one.

Had Lazarus forgiven Cameo for saving his tormentor's life?

Hell, no. Otherwise he'd be here.

Lost him before I had him.

Cameo's friends filed into the great room. She claimed a spot up front, her arms crossed over her chest as she met the gaze of every occupant: Torin, Keeley, Maddox, Ashlyn, Sienna, Sabin, Gwen, Gideon, Scarlet, Amun, Haidee, Danika, Kaia and Olivia, a Sent One.

Aeron, former keeper of Wrath, was out tailing Galen, who was out searching for Legion, a former demon turned human who'd suffered unimaginable horrors in hell.

Legion was and would forever be under Aeron's protection. Aeron considered her a daughter.

Lucien, Anya, Paris, Reyes, Kane, Josephina, Strider, Baden and Katarina were currently in the underworld with Hades.

Redheaded Kaia nudged Cameo's shoulder, all *I've*

got this. "Pipe down and listen up. The entire Eagleshield clan has declared war on our girl Cam. They expect all Skyhawks to do the same because we've always held a grudge against Cam's man-candy-liciousness Lazarus."

How dare the Eagleshields try to recruit her friends!

You have no friends, Misery whispered.

I do! I know I do.

A chorus of "boo" rang out from the crowd.

See? she told the demon. *Friends.*

"We declined, of course. With blades." Cheers erupted, and Kaia took a bow. When the room quieted, she added, "Ages ago, Lazarus destroyed one of our villages, but today, we officially forgive him. For Cameo's sake and also because we'd like an opportunity to torture him slowly. In the most nonviolent ways." Her gaze darted to Cameo. "Death is too fast and definitely too permanent."

"Word is Lazarus actually came back from the dead," Gwen said. "How is that possible?"

All eyes landed on Cameo. "I don't know." His physical appearance had changed, the lines etched through his arms thicker and darker, his hatred of them worse. "Neither does he."

Her friends cringed at the sound of her voice. Worse, they cringed with more force than usual.

Told you, Misery taunted.

She pressed her lips together. She'd had no plans to tell anyone about Lazarus's lines, anyway. His secret was his to share.

"I'll ask around," Sienna said. "Someone knows something." As the new keeper of Wrath, dishing punishments had become her favorite jam. She cracked her knuckles. "That someone will sing like a canary."

"Inquiring minds want to know." Kaia hopped up

and down. "Does every inch of the new, living Lazarus work?"

Like, did his heart beat? She nodded.

Kaia offered a sly grin. "How many inches are we talking about? Huh, huh. Tell me!"

Try: gigantor. *And mine. All mine.*

Cameo silently mouthed, *"Focus, people!"*

"So less than six? Seven?" she insisted. "Juliette bragged about keeping his balls in her trophy case. Apparently she cut one off every now and then to remind Laz who was boss. Got a new one during the last battle. I just wondered if he's experienced shrinkage."

He'd been injured? She'd assumed the blood he'd worn had belonged to his victims.

How could I leave him behind?

Before Misery could use her guilt against her, she turned to Olivia. "After Aeron died, the Most High gave him a new body. The Most High the only being capable of such a feat, yes?" He'd created Sent Ones, angels and even humans from stardust.

As for the other species?

Stories claimed fallen angels had once mated with humans to create demigods—the Titans, Greeks and Unspoken Ones. Though they'd chosen to drop the word *demi*. Those demigods had mated with other demigods, and different immortal races were born. Shifters, Berserkers, sirens, nymphs and a handful of others. Still other demigods had mated with demons, creating Harpies, vampires and witches. However, none of those beings knew how to create flesh from dirt—or anything else.

"To my knowledge, yes." Olivia's voice was as sweet as ever. "I don't know how He did it, though. Aeron woke up in the heavens, his spirit already bonded to his new body."

So we're still at square one. Awesome.

Sorrow wafted from Misery, a poisoned perfume. Sienna sniffled. Kaia and Gwen turned away to stealthily wipe their tears.

Here I go, making everyone around me miserable again.

"I'm out." Head down, Cameo strode into the hall.

"We need to discuss the box," Sabin called after her.

She paused long enough to answer. "Don't worry. Juliette Eagleshield will tell me everything she knows before I remove her head." No more playing nice and stopping with a hand removal.

Cameo descended the stairs. Along the way, she passed a butterfly in flight and ignored the prickling unease. She shut herself inside her bedroom and eased onto the cushioned seat in front of her vanity...where Lazarus's mirror now hung.

At first, she'd had no idea the mirror was in her room. She'd seen a blow-up doll. Then she'd touched it and the illusion faded, the glass appearing before her eyes. A gift from Lazarus. She was awed by his thoughtfulness... and terrified of what she would next see.

History had proved only heartache awaited her.

Tears slipped down her cheeks as little sorrows began to nibble at her soul like starving mice who'd finally found a hunk of cheese. Sadness and regrets scurried across her mind, little cockroaches that dwelled in the shadows.

Despite their explosive goodbye, she missed Lazarus more with every second that passed. Missed his touch. His taste. His bark of a laugh, a bit rusty at the edges.

Not many people could make him laugh; she was one of a rare few. She even missed his irritating comments.

With him, she felt alive for the first time since her possession, so close to happiness she could almost bark out a laugh of her own.

Lazarus has abandoned you, wants nothing to do with you. Misery purred like a well-fed kitten. *Perhaps you would feel better if you forgot him.*

Never!

Maybe…

Lazarus believed the demon needed permission to wipe her memory. At first, she'd discarded the idea as ludicrous. Not knowing the things she'd done and said was torture. Now, however, she was possessed by an even worse torture. Knowing the wanton things she'd done and said, the wanton things *Lazarus* had done and said—and knowing she would never experience them again.

No, no. The loss of memory would be worse, guaranteed, and she couldn't let sorrow convince her she'd finally know peace.

No "peace" could compare with the memory of their first kiss. The little details as much as the big. The sardonic gleam in his dark eyes when he teased her. The huskiness of his voice when she pleased him. The way beads of sweat trickled down the ripples of his muscles.

Cameo stared into the mirror, desperate. "Show me the future," she whispered. "Please."

To her surprise, the glass liquefied, waves rippling from top to bottom. Those waves split, two images appearing, one on the right, one on the left. In the first, Lazarus stabbed Hera with a miniature version of the Paring Rod. The shaft had been cut in two, the bulbous tip now to the center to make room for a retractable dagger. Vision Cameo watched the murder with an air of relief. He'd done it. He'd gotten vengeance and survived.

The scene morphed, revealing the consequences of his victory. Cameo's motionless body burned atop a pyre. Her friends surrounded her, their heads bowed with sorrow and grief—funny, the terrible emotions were still courtesy of her.

"If Lazarus kills Hera, I die?" she asked the glass.

Trembling, she focused on the other half of the mirror and blinked in shock as she watched her image act out the second scene. In it, she stepped in front of Hera, saving the former queen's life—and causing the end of her own.

No hope, then. *Doomed if I do, doomed if I don't.* Unless she could somehow change her future.

Why would Cameo protect the goddess who'd killed Lazarus's mother?

The scene changed, revealing the consequences of this new choice. This time, Cameo lay in bed, laughing as a kaleidoscope of butterflies danced overhead.

Whoa. She survived? And *laughed*? At *butterflies*?

Maybe she shouldn't try to change her future, after all. Following the mirror's lead the first time had worked out *very* well for her.

But...butterflies?

If one leaves her chrysalis too easily, her wings are weakened. She must struggle to exit, or she will never have the strength to fly.

She remembered Lazarus's words, and twisted to peer at a flurry of butterflies perched outside her window. What if the insects weren't a symbol of doom but instead—she swallowed hard—a portent of success?

What if they signaled Lazarus's approach? He'd said they gravitated to him.

Her heart leaped. Had he forgiven her for Juliette's temporary stay of execution?

Maybe so, but… She rested her elbows on the vanity and leaned her forehead against the heels of her palms. He would forever despise her for saving Hera. Therefore, saving the goddess could not possibly lead to Cameo's happiness.

But come on! What if she lost Lazarus either way? The first vision showed Cameo's death, and in the second vision Lazarus hadn't been anywhere near her.

And yet I laughed. Why?

Had he been nearby?

So many unanswered questions.

A knock sounded at her door. The glass cleared, revealing her reflection and the disarray of her bedroom. Good, that was good.

She stood on shaky legs and croaked, "Enter."

Viola swept inside, her pet nipping playfully at her heels. Today Viola wore a grungy T-shirt that read "I'm Dating a Supermodel. Me!" The collar was ripped and the hem frayed. Her short shorts were streaked with grass stains. Mud caked her cowgirl boots.

Fluffy wore a matching outfit.

The pair had returned to the fortress yesterday. The goddess had refused to talk about what had gone down at the club, and Cameo hadn't pushed for answers.

"Since I'm your best friend," Viola said, "I've been elected to tell you the bad news."

Oh, no. "What happened? Did someone die? Who died?"

Misery snickered.

"Wow," Viola said. "Your mind immediately goes all worst-case scenario, doesn't it?"

She forced herself to inhale and exhale with purpose. "What happened?" she repeated as calmly as possible.

"Gwen and Kaia just got a bead on Juliette." Viola's gaze landed on the mirror and widened, her mouth parting on a dreamy sigh. As if in a trance, she walked forward, her arms extending to touch. "Oh! A pretty!"

Cameo grabbed a blanket and rushed toward the mirror, intent on intervening before Viola lost herself to her reflection. Mission accomplished.

"How is finding Juliette bad news for me?" Cameo asked, wiping her hands together in a job well done.

"Who said anything about it being bad news for *you*? It's totally bad news for *her*. Did I forget to mention the silly Harpy has issued you a challenge? She wants to nix pitting family against family and fight you one-on-one. Winner gets to keep Lazarus."

Cameo's hands balled into fists. "One-on-one? Done. But Lazarus is no one's pawn. He will choose the woman he's with."

It won't be her, and it won't be you, the demon piped up. *That plane has already left the runway.*

"She doesn't care about free will, so you need to prepare. Come." Viola walked away, clearly expecting Cameo to follow.

Feet as heavy as boulders, she trudged after her friend. They entered the artifact room, where the Paring Rod, Cage of Compulsion, Cloak of Invisibility and paintings created by the All-Seeing Eye were stored.

Power thickened the air. And dust. Lots and lots of dust. Cameo coughed.

Her gaze fixed on the Paring Rod. It had a long,

metal shaft and a bulbous stained-glass tip. One touch, and she would end up in another realm.

"Why are we here?" she asked. "I don't want to leave the mortal world."

"Duh." Viola pulled a piece of cloth from her pocket and carefully sheathed the bulb. "As you know, I made it my business to learn more about the Paring Rod while trapped inside the spirit realm—"

"You weren't trapped. You willingly entered the second time. And you had the ring!" Cameo reminded her.

"*Anyway.* The Paring Rod. I have a feeling you're going to need it." As Viola spoke, she bent and twisted the Rod…in natural grooves Cameo had never noticed, shortening the staff, causing a sharper edge to emerge from the tip.

Her stomach twisted into a tight knot. The Paring Rod *had* shrunk into a miniature version of itself, becoming the sword she'd seen in the mirror. Which meant the artifact had just become the weapon Lazarus would use to kill Hera…or Cameo.

Sooo. The mirror *had* shown two possible futures, and now Cameo had to choose which one she desired to fruition.

No need to ponder. The second. Of course she picked the second. She'd laughed!

But what about Lazarus? Would her happiness ruin his?

21

"Your kingdom will never experience peace while your ~~enemies still live~~ woman is upset."
—*The Art of Keeping Your Female Happy*

Lazarus strode into the Budapest fortress as if he owned it. In his mind, he did. He'd decided to go all in with Cameo, so she had to go all in with him. No other outcome was acceptable. What belonged to him now belonged to her and vice versa. Therefore, he owned the fortress.

He paused in the foyer. Maybe close proximity to Cameo strengthened him in some ways while weakening him in others, because his testicle finally finished regenerating. An agonizing process he betrayed by neither word nor deed.

"Welcome." A disembodied voice spilled over an intercom system. A voice he knew belonged to Torin, puppet of Disease, who had once dated Cameo. The male would live only because he'd never actually touched her.

With the cameras placed around the perimeter, Torin

had known of his arrival the second he'd flashed in front of the door. Lazarus had opened his mind to the occupants before entering and had sensed no desire to attack.

Maybe because Torin had announced, "We have a guest. Don't kill him."

Lazarus flipped off one of the cameras as he kicked into motion. Urgency rode him, whipping his flank; he increased his speed as he pounded up a flight of stairs.

On the second floor, he spotted a woman he'd met long ago. He'd been a young boy and she'd been engaged to Hades. Keeley, the Red Queen. Typhon had dragged Lazarus to the underworld to pay his respects.

Back then she'd had red hair and brown eyes. Today her long locks were pink, her eyes as green as grass. Tomorrow? Who knew what color they'd be. Her features were tied to the calendar and changed with every season.

He watched as the woman wove in and out of bedrooms, stuffing different items into a bag. "She's going to need this—" a vase "—and this—" she pulled a nail from the wall "—and definitely this!" A pair of swimming goggles.

Her fathomless gaze landed on him, and she offered a distracted smile. "Hey, Lazy. I've been meaning to tell you…something? Need to search the old corkboard. If you're looking for my girl, she's in her room, preparing for the challenge. Good news! She accepted."

What corkboard? What challenge? And accepted what, exactly?

Lazarus didn't wait around to ask. Instead, he took off at a swift pace down the hall, passing an open doorway where Sabin, keeper of Doubt, stood in the center of the frame, sipping a cup of coffee and staring him down. Or up. The male topped out at only six-seven. Shirtless, the huge butterfly tattoo on his right side couldn't be missed. The mark of his demon.

Soon I will see—and lick—my sunshine's mark.

"You hurt Cameo," Sabin said, "and I'll remove *both* of your heads."

Under any other circumstances, Lazarus would have attacked without warning. *Threaten me, die.* But he said, "Fair enough." If he hurt Cameo, he deserved whatever pain these warriors dished.

Frowning, Sabin rubbed his arms. "There's something different about you. You're making me...tingle."

Lazarus ran his tongue over his teeth. The warrior sensed Pandora's box, despite the leather sheath and chain mail. With Hera hot on his trail, he'd had to bring the pendant with him. "What you're feeling is called sexual attraction. Sorry, but you're just going to have to deal with it."

Sabin's consort, Gwen, sidled up to him and flashed her fangs at Lazarus. "I don't feel any different, but I'll be happy to rip out your throat with my teeth."

Gwen was a Harpy from Clan Skyhawk, but he bore her no ill will. He knew better than to hate an entire race for one person's sins.

Every other open door had another warrior in place, waiting to terrorize him. This was a Walk of Promised Pain, wasn't it? Whatever. He was dating Cameo. This had to happen sooner or later.

"I'm tingling, too, and it's definitely not sexual attraction." Maddox, keeper of Violence, had black hair and violet eyes, a male as lethal as he was pretty. "Might be rage. Upset Cameo, and I'll play Go Fish with your internal organs."

"I don't feel your new mojo, but I do want to jump your bones." Gideon, keeper of Lies, had a punk rock vibe, with multiple piercings and blue hair that was a perfect match to his eyes. He couldn't utter a single truth without suffering debilitating pain. He added, "And FYI, Cameo isn't like a sister to me. Use and abuse her if you'd like. Whatever. I certainly won't use your severed skull as a masturbatory aid."

A pregnant dark-haired woman wound her arm around Gideon's waist. She offered Lazarus a soft, sweet smile. "My husband might see you as a masturbatory aid, but I see you more as an outhouse." That sweet smile never wavered.

Well. Lazarus had a new admiration for these people.

Amun, keeper of Secrets, stood beside his woman, the heavily tattooed Haidee. Using sign language, he said, "Hurt Cam? I'll slit your throat while you're sleeping and dance in your blood."

Nice.

Olivia, a dark-haired Sent One, met Lazarus's gaze. "However you came back from the dead…you won't be doing it again if you screw over Cameo. Aeron will tear you into so many pieces, no one will ever be able to put you back together."

"Great chatting with you guys." Lazarus reached Cameo's room and entered without knocking. He shut the door with a soft snick, nearly overcome by an oppressive taint of sorrow.

Not yet noticing him, his μονομανία hurried here and there. For the first time since they'd parted, he felt like he could breathe. Despite her dark mood. He was finally home. Tension evaporated, arousal taking its place.

"I want more than a night with you," he announced.

She spun, jet-black hair dancing with the movement. Her delicate cheeks flushed prettily, but her thick lashes were spiked and damp, her silver eyes rimmed with red. She'd been crying?

A growl rumbled deep in his chest.

"Lazarus. You're here." The sorrow in her voice contained a sharp edge and utterly ripped him up inside. "I wasn't sure I'd ever see you again."

Remaining in place proved a Herculean feat. If he touched her, the conversation would end. "Tell me what's wrong, sunshine, and I'll fix it."

A fresh round of tears welled, and her chin began to tremble. "I'm so sorry I ruined everything for you. I missed you…going to lose you soon…our time together is limited, even tainted, and…and…"

Misery had used their separation to strike at her, he realized. Teeth gnashing, Lazarus reached up and wrapped his hand over the apple, still hidden under his shirt. More and more he longed to kill the demon, to teach him the error of his ways.

Can't risk Cameo.

"If you kill Hera," she said, and sniffled, "I die."

His brow furrowed. "How do you know?"

"The mirror showed me."

"Remember, the mirror shows *possible* futures." But he could not tolerate the thought of her death in any capacity. "Now that I know, I can take measures to ensure you remain safe." And he would. "I have always refused to ask anyone for help. I believed needing help meant I was weak. But I'm asking you. Help me find Juliette. We'll kill her together. The faster the better. I'm sure there's a study out there that will confirm couples that slay together, stay together. Besides, if she knew where to find Pandora's box, she would have used it to kill you already. When Juliette is rotting in a grave, we can focus on Hera. Lock her away, if necessary. And once she's defeated, we can find and kill my father."

Hope flared in her eyes, only to be snuffed out. Tears streamed down her cheeks, wrecking him. "You want your father dead? That's so sad. I mean, I knew he was a brute, but surely you have some fond memories."

If she weren't so upset, he would have been amused. Such a soft heart for such a hardened warrior. "Typhon enslaved and raped my mother. I will celebrate his demise."

"Oh, Lazarus. I'm so sorry. No wonder you want to wed a queen for an army. An army I can't give you." Sniffle, sniffle. "And thanks to me, you're missing a testicle—"

"You, sunshine, are an army of one," he interjected. "I'll lead you. And your friends."

She snorted now. "You'll *lead* me? Lead us? Wow. What an honor. Everyone will be…pleased. I foresee *zero* problems with your plan."

He feigned shock. "Did the Mother of Melancholy just crack a joke?"

"She most certainly did, and her joke even has a punch line. Guess what? It's *you*. Because the first time you issue an order to my friends, they'll take turns punching you. A few might even kick you in your ball."

His gaze slid over her, lingering on his favorite places. "You'll be pleased to know my testicle has regrown. Perhaps you should give it a welcome back kiss?"

She wrapped her arms around her middle, suddenly swept away by a new tide of sorrow. "You shouldn't let my lips anywhere near your jewels. Did I mention I ruin *everything*?"

Cursed demon. Time to pry his claws out of her emotions.

Lazarus sighed. "You're right. You ruined my well-ordered life, my plan to wed a queen I wouldn't love and probably wouldn't even like, and you destroyed any chance I had for a peaceful existence. You're terrible. You have zero positive qualities."

Her jaw dropped. "I must have *a few* positive qualities."

"Please. You're only kidding yourself. You're hopelessly irredeemable. Go on, admit it." He put enough sneer in his voice to aggravate a saint. "Admit it so I can pity-kiss the hell out of you."

"I'll do no such thing. Go pity-kiss *yourself*!"

Unable to stay away—and unsure how much longer he could hide his smile—he closed the distance and hauled her against the solid length of his body. "Accept my offer, and I'll give you a *panty-melting* kiss."

Shivers caused her nipples to rub against his chest. He stilled, his every cell catching fire and burning his control. *She* stilled, though the pulse at the base of her neck raced.

"I suspect you'll give me the panty-melting kiss, anyway," she whispered.

He loved when she was right.

Lazarus claimed her lips with fierce demand. She welcomed the hard thrust of his tongue but she didn't return his volatile passion. Unacceptable. When he opened his mind to hers, he heard the demon wail.

Vengeance will be mine.

He lifted Cameo into his arms and carried her to the bed—where he tossed her onto the mattress.

"Right now, we're the only two people in existence." Reaching overhead, he pulled off his shirt. After removing the apple pendant, he placed it in the top drawer of her nightstand.

Later, he would create an illusion to better hide it. And he would *not* feel guilty.

She stared at the drawer, the wheels in her head clearly spinning. "You still haven't told me—" she began.

"Concentrate on your man. Or rather, my smorgasbord of masculine delights."

Her gaze stroked over him, black pupils spilling over silver irises. She licked her lips, and the sight of her little pink tongue nearly unmanned him. "The biggest thing about you…is your ego. Which is why I shouldn't admit this, but what the hell. You are so beautiful."

"*You* are the beautiful one." His tattoos failed to hide the onslaught of crystal.

Desperate for any contact she would allow, he crawled on top of her. She traced the human heart etched into the center in his chest, and the daggers piercing each of the chambers. Then her fingertip circled his navel, and his gut clenched with desire.

"You want another orgasm, sunshine?" The question was nothing more than a croak. He wanted to give her orgasms. Plural. As in, thousands.

Breath hitched in her throat. "I do. I really, really do. But first I want to see those testicles you mentioned. A girl's gotta inspect her merchandise."

The struggle to hide his smile intensified. "What will you give me in exchange for my cooperation?"

As he'd hoped, the rest of her sorrow gave way to determination. "How about the opportunity to survive this encounter?"

"What's my other option? Dying of pleasure?"

"Yes. No!" She shook a fist at him.

Laughing, he rose to his knees. Their eyes locked, liquid silver against black. Slowly, he unfastened his pants, letting the anticipation build. As need overtook her exquisite features, his amusement drained. Even more slowly, he drew down his zipper.

She gulped. "No underwear?"

"Why bother? I suspect my woman prefers me bare." He pushed the material apart, his erection springing free. He gave his testicles a tug before wrapping his fingers around the base of his shaft. "See. Your merchandise is perfect. Happy now?"

"I think I'm getting there." The husky rasp in her voice drew a bead of moisture from his erection. "I know you're all healed up, but I'm going to write you a prescription for a little Cameo, and I'm ordering you to take me twice a day."

His grip flexed of its own accord. Bloody hell. With a fierce growl, he swooped down and fed her another fiery kiss. He devoured her, and she devoured him right back, the kiss quickly spiraling out of control. His insides turned molten, and his shaft ached. Cameo was more addictive than any drug.

He couldn't get enough of her, this woman who'd enchanted him past all reason. She was passion and pleasure, suddenly his sole reason for breathing.

Fighting tremors, he stripped her. His mind almost couldn't compute the majesty of her beauty. The alabaster skin. Those dusky nipples already hard and ready for him. How delicate her bone structure appeared...a deception. There was no woman stronger.

Between her legs, a small thatch of damp curls begged for his attention. *Helpless to obey...* He sat back on his haunches and placed her legs outside his. The woman who claimed she couldn't come was pink and wet and so very eager.

He ran his finger down her center before slipping it inside her. Her hips arched, and she cried out. When he pulled that finger out of her, she moaned in disappointment.

"Going to give you more. In a bit." He flipped her over and received his first full view of her butterfly. Its antennae rested between her shoulder blades, its thorax perfectly aligned with her spine and its abdomen ended at the crack of her ass. Forewings wrapped around her hips while hindwings wrapped around her thighs. The colors...a thousand colors glittered within a jagged black outline: a feminine blend of purple and pink, with flecks of silver to match her eyes.

Entranced, he traced the butterfly with his tongue and slid his finger back inside Cameo. Wet heat greeted him, and he grunted with satisfaction. She gasped, her inner walls squeezing him, creating a prison he adored.

He worked in a second finger, and she whispered his name. "Lazario." The wonder in her voice puffed up his chest with pride. "Don't stop. Please."

"Never." In... He angled his wrist. Out...

Now she *shouted*. A curse or a request, he wasn't sure. He quickened his pace. In and out, in and out. Her hips rolled as his fingers slid back in. Her head thrashed over the pillow, ribbons of black silk tangling. She gripped the sheet and chewed on her bottom lip, her nails slicing through the cotton. She was the picture of passion and bliss.

In, out. In, out. In, out. Faster and faster. He brushed his thumb over the scorching heart of her, and she quivered. So he did it again...and again.

"Lazario!" She climaxed, her inner walls clenching and unclenching.

"My Cami."

When she went limp, he rolled her over. Satisfaction radiated from her as she smiled up at him, wanton and languid.

That smile...the stuff of dreams.

Savage need pulsed within him, his own orgasm almost shooting from him. He gripped his erection, roughly commanding, "Touch me, sunshine. Please."

She drew a fingertip along her red, kiss-swollen lips. "With my hands or my mouth? I owe you a reward, after all."

"Hands. Mouth." *Give me.* "Both." He would take anything she wanted to give. He would take *everything.*

"I'm going to eat you up," she promised, and he tensed, ready, so ready. "But only after you remove your leathers."

A flicker of panic cooled his ardor. "I want you now. Just like this."

"Off," she said with a shake of her head. Gaze locked on him, she sat up. Her perfect breasts jiggled, and for a moment, he forgot his own name. "Or I keep my lips to myself, and you wish your testicle never grew back."

"Why do you want the leathers off?" he demanded.

"I want to see all of you." Luminous silver eyes beseeched him, her lashes so long they cast shadows over her cheeks. "The way you've seen all of me."

Yes, but he had seen her beauty and strength. She would see in him both his shame and weakness. He would have to explain what had happened to his father, what would one day happen to Lazarus. She might insist they part. On some level, she cared for him. Why else would she trust him with her pleasure? She would want him healthy and whole. She would hate how thoroughly his sense of self-preservation eroded every time he neared her.

Fear of losing her consumed him.

Calm. Steady. She was here, in his arms. Alive and well. He needed her in a way he'd never needed anyone or anything. And he owed her. He had Pandora's box. He couldn't risk telling her about the artifact, but he *could* risk this. His secret shame. If she thought to break up with him, as humans liked to say, he would find a way to change her mind.

"Very well." He stood, embarrassed by his tremors. He kicked off his boots and—*do it, just do it*—removed his leathers, leaving his legs bare.

For several agonizing seconds, she looked her fill. The crystals had spread, branching from his hips to his ankles, every glistening river a burning reminder of his hated fate.

"You are...magnificent," she said, her voice heavy with...awe? "These lines. They're like the ones in your arms. The ones you called wounds. Will I hurt you if I touch them?"

"You'll hurt me if you *don't*."

"Why hide them, then?"

"The lines...they signify a change I cannot stop." Unwilling to meet her gaze, he returned to the bed to settle against a mound of pillows. "A change that overtook my father and ultimately led to his destruction."

"You mean the day Hera attacked him?" Her head tilted to the side. "I don't understand."

And he wasn't going to help her do so. Not here, not now. The demon would use the information against her.

"Later." Lazarus waved an imperial hand at his swollen shaft. "I did my part. Time to do yours."

"Very well." She settled between his legs, remaining on her knees, and pressed her hand over her heart. "Give me a moment to recover from the onslaught of romance."

Her dry tone earned a glower.

Her eyes glittered with a hint of amusement, and his panic receded. His irritation, too, until only arousal remained. Down, down she leaned and flicked her tongue over one of his nipples. Pure, raw sensation blazed through him, and he sucked in a breath.

Her lips left a trail of fire down the ropes of muscle lining his stomach. "You say you are like your father. He's known as the Monster. Is it because of the size of his penis?"

Lazarus nearly choked on his tongue. "Why do you ask?"

"Because yours could qualify as a monster, too. Tell me the truth. You thought I'd be afraid of it, didn't you?"

"No. I feared your reaction to the marks in my legs. They are—"

"Lethal to my inhibitions? Exactly right."

"I...don't know what to say right now." She baffled him.

"Well, that's a first, isn't it?" She turned her attention to his thigh and licked the crystallized vein running from his groin to his knee.

The contact was a shock to his system. His entire body shuddered with pleasure.

As she followed another vein, she reached up and wrapped her fingers around the base of his erection. Groaning, he arched into her touch—and at long last her lips closed around him. She sucked him down, down, all the way to the back of her throat. He roared. The fiery heat…the wet, silken depths of her mouth…too much to survive and yet not enough to save him. Drops of sweat trickled over him. He fisted the sheets. Inside him, ecstasy and pressure combined, tormenting him.

My woman. Mine. Never giving her up.

She sucked on him as if he were a tasty treat. As if she couldn't get enough of him. As if she would *never* get enough of him.

She owned him.

"Yes. Yes!" He wanted to give her the world. Every kingdom. Every jewel. Wanted to throw her enemies at her feet. Wanted to make love with her every night and awaken with her every morning.

Her teeth scraped lightly over the head of his shaft. His hips shot up of their own volition, sending him deeper down her throat. As she moaned her acceptance, the sound sending soft vibrations along his erection, satisfaction crept through him, demanding its due.

Lazarus erupted, climaxing harder than ever before.

Cameo nestled into Lazarus's side. Anyone who'd ever dated anyone would probably tell her clinging was a deal breaker, but she tightened her hold, refusing to let go.

I think I'm falling for him.

Well, why wouldn't she? Each time he'd fought—either the Amazons, bear shifters or Harpies—he'd checked on Cameo first to make sure she was unharmed. When Misery barraged her, he moved heaven and earth to make her happy. He ensured her orgasm before seeking his own.

In many ways, she came before his vengeance, and the realization thrilled her. Maybe they had a chance to go the distance, after all.

What about the visions?

The demon beat at her skull, and a familiar but still strange tingle resonated below the surface of her skin. A tingle she'd experienced since Lazarus's arrival. A tingle she didn't understand—just like she didn't understand his fear of the glistening rivers that ran through his legs.

"Tell me about the change that overtook your father," she said. "What led to his destruction?"

He tensed, but admitted, "The lines you see in my limbs…they are crystals, and they are slowly killing me."

She jackknifed into a sitting position. He tugged her back to his side before she could leap from the bed. "But…you can't be killed. Not for long. Your resurrection is proof."

"Destruction doesn't have to mean death. How do you think Hera was able to capture my father, the strongest man in existence? Because he, too, had begun to crystallize."

Horror turned her blood to icy sludge. "What causes it? Is there a way to stop it?"

"Doesn't matter." He combed his fingers through her hair, petting her. "I've accepted my end. You will, too."

She gave a violent shake of her head. "I will *never* accept your end."

He kissed her temple, sighed. "You must."

"The way you accepted mine when I told you about the vision?" she snapped.

"That's different. Yours can be prevented by a change of action. The crystals are spreading, limiting my range of motion. One day they'll cover me."

Lose him, after she'd only just found him? No! "There must be an antidote."

"Trust me. I exhausted my resources during my search. There's not. And now, I'm turning my efforts to something else. Before my last breath, I will see to the destruction of our enemies."

Not *my.* Not *your.* But *our.* "Lazarus." *I don't want to go on without him.* "We can talk to Torin and Keeley. They can help you—"

"No. I will accept help from no one but you. To do so would reveal my weakness. I will risk being abducted like my father, doomed to live out an existence in paralyzed awareness, unable to change my fate in any way. And you will not break up with me over this," he said. A command, not a question.

"Of course I won't." Why would he think such an awful thing? And was he serious about accepting no help? His pride was *that* great? The reward—more time with her—not enough? "But I *will* find a way to save you."

Already an idea took root. Pandora's box…the Morning Star supposedly still trapped inside. What if the being could remove the crystals?

To free the Morning Star, Cameo would have to find and open the box. She would end up killing herself and her friends in the process. There had to be another way.

"Hope you don't mind," he said, "but I've already planned our week. First, we'll hunt and kill Juliette. Second, we hunt and *imprison* Hera. See? A change of action, a new outcome. You will live. Third, we'll spend every spare minute in bed, making memories to last a thousand lifetimes."

She *had* to convince him to talk to Keeley, the oldest woman in creation, and Torin, the best researcher on the planet. "Actually, *I'll* be attacking Juliette. I tried to tell you earlier, but you distracted me. She challenged me to a duel and claims the winner gets to keep you."

Tension radiated from him. "There will be no duel. The deathblow is mine to mete."

At least he hadn't assumed Juliette would win. Hardly a silver lining, but hey, silver linings of any sort were new to her, so she wasn't going to complain. "I thought you said we'll be working together."

"We will. I will give orders, and you will obey them."

"Dream on, Neanderthal Man. I've been managing my calendar without a Secretary of War for centuries, thanks."

"Too bad. I've dreamed of killing the Harpy for centuries."

Cameo fluffed her pillow. "Before, you were alone. Now you have me. Therefore, your dreams need an overhaul."

"I *do* have you." He nuzzled her cheek. "And I like you like this. Openly admitting you're mine."

Trying to distract her? "You're going to give me your blessing. You're going to watch me fight your enemy on your behalf. You're going to cheer me on while I kick her ass. Consider it your gift to me…since I've given you the gift of my presence."

He gritted his teeth. "Someone's been hanging out with Viola, I see."

Another silver lining: he hadn't contradicted her!

"I have. I like her," she admitted. "I might want to be her when I grow up."

He pinched the bridge of his nose. "You do realize what you're asking of me goes against every fiber of my being, yes?"

"Yes."

"And yet still you ask."

"Wrong," she said. "I don't remember asking, only telling. I mean, what else am I getting out of our deal? Your to-do list benefits only you. What about my list? Talk to Juliette, find Pandora's box. Find a way to free the Morning Star. Maybe, just maybe, save you in the process." *Because I don't want to remember you only to live without you.*

"You can't trust anything the Harpy says." As rigid as steel, he released a sound that was part growl, part sigh. She noticed he had no questions about the Morning Star. He must have heard the rumors. "I did mention we would spend our free time in bed, yes? Orgasms should be numbers one through ten on your list."

"Orgasms are two through ten."

"At least they rate." He scrubbed a hand down his face. "I probably should have hooked up with a weaker woman."

"You *have* hooked up with weaker women. Everyone you dated before me." Cameo rolled on top of him, something odd happening to her face. The corners of her lips were…lifting? A smile was about to bloom! A miracle only Lazarus could perform.

Misery seemed to reach through her mind to petrify the muscles around her mouth, and the urge to smile faded.

"So," she said, and sighed. "Give me your blessing."

He framed her jaw with his big, strong, callused hands. "You will not trust her?"

"Of course not." But even still, Cameo would be checking out any leads about the box.

Lazarus looked up at the ceiling, as if praying for patience. "When you look at me like that, sunshine, I can deny you nothing. You have my blessing."

22

"If you are truly king of your castle, your woman is queen. Treat her like one."
—*The Art of Keeping Your Female Happy*

Lazarus kept Cameo in bed until the last possible second. When he could postpone the inevitable no longer, he flashed her to a remote part of Alaska. A forest surrounded by ice-mountains and supposedly neutral territory for Harpies. They were the first to arrive.

The duel would kick off in an hour. Just enough time to study the terrain, check for traps and ensure Cameo had every advantage.

He erected two tents side by side, since four of Cameo's friends had insisted on coming to force the Eagleshields to play by the rules. Kaia and Gwen, Keeley and Viola. He felt…indebted.

A strange sensation. Especially since he still believed killing Juliette was *his* job. His privilege.

His hands curled into fists. *Has to be this way.* He understood the Harpy way of life better than most. The clans were predatory; when they sensed weakness, they pounced. One way or another, Cameo was going to have to prove her strength, or the Eagelshields would forever view her as easy pickings. And then they would pick, pick, pick at her, even if Lazarus beheaded Juliette before the fight.

"Do you have a pre-battle ritual?" he asked Cameo.

"Doesn't everyone?"

"Do it." He kissed her, lingering as long as possible before his body began to insist he do more. "I want to do another sweep for traps."

"Sir, yes, sir."

He tweaked her nose before taking off and hiking a one-mile radius around the campsite. Mist danced in front of his face every time he exhaled. Perhaps the territory *was* neutral. There were no land mines, no hidden pits or armies lying in wait, ready to attack.

Satisfied, he returned to the tents to find a handful of Eagleshields had arrived at last. They were drinking beer and climbing trees, and they waved when they spotted him.

"Juliette brought a saddle," someone called. "She's planning on riding you hard tonight."

Red winked through his vision. *Keep walking.* If he killed a Harpy now, the clan could cry foul later.

He entered the relative warmth of the tent and took stock.

The box—once again hanging around his neck.

The ring he'd gotten from Viola—hanging right beside it.

The jewels he'd procured for Cameo—still burning a hole in his pocket.

More and more, the first item filled him with sizzling guilt he couldn't escape. If ever Cameo discovered he had the box, she would despise him. She would never forgive him.

I'll be frozen in my crystal form. What will it matter?

He could deal with her hate, but not her death.

Problem: in a frozen state, he would be unable to protect her or the box. If someone stole the relic and used it against Cameo…

He cursed. Maybe he would give the box to one of the Lords on the condition Cameo never know about it, see it or touch it. Amun, keeper of Secrets, had perfected the art of staying quiet. During his possession, he couldn't utter a single word without spilling countless confidences, so he'd said nothing.

Could Lazarus trust him?

Maybe. Probably. Unless Amun's own guilt drove him to confide in his friends. Word would reach Cameo.

Lazarus was unwilling to take chances with her life. If he was going to spend eternity locked in place like the statues he'd created, he had to know Cameo not only lived but thrived.

"You're pacing," Cameo said, calm and cool but not exactly collected. Sorrow dripped from her tone.

His gaze sought her. His gaze always sought her. She sat in front of a crackling fire pit, sharpening a sword he'd never seen her use. A piece of black cloth covered a portion of the hilt.

"Nervous for me?" she asked.

"You will win." A command. He sat beside her, removed the ring from around his neck and drew the chain over her head. If she died today—

She wouldn't die today. He wasn't ready to let her go. Would he *ever* be ready?

Even still, he had to prepare for the worst. The ring might be her only way out of the prison realm. He tucked its weight underneath her shirt.

If the worst happens, I will find her. I will always find her.

"If you think I'll win," she said, "why are you—"

"Always have a backup plan." He dug into his pocket and withdrew the diamond knuckles. "These are for you. Do me a favor and drench them with Juliette's blood."

Her hand trembled as she slid the beautiful weapon in place, the jewels glittering in the light. How lovely they looked pressed against her fair flesh.

"Thank you for the gift and for entrusting me with your wrath," she said. "I won't let you down."

"No, you won't." Her gratitude affected him in an unexpected way, making him feel as if he'd just taken an arrow through the heart. "You are the strongest warrior I know."

She set the sword aside and kicked her leg over his to settle onto his lap. Her luscious fragrance enveloped him as she combed her fingers through his hair.

"Will you grow to resent me for stealing your vengeance?" she asked.

He gripped her waist and pulled her directly against his hardening shaft. They both sucked in a breath. "I've waited a long time to kill Juliette, have dreamed of it, craved it."

Pinching his chin with two fingers, she angled his head, forcing his gaze to meet hers. Arousal had deepened her silver irises to a gunmetal gray. "You didn't answer my question."

Because he had no answer for her. He only knew he

couldn't stop her from fighting without hurting her; therefore he wouldn't stop her.

He cupped her jaw, simply enjoying the look of her, the softness of her skin and the astounding connection they shared. Then he slid his hands into her hair and fisted the silken strands. "Why are you so determined to have a conversation when we could be kissing?"

Her eyes narrowed in slow motion, as if her body had to catch up to her thoughts. "Why do you use kissing as a means of stopping every personal conversation?"

"With you, I'll use any excuse to kiss." He turned swiftly, placing her on her back while he hovered over her. She gasped; he pressed his mouth to hers, stealing a swift taste.

"We shouldn't," she whispered, sounding deliciously scandalized. Need shivered through her. "There's not enough time. People are outside. They'll hear us."

"There's always time. And let the people hear."

Let Juliette *hear. Let her know.*

A petty means of vengeance, but if it served to rattle the Harpy? Sex for the win would make Cameo's victory that much sweeter.

He knelt between her legs, yearning to undress her fully, to devote hours to the butterfly etched into her back, but she was right; time wasn't their friend.

He unsnapped her pants, lowered the zipper…then twisted a finger into the edge of her panties to draw the material away, revealing the hottest, pinkest playground he'd ever seen.

She rasped his name. A plea. One he heeded. He bent his head to lick her, and she screamed his name.

The woman was sweet everywhere. He wasn't content to lick. He sucked and nibbled, and she writhed against him, even began to chant his name. He reveled as the sorrow easily faded from her voice; he *heard* her passion.

He would willingly give up his vengeance for this. How could he resent her?

"Going to have you every day we're together. Just like this," he breathed against her tender flesh.

"Yes." Goose bumps covered her thighs. "Yes!"

His ear twitched as footsteps sounded outside the tent. Roughly fifteen seconds until someone breached the door of the tent. He growled with frustration.

Not ready to stop. Will never be ready!

Lazarus…utterly…devoured her. With a hard press of his tongue, he brought her to a swift and brutal climax. As she convulsed with satisfaction, he righted her clothing, adjusted his hard-on and drew her to a sitting position. Dark hair fell down her arms in tangles.

Perfect timing.

"Yo!" Kaia stuck her head through the flap. "The starting bell is about to ring."

Cameo struggled to calm. Her cheeks possessed a rosy glow, and her lips were slightly swollen from being chewed on.

The redhead winked at him. "Properly motivating our girl, eh?"

The color in Cameo's cheeks only deepened.

"Something like that," he muttered.

Kaia had reason to hate him. As a child, she'd freed him from Juliette's chains. In return, he'd slaughtered many of her friends in his maddened bid to escape. Not that it had done him any good. Weakened as he'd been, Juliette had found—and punished—him soon enough.

But. Years later, Juliette commanded him to break

up Kaia and Strider by any means necessary. The gorier the better. Compelled by the Paring Rod, Lazarus would have plagued the pair forever. He regained free will only long enough to allow Strider to behead him, ensuring the happy couple received their happily-ever-after.

His debt to Kaia had been paid in full.

Lazarus claimed Cameo's hand and pulled her to her feet. With mesmerizing grace, she sheathed her new sword in the pouch hanging from her back.

Acting on instinct, he yanked her against him. "Don't think about me while you're out there. Keep your mind on the task at hand and only the task at hand—winning. Nothing more, nothing less."

While part of him would have enjoyed watching Juliette suffer for hours, the other part of him would rather have Cameo safe…and back in his arms. "Also, if you kill her in under five minutes," he added, "I'll reward you."

Her eyelids grew heavy, her gaze sultry. "With your hands or your mouth?"

"Don't be silly. My cock."

As she mewled her approval, he bent his head to press a hard kiss into her lips, giving her the air from his lungs. He would never get enough of her. She softened against him, thrusting her tongue against his and—

She wrenched from his embrace. Panting, she said, "Juliette will be dead in under five minutes, you have my word. Make sure your zipper is down and your monster is ready." Head high, she stalked from the tent.

He palmed two daggers and followed her out, cold air slapping at his cheeks. The entire Eagleshield clan had arrived, hundreds of Harpies congesting the area.

Cameo's friends stepped from the shadows to lead

the way. Their group stalked forward, menace in every step, and he'd never been prouder. *My woman has this.*

Up ahead, an even larger crowd of Harpies formed a circle—a booing circle.

"Out of our way," Keeley commanded. "I'm not called the Red Queen for nothing. Bodies explode in my presence."

"Or they could stay in our way, and I could use their severed skulls to create designer hag-bags," Viola said.

Kaia and Gwen didn't say a word, just pushed and shoved anyone foolish enough to remain in place. Cameo reached the center of the circle, where Juliette waited.

The sight of his former tormentor gave new life to the fury he'd lived with since their first meeting.

As in the days of old, she wore a bronzed breast-plate, leather wristbands with a matching loincloth, and bronzed thigh and shin guards. How many times had he dressed and undressed her?

Cameo wore black leather with chain-mail inserts to cover her most vulnerable areas: heart, stomach, biceps, thighs and calves. The inserts were lighter than Juliette's bulky armor. Even better, Cameo had made every piece herself, the craftsmanship remarkable.

As she walked, she anchored her hair in a braid. A braid he would later unwind. He would fist the strands as he kissed and licked her from head to toe. She would shout his name, her nails digging into his back. She would demand he take her—fully, nothing held back.

An Eagleshield stepped between the combatants to say, "All right. Let's get this party started. There are no rules. The fight will last as long as it needs to last, and only one woman will walk away. The winner *re-claims* ownership of Lazarus the Cruel and Unusual."

As Harpies cheered, he flared with indignation.

"Enjoy your thoughts about reclaiming him—they're all you'll have. Not that you ever had him. But I do. I have him. He *chose* me of his own free will. No Paring Rod or compulsion necessary." Cameo unsheathed her sword, the metal whistling.

While most of the crowd flinched or cried, he smiled and blew his woman a kiss. She'd just claimed him publicly.

Juliette screeched as she unsheathed her own sword. "The Mother of Melancholy dies today!"

Cheers resounded once again.

"What are you waiting for?" Grinning, the announcer rushed backward. "Go!"

The starting bell. The crowd whistled and called out advice as Cameo and Juliette circled each other, two hungry predators with a meal in sight. Cameo slipped but managed to remain upright, the tread on her boots offering little protection against the slick ice covering the ground.

He cursed. Why hadn't he considered her shoes?

"Curious about Pandora's box?" Juliette asked her. Her boots possessed small metal spikes, making her gait smooth and graceful.

"Where is it?" Cameo demanded, and Juliette cringed. "Do you know?"

Lazarus stiffened. She'd asked. Why had she asked? She'd said she wouldn't trust the Harpy.

"You should question my consort," Juliette said, smug now. "According to Hera, he stole it."

He cursed. Cameo jolted and lost her footing. Of

course, Juliette chose that moment to strike, lunging at Cameo and swinging her sword.

"No!" he shouted.

At the last second, Cameo spun out of the way and blocked. Impact caused her to slip, and this time she couldn't stop her fall.

Juliette thrust her sword with deadly precision, but Cameo rolled the second she hit the ground and the sharpened tip hit the ice.

With a push of her legs, Cameo slid between Juliette's legs and jumped up behind the Harpy, a semiautomatic palmed and aimed. *Boom! Boom!* Even at close range, the bullets pinged off Juliette's armor without causing her any bodily harm.

Scowling, the Harpy turned and tossed a dagger. The weapon sliced into Cameo's wrist. She dropped the gun, and a smug Juliette picked it up.

Lazarus settled his weight into his heels. *Do not move. Do. Not. Move. Cameo has this.*

Juliette fired at Cameo, emptying the magazine. Miracle of miracles, Cameo managed to dodge every bullet.

Dropping the empty gun, the Harpy stalked closer to her target…closer still. Cameo wrenched out the dagger and blocked Juliette's next sword thrust. She parried, spun and delivered an attack of her own. *Clang, clang, clang.*

The females began a brutal dance, moving almost too quickly to track. Almost. Still he looked away, lest he step between the two combatants and snap Juliette's neck like a twig. His gaze landed on a woman gliding on the ice just outside the circle, and he stiffened.

Hera.

She watched him with steady intent as she traced a

fingertip down her biceps, letting him know she had noticed the crystals on his arm.

The red dots returned to his vision. *Remain in place. Do not move.* A command from the depths of his soul. If he distracted Cameo, heralding her harm, he would forever regret it.

Was that Hera's hope? Propel him into action, make him become the catalyst to Cameo's doom?

Bitch. He tightened his grip on his daggers but did nothing else. A task easier than it should have been, considering the wrath that lived inside him. But then, he remembered the vision of Cameo's future. Kill Hera, kill Cameo.

One enslavement, coming up. He would defeat the queen and save the girl.

When Cameo grunted in pain, his attention returned to the fight, though he kept Hera in his periphery. If she made a play for his woman, he would be ready.

Juliette had landed a blow, slicing into Cameo's vulnerable neck. Blood poured from the wound, crimson splatters decorating the ice. He inhaled sharply, unsure how deep the wound reached. She collapsed to her knees, the next collision knocking the dagger from her hand.

Her motions slowed, but still she managed to flip backward, avoiding another wound. When she straightened, she was covered in ice shavings, her body stripped of weapons. The diamond knuckles and few daggers she'd had left had been stolen by Eagleshields.

Kaia and Keeley managed to retrieve the diamond knuckles, and tossed them to Cameo. She caught them as a smiling Juliette dived for her.

Just before impact, Cameo crouched. The Harpy

soared over her head, and Cameo latched onto the edge of her breastplate, jerking her to a stop and flipping her midair. Juliette lost her grip on her sword as she landed and gasped for breath.

Cameo straddled her shoulders and whaled, the diamond knuckles shredding the Harpy's once-pretty face. Blood sprayed the ice. A tooth soared through the air. Finally, though, Juliette bucked free, tossing Cameo to her back.

In unison, they stood and faced each other.

The Eagleshields offered suggestions to Juliette. "Rip out her still-beating heart!"

"Kick her in the baby maker!"

"Take her eyeballs as trophies!"

Juliette raised an arm, and cheers rang out.

Cameo looked around, a look of resignation darkening her features. She raised her chin…and hummed a soft, haunting melody.

Curses sounded. Harpies covered their ears. Hera flinched.

Cameo continued to hum. Some of the Harpies dropped to their knees. Others sobbed and raced from the clearing. Even Kaia, Gwen and Keeley cried. Viola paled.

Lazarus began to *tremble*. In seconds, sorrow washed through him, filling and nearly drowning him. And when it finally drained, it left a sticky film behind. Cameo's voice had never hit him so hard or so deep. He'd only ever wanted to take her into his arms and protect her from the travesties she'd had to live with every day, every hour, every minute.

This time was different.

He had no defense against a sudden onslaught of memories. Every action he'd ever regretted. Flashes of everyone he'd ever loved and lost. Dark thoughts followed: *I will never have what I crave most. Will only be strong enough to defeat Hera without Cameo at my side. I'm weakened already...but I don't think I can survive without Cameo. This is an impossible situation. There's no hope. No hope.*

"Stop," Juliette commanded, pressing her palms against her ears. "You have to stop this!"

Cameo sang her response, the words sharper than any weapon she'd wielded. "There are no rules, remember?" She picked up the Harpy's fallen sword and slowly approached.

Juliette hunched over and sobbed. Cameo's voice contained a thousand disappointments and regrets, each bleeding into Lazarus's own...offering an invitation to at last end his suffering. Here and now. The world would be a better place without him. So much better.

The eerie melody had a life of its own, a dark life, bleak. And so powerful it cast a terrible shadow over the land. Already cold air became frigid. Birds squawked and flew from the trees. No, not from the trees but *into* the trees. Trying to kill themselves? Anything to escape the brutal spiral of hopelessness and despair!

Lazarus trembled harder when he realized he'd pressed the tip of a dagger into his chest, ready to plunge the blade into his heart.

Death...the only way to experience peace...

He couldn't stop himself. Stop, had to stop...

At the last second, he lifted the dagger and stabbed one of his ears. He repeated the motion with the other ear. Sharp pain exploded inside his head and warm liquid trickled down his neck; at least the sense of hopelessness faded.

He ground his teeth, knowing soul deep he'd just experienced a taste of what Cameo experienced on a daily basis. How had she managed to survive as long as she had?

His poor, darling female.

Words had power to build up or tear down, and she'd certainly proved it this day. She'd torn down his every defense, leaving only raw vulnerability. For Juliette, too.

The Harpy dropped to her knees as tears streamed down her cheeks. She crawled to a fallen dagger, though she stopped midway to dry-heave. With a quick jab, jab, she stabbed herself in the ears. But she was too late.

Cameo struck once, twice, and both of Juliette's hands thumped to the ground. The Harpy screamed in agony, clutching the gushing stumps to her chest.

With a cold smile lacking any hint of amusement, Cameo dropped the sword and caught the odd little weapon Viola tossed at her. She removed the cloth over the end, and Lazarus stilled, not even daring to breathe as recognition slammed into him. The Paring Rod.

"No," Juliette cried. He couldn't hear her voice, but he could read her lips.

In a desperate bid to escape Cameo and the Rod, she scrambled toward the crowd. When no one stepped forward to help her, she climbed to unsteady legs, swayed.

"This is for Lazarus." Cameo stabbed the Harpy in the throat. "You enslaved him in the Harpy camp. Now I enslave you in the spirit realms."

Again he had to read lips.

With another push, Cameo caused the bulbous tip to come out Juliette's other side. Blood gurgled from her mouth. A second later, she vanished, the tip of the

Rod glowing bright blue, charged by the passing of a new life force.

All that remained of Juliette was the pool of crimson she'd left behind.

And it was done. Just like that. One of his greatest enemies had been slain. He expected to feel pleasure and contentment, or barring that, disappointment and resentment. As he stalked forward, he experienced only relief. Cameo was unharmed.

After carefully sheathing the Paring Rod in leather, he pried the weapon from Cameo's grip and drew her into his arms. He refused to contemplate what this meant for him. What this meant for their relationship.

Over Cameo's head, he met Hera's gaze, and he smiled. Tears glimmered in her eyes. Because she'd just lost a friend, or because Misery had filled her with sorrow, too?

The goddess vanished. Weakened? *There must be a chink in her armor...*

There might not be a better chance to strike. He should give chase. But as he prepared to flash away, he realized Cameo hadn't returned his embrace. He frowned and pulled back to look her over.

Misery pulsed from her. Her silver eyes were dull, her expression contorted with pain.

The demon had taken over.

Her gaze met his, tears trapped in her lashes. "Kill me," she whispered. "Please."

23

"You cannot take a strong man's castle without first weakening him. Once you've taken it, give it to your woman for safekeeping."
—*The Art of Keeping Your Female Happy*

Misery consumed Cameo. In every sense of the word. The demon reminded her of a family of termites; she was the crumbling house, her foundation already riddled with holes. Every hour—every minute—he reminded her of every torture she'd ever endured. Of Alex's death and Lazarus's doom.

My fault. All my fault.

One hundred percent of the population feels they would be better off without you...

During the fight with Juliette, Cameo had done the unthinkable. She'd allowed Misery to fill her with the worst of his sorrows, pricking the worst of her regrets. The overflow had spilled out, vanquishing her opponent. But victory had come at a terrible price. Dark thoughts now mired Cameo's mind, and no matter how hard she tried, she couldn't escape them.

No hope, no hope. She no longer believed she could live a better life. Lazarus was dying, crystals growing inside his veins, and she had no idea how to save him.

Her mind hurt. Her *soul* hurt. Who was she kidding? *Every* part of her hurt. Misery used her fear and grief for Lazarus, playing her heart like a violin.

"A terrible melody haunts her," she'd heard Lazarus explain to her friends. He was right. She'd never felt so alone or helpless.

Logically she knew the feelings were a lie. Of course she knew. Her friends loved her and would do anything in their power to aid her. Lazarus had said he planned to stay with her for the remainder of his days. But truth and logic meant nothing right now.

Tears spilled down her cheeks and tremors rocked her. She lay in bed with no idea how Lazarus had gotten her home. Not because the demon had wiped her memory, but because she had retreated mentally. One day bled into another, the agony inside her never easing.

Through it all, she had no desire to eat or drink—*just let me die*—but Lazarus the Cruel and Unusual forced food and water down her throat. She would have fought him, but she lacked the energy.

She had no desire to shower, either, but more than once he'd carried her to the bathroom stall, stripped her and soaped her off. Again, she'd lacked the energy to fight him. Not that it mattered. He'd never made a pass at her and she…hadn't cared. *Didn't* care. Really.

He often paced through the room with swords strapped to his back and daggers in hand, as if he expected Hera or his father to pop in. His last two enemies, not counting Misery, who he'd threatened a time or twenty.

Cameo dozed fitfully, her dreams turbulent. The demon loved to show her ways she could be hurt. For the past few nights she'd seen Lazarus's funeral on constant repeat.

When she awoke, Maddox sat in a chair beside her bed and glared at her. "Want me to throw your visitor out the window?"

"You may try," Lazarus responded on her behalf. "Also, I'm not the visitor here. You are. What's hers is mine."

"You speak like a husband," Maddox snapped. "I don't recall attending a wedding."

"I speak like her man. Exactly what I am."

"Then do a better job of taking care of her."

Lazarus unleashed a string of curses, and Maddox responded in kind. Both males were vicious beasts clearly vying for the title of king of the jungle.

As keeper of Violence, Maddox had a temper more volatile than most. The big brute stomped toward Lazarus, menace radiating from him. Cameo watched, detached from the situation...but also enraptured by it.

Lazarus met him halfway, completely unfazed. As soon as they were within reach, he used Maddox's thigh as a step stool, wrapping a leg around the warrior's neck, shifting his weight and pushing the warrior to the floor. Upon landing, he rolled, tossing Maddox onto his back and standing to loom over her friend.

With a roar, Maddox kicked him in the chest, sending him flinging backward. In seconds, both males were on their feet and throwing punches. A spectacular display of masculine aggression, yes, but one she should stop.

To do so, she would have to speak. If she spoke, she would only make things worse.

Can't win for losing. Face it, I'm destined to hurt everyone around me.

Besides, if Lazarus wanted to kill Maddox, the male would be dead. Ripped to ribbons like the griffin.

The guys continued fighting, razing her room, destroying every piece of furniture, including the bed. One of the posters toppled and the footboard cracked, jamming the mattress at an odd angle. If Lazarus hadn't locked her mirror in her closet earlier, she would have lost it, too.

In the end, Lazarus snapped Maddox's neck—a fact that sent the other warriors in residence over the edge. Gideon and the newly returned Paris rushed into the room.

"You had no right," Paris grated.

Gideon smiled. "I'm going to hate what comes next."

Another battle broke out, but Lazarus won that one, too. Though not as quickly or as easily. His motions had slowed as if he'd been weakened. Maybe he had. Those crystals…

Going to lose him one way or another.

The rest of her family raced into the bedroom, spotted the unconscious Maddox, Gideon and Paris on her floor—and gales of laughter soon rang out.

The laughter only darkened her mood.

No fair! They do what I can't.

What you will never *do*, Misery vowed.

Lucien, keeper of Death, patted Lazarus on the shoulder. At some point, he, too, must have returned from the underworld. "I like you. I like you a lot."

The balcony doors swung open, and Galen stormed

inside the room. Tall, blond and tanned with white wings still in the process of growing back.

"Well, well. Look who's back." Reyes cracked his knuckles.

Galen had been coming around more and more lately, and so far, no one had killed him. He was trying to make peace, if not amends.

He must not have had any luck with Legion.

Aeron dropped from a wire and landed on the balcony, then trailed after Galen. Dude. Had he rappelled from a helicopter? Wind blistered in, and the sound of whapping hit her ears.

Lazarus pointed an accusing finger at Galen. "Your Hunters once cut out Cameo's tongue."

"I know." Unrepentant, the blond spread his arms wide. "You're welcome."

A ferocious growl echoed, the promise of a bad, bad death. The most feminine part of Cameo responded to the masculine resonance, and she thought, hoped, she would pull herself from the depths of sorrow…but she failed.

Galen scrubbed a hand down his face. "She is who she is because of her past. Do you like who she is or not?"

Her ears perked. Good question.

"I…do," Lazarus admitted grudgingly.

Again she tried to pull herself up. Again she failed.

"Wow. Galen isn't wrong." Anya leveled a disgusted look at Lucien, her fiancé. "Does this mean I have to forgive him for spearing me to a wall?"

"No," Lucien said with a shake of his head.

At the same time, Galen said, "Yes. I'm going to be

part of your group whether you want me or not. I will win Legion. One day," he added with a grumble.

Torin, who used to remain inside his own room no matter what happened, stood in the midst of the crowd. Since he'd learned his blood contained the antidote to his demon's disease, he'd become a lot more social.

"Looks like *Legion* doesn't want you," he said. "Otherwise you'd still be with her."

Galen flipped him off. "Maybe I'm taking my time. Slow seduction versus bull in china shop."

He stalked out of the room, and Torin followed.

Lazarus eased onto the mattress, sitting beside her, and linked their fingers. He rubbed his thumb over her bruised knuckles. "Come back to me. Please."

She tried. She tried so hard, desperate to do this for him. But the sorrow remained, clawing and ripping at her, leaving her insides bloody. Tears filled her eyes, and her chin trembled.

He opened his mouth to say more, but Sabin stepped forward and clapped once, twice. "All right. The party is over. We're all part of the same team, and we've got things to discuss." He was the original warmonger, always putting business before pleasure. "Over the past week, two new battles have waged between Hades and Lucifer. Hades won the first round, thanks to Katarina's hellhounds. They enjoyed a sweet little game called Fetch the Femur, ripping through enemy ranks to collect their prizes. The second round was a draw with massive losses on both sides."

Murmurs and speculations arose. How to ambush Lucifer, leader of the Harbingers—those who granted foreknowledge. How to achieve maximum results. The interaction only saddened Cameo further.

These men and women were a unit. Part of the same team, as Sabin had said. Cameo had forever been on the fringes.

"Out," Lazarus bellowed, his hard voice echoing from the walls. "Now. Everyone."

Protests erupted. When he leaped to his feet, those protests ended and footsteps sounded.

Ashlyn alone remained. Well, Ashlyn and the unconscious men on the floor. No one had bothered to drag them out. The woman took Lazarus's place on the bed.

He stared at her, doing his best to intimidate her, but she remained far from cowed.

"My husband is napping a few feet away. I'm staying, and I'm going to help my friend," she said. "Try to stop me. Dare you."

She had a gift. When she stepped into a room, she could hear every conversation that had ever taken place inside it. Considering she'd just used Lazarus's own words against him, she must have heard some of the things the warrior had said to Cameo.

"Fine," he grumbled.

"So gracious." For over an hour, Ashlyn read from the pages of a romance novel. Fairy tales for adults, she'd once called them. Oh, to be part of a fairy tale with Lazarus, destined to have a happily-ever-after.

Impossible. This is it, Misery said. *The best you're ever going to get.*

Cameo believed him.

The next day, Lazarus fed and bathed her, as usual, remaining impersonal and personal at the same time. He touched her without any outward sign of emotion, but his fingers lingered on her breasts and between her legs. At first, she experienced a tingle of arousal. With arousal came hope.

The demon whispered, *He's going to die. I wonder if you are the reason.*

She cried. Lazarus dried her off and carried her back to bed.

How much longer would he live? How much longer would he put up with her?

Viola visited her and minded her manners, stretching out beside Cameo to tell her all about the armor she had designed, intending to keep herself and her pet safe from a winged beast with death on his mind. All she needed Cameo to do was make it.

Cameo drifted into a light doze, waking when she heard Lazarus's voice. He spoke in Typhonish, and he sounded angry. Through the shadows in the room, she glimpsed him standing on her balcony, wind whipping his hair as a storm raged. No sign of Viola or anyone else. Until lightning struck the sky. For a split second, she saw a sky serpent perched on the railing, his claws wrapped around the iron bar.

Her heart fluttered and—

Nothing. She closed her eyes. When next she woke, the storm had stopped.

Lazarus opened the bedroom door and a laughing Urban and Ever rushed inside. The little boy jumped on the end of the bed. When Cameo failed to react, he set her covers on fire. Ever doused the flames with a glaze of ice.

Life continues without me.

Cameo sighed, and the twins stopped laughing. Ever sobbed, and Urban teared up.

With a sigh of his own, Lazarus rushed the children into the hall and shouted for their parents.

What kind of monster are you, making those sweet babies cry? Misery asked.

Claw, rip. The sorrow sharpened, and her internal wounds hemorrhaged.

Lazarus returned to her side and smoothed away the hair that clung to her dampened cheek. "What am I going to do with you, sunshine?"

The demon had a million answers, none of them good.

Cameo's mind played a word-association game, making the leap from "none of them good" to "nothing good can happen" to "remember he's destined to die," to "everyone's going to die at some point" to "Pandora's box will kill us all." Juliette had said Lazarus already possessed the box. Had she spoken true, or had she sought to drive a wedge between her consort and his new slice?

Definitely a wedge. No way would Lazarus keep such a huge secret. He knew how much Cameo wanted— *needed*—that box. How the very survival of her loved ones depended on it.

Why would he want Pandora's box, anyway?

Well, that question was easy to answer. The Morning Star.

But if Lazarus had the box and wanted the Morning Star, why not open the box and *take* it?

Another easy answer. He feared killing Cameo the instant he lifted the lid.

He should kill me. I'm better off dead. Everyone *will be better off.*

"Enough," Lazarus said, the fury in his voice unmistakable. "Do not ever think like that again. *No one* is better off without you. Understand?"

With his words, something inside Cameo broke. His gaze had so often smoldered at her, promising her untold delights. His hands and body had touched her naked curves on more than one occasion, willing to dish those delights. Now all she could do was pray for death?

Cameo curled into her pillow and sobbed until she had no more tears to give. "My pleasure-feeling days are over." It was the first time she'd spoken in days—weeks?—and her raw throat protested.

"They are only beginning. You know this." Soft fingers combed through her hair, traced down the ridges of her spine before forcing her to roll to her side and gaze up at him. "This isn't you, sunshine." He cuddled behind her and kissed her nape. "Fight the demon. Fight for *me*."

What good had fighting ever done her? Always she ended up in this condition. "Go away. Please. Just go away."

For the first time in their acquaintance, he cringed at the sound of her voice.

No, not the first time. After the battle with Juliette, she'd seen the blood dripping from his ears. Like the Harpy, he'd stabbed himself to escape Cameo's voice.

He said nothing more.

Ensuring you won't utter another response.

"That's a lie of the demon," he grated. "I hate seeing you this way."

"Don't worry. You'll grow tired of this—of me—soon enough. Then you'll leave, and you won't have to see me at all." Though she thought her tear ducts dry, a new rain poured down her cheeks, scalding her skin.

The bed bounced, signaling Lazarus had risen. Footsteps pounded, creating an ominous soundtrack. Lights deluged the bedroom, chasing away precious shadows.

She cringed, blinking rapidly to soothe the burn in her tired eyes. "Off," she commanded.

"You want them off, you get your ass up and turn them off. I've coddled you long enough." With a dark scowl, he stomped to the bed.

The sight of him and his crackling fury cowed Misery, the demon hiding in the back of her mind, the cloud of oppression lifting… But he'd tasted the sweet reins of control and refused to relinquish them so easily. He hissed and clawed, and doom's tempestuous storm rolled back in.

Lazarus ripped the covers from her, cool air suddenly enveloping her. After the last shower, he'd dressed her in a tank top and a pair of panties. Motions firm and without a care for her tender flesh, he picked her up and draped her over his shoulder in a fireman carry. His stride long and without grace, he made his way to the door and threw it open.

One by one, her friends exited their rooms.

He growled, "This is happening. Don't try to stop me."

"Stop you? I'm too busy cheering you." Maddox, who had recovered from his broken spine, sounded downright friendly just then. "You should have done this days ago."

Lazarus smacked Cameo on the butt. Right there. In front of everyone. The sharp sting made her gasp.

"Can I keep him, Lucien?" Anya clapped. "Pretty please with a cherry on top of me. For the last five seconds, I've always wanted one!"

"Only if I can keep him, too," Lucien replied. "Although there's still something off about him. Death goes crazy every time he's near."

"Lies doesn't." The denial came from Gideon.

"You took the words right out of my mouth," Strider said. "Or you would have, if you'd told the truth and mentioned Defeat. So what's the problem? How do you provoke the demons, dead man?"

Her friends sensed the box, too?

Lazarus ignored the question and gave Cameo's butt another smack. Her back teeth ground together.

"What did you do with her the last time she got like this?" Lazarus asked no one in particular.

"We waited," Sabin said. "Everything we tried made her worse."

"Well, I'm done waiting." Lazarus bypassed the group and pounded down the stairs.

To her annoyance, everyone followed him, eager to discover what he'd do next. Kane, the newly crowned king of the Fae, was among them. When had he returned from the underworld? Even Torin tagged along, the traitor!

Why had he dated her, anyway? What an ill-matched pair they'd been, unable to touch. Or rather, unwilling to touch, because she *could* have touched him; she wouldn't have gotten sick—probably—but she would have become a carrier, like him. They hadn't known about his cure back then.

They'd pleasured themselves while the other watched. Well, she'd pretended to pleasure herself. She'd faked every orgasm. Should she tell him? He would return to his room in a huff, and she'd have one less spectator.

"Don't worry, sunshine," Lazarus said. "I'll make sure he knows by the end of the day."

Her teeth ground together with a little more force. She erected the shield around her mind. "Unlike Misery, I find no enjoyment in hurting others. Don't say a word to him."

Groans swept through the crowd, but this time Lazarus gave no notice of her voice.

The demon prowled from the shadows, desperate to recover every inch of ground he'd lost. *Couldn't keep Kane, couldn't keep Torin, won't keep Lazarus.*

She whimpered. Lazarus gave her butt another smack.

Now she huffed and puffed. How dare he! "If you liked and respected me *at all*, you wouldn't treat me this way."

"It's *because* I like and respect you that I'm treating you this way." And just to be contrary, she was sure, he gave her another smack. He used more force, most definitely leaving a palm print.

Anger sparked. Why was he doing this? Where was he taking her?

He kicked open the front door and strode outside. Sunlight seeped into her skin, warming the bone-deep chill she hadn't realized she had felt. He stopped somewhere in the front yard and dropped her.

Splat! Thick, gooey mud bespattered her from head to toe, droplets snagging in her hair and even her eyelashes.

How dare he! A prolonged lack of mobility had left her weak, and her legs trembled as she stood. Mud oozed from her hands.

Lazarus poked a finger into her chest, and her feet

slipped out from under her. She fell, and this time she stayed down, glaring up at him.

"Is this supposed to send me into a fury?" she demanded. *Because it's working!*

"Don't be silly. What happens *next* is supposed to send you into a fury."

24

"~~With an enemy, death should always come be-~~
~~fore surrender~~ With your woman, your surrender
will happen one way or another. Why fight it?"
—~~The Art of Keeping Your Female Happy~~
—*The Secret to My Success*

Viola couldn't believe the turn of events. She whistled
and cheered. The guys clapped.

"Take it all off!" Anya cheered.

"What happens next?" Cameo asked Lazarus.

A slow smile overtook his gorgeous face, and he
cracked his knuckles. "I'd rather show you."

Viola watched as he pelted the keeper of Misery
with one mud ball after another, envy creating a vise
grip around her heart. *I want this...this...fun. This acceptance.*

As Cameo ducked and dodged the missiles, sput-
tering with indignation and spitting out dirt, Lazarus
barked out a laugh.

The rusty sound enchanted everyone around him.

The women preened as if he'd just morphed into the fairy-tale prince of their dreams. The men simply stared.

For the first time since her return from the Alaskan wilderness, a cloud of darkness lifted from Cameo. "Darkpit," she said, "you're going to pay for this."

A miracle happened. No one flinched or cried at the sound of her voice. Not that Cameo or Lazarus seemed to notice. They were too absorbed in each other.

"If you'd like this *savage* attack to end, you're going to have to stop me," Lazarus said. "I respond only to kisses."

The onlookers waited with bated breath for her response.

"Don't you dare—" she began. A mud ball splattered in her face. "You're going to regret—" More mud in her face.

Lazarus's smile was smug. "I regret nothing."

Cameo's screech of fury caused everyone to cheer. Then the dark-haired beauty hurled a mud ball at her man. The ooey-gooey substance drenched his shirt, and a wicked light glowed in his eyes, mixing with relief.

He truly cared about Cameo's well-being, Viola realized. Those two crazy kids just might go the distance.

Lazarus knocked Cameo into the puddle, dirty water splashing around them. They struggled and strained together, vying for supremacy, doing their best to pin the other down. They were acting like children and—dude! So were the others.

Maddox, Sabin, the Harpies and everyone else who'd followed the unlikely pair outside rushed into the pond to launch their own missiles.

Viola, the sole (intelligent) holdout, remained in place. She practiced decorum in all situations. *When*

*you think class and sophistication, you think goddess
of the Afterlife and her pet Tasmanian devil.* Every—
freaking—time.

Urban, the rat, threw mud at her, but she performed
an expert duck and slide.

Even Strider, keeper of Defeat, joined the festivities.
How foolish! If he lost a single challenge, even one as
innocent as this, he would suffer unimaginable pain.
Why risk it? And yet, he laughed as he pinioned his
consort to the ground and stuffed her pants with mud.

Maddox held his squirming, laughing children upside down and threatened to dip their faces into the
puddle. "You've got to stop pestering Viola. I mean it."

"I don't pester," the boy protested. "I woo!"

Gwen pounced on Sabin, sending him to his knees.
"You deserve this. You know you do. Take your punishment like a good boy."

Torin covered his mouth with a gloved hand, trying
to hide a smile while his wife—girlfriend, whatever!—
did the backstroke in the pond.

"Come on in. The water's warm," Keeley called. As a
Curator, the beautiful pink-haired babe had been created
long before humans. Once a spirit of light, she had been
tasked with the safekeeping of Earth, bound to it and its
seasons. She was still bound to earth itself. Dirt healed
and revitalized her. "Don't worry about getting dirty."

"Yes, but my mind is *already* dirty," Torin responded. "I should probably keep my body clean. You
know, to balance things out."

A mud-drenched Cameo raced around the edge of
the pond as Lazarus launched handfuls of sludge at her.
She hollered like a loon and flipped him off.

"Be still, woman, and experience the full breadth of my wrath," Lazarus commanded with mock ferocity.

"Never!" Cameo shook a fist in the air. "You can take your wrath and shove it where the sun doesn't shine!"

Absolutely, positively, horrifically *children*. And yet, within Viola the vise grip of envy only sharpened.

No one cares enough about me to toss mud at me, she lamented. *I'm practically invisible. These people would be happier without me...*

Oh, no. Since Cameo had fully given in to her dark side, those kinds of thoughts had been coming more frequently, as if Misery had trumped Narcissism and spilled into Viola. Or maybe the two now worked together?

She missed the days when Narcissism loved her self-pride, even as it destroyed her. But she supposed the fault was her own. As she'd ruined one relationship after another, she'd grown to hate herself, and her demon discovered a new love: building *himself* up while tearing her down. Sadly, he would never grow to hate himself.

She deserved his rancor, really. She'd torn down others for centuries. This was payback.

"Jerk!" someone called, drawing her from her thoughts.

A pair of gorgeous white wings flared from Olivia's back as she laughingly pushed Aeron into the mud.

Fluffy ran circles around Viola's feet, chasing his tail. The excited atmosphere had jacked up his energy level.

She scanned the yard. Galen stood off to the side, leaning against a tree, his arms crossed over his chest. He was as much of an outsider as she was, unsure how to insert himself, not sure where—or if—he fit in the mania.

If you want different results, you must do something different.

Very well. She would force herself to play.

With a grimace, Viola inched toward the disgusting pond. Before she could talk herself into dipping in a toe, Cameo, the sneaky bitch, moved behind her and shoved her in.

When she sat up, mud sticking in her lashes, her once-depressed best friend fist-pumped the sky. "I'm queen of the jungle pond. Hear me roar!"

A smile teased the corners of Viola's mouth. Perhaps playing wasn't so bad. "You may have won the battle," she said, gathering a mud ball of her own, "but you'll never win the war." She launched her abundant supply, but Cameo managed to dodge.

"I'm untouchable! Unbeatable! Too hot to handle!" The overly confident darling performed a ridiculous little dance, earning another rusty laugh from Lazarus.

See! I'm someone. I'm needed here. No one *would be happier without me.*

Movement in the distance drew her focus. Viola stilled, scrutinizing the thick, vibrant forest with massive hickories, oaks and a willow. The sky created a dark gray backdrop; the storms might have ended, but the sun hadn't yet gotten the memo.

Fluffy sensed her unease and stilled, the hair on his back lifting. Tasmanian devils were known for their wild rages and propensity for biting.

Where had—

There! Two oaks towered side by side, and despite

the lack of wind, a branch on each tree jiggled, as if the two were shaking hands, a deal made with the devil.

Threat? A wild animal? Had the fallen Sent One found her?

Why did her blood warm at the thought?

Fluffy issued a soft but fierce warning growl as he moved in front of Viola, standing guard. She vaulted up, slipped and fought to right herself. Meanwhile, the leaves gave another jiggle, the offender—offenders?—hidden by shadows.

Multiple things seemed to happen in a blink of time.

A thin twig rocketed from the shadows. No, not a twig. An arrow. The deadly missile sliced through the air with a speed no human would have been able to track. Destination: Cameo's heart.

Acting on instinct, Viola flashed in front of her friend—and caught the arrow in a tight fist.

Narcissism bellowed with indignation. She'd dared to place herself in danger to save someone else? The horror!

That's right, she snapped, the arrow breaking in her fist. *And I'll do it again.*

I'll punish you...

She shuddered.

"Viola," Cameo gasped out. "You... I..."

Around her, the warriors stopped laughing. Everyone froze. Then chaos erupted.

"You're the target," Lazarus barked at Cameo. "Get down and stay down." With the stealth of a predator, he bolted from the pond, not heading for cover but for the trees. His arms and legs pumped quickly, fiercely, his speed soon rivaling the arrow. And yet, his motions were...stiff, lacking his usual grace. Was he injured?

Maddox and Ashlyn hurried the children inside the castle while everyone but Cameo and Viola rushed after Lazarus.

"Thank you." Cameo approached Viola's side. "If the arrow had hit its mark, I would have been in pain, and the demon would have pounced, desperate to regain his power over me. I owe you big-time."

"What can I say?" She fluffed her hair, an action as ingrained as breathing. "Saving lives is what supermodel-heroes do. We can't help ourselves."

Cameo's gaze darted to the path Lazarus had taken. "I think I'm into supermodel-heroes. If you aren't careful, I'm going to fall in love with you and ask you to marry me."

The praise was better than a warm bath. "You wouldn't be the first. Or the last."

Cameo picked up the broken part of the arrow, studied it and pursed her lips. "I recognize this craftsmanship."

In the distance, a mud-splattered Lazarus emerged from the line of trees. He carried an Amazon under each arm. The Lords and their ladies trailed behind him, and oh, wow, that was a whole lot of sexy to behold.

"What do Amazons want with us?" Anya demanded.

Lazarus dropped the Amazons at Cameo's feet. Twine had been used to truss up the pair like pigs on a spit. Probably thanks to Keeley, who could grow a plant from seed to maturity in a heartbeat.

As the Amazons fought for freedom, Lazarus grabbed them by the hair, holding their heads at an uncomfortable angle. A position the two *couldn't* fight without breaking their necks.

The other warriors aimed semiautomatics, swords, and the very bow the Amazons had used.

"Dare you to make another move," Strider said with an evil grin.

"Please make a move," Kaia begged. "I love to see my guy in action. Plus? Post-battle sex. 'Nuff said."

Lazarus peered at Viola, his black eyes fierce. "Thank you for saving Cameo from harm." His tone had a ragged quality, as if the words had been pushed through a window of broken glass. "I owe you a boon. Whatever you wish."

Some of his fury was directed at himself, she could tell. He'd failed to sense the Amazons before they'd lobbed off a shot at his woman, after all.

"Yes, you do owe me." Viola rubbed her hands together. What should she choose? The heart of McCadden's brother? A sky serpent of her own? Lazarus's life force?

Oh! There were too many options. "Perhaps you owe me two boons?" she said, nails tapping against her chin. "I mean, I saved more than Cameo. I saved *the day*."

He ran his tongue over his teeth. "One boon. No more."

Her shoulders drooped a little. "Fine. I'll name my prize at a later date." She needed time to think this through.

To Cameo, he said, "You remember the woman who killed my guard, I'm sure. Her tribe—those who still live—received word of her placement in my Garden of Perpetual Horror. They seek vengeance."

"The statues," Cameo said, her eyes widening. "You turned the Amazons to stone."

He gave a curt nod.

He could turn people to stone? How cool was that!

These newest Amazons looked to be from one of the Asian clans. Their beauty was jaw-dropping. They'd branded their faces and bodies with symbols she didn't recognize.

The older one spit at Cameo. "You choose to be with a murderer. You will suffer his same fate."

Lazarus unleashed an unholy sound before bellowing, "Hypocrite! You tried to murder a woman who never hurt you. Make no mistake. You will be the centerpiece of my newest Garden of Perpetual Horror, a cautionary tale for any others who think to harm what's mine. Your next actions simply decide how you are posed. I suggest you apologize."

Silence.

A bird squawked. A dog barked. The circle of warriors surrounding the Amazons began to shift from one foot to the other. Eager?

Amazons were known throughout the immortal world for their unwillingness to give up, no matter the odds stacked against them.

Lazarus tightened his hold on the spitter's hair, tilting her face higher. She cried out.

"Apologies," she snarled at Cameo.

Viola's hand fluttered over her heart. Oh, to have a man as strong and menacing as Lazarus devoted to her!

He stared at Cameo, his dark gaze searching. Did he seek permission for his next deeds? Awareness smoldered between the two, heating the air. Sweat actually beaded on the back of Viola's neck, her body aching for what it had never known—passion born of authentic desire rather than her demon's trickery.

Finally Cameo nodded. She had to suspect what

Viola knew. If freed, the Amazons would attack again and again, and they wouldn't care who was harmed so long as their objective was accomplished.

Lazarus smiled his most lethal smile.

A strange and terrible tension descended over the Amazons, and their skin began to gray. One gasped with shock while the other cursed. As their flesh hardened into stone, both screamed with horror.

When the process was completed, Lazarus rubbed his hands together in a job well done.

Murmurs rose from the crowd.

"Whoa," Kaia said. "Did Lazarus just do what I think he just did?"

"We need more statues! Naked statues!" Anya jumped up and down. "Everyone, lure your enemies here el pronto."

"If Cameo doesn't have his babies," Sabin said, "I will."

Viola was practically shoved out of the way as the warriors surrounded the statues, admiring the exquisite detail.

Well, this was lovely, going from hero to zero in a snap. She huffed and puffed until her gaze collided with the silvery-white eyes of the monster she'd first seen in the spirit realm.

Brochan had returned. He stood just beyond the circle of her comrades. No one else noticed him.

Forsaken, he mouthed, and her heart rioted in her chest. The deep ebony in his feathers had spread. Barely any white remained. Two horns had sprouted from his head.

Fluffy crawled up her body to perch on her shoulders. He mimicked Lazarus's growl, daring the monster to take a single step closer.

Though Brochan had come to steal McCadden's life force from Fluffy, had vowed to do it, he remained at a distance once again. Did he fancy her?

Can't blame him.

She blew him a kiss, testing his reaction. He blinked in confusion before his expression hardened. He took a step toward her, only to stop. At his sides, his clawed hands curled into fists.

He launched into the air, soon disappearing in the clouds. Too many people around to mess with her?

No matter. Viola forced him out of her mind. For now.

A kaleidoscope of butterflies had appeared above Lazarus. Cameo stiffened before extending her arm and allowing one of the insects to perch at the end of her finger.

Watching her, Viola suddenly wanted to vomit. Neither Cameo nor Lazarus could see into the invisible world around them, where ghosts and bodiless demons walked. As the goddess of the Afterlife, Viola had powers and abilities few—okay, none—could match. Her skills were unsurpassed. Legendary. She was one of a kind, one in a billion, and had—

Lost track of her thoughts. A black mist now surrounded the couple.

Horror radiated from Lucien. As the keeper of Death, he must see the mist, too. Must know exactly what it meant.

One way or another, Lazarus or Cameo would die. And soon.

25

"What you love, your enemy loves to take from you."
~~*The Secret to My Success*~~
—*The Secret to Survival*

Despite the arousal nearly burning him alive, Lazarus hadn't been able to shake his self-directed fury. Over the past week, he'd been dedicated to Cameo's recovery, too afraid to leave her side, constantly beleaguered by the fearful thought, *Will she harm herself?*

He'd been struck by helplessness and savage possession. *Can't lose her.*

Kill the demon, revive the girl.

He should have left when his sky serpents told him about Hera, how she'd attacked his former allies and destroyed every home Lazarus had ever known in the mortal world, all in an attempt to find Pandora's box. But he'd stayed put, determined to protect Cameo. Determined, and yet he'd still failed to prevent an enemy attack.

He was ashamed. She was his μονομανία. He should have taken better care.

She doesn't just ruin my body, she ruins my concentration.

Before playing in the mud, he should have opened his mind to ferret out the Amazons. He should have erected defenses. The fact that he hadn't planned ahead…had only concerned himself with Cameo's happiness…

He should walk away. No, he should flash. The act would take him farther, faster. *He* wasn't good for *her*. Soon he wouldn't be able to protect her at all. The crystals had thickened on his arms and legs and had crept deeper into his chest. The moment they breeched his heart, he would have no defense against anyone, even bunny shifters and puny humans.

He still couldn't bring himself to leave.

Later. He would deal with the worst decisions later. But not today.

He led Cameo through the fortress halls and into their bedroom, where he locked the door, sealing them inside. He tugged her into the bathroom, his intention clear. She offered no protest.

He'd bathed her every day for a week, every shower an exercise of his strictest control. Having her naked curves in his arms had been as much heaven as hell.

He turned the knobs, water pouring from the spout.

"Wait." She placed a hand on his biceps and squeezed gently. "Now that I'm thinking clearly…or somewhat clearly…Juliette's words keep replaying in my mind. Tell me, Lazarus. Please. Do you know where Pandora's box is?"

He ignored a flare of panic, barely resisting the urge to cup the leather-covered pendant hidden under his shirt. It had left his possession only when he'd bathed Cameo; he hadn't wanted to risk contact with her skin, had feared the worst. But he now feared Hera finding it more, so he always kept it on a chain around his neck or within his sights.

The former bitch queen had to know what Cameo meant to him. Worse, she knew how the crystals had weakened Typhon, allowing her to strike at Lazarus's mother. She already suspected the same change was overtaking Lazarus. Now she waited for the perfect time to strike.

Every day he'd expected her to show up at the fortress.

"Lazarus," Cameo prompted, and worried her lower lip.

"The time for talking has ended." He stripped, grace beyond him. Weapons thudded to the floor. He ripped the necklace over his head and dropped it beside a dagger. His shaft was long and thick and harder than the titanium they'd found inside the griffin cave.

She stood before him fully clothed, her gaze heating as it roved over him. The distraction had worked. She trembled as she traced her fingertips along the crystal veins draping his shoulders. "There has to be a way to save you," she croaked.

Sorrow would not intrude. "There is," he replied. Leaving her. An impossible feat, as he'd already proved.

Hope brightened her features. "How?"

"We'll talk. Later." Steam escaped the stall and enveloped them. Outside, thunder boomed. A new storm brewed. Through the window, lightning flashed. "I want you," he rasped. Every inch of her. Nothing withheld from him.

Her tongue glided over her red, red lips, leaving a trail of glistening moisture. The shield around her mind vanished without any probing, her thoughts inundating him. She wanted him to feel the lust sizzling inside her, wanted to be vulnerable to him and for him. Her nipples ached for his touch, his tongue—only his. Her belly quivered, and between her legs, she throbbed with need.

She imagined him thrusting inside her, and she loved it. *He* loved it.

Lazarus's iron control utterly snapped. With an animal-like snarl, he backed her into the wall. *Beautiful female. My willing captive.* He ripped away her clothing, filling his hands with her beautiful breasts, her sweet little nipples beading against his palms. *My female.*

Must slow down.

Must savor.

"I will do *anything* you desire," he breathed into her ear. "Tell me, Cami. Tell me what you want."

Shivers cascaded through her. "I want to get clean… so we can get very dirty."

The longing in her voice eroded the edges of his calm facade. He'd missed this. Missed her so deeply he wasn't sure how he'd breathed without her.

He nipped her earlobe before picking her up and placing her inside the stall. The steam had thickened, enveloping them both with sultry abandon, turning the small enclosure into a dreamworld.

"I'm going to make you come so many times you lose your mind."

"Lazario!" Her nails scoured his shoulders.

"My Cami."

Hot water rained over them as he soaped the mud from her exquisite curves. Little moans and mewls escaped her, driving him insane with lust.

He pressed her against the cool tile and kissed her with bone-deep ferocity. She alone held the power to give him breath. She was the only anchor amid a violent storm.

She melted against him, her nipples abrading his chest, the friction maddening. Grinding his erection against her, drawing new mewls from her, he cupped and kneaded her beautiful breasts. But the contact wasn't enough. With her, nothing would ever be enough. He would always crave more.

"I'm desperate to get inside you." He needed to brand her, needed to bond her body to his, now and always. "You haunt my every waking hour, star in my every dream."

She nipped at his lower lip. "You *are* my dreams." Her arms wound around him, and she rubbed her thigh against his.

He caught the underside and lifted her off her feet, forcing her to wrap her other leg around his waist. Then he ground his shaft against her core with greater force.

With her mental shield down, Lazarus heard her demon whisper words of discontent—*going to forget this*—in an effort to sow discord and therefore sorrow. Rage surged through him, setting the crystals in his veins on fire.

"I'll make this so good the demon *can't* erase it, love."

Love. He'd called her *love*. Was that what she'd become to him? And he'd meant his words as a vow. Even if she *begged* the demon for a total memory wipe, the image of Lazarus would forever haunt her.

"Yes. Please, yes."

He kissed her, greedily drinking from her. Her nails combed through his hair and sank into his scalp. An action born of the same desperation he'd battled since returning to the fortress, making his heart careen against his ribs. Her passion stoked his own.

"I'm so close already," she rasped. "I'm going to…"

He stilled, ending her quick descent into oblivion. Screeching in frustration, she pounded her fists into his shoulders, hitting with enough force to bruise him.

"Now, now. There's no reason to fret. You killed Juliette in under five minutes." He licked the corner of her mouth, the seam of her lips, before his tongue played a carnal game with hers. "I owe you a reward…"

He forced her legs to lower. Then he did something he'd only ever done with her. He willingly dropped to his knees, granting her a position of power. Why not? She'd enslaved him in ways Juliette hadn't. Ways he relished.

Through his lashes, he looked up at paradise. The tantalizing dip of her navel. The strength in her stomach. Her breasts crested by hardened peaks. A pink flush stained the surface of her skin as water droplets rained over her. His tongue captured one on her outer thigh.

Her fingers combed through his hair. Nibbling on her lower lip, she applied pressure to his nape to draw him toward her. "Take me, then." The command of a queen. His queen. "Take me well."

Lazarus leaned in, so close he could scent her unique musk…she held her breath, waiting, eager…before he lifted to his haunches and sucked on her nipples, teasing and taunting her. She made a sound of frustration followed by a sound of ragged need.

He flicked his tongue over the swollen crests until both were swollen and hopefully throbbing. As her hips writhed, he kissed the outside of her navel, dipped inside it…then licked down, down, as if finally giving her what she wanted most…only to turn his head and bite her hip, where the wings of her butterfly tattoo glittered on her skin.

"Enough! I need to… *Pleeease*."

"Can't resist such a sweet plea." He slid his hands up, up her legs. When he reached the source of her desire, he thrust a finger deep inside her, at the same time licking her little bundle of nerves.

She screamed his name, just the way he liked.

Mmm, she tasted so good. Was more intoxicating than ambrosia. His perfect little lollipop. His tongue and fingers worked in tandem, propelling her need higher—propelling his own need higher. Her inner walls were hot and wet and so wonderfully tight around his finger.

His shaft ached with pain and with pleasure.

"Lazarlo…" A groan.

My woman desires more. He wedged another finger inside her, stretching her, preparing her for a more intimate penetration.

Then her soft lips parted, and she *moaned* his name. "Please…please…"

Frenzied, he shot to his feet and shut off the water. He picked her up, his motions shockingly unaffected by the crystals. His passion was simply too great. He carried her to the bedroom and laid her across the bed, pinning her body beneath his. Wet skin against wet skin. Long ebony hair spilled over the pillows like ribbons drenched in a rainstorm. Her arms and legs wrapped around him. With no other preamble, he surged inside her.

Her back bowed. She closed her eyes and cried out

as she climaxed around his shaft. Pleasure morphed into agony as he fought his own need to come. Nothing had ever felt so good, so right, but he forced himself to remain still.

Savor. He wasn't ready for this to end.

When she sagged against the bed, a panting, boneless heap, he had a flash of rational thought. "Should have covered this earlier. Birth control?" Sweat trickled down his back, only to steam off his overheated skin.

If he had to withdraw from her, he would. He would suffer, but he would do it. He'd never wanted children, had never wanted his love for his child used against him, had never desired to sentence a child to a cursed eternity weakened by something as innocuous—and insidious—as crystals.

"I'm given a shot every three months." She practically purred the words. "I'm good to roll."

Heady with relief, Lazarus hooked his arms under her knees and angled her body for deeper penetration. With his first thrust, her languid contentment vanished. Moaning, she arched to take him deeper still.

He slid out with slow reverence and then thrust back in. The ecstasy! His skin pulled taut over his bones. Out...in. Out, in. The pressure inside him built. Her inner walls slick and hot, he increased his speed until he was pounding inside her, again and again. The bed rocked, headboard slapping the wall. Pictures fell, glass shattered.

"One more kiss. One more touch," she pleaded. "One more everything."

He slammed his mouth into hers, finesse beyond him. She met his ferocity with pure feminine aggression. Their breaths mingled. Through the connection of their minds, he knew how close she was to a second climax. How desperately she ached, as if she'd never experienced satisfaction.

He lifted his head and rasped, "Look at me, my beautiful μονομανία."

Her eyes opened, meeting his, her silver irises wild with lust. Then she screamed his name, her inner walls squeezing his length. He *felt* her pleasure, both physically and emotionally, and his own climax ripped through him.

With a roar, he jetted inside her.

Cameo opened her eyes, roused from the sweetest sleep of her life. Lazarus dozed beside her, his arms wrapped around her, and her heart melted. Was this the first time he'd slept since her bout with depression?

A tender smile shaped her lips. Poor, sweet darling. He'd taken such good care of her. She stretched and grinned at the lovely soreness in muscles long unused. Yes, he'd taken *very* good care of her, and in more ways than one.

Sex with him had been eternity changing. He'd catapulted her to heights she hadn't known existed. He'd done the impossible and quieted Misery. And through it all, he'd looked at her and touched her as if she were a precious treasure rather than a hated anchor.

Living without him would not be possible now.

Perhaps he felt the same about her? He'd called her *monomania*. Spelled μονομανία, the Greek word for *kink* or *obsession*.

A single doubt nagged at her, however. When she'd mentioned Pandora's box, some dark emotion had flashed in his eyes. Guilt? Anger? If she were his obsession, he would have told her if he'd found the artifact. He wouldn't allow her to wonder and worry needlessly.

Despite his moniker, Lazarus was kind and caring. At least, he was kind and caring with her.

Fear prickled along the nape of her neck when she saw that the crystals had spread farther down his chest. She wanted so badly to talk to Torin and Keeley, but she wouldn't betray her man's trust. Not even to save his life.

After all, there was a way to stop this. He'd said so.

Whatever he needed to do, he would do. Whatever *she* needed to do, she would do. End of story.

As carefully as possible, she extracted herself from his embrace. Already mourning the loss of his heat and hardness, she donned a robe and tiptoed to the vanity, where she sat and peered into the mirror.

"Help me help him," she whispered. "Show me what to do."

The glass remained intact.

"Please," she said, desperate.

Nothing. No change.

Why! Why would the mirror deny her now?

Misery laughed, and her shoulders rolled in. But she caught the action and forced her shoulders to square. No! No more sorrow.

The demon stopped laughing.

A soft knock sounded at the door. When Lazarus gave no notice, Cameo stood and tiptoed to the entrance. Torin stood in the hall, his white hair in complete disarray and his expression grim.

Nerves suddenly razed, she closed the door behind her. "What's wrong?"

He couldn't mask his flinch. "I've wanted to speak

with you for a week but…yeah. Anyway. As soon as you took off to find Lazarus, I started digging into his past. When Keeley saw my notes, some memories clicked into place for her."

Her stomach churned with an influx of concern. "I won't tell you anything I know, but I will listen to what you discovered."

"He's dying," her friend announced, and she stumbled backward, hitting the door. "A few hours ago, Lucien and Viola confirmed it. As Death and the Afterlife, they see what we can't. And they saw an end for either you or Lazarus. But I know the unlucky victim is… Lazarus. I'm sorry, Cam. But his veins are filling with strange crystals, yes? Keeley informed me the same transformation happened to his father…soon after he met Lazarus's mother."

Horror petrified Cameo's muscles. She couldn't move, couldn't breathe. Torin's emerald eyes filled with pity, but he said no more. No other words were necessary.

After he met Lazarus's mother…

Cameo was Lazarus's doom. She had caused the crystals to spread.

In the back of her mind, Misery began to laugh again. *Only a matter of time before you* want *to forget the male, eh?*

"I didn't want to tell you," Torin said, "didn't want to cause another episode."

Episode. What an innocent, *insufficient* word for the deluge of sorrow she'd so often endured.

He continued. "I asked Keeley if there is a way to save him, but every time she thinks about him, she gets wrapped up in two words. Well, three words if you count his name. *Lazarus, king* and *butterflies*."

So. Cameo had been right all along. Butterflies did herald doom.

Light-headed, she reached out, found and twisted the doorknob, closing the door in Torin's face. Tears filled her eyes as she raced back into the room and found Lazarus sitting on the edge of the bed.

He wore a wrinkled shirt and a pair of pants. His weapons were already in place. As he tugged on his boot, rage shimmered in his eyes.

"You know," he said, his voice flat.

"Know that I'm the one killing you?" A barbed lump grew inside her throat. "Yes. I want you to go, Lazarus. Now. Never come back. You aren't welcome here anymore."

He yanked on the second boot and stood to his full seven-foot height. Unwilling to meet his gaze, Cameo strode to the closet, where she discarded her robe and dressed in a sports bra, a pair of fighting leathers and a tank top.

When she emerged, he was right there to greet her, backing her into the wall. "I won't give you up," he grated.

A promise. A promise that caused her heart to split down the center and bleed into her chest. "You don't have a choice."

"I always have a choice."

Oh, really? She slapped him with every bit of her strength. Crimson leaked from his mouth as his head whipped to the side. His gaze narrowed to tiny slits.

"I attacked you," she spit at him. "Go ahead. Tell me I'm your enemy now."

His hands wrapped around her vulnerable neck. Instead of squeezing, he grazed his thumb over her wild pulse. "You will never be my enemy. Hit me all you want, love. I will never hit back."

"Don't call me your love." He didn't mean it. He couldn't. The man who loved her would not betray her. "You are choosing to let me destroy you. You are choosing to let me deal with guilt and misery when you're gone. You are choosing to—" *Leave me.* Her chin trembled. She quieted before she began to sob. *Can't do this.*

She pointed to the door, her message clear.

Lazarus released her. Rather than leaving, he flattened his palms at her temples and leaned in until they were nose to nose, breathing each other's breath the way they'd done when they'd last kissed. The memory would forever—

The memory. Her eyes widened. She could allow Misery to wipe her mind. And she would leave herself a note, warning herself about Lazarus. No, a note could be disposed of too easily. She could tattoo herself. Then Lazarus would have no reason to stay.

With the thought, she couldn't breathe. Forget the bliss she experienced with this man? Forget his every kiss, his every touch and the feel of his body filling hers? Forget how she'd had hope for a better future, if only for a little while?

A fierce growl rose from him. "You will not forget me, Cameo."

"My choice," she said softly.

"Do it, then. Go so far as to tattoo yourself. I won't leave you. I'll stay here and romance you back into my arms."

Have to stay the course. It's for his own good. "You can try, but I'll resist you." She would find a way.

His hands fisted. "You want to keep me around, love. Trust me."

"I don't, I can't—"

"Cameo, I have the box."

No…he couldn't. "You're lying."

"I often misdirect, misguide and mislead, but I never lie. I found it, fought for it, and now I guard it to save your life."

Her earlier doubt resurfaced, but still she shook her head. "Keeley would have known—"

"Wrong. I used an illusion to hide its presence from her."

"Your illusions aren't strong enough—"

Suddenly the entire room erupted into orange-gold flames. They crackled around her bed, underneath the mirror Lazarus had given her, and on her curtains and rug. Heat enveloped her, and sweat popped up on her upper lip. She opened her mouth to shout for an extinguisher, but the flames vanished, taking the heat with them.

"You were saying?" Lazarus asked quietly.

"You…you bastard! You let me worry other immortals would find and destroy the box before I could find it. You let me stew over Juliette. Did you secretly laugh at me behind my back?"

"Never. I've only ever laughed at you to your face."

Jokes? Now? Cameo slapped him again. "Where is it?" she demanded. "Tell me."

"That, I won't do." He wiped the new stream of blood from his mouth before placing his hands against the wall behind her, caging her in. "You would use it to kill yourself."

"I would never—" She pressed her lips together.

Wouldn't she? If Misery made her miserable enough…
"Give the box to Torin. He won't let me near it, and my
friends will be protected from it."

"And what will I receive in return?"

The question hung between them, a noose around
her neck. After everything he'd done, how dare he try
to bargain with her?

Knock, knock, knock.

"Go away," Lazarus shouted, never looking away
from her. "Well?"

Needing time to think, she ducked underneath his
arm to open the door, expecting to find Torin. William and Hades stood before her, armed for war and
unsmiling.

"We want the mirror." William was steady on his
feet. Actually, he'd never looked steadier. Determination cloaked him. Had he found Gilly, or a new reason
to live? "We're willing to trade for it."

Can't deal with this right now. "No, thanks," she replied, and tried to shut the door.

Neither male flinched at the sound of her voice. Both
slammed a hand on the ancient wood, ensuring the entryway stayed open.

Lazarus moved directly behind her, his heat enveloping her. She had never been so furious with another
being. Not even Galen, after he'd removed her tongue.
The man she'd accepted into her bed, her body and her
now decimated heart, had betrayed her. Had kept secrets from her. Had let her worry for nothing.

"What do you offer?" Lazarus asked.

Hades arched a brow, his mien as beautiful and sardonic as it was deadly. "What you desire most. Two
round-trip tickets to Hera's secret temple."

Cameo inhaled sharply. The one thing Lazarus couldn't refuse. His vengeance.

He stiffened, seconds eking by in silence. Finally, he said, "No. You want the mirror, you have to release me from your service. I'm done with war, done with vengeance. I wish to spend the rest of my days with Cameo."

What? No! He was giving up, preparing to die? "The mirror is mine, not his," she said through clenched teeth. "He gifted it to me. You guys want it, fine. It's yours." The cursed thing had given her hope. Had misled her as thoroughly as Lazarus. Laughing while butterflies flew overhead? Like hell! "But you will release Lazarus from your service, just like he asked—" he wasn't in any condition to fight "—and you will give him Hera's head on a pike."

If Lazarus was the one to kill the former queen, Cameo would die. Somehow. If she had Hades see to the task, she would survive. Possibly. Plus, she would vengeance-block Lazarus, a prospect that came with two perks. One, she would teach him the error of his ways. Mess with the Mother of Melancholy and suffer. Two, he would grow to hate her and leave her. Then she could forget him, and he could live a long life without being hunted by the former queen.

Even as furious as Cameo was, she wanted him to live forever.

"In war, you pick a side. That hasn't changed. So," Hades said, "I will not release him from my service. Victory is too important. Also, I will not give him Hera's head. She and I have an understanding. My offer stands as is. Two tickets to her realm."

Playing hardball? "No, thanks," she repeated, and tried once again to shut the door in his face.

"Okay," he said in a rush, holding the entrance open with more force. "I can add a sweetener. I'll give you the tools to defeat her on your own." His gaze lowered to the necklace around Lazarus's neck. He frowned, reached out.

Lazarus knocked his hand away, and the two males glared at each other.

"Just one ticket, then," she said. "For me." She would use her ticket to kill Hera without Lazarus and hopefully reap the same benefits. "And the tools."

Misery started laughing again. *Going to regret this...*

Feeling as if she were dying inside, Cameo wrapped her arms around herself.

Hades smiled at her. "Sorry, poppet, but I won't send you into the lion's den without a lion. You're getting two tickets." He waved his hand in the direction of her vanity.

She glanced over her shoulder, wide-eyed when the mirror vanished from the wall.

"While I can't get you past the blocks inside Hera's temple," he continued, "I can put you a few miles outside it. But be careful. There are traps everywhere. Oh. And remember. You can't spell funeral without the word *fun*."

There was no time to respond. Like the mirror, the bedroom vanished. A second later, a golden paradise appeared.

26

"Do what's right today or suffer the consequences tomorrow."

—*The Secret to Survival*
—*Memoir of a Maddened King*

No one could flash Lazarus to a new location when he had no desire to flash. Today, he'd had no desire to flash, and yet the king of the underworld had managed it, anyway.

His weakness must be manifesting in other ways. Would he have the strength to defeat Hera, even with the proper tools?

Maybe. Maybe not. But he couldn't bring himself to regret a second spent with Cameo. There was no greater misery than being without her. He only regretted her presence here. If he failed to protect her…

Fool! She can protect herself. She'd proved her skill time and time again. He would pick her over a queen with an army any day of the week; he could ask for no better partner.

Unfortunately, his partner currently hated his guts.

And why wouldn't she? He'd placed her directly in Death's sights. If he killed Hera, Cameo died.

Only a possibility. One he'd planned to prevent... somehow. Perhaps he could use the Paring Rod to enslave the queen?

Except the Paring Rod was back at the fortress.

Fine. He would find another way. He hadn't earned the moniker "Unusual" without due course. He could do anything. Today, he and Cameo had become one. In body...in soul. She had clung to him, welcomed him, while he'd pounded inside her, had shouted his name in passion and supplication, and begged him for just one more kiss, just one more touch, just one more everything. Her lust for him could not be denied.

Lust means nothing. Only love matters.

He stiffened. He wanted her love, he realized, but he couldn't fight for it. To do so would be cruel and unusual, and for once, he wanted to be more...to be better. Because one way or another, life as he knew it was going to end. Did he really want to leave her with a broken heart?

Going to do so, anyway. Might have done so already.

His hands fisted as he scrutinized the terrain. This was Hera's secret realm? An overgrown forest with gold trees, gold birds and gold monkeys.

The ground shook beneath his feet. Danger approached? He opened his mind but sensed no foe. He listened but heard no footsteps. Then he looked down. He stood within a small circle of cut grass, Cameo at his side. Behind them, tall grass was interspersed with multicolored wildflowers, the petals dotted with dew. He sniffed. *Poisoned* dew.

Hades had flashed Lazarus and Cameo into the middle of a trap. A land mine, to be exact. It had been an accident, no doubt—otherwise the male would have flashed them onto the end of a pike—but it was still irritating.

"What's happening?" Cameo demanded. "Earthquake?"

"Worse." Lazarus grabbed the go bags resting at their feet and snaked an arm around her waist. Inside had to be the tools they'd need to defeat Hera. "We activated a land mine."

She went rigid, as if he'd just turned her to stone. He tightened his hold, lest she try to escape him and lose a limb.

"No worries, love. I'll flash us to safety before it blows." He attempted to flash…and failed. His irritation sharpened. Another weakness? Or had the realm negated his abilities? To his knowledge, only a handful of realms possessed the power to do so.

There was only one other way to clear the land mine; they'd have to dive through the poisoned wildflowers.

"Well?" Cameo demanded.

"New plan." He removed the ring from its chain, jammed the metal down his finger and waved his hand through the air, intending to open a portal to safety.

Nothing happened. Because they weren't in a spirit realm.

"All right. New *new* plan." He lifted Cameo, cradling her against his chest. Even as light as she was, the action challenged his stamina, and he grimaced. "Curl into me and cover as much of your skin as possible. The dew will burn holes in you."

"Put me down. I'm hurting you. The crystals are strengthening, aren't they? You shouldn't—"

He liked that Cameo still cared about his well-being,

but another quake had just rocked the ground at his feet, the vibration like a giant second hand on the countdown clock. *Running out of time.* With no other recourse, he jumped.

Boom!

Rocks and dirt exploded as the white-hot blast flung him through the air. Fire and acid licked at him, quickly burning through his clothing and shoes. A tree stopped his flight. He curled inward, protecting Cameo as his shoulder slammed into the trunk. Bone shattered. Muscles tore. His lungs emptied and flattened. He crashed into the ground, pain and dizziness assaulting him. His vision blackened.

When the world finally came back into focus, a loud chime wailed in his ears.

Cameo crouched at his side, shaking him. Concern had turned her cheeks pale and waxen.

He searched her and found no acid burns in her clothing or on her skin. However, soot streaked her face and arms.

"—okay?" Her voice penetrated his awareness as the chime faded. "Where do you hurt? What can I do?"

"I think…I think I strained my cock. Kiss it and make it better?"

Concern gave way to relief and annoyance, and she slapped his chest.

"You're not funny." She turned away from him and dug through the bags.

"I kinda am."

"Let's check out our supplies. We've got— Yes! Hades packed the Paring Rod," she said.

Beautiful bastard. He'd solved Lazarus's biggest problem. "What else?" He eased into a sitting position and rolled his healing shoulder to pop the joint back into place.

"A change of clothes, a box of condoms with the name Spawn Be Gone, two canteens of water, a can of caviar and a box of organic crackers, toothpaste, wet wipes, a backscratcher, a small bottle of Febreeze, a package of earplugs—" She stiffened, ground her teeth. "What a dirty rat. He only packed one pair of plugs, implying *your* voice isn't upsetting to *me*."

Lazarus hid a smile behind his hand. "I'd punish him for you, but, you know, I'm dying." When she glowered at him, he said, "What? Too soon?"

She snapped her teeth at him before holding up a spotted stuffed leopard. "A toy version of Rathbone the Only. I wonder why he sent it."

Lazarus could guess. With a snarl, he confiscated the doll and tossed it into the pit the land mine had created.

"Hey! What'd you do that for?" Cameo demanded. "He was cute."

"And he would have loved hearing you say so, which is why he had to go."

Lazarus scanned ahead and spotted a crystalline river rushing over precious gems the size of boulders. A crystal bridge led to the only splash of white on the horizon. A twisting staircase that wound up a moss-covered hill and ended in front of alabaster columns. The entrance to the temple? How long since Hera had visited?

Hidden within the spectacular beauty were signs of neglect. Overgrown weeds, chips in the precious gems and a section removed from the middle of the bridge.

"Anything else in the bags?" he asked.

"Yeah. A pair of binoculars. A square cloth." She

gasped with excitement. "Not a cloth, but the Cloak of Invisibility. And this! This belongs to Danika, the All-Seeing Eye." She held up a small four-by-four square tile with only one marking. A name in the corner. Danika Lord. "But aren't there images?"

Brow furrowing, he claimed the tile and held it under a beam of light. The surface… Something struck him as odd. The slightly yellowed spots, perhaps?

Cameo withdrew a metal pipe from the bag, looked it over and squealed. "I think this came from the Cage of Compulsion." She snatched the tile from him and clutched all four items—the Cloak, the Rod, pipe and tile—to her chest. "These are mine. Try and take them and I'll—" Her lips pressed into a firm line.

Couldn't think of a threat great enough?

No matter. He'd already thought of the worst-case scenario. If something were to happen to Lazarus out here or anywhere and his woman didn't know where the box was or what it looked like…anyone could steal it.

His silence could have cost her big-time.

No more hiding it. He pulled the necklace from under his shirt and stroked his thumb over the leather casing. "This…is what you've spent centuries searching for."

She eyed the leather-bound pendant and snorted. "Nice try, but I'm not buying your bull anymore." But even as she spoke, her gaze remained glued to the artifact he'd once called "dangerous." Frowning, she rubbed her nape. "What is it? Really."

He opened his mind, desperate to know her thoughts, but she'd erected her shield. He wasn't surprised, but he was still disappointed. He craved a connection with her. "It is the box, I assure you. The bones were crushed and reshaped."

"Impossible. To be remade, it would have to be opened. I would be dead."

"It *was* opened. By you and your friends. I'm willing to bet Hera is the one who stole it while you were distracted. Then, before she hid it, she remade it to ensure no one would recognize it if ever it was found."

"Then how did *you* recognize it? What about the Morning Star thought to be inside?"

"It was concealed inside a skull, next to what I thought was the box. I knew Kadence, the goddess of Oppression. Her bones were used to make it, and I felt her power. As for the Morning Star, I don't know."

Cameo leaned back, balanced on her haunches, her nails digging into her thighs. "All this time, you've had the box, the artifact capable of killing the only people I love, hanging around your cursed neck?" Rage crackled in her tone.

Tread carefully. "You sensed it. You and all the others." The others. The only people she loved, as if Lazarus had no place in her heart. *Calm, steady.* "It never harmed you. Not really. In fact, it might have helped you suppress the demon. That's why it was made, after all. To stop evil."

He should have considered the possibility before, but hadn't let himself. His conscience would have insisted he give the box to Cameo…then she would have had no need to keep him around.

An eternity passed, the only sounds coming from the rushing river and howling monkeys. The branch above them shook, golden leaves raining around them. Finally, she placed the other artifacts on the ground and held out her hand, palm up.

She waved her fingers. "Give me the apple. Or box. Whatever."

He met and held her gaze, saw a deluge of hurt and anger and felt as if the daggers tattooed on his chest had manifested and stabbed him. "I'm sorry I hurt you," he croaked. Before her, he'd never issued a sincere apology; now he couldn't do it enough. "I'm sorry I waited to tell you about the box."

"How ironic. You seek my forgiveness, and yet you refuse to forgive those who have wronged you." Another wave of her fingers. "The apple."

Still he hesitated, grating, "Our situations are not the same."

"Aren't they?"

No! How could he make her understand her safety meant more to him than his own? How could he prove the intensity of his feelings for her? "When Hades offered vengeance on a silver platter, I declined. I chose you."

"You chose death!"

With her, they were one and the same. However, he kept those words to himself. "Do you *want* me to kill Hera? I won't. I won't risk you."

"No. *I* will kill her."

And change the future.

"She's a threat to you, and threats get cut," she said, her voice firm but hollow. "Afterward, you and I will part."

Never! He scrubbed his free hand down his face, clearing the soot from his eyes. "I will stay with you until the end."

The color drained from her cheeks.

Have to make her understand. "Let me stay with

you, and I will trust your friends, allow them to search for a cure." A major step for him.

"There isn't a way to cure you, only a way to save you," she croaked. "By staying *away* from me."

"I want a cure, and you," he said. "If I can't have the cure, I'll have you. When we're back at home, the box is yours. I'll trust you not to hurt yourself, and you'll trust me again."

"Or I'll simply *take* the box."

In the distance, a flock of golden birds took flight. He palmed a dagger and jumped to his feet. "We should go, shouldn't stay in one place too long."

Ever the warrior, Cameo moved beside him. "If Hera is here, she'll be inside the temple. On the flip side, if she were here, she would have sensed our presence and ambushed us."

"Not necessarily. If she could sense a breach, she wouldn't have bothered with traps."

He opened his mind, searching for other living beings, hoping to summon a sky serpent or two. He ignored the birds, monkeys, insects and an assortment of other animals, and concentrated on a dark presence... hungry, so hungry...and closing in fast. Enemy!

"Time to beat feet," he said.

He anchored the go bags to his shoulders, grabbed Cameo's hand and sprinted toward the river.

What was she going to do?

Cameo couldn't escape the tumultuous storm of emotions raging inside her. Lazarus had carried Pandora's box around his neck all this time. He'd told her he would never lie to her—while already trapped in the midst of one. He'd denied her the opportunity to make an in-

formed decision with her friends: attempt to suppress
the demons or to destroy the box.

The bastard had box-blocked her!

Lazarus ground to a halt, and she slammed into his
back. At the top of her to-do list: *remain aware*.

Steam thickened the air, making it harder to breathe
as she scanned the newest terrain. A field of wildflowers stretched before them, lush and lovely and without
the poisoned dew, except…it was a trap. Upon closer
inspection, she realized the ground was murky marsh.

"Quicksand," Lazarus said. "And there." He pointed
to the right. "The flowers cover another land mine."

Misery laughed as he led her to the left, *away* from
the temple. Unfortunately, there was no other way to go.
They had to bypass the marsh and circle back.

They remained on the fringe of the field, caught
between the forest and the marsh, careful not to step
anywhere they shouldn't—

An eel-like creature burst from a muddy puddle of
water, his fangs bared. Cameo caught him by his slimy
neck, preventing him from biting her. His slippery body
wiggled.

"Um, a little help, please."

With a slash of his dagger, Lazarus removed the creature's head. Grimacing, she tossed the still-wiggling
body back into the puddle. Other eels—or whatever
they were—jumped up to snack on the remains.

Here you were either predator or prey. *Got it*.

"The tile Hades packed," Lazarus said.

"Yeah? What about it?"

"I have an idea." He stopped under a golden tree
and fished out the tile. He angled it toward the light,
then angled it toward the shadows cast by the forest.

"Everything he provided serves a purpose, except the tile. Why?"

"Maybe it *does* serve a purpose. We just can't see it."

"Exactly. Hades has been known to use invisible ink and paints."

A spark of excitement. "How do we make the invisible visible?"

"That, I don't yet know."

"Well, let's think like Hades." *I'm a self-important male with a warped sense of humor. I enjoy torturing my enemies, taunting my friends and winning, whatever the cost.* Wow. Hades and Lazarus could be brothers from other mothers. *I have an unhealthy obsession with making other people bleed. I—*

Bleed. Blood. The source of life. Excitement heating up, Cameo whipped out a dagger and dragged the blade over her palm.

Lazarus snatched the dagger from her grip, as if she had no right to injure herself—or better yet, his property. "You do *not* harm—"

"Too late." A pool of crimson welled. She held her fist over the tile, letting the thick droplets slide down… down…and splash over the surface.

Images began to appear on the tile.

"You did it," Lazarus said, his pride unmistakable.

She ignored the urge to preen under his praise and studied the images. A…map? Yes! The forest, marsh and temple were clearly marked. So were the different traps.

"If we continue on this path for roughly two miles," Lazarus said, "we can use this bridge to reach the temple."

"The bridge is booby-trapped."

"Yes, but we can go over them."

"How? In case you haven't noticed, neither one of us has wings, and the birds aren't big enough to saddle and ride."

He gently chucked her under the chin. "Have a little faith in your man."

Her skin tingled, and her newly awakened lusts surged. She trembled. *He's more dangerous than the realm.* Cameo wrenched away. "You mean the man who lied to me?"

"I believe you mean the man who admitted to his crime, even though he could have taken the secret to his grave." His gaze slid past her, and every muscle in his body stiffened. "We're being followed. Come on."

As he linked their fingers and trudged ahead, she glanced backward. About a hundred yards away, a storm cloud rolled across the sky, spraying the land with mist. Birds fell from the sky like feathered missiles. Trees withered.

"Go, go, go," she commanded.

Lazarus picked up the pace—until a vine darted out, wrapped around his ankle and jerked him high into the air. He hung upside down, the bags slipping from his shoulders and crashing into Cameo.

A stream of curses burst from him. There wasn't enough time to cut him down *and* escape the death mist.

"Go." *He* issued the command this time. "Leave me."

Misery snickered.

Determined to save Lazarus, Cameo dug through the bags, withdrew the Cloak of Invisibility, the Paring Rod and the pipe that was taken from the Cage of Compulsion. "Leave it to the woman to save the day—and the *man*sel in distress."

27

"A man cannot be led by two opposing forces, for truth cannot coexist with a lie. Love cannot coexist with hate."

~~*Memoir of a Maddened King*~~
—*Memoir of a Besotted Fool*

Plagued by urgency and fear, Lazarus lifted his upper body and stretched out his arms, his muscles screaming in protest. In the last hour, the crystals had spread and thickened, slowing his reflexes considerably. His fingers found the dagger in his boot. With one hand, he grabbed hold of the vine that was wrapped around his ankle. With the other, he used the dagger to saw.

At last the vine broke. Bracing for impact, he tumbled toward a bank of moss—only to be caught by another vine and hang upside down a second time. He unleashed a stream of obscenities. Still the dark cloud approached, headed directly for Cameo.

As graceful as a swan, she unfolded a piece of gray cloth until it formed a hooded cape. When she placed the cape over her shoulders and lifted the hood, she vanished. Not even Lazarus could see her. Good, that was good. The cloud couldn't see her, either.

"Run," he told her. "Run, and I'll find you." Always.

But he knew she wouldn't obey. She was Cameo, stubborn to an extreme. When the cloud reached the spot he'd last seen her, it screeched. Lazarus cringed, the high-pitched sound nearly bursting his eardrums.

Ignoring his own pain, he pulled up and sawed at the new vine.

The cloud thundered and flashed bolts of lightning, all the while shuddering. What was Cameo *doing*?

Yet another vine snatched the dagger from Lazarus's grip and aimed a sharpened tip at his heart. He cursed his distraction.

Just before impact, a tar-covered vine batted at the blade, saving Lazarus from injury. He shook his head, confused. The tar-covered vine coiled around the one holding his ankle and squeezed. He was released. He toppled, expecting to crash-land. The tar-covered vine caught him, easing him to the ground.

It's...aiding me? Why?

Think about it later. Ready for battle, he popped to his feet. Cameo materialized, the Cloak of Invisibility in a pool at her feet. She stood underneath the cloud, her arm extended high, her hand hidden by the gloom. No, not hidden. The cloud thinned, revealing her hand and the pipe she held.

Pride overwhelmed him. *My woman. So strong. So capable.*

When every speck of darkness vanished, she lowered her arm. Her eyes sparkled like diamonds, and her cheeks glowed with rosy health. Brittle leaves tangled in her hair.

"What happened?" he asked.

"The Cloak of Invisibility protected me from the mist as I snuck under the cloud, inserted the pipe into the center, and commanded the thing—whatever it was—to die. And it did! It had to. The pipe is from the Cage of Compulsion. It was a gift, so we own it, and anything inside it has to do whatever we command."

Her excitement…

Beneath his fly, his shaft hardened. With her, it proved inevitable. "You are a true warrior." Even though she was upset with him, she had done everything in her power to ensure his safety.

No one had ever acted so selflessly on his behalf. No one had ever placed him first. Not even his parents. Their hatred for each other had trumped their love for him.

Desperate to touch her, to assure himself of *her* safety, he closed the distance between them. "You endangered yourself to save me. Can you really fault me for doing the same for you?" He reached for her.

"It's not the same." Avoiding contact, she bent to sheathe the pipe in one of the bags.

His heart shriveled, but he pressed on. "Why?"

"The outcome of my action is life." She folded the cloak and hid it in her pocket. "The outcome of yours is death."

"You speak as if I'm wasting what time I have left. The truth is, time with you is not wasted but cherished."

Scowling, she tossed a bag at him. "Shut up. Just… shut up."

He crouched beside her. He was getting to her, cracking her internal armor. He had to keep pushing, couldn't allow her to refortify her defenses against him. With her, he had no defenses of his own. Because he loved—

He sucked in a breath. He did. He loved her. Not because of *what* she was to him. Because of *who* she was. Period. She was a wealth of contradictions. Kind but fierce. Caring but stubborn. Witty but morose. Protective but easily provoked. Compassionate but violent.

Despite the demon, she was the light in Lazarus's darkness. She was smart and she was…everything. Before her, he'd known rage. Somehow, she had filled him with joy.

"Cameo," he croaked.

"No." She stood. "That isn't what I want. I want you to live. Free of the crystals. Free from danger."

He stood as well, hope shining like a brilliant beacon inside him. She loved him, too. To put herself at risk as she had? To make the sacrifices she'd made for him? To give herself to him so unconditionally? She must. "I don't want to live without you." He followed the gruff admission by removing the apple from his neck and placing it around hers, the leather and chain mail touching her skin, rather than the bone.

She raised her chin.

"It's yours," he said. "I trust you not to harm yourself. I trust you to make the call—remove the covering and touch it, open it, hide it or destroy it. Whatever you want. I give it to you, free of obligation or expectation." His knuckles brushed her nipple as he ensured the pendant hung between her beautiful breasts, drawing another hiss from her. "I give you my love, my time, my everything."

* * *

He's shattering what remains of my resistance.

Cameo reeled, Lazarus's declaration ringing in her ears. He loved her? She shook her head and backed away from him. "You'll give me everything…except a future with you. A family."

He moved with her, saying, "You *are* my family."

She turned away. Looking at him hurt. She wrapped her fingers around the apple. Even with a covering, she felt the heat radiating from the bones. Felt the power.

Misery screeched and scrambled to the back of her mind. Subdued? Precious silence reigned…and yet still she experienced a deluge of sadness.

Lazarus knew her, knew who and what she was, and he wanted to help her, not destroy her. He loved her, despite her many flaws. And she lo—

Nope. Not going there. If she gave in to either him or her emotion, she would curse him to an eternity encased in crystal. So she had to let him go. No ifs, ands or buts. What's more, she had to force him to leave her. And thanks to the mirror, she knew there was a way to do so…

Dread slithered down her spine.

Lazarus stiffened and said, "We need shelter. Another cloud approaches." He gathered the packs and pushed through a thick shield of foliage.

She followed, passing a tree of some sort. Maybe. It was nine feet tall and oozed a thick black substance. Tar? The substance covered two vines—two vines that could pass for arms. Butterflies flew above it, creating a colorful canopy.

Doom and gloom…

"This thing…whatever it is, it helped me," Lazarus

said. "I don't trust it, though. I don't trust anything in this realm."

They traveled for over an hour, successfully avoiding other traps, sneaky vines and biting insects. The new death cloud continued to trail them, but never caught up.

Lazarus rejected two caves before settling on a third that was smaller than the others. So small, in fact, they both had to crawl inside. Deep into the bowels of the earth, however, the cavern opened up, allowing them to stand. The enclosure had only one entrance and, as such, only one exit—the one they'd crawled through.

He dropped the packs and dug inside. With a snarl, he extracted the stuffed leopard he'd discarded earlier. "I'll be right back."

"Right back" turned out to be fifteen minutes, no toy in sight.

"What'd you do with the leopard?" she asked.

"Tossed it into a puddle." At her side once again, he offered her a canteen. As she quenched her thirst, he opened the caviar and crackers. They ate in silence.

Was he upset with her? He'd offered her love, and she'd spurned him.

Had to. Won't be his downfall.

But…she *could* have one more night with him. Just one more. And what better night? If she waited until they found Hera, the crystals could overtake him, or he could use his masculine wiles to convince her to ignore his doom in favor of her temporary happiness. How close he'd come already.

"Do you love me, Cameo?"

The question came out of nowhere. Or maybe not. Maybe he'd read her mind. Maybe he'd asked to begin working those masculine wiles she had no defense against.

There was no denying the truth any longer. She loved him with every fiber of her being. He pleasured her spirit, mind and body. His irreverence amused her. His stubborn determination kept him by her side during the worst of her depression. His care of her made up for every second of sorrow she'd ever endured.

Somehow, he'd become her anchor in the storms of life. He'd become the sun, always chasing her darkness away. He'd filled an empty vessel with hope. He'd fought for her when she couldn't—wouldn't—fight for herself.

She would not put her wants before his needs.

"I'm not going to talk about this," she said.

In the morning, she would do what she needed to do, no matter how bad it hurt. She would let Misery take her memory. Lazarus would kill Hera, as he'd always wanted. That way, Cameo wouldn't try to kill the goddess on her own or save her.

That way, Cameo died, too. Better to go with a known outcome this go-round, too, than try to change the future and possibly make things worse. For herself, and for Lazarus.

She hated the thought of leaving him to deal with guilt, probably shame, on his own. But better he live with guilt and shame than die once again.

I'll gladly give my life for his.

Without her, the crystals would stop growing inside Lazarus. He would have the strength to live forever.

Sadness rose like a midnight tide, attempting to drown her, but she quickly built a dam around her heart. It would hold. For now. He came first.

Cameo used the toothpaste and wet wipes to clean up. Lazarus did the same, tension arcing between them. Outside, a storm erupted, the faint scent of rain filling the cavern. Thunder boomed and, through cracks in the earth, lightning flashed.

"I don't want to fight with you anymore," she said. Warmth spilled through her. "I just want you."

Pulsing with vitality and masculine aggression, he framed her face with his big hands. His titillating scent consumed her senses. The essence of seduction.

His gaze locked on hers, his pupils expanding and overtaking his irises. "You want me as your man? You want endless kisses? Sweat-slicked skin? Heated whispers? Wandering hands? Moans of pleasure? Grinding bodies? Intertwined limbs? The rest of my days?"

She shivered, and oh, how she ached. But then, his ability to paint such a deliciously carnal picture...to make her want what she couldn't have...was as well honed as her daggers. "I want here and now."

His grip tightened. "Do you love me?" he demanded again.

Refusing to answer had done her no good. "I do. I love you." Later he would find that admission had done *him* no good.

"Prove it, then. Give me everything."

Lightning shot through the cracks and illuminated the small space with bright gold flashes. The air charged, electrified, sensitizing her nerve endings.

With a moan of surrender, Cameo smashed her lips into his. Finesse was beyond her. She thrust her tongue against his, offering love...passion...tonight. Only tonight. The feel of his muscled strength was a high like no other.

A high she would never experience again.

He pressed her to the ground, heat to searing heat, and she rolled on top of him. Her hair created a dark curtain that hid them from the rest of the world. His hardness contrasted perfectly with her softness. Her nipples ached, and she quaked with longing.

She *felt* his love for her, a rushing river winding through them both. Her love for him sprouted like a tree planted beside the water, growing taller, wider, greater.

Desperate for skin-to-skin contact, she tore at his shirt until the material gave way. Bronzed skin. Magnificent tattoos on display. Savage hunger frothed inside her as she licked and nipped his collar…the center of his chest. She took the time to pay proper homage to his nipples.

He cupped her nape, offering himself in supplication. A masculine buffet of sensual delights, he was hers for the taking. And take she did, lost in her addiction for him.

Yes, I'm addicted. Obsessed, even. Blissfully so.

With the rising of the sun, everything would end.

The thought filled her with sadness.

No, no. Not here, not now. She checked the shield around her thoughts. It held, and she breathed a sigh of relief. Tonight she made memories to last a lifetime. Tonight she enjoyed the gift she'd been given: a marvelous male who saw her as a treasure rather than an anchor. Tonight she pretended she had a tomorrow.

"You are worth every hardship I've ever endured," he rasped. "You are my prize."

See! A treasure. "And you are mine."

"I love being claimed by you." *He* rolled on top of

her, taking the reins of their lovemaking and claiming control.

She ceded to his power, no part of her body off-limits to him. The muscled weight she so admired pinned her in place, a welcome cage.

"Where do you want to love your man?" he asked. "A beach hideaway? In front of a fireplace?"

Role-playing to help her forget the direness of their circumstances? "No illusions. Nothing false between us ever again. I want you here. Now. As you are—as *we* are."

He smiled down at her, tender and sweet, and she swore she could have an orgasm simply by looking at him. Beautiful man.

He nuzzled her cheek with his own before his mouth descended, devouring hers as if she were a meal, the last meal…until he was no longer kissing her but making a promise to her: *never letting you go.*

With deft movements, he stripped her of her top and bra, and tossed both garments aside. Then he cupped and kneaded her breasts. She arched against him, loving the friction…heat…fire. Mmm. *He's burning me from the inside out.*

"You're mine, and we're in this together." His fingers linked with hers and squeezed before stretching her arms over her head, pinning her more effectively, leaving her vulnerable to him. "Tell me."

"You're mine," she echoed, "and we're in this together." Until morning…

28

"Making your woman happy = making yourself
happier."

—*Memoir of a Besotted Fool*
—*How to Give Mind-Blowing Orgasms*

Primal hunger ruled Lazarus. He had his woman in
his arms. His one and only. Finally she would belong
to him body and soul. As he would belong to her. Now
and forever.

More than taking pleasure from Cameo, he wanted to
give. Wanted to give *himself* to her, the woman he loved
above all others. Above himself. Above his vengeance.

His father was wrong. Love wasn't what weakened
a warrior. It was the fear of losing what you loved that
weakened; Rathbone had tried to tell him that very
thing, that fear ruined and destroyed what love em-
powered, protected and enhanced. Love picked up the
shattered pieces of a broken heart and welded them back
together, making it stronger than ever before.

Once a weak link, now indestructible.

The truth had struck him when Cameo had said those three beautiful words. *I love you.* She affected him as no other, her passion a blazing match for his own. She wasn't just his lover; she was his partner.

The knowledge had only solidified as he'd stared into her luminous silver eyes—eyes that saw past the dark stains splattered across his past to the child who'd lost so much that the man he'd become had refused to relinquish possession of anything else. Even a piece of his fragmented heart. A piece Cameo could have easily stolen. Instead, she'd waited for him to give...and give freely.

In return, I will give her the world.

Lazarus plundered her mouth, stoking her desire as well as his own. Her lips were soft and plump, so giving beneath his. There was the word again. Giving, give. *Give her more...*

As he deepened the kiss, she *clung* to him, as if he were a life raft and she a shipwrecked sailor. She moaned and breathed his name. All the while she writhed against him, rubbing her core against his throbbing length. Every point of contact heated the blood in his veins to a boiling point. The steam only fortified the crystals, but he didn't care.

He nipped at her chin, licked the elegant length of her jaw...sucked on her exquisite neck and the pulse racing as quickly as his own. He left a mark. His mark.

"I love you," she whispered.

His heart leaped with joy. "You'll remember this. And this." He kissed a circle around each of her breasts before bathing her nipples with the wet heat of his mouth. "And this."

Her hips continued to writhe, an irresistible flush

spreading over her flesh. She was like a delicate pink rose, silken and sheened with dew. *She blooms for me and me alone.*

With his tongue, he traced a heart around her nipple and blew.

"Lazario!"

He heard no sorrow in her voice, only passion. How far this wonderful woman had come, from the deepest depths of misery to the highest pinnacle of joy. The true power of love.

He suckled her. "With my mouth and body, and my very soul, I honor and claim you." He moved to her other breast and flicked his tongue back and forth, every swipe proclaiming *mine, mine, you are mine*. "Today, tomorrow and every day after."

"I'm yours." Her nails scraped over his back. "I'll always be yours."

Lightning flashed over the rocks, and for a moment, golden light spilled over her. Her beauty was ethereal, otherworldly. Raindrops found grooves in the rocks and dripped from the ceiling, landing on him and splashing onto her. Cool and sweet, no hint of burning acid. Her passion fever quickly heated the droplets, creating a fine wine and an even sweeter candy. He lapped every bead from her skin, drinking from her.

What they were doing wasn't just an act of intimacy meant to slake a momentary desire. What they were doing was solidifying a promise they'd made for their future.

A future together.

Overcome, desperate for more, he released her hands, removed her boots and tore at the waist of her leathers. As soon as the zipper gave, he yanked the material down her legs with a single flick of his wrist.

As his gaze perused her, she cupped and kneaded her breasts, her thumbs brushing over her nipples. Weapons were strapped to her thighs and ankles, turning her into a goddess of sex and war. *My goddess.* He could only stare at her in amazement—until his body demanded he act.

He discarded every gun and blade, though he ensured each remained within reach. Her panties received the same treatment as the leathers, leaving her bare. His gaze perused her once again, languid yet wild, savoring yet desirous of more.

He'd beheld her nakedness before, yes, but every time was like the first: a revelation.

The leather-sheathed apple rested between her plump, pert breasts, where her satin skin displayed a rosier flush. Her body possessed a graceful muscle tone as well as mesmerizing curves. The edges of the butterfly's wings hugged her hips and thighs.

"Spread your legs for me, Cami." The rasp of his voice drifted between them. "Let me see every inch of my love."

She obeyed, revealing the pretty pink paradise that awaited him. He groaned his approval—and reverence. She wasn't just wet; she was soaked.

Driven by ferocious arousal, he slid a finger inside her, deep, deeper, and inhaled sharply. Her hips lifted, her inner walls tightening on him, driving him mad.

"You were created for me, sunshine."

She placed her foot on his chest, just over his heart, and gently but insistently pushed him. "Get naked. Now. Show me every inch of *my* love."

Before, when she'd wanted to see his legs, he'd hesitated. This time, he stood and stripped in a hurry, overcome by anticipation. He kicked off his boots, shucked off his pants and dropped his weapons next to hers.

Her gaze lingered on his aching shaft, and she licked her lips. "There's my monster."

The huskiness of his laugh turned her silver eyes molten. "Yours," he said, gripping the base of his erection. "He doesn't just love his woman. He adores her."

"Good. Because there's no other male I would rather call my own."

Cameo thrilled as Lazarus knelt between her legs. Her nerve endings blazed. What little air she managed to draw in smelled of Lazarus, champagne and chocolate. Temptation and carnal indulgence.

He flipped her over and positioned her on her hands and knees. His fingertip traced the butterfly, the touch sending currents of raw passion through her. He rubbed his erection in the crevice of her thighs, her wet heat offering an easy glide. A perfect glide. He wasn't inside her, but even still, rapture beckoned...

Pressure built inside her, making her need for release—for her man—a thousand times stronger. "That feels good," she rasped, "so good, but I want more."

He leaned forward to nibble on her earlobe. "Must get you ready first."

"I'm ready. Promise!"

"Let's find out." He kissed a path down her spine, paying every ridge equal attention. By the time he reached the end of her tattoo, shivers racked her. He curled one hand around her thigh, spreading her legs farther apart. He glided his other hand around her hips...and between her legs, where he played with her, circling where she needed him most. She rocked her hips, seeking his shaft. "Mmm. I think you're right."

"Need to be filled," she said with a moan. "Please, Lazario. Now."

"A plea and a command all rolled into one." His soft chuckle fanned his breath on the back of her neck, tickling her. "Do you want my fingers?" He thrust one in, out, in, and she gasped...then he eased in a second, stretching her, delighting her. In, out. In-out. The heel of his palm pressed against her core, driving her need higher...higher still.

Her breaths were coming faster now, so fast she could barely speak, but still she managed to say, "I want...you...all of you. Please," she repeated.

"Then all of me you shall have, my Cami." Lazarus placed the tip of his erection at her entrance—and plunged inside her. He stretched her. Filled her. Branded her.

Owned her.

Never going to be the same. Her back arched, her nails cutting into the cavern floor, and she shouted his name. "Give me hard and fast."

Lazarus unleashed the full brunt of his passion. He pounded in and out of her with no hint of gentleness, tossing her into a great and mighty storm. Pleasure saturated her bones...sweet...as potent as a drug, going straight to her head.

He pressed his chest to her back and laved the shell of her ear. His pace never slowed, the force he used never easing. Too much. Not enough.

"My Lazario." Lost in abandon, she chanted his name now. In her tone, she heard no sorrow. No regret or sadness. She heard wonder, and his entire body jolted in response; he pounded into her harder, faster, in and out. She was almost there… "So close."

He hooked his hand around her knees to push her legs farther apart, at the same time pressing her head forward, causing her back to arch, granting him another inch inside her, hitting her where she needed him most. She screamed in bliss, in agony, her inner walls clenching and unclenching on him, demanding a reward. A reward he freely gave.

As satisfaction punched through her, Lazarus roared. A guttural, animalistic sound that echoed through the cave long after he'd collapsed atop her, tremors still working through both their bodies.

As Lazarus slept, Cameo remained cuddled into his side, toying with the apple—Pandora's box. Soon, the sun would rise. Today would be gone, and tomorrow would be here.

Her life with Lazarus would end.

Her *life* would end, period.

What would happen if she touched the apple skin-to-bone? She had to know.

If she died this way, she died, the end coming sooner than she'd expected. Lazarus could warn her friends. And live. He would live.

Not giving herself time to think or worry, she purposely slipped her fingertips under the leather casing. In an instant, fiery heat arced through her, and she grunted.

What didn't happen? Death. Misery remained at bay, hidden in the back of her mind. Suppressed more forcefully? Perhaps even injured?

Lazarus shifted against her, and she stilled. Only when he resettled, his breaths even, did she begin to breathe again. His strong arm was draped over her, his hand cupping her breast, as if he couldn't bear to sever their connection.

A fierce need she understood.

Tears burned the backs of her eyes, and a knot of grief grew in her throat. The dam around her heart threatened to break at last. *Not yet, just a little longer.* Sorrow beat and battered her. How could she proceed with her memory-wipe plan? How could she willingly part with her only source of happiness?

Easily. To save Lazarus's life.

He would kill Hera. Cameo wouldn't stop him. She would die, somehow, free of Misery, no longer a threat to Lazarus's life.

Win-win.

Lazarus...king...butterflies.

The words Keeley had spoken to Torin played through her mind. Perhaps Lazarus was right. Perhaps butterflies represented hope. Without Cameo and her butterfly, he would thrive.

The tears overflowed, streaming down her cheeks, burning her skin. For so long her memory had been everything to her. She'd cherished what she retained and mourned what she'd lost. Meeting Lazarus—loving Lazarus—had made her memories even more precious to her.

His every smile. The way he teased her. His every touch. The way his muscles rippled when he moved. His every kiss. The way he tasted, intoxicating her senses. His every claiming. The way he looked at her, lust and affection in his dark eyes.

Can't live without the memories.

Don't have to.

Yes, she did. For him.

Hands shaking, Cameo removed the necklace and gently placed the chain around Lazarus's neck. Misery couldn't wipe her memory while she wore the box.

The demon surged front and center, pissed as hell and determined to ruin whatever happiness she'd achieved in his absence.

Too late. "Take my memory of him," she whispered.

Part of her expected him to refuse. As miserable as she was, as miserable as she would continue to be, her sorrow would surely empower him for centuries to come. But he had to know as well as she how deeply the loss of her memory would devastate her. Lazarus's reaction would finish her off, because she would know, deep down, her mind had been violated, something precious taken from her.

With a gleeful laugh, Misery sliced his claws into her mental files, cutting away the most beloved moments of her life. She cringed, the pain sharp and sure.

Necessary.

Cameo turned her head to peer at Lazarus, to say goodbye a final time. To—

She frowned. A naked male lay beside her; he was cut with muscle and heavily tattooed. Thick lines stretched across his arms, chest and legs, as if his veins had been filled with glitter. He was gorgeous. Magnetic. Dangerous?

Heart thudding, she scrambled away. The demon had taken her memories again, hadn't he?

Bastard! She reached up to punch her fists into the sides of her head, perhaps shaking the demon.

Her bedmate blinked open his eyes—dark eyes, framed by incredibly long lashes. He was more than gorgeous. He was rugged and strong, and she wondered if she'd fallen for his looks. Because wow. But…she hated sex. What if he'd forced her?

"Sunshine?" He reached for her. "Come back to bed, love."

She scrambled backward, widening the distance between them.

Love. He'd called her *love*. He hadn't forced her. He'd romanced her. Had probably made her happy, and the demon had decided to strike.

Can't live like this.

"Who are you?" she whispered.

As Lazarus dressed and weaponed up, Cameo did the same while keeping him within her periphery. Her intent was clear: she wanted to maintain distance.

A blistering curse left him. Only hours before, she'd promised to love him always. Now Pandora's box hung around his neck. Which meant she'd returned her prized possession, and forgotten it —forgotten him. She'd *will ingly* allowed Misery to wipe her mind.

Why?

He wanted to hate her. He fell deeper in love with her instead. Whatever her reason, she'd put him first. Clearly. No one had ever put him first before.

But though he loved her, fury frothed inside him. With one act, she'd shredded the heart he'd entrusted to her. He wanted his Cameo back. His sunshine. He felt as if she'd perished today, along with his dreams. The remains were here, in a cave that had become a grave.

"I'm your man." *Believe me. Remember.* "You love me, and I love you."

At his declaration, her eyes rounded like saucers. Her mind remained open to him, the shield down. She could see the torment etched in every line in his face, sensed it was genuine, and hated that she'd hurt the man who'd probably shown her the meaning of happiness. Probably. He had!

"Where are we?" she asked.

"Nowhere important." He gnashed his teeth as he approached her. With every step, pain ricocheted through him. The crystals had thickened and spread, so close to his heart. His end neared.

Cameo retreated. A muscle jumped beneath his eye, but he continued moving toward her, anyway. When he had her pressed flat against a rocky wall, he fought the urge to kiss her—couldn't stand the thought of a rejection after her complete surrender—and removed the chain to drape it over her head.

"This is yours." He settled the box between her breasts, hoping the familiar action would spur a flicker of her past.

She blinked with surprise and relief, her head suddenly her own. Peace and quiet reigned. "The demon—" She pressed her lips together.

He read her thoughts, knew she feared his reaction to discovering the truth about her evil. "I know all about him." His voice snapped like a whip. He resented the need to explain. "When you wear the pendant, its power suppresses the demon. When you're near the pendant, its power aggravates the demon, but it isn't strong enough to suppress him."

Out came her tongue to swipe over her bottom lip.

Before she'd wrecked him, he would have leaned down to capture her tongue with his own. If he kissed her now, she would bite him.

"What's so special about the pendant?" she asked.

"Only everything." Frustration and anger raged inside him. He wanted his Cameo back. The one who melted when she looked at him. Who kissed with passion and awe. Who clung to him. The one who loved him.

The one he couldn't live without.

The demon had wiped her mind. Permission or not, the demon would pay.

Lazarus pressed his forehead against Cameo's. Though she stiffened, she allowed the contact to continue without protest. He breathed in her scent. Roses, bergamot and neroli.

He hadn't cried when his mother died, her body in pieces at his feet. He hadn't cried when Juliette hacked off his hands or his testicle. Hadn't cried when he'd been beheaded and sent to the spirit realms, his future forever altered.

He'd always considered tears a weakness.

Here, now, tears flowed unchecked down each cheek. He'd lost something precious today.

Maybe her memory loss was for the best?

While the thought angered him, he couldn't deny its veracity. This way, when Lazarus told her goodbye, when he ended up encased in stone for eternity, she wouldn't cry, breaking him. She wouldn't feel anything at all. She could live her life without regret.

He would do anything to save her from a moment's pain.

"Let's get you home," he croaked. "There are things

you and your friends need to know." Forget Hera. Forget vengeance.

Hate had ceased to matter. Life wasn't about who he killed but about who he loved.

Boom!

An explosion above the cavern shook the walls. Hunks of rock rolled from the ceiling. Dust clotted in the air.

Can't break down now. Must get Cameo to safety.

Cameo reached out to brace herself against the wall.

He stalked from her *without* kissing her or shouting obscenities. The hardest thing he'd ever done. Despite the pain that escalated with every move he made, he gathered the go bags. "We can't stay here." He couldn't leave her behind while he scouted the area for a portal. She had no idea how many dangers surrounded them. "Stay directly behind me."

"Wait," she called as he marched to the narrow entry.

He stilled, daring to hope she had remembered something about him.

"You never told me your name."

The fragments of his heart withered. "I'm Lazarus, known to all as Cameo's man."

29

"When everything has gone wrong, rejoice. Something must now go right."

—~~How to Give Mind-Blowing Orgasms~~
—How Boys Become Men

Siobhan's glass hung in Hades's private bedchamber. The bed had a six-foot-tall panel at the footboard, and he'd placed her in the center, giving her a direct view of his mattress while he lounged against a mound of pillows.

She'd beaten at her prison wall until the flesh had ripped from her hands. She'd screamed until her throat had become as raw as ground meat and breathing became an act of sheer torture. Hades had simply peered at her, waiting for her to break and show him different possible futures.

The ultimate staring contest. Who would flinch first?

Well, there was no reason to engage. No reason to help him. She scanned her new surroundings. The spacious room was filled with fine velvets, antique furnishings and mystical artifacts. A bouquet of red roses decorated the nightstand. A glowing blue sword rested on the dresser. A portrait of a pink-haired woman hung over the bed's headboard—Keeley, the Red Queen. Once Hades's fiancée.

Why did he have a portrait of his former fiancée? Did he love her still?

Siobhan hated the woman on principal. Loving a man like Hades made you a fool.

"I can do this all day," Hades said, his voice a silky purr. He looked every inch the pampered male. A bowl made of incandescent dragon glass rested beside him, overflowing with grapes. He tossed a piece of fruit into his mouth and chewed, the movement of his jaw somehow sensual, indecent, even. "Give me what I want. Show me who wins the war and how victory is achieved."

He wanted an edge over his enemy. She wanted to show him a devastating loss.

Strategize. Lead. Strike.

She had to proceed with caution. Hurting him under the guise of helping him meant hurting herself. If she brought about his death, without finding his true love, she added time to her sentence. If she aided him now, she could maybe, finally, gain her freedom.

Help now, hurt later.

Decision made.

She helped. The first problem arose. Siobhan couldn't see Hades's futures. *Because I escape and force him to take my place?* Fingers crossed!

As glass rippled and split, Hades jolted upright, his fruit forgotten. With no other recourse, she revealed the same futures she'd shown to Cameo. This time, however, Siobhan's vision launched further into the future. She saw what would happen if Lazarus killed Hera and shuddered.

Demons. So many demons.

In a strange, tangled loop, the past began to blend with the future. Long ago, the former queen of the Greeks made a deal with Lucifer the Destroyer. Help him capture the Morning Star, and Lucifer would do what Hera couldn't. He would punish her husband, Zeus. She'd agreed to his terms and sneaked a thousand demons from the hell realms...by hiding them inside her own body. She'd planned to release the fiends upon Earth, where the Morning Star roamed, so that they could hunt the being. But the demons hadn't wanted to leave her. They'd liked their new home. Liked driving her mad. They bonded to her.

In a rare moment of lucidity, she'd created a box made from the bones of her friend, the goddess of Oppression. Hera used the box to extract a quarter of the fiends inside her, not realizing the box had a limited capacity. Lucky her. The culling process nearly killed her. But as she lay dying, she somehow found a way to save herself...

Again, Siobhan couldn't see how.

How had the Morning Star gotten trapped inside the box? Siobhan couldn't see. Also couldn't see how Hera had saved herself. Too many snags between past and future...

Past: Lucifer betrayed Hera and told Zeus what his wife planned. He offered the demigod the world in exchange for the box.

Zeus stole the box, but rather than give it to the Destroyer, he placed it in the hands of a woman Hera wouldn't kill, thanks to her warped morals, and a woman Lucifer couldn't tempt. The loyal Pandora. Then the Lords of the Underworld stole and opened the box.

In the ensuing chaos, Hera retrieved the box and spirited it away. Since it had been emptied, she was able to remove another quarter of the remaining demons possessing her, leaving her with only half of the demonic squatters. That meant five hundred remained inside her, and two hundred and fifty still filled the box. As for the Morning Star? No one knew if the being had escaped or remained inside. Not even Hera.

Present: if Lazarus killed Hera, as one of Siobhan's visions predicted, Hera's demons would be let loose upon an ill-prepared world. The fiends would be crazed, free to wreak havoc on innocents.

Lazarus, Cameo and even Hera had made decisions that resulted in a defined outcome. One way or another, Lazarus would face his nemesis, and he would face her today.

A pallid Hades leaped from the bed. "William!" he shouted. His son had taken off hours ago to search for Gillian, a female he hoped to steal from her husband. "Return to me. Now. There's going to be trouble."

Lazarus's final words played inside Cameo's mind again and again. *Lazarus, known to all as Cameo's man.* He'd meant what he'd said. The way he'd looked at her with no attempt to disguise the fire and lust and longing in his eyes. She shivered. Mostly, though, he'd looked at her with betrayal.

Her shoulders sagged. She had hurt this man. Badly.

Since they'd left the cavern, he hadn't looked at her at all, and she didn't have to guess why. Her eyes regarded him as the stranger he'd become, and every glance reminded him of what he'd lost. What they might have shared. He must feel like he was taking a dagger to the gut.

She did!

How had he convinced her to sleep with him? Had he enjoyed himself? Had Cameo climaxed?

No need to wonder. Yes. Yes, she had. Satisfaction still sang in her veins, a soft vibration against her bones.

Her first orgasm, and she couldn't remember it. How she loathed Misery! He'd taken something precious from her. He would *always* take from her.

There was no escaping him. Except through death.

When the forest opened up, revealing a bank of moss, a rushing river and a wide, mile-long marble staircase leading over the water, Lazarus stopped. Every mile they'd gained, his pace had slowed a little more and his steps had become a lot more labored. He had to be injured, but when she'd questioned him about possible wounds, he'd said, "Want to know what's wrong with me? Remember."

"I can't," she'd snapped. "The demon—"

"He can't take your memories without your permission."

The claim still rattled around in her head.

Lazarus, known to all as Cameo's man.

Without your permission.

Lazarus. Permission.

A lie, surely. Why would she ever grant permission? There was no reason great enough.

And yet, a terrible suspicion struck her. If she couldn't remember the reasons she'd allowed Misery to wipe a select portion of her past, she would be destined to repeat the same mistakes, right? Wasn't *that* the true definition of misery?

"The portal that will take you home is close," Lazarus said. He clutched a dagger in each hand as he scanned for traps.

Clearly on guard, he began to climb up the steps, approaching the entrance of a temple.

Cameo stuck close to his heels. "How do you know?"

She'd noticed he never flinched when she spoke, and it had thrilled her every time.

"Portals radiate a certain type of power. I've been around enough of them to notice." The formal tone he used disconcerted her.

She missed the warmth he'd expressed in the cave. Maybe *he* needed a reminder of their past. "You said… you love me?" The words were more of a question than a statement. How could *anyone* love her? "What made you fall for someone like me?"

Underneath his shirt, the muscles in his back knotted. "You mean someone strong and courageous? Someone who doesn't cave to fear but overcomes it? Someone who is as much a weapon as the swords she creates? Someone as lonely as I've been, who dreams of a happily-ever-after? Someone who smiles for me and me alone? Someone who empowers me with only a glance? Someone who has never placed a condition on her feelings for me, who loves me and wants the best for me?"

She sucked in a breath. He'd thrown the last one at her as if the words were bombs set to detonate.

"Why would I ever fall for someone like that?" he asked softly.

Her heart thudded. The things he said to her… "Someone who inspires sorrow."

"You didn't inspire sorrow in me…until today."

* * *

Lazarus lapsed into silence. If he continued to speak, he would rage. *Control is fraying.* As he'd led Cameo through the forest, bypassing different traps and predators, his mood had only darkened. *Want what's mine!* Namely her affection. She'd become the best friend he'd ever had. Someone Lazarus trusted with every aspect of his life.

She had become his family.

But he didn't have much time left. His every step had become an exercise in agony.

Get Cameo home to safety. Say goodbye. Would she kiss him one last time? Or would he spend the rest of eternity remembering her blank stare?

He trudged another step, then another. Despite every hardship they'd already endured in the forest, Lazarus suspected Hera had saved the worst trap for the temple. A means of guarding the portal. Except, he reached the top without a single incident.

The temple itself had been emptied. No furniture, and no portal, either. No pulse of power. No sign of Hera or his father. The only indication anyone had *ever* been here was a rust-colored stain beneath a huge cobweb on the marble floor.

A flame of rage escaped its tether, and he slammed a fist into a towering alabaster column. How was he supposed to get Cameo home to her family? He'd promised her. He could not fail her!

"Lazarus?"

And he could not bring himself to peer into those liquid silver eyes again. "What?" he bit out, staring at the ground between them.

"There's a stuffed leopard attached to your go bag. It wasn't there before. Or if it was, I failed to notice."

Rathbone! Lazarus pulled the pack forward and sure enough, the toy smiled up at him. No matter how many times Lazarus had tossed the warrior's newest incarnation somewhere in the jungle—in pits and quicksand—the immortal sovereign had returned.

With a flick of his wrist, Lazarus hurled the stuffed animal down the temple steps.

"What's your beef with toys?" Cameo asked. "And why did you pack this one if you didn't—"

"You want answers? Remember," he snapped. Then he scrubbed a hand over his face. At this rate, he would scare her away.

Time to plan his next move. He'd sensed the portal from the forest, even on the steps. The power had only intensified as he'd ascended. Unless Hera could cast illusions? When she'd shown up at the Downfall, he'd suspected it.

Had she tricked him the same way he'd tricked so many others?

Cameo stalked through the empty chamber, tracing her fingertips over the columns. "Whose temple is this?" She asked the question hesitantly, as if she had no desire to set him off again.

"Hera, former queen of the Greeks. Never trust her. She wants to kill you."

"Me? Why?"

"Many reasons." Why not tell her? When he left her, she needed to remain on constant guard. "I vowed to kill her. You are my woman, the only leverage she has against me. And you have Pandora's box."

She snorted. "Yeah, right."

"I have *never* lied to you, love. Never will." His ear twitched as a pebble rolled in the distance. He had two daggers at the ready as he turned—

A whirlwind gusted between him and Cameo, knocking them apart. Any other day, he could have stood strong against such a blast, but not now, not like this. He flew through the entrance and tumbled down several steps, his damaged body screaming in protest.

Adrenaline surged, dulling the sharpest edges of pain, allowing him to jump to his feet and race into the temple once again.

The whirlwind stopped at the far edge, revealing a smug, grinning Hera. She'd pinned a surprisingly calm Cameo to a column, a sword tip pressed to her neck.

Terror wrapped its claws around his neck and squeezed. He stilled, not even daring to breathe, lest he goad the goddess into striking. This. This paralyzing fear, born as a boy forced to watch as his mother was murdered, was why he'd always abhorred weakness.

Cameo's gaze remained steady, the color in her cheeks deepening rather than draining. She planned to fight back, didn't she?

"Let her go," he commanded the goddess. *Must protect Cameo at all costs!* "She's done nothing to you."

Hera raised her chin. "I loved your mother, and yet I tore her limb from limb. I will do the same to the keeper of Misery without a moment's hesitation."

"You want Pandora's box, and you want me dead so you'll be safe from my wrath." She had no idea how close she stood to the object of her desire, the pendant hidden underneath the truth of Cameo's shirt and his illusion. Finally, Lazarus forced himself to move, placing the tip of a dagger against his own throat. "You will never have the first, but I can give you the second."

Now Cameo paled. "No! Don't."

"Quiet!" Hera squeezed her eyes closed and shook her head. With her free hand, she slapped her forehead once, twice, as if to dislodge a thought…or a voice? Lazarus had witnessed the same action by each of the Lords at some point. "Why would you want to save this woman from me, anyway? She is your weakness."

"Wrong. She is my greatest strength."

Hera blanched. "Impossible. Zeus did not create her to be a warrior. Oh, no. Not my husband. He's always considered women an inferior species. He created her and Pandora to be whores, responsible for pleasing the—quote, unquote—real soldiers. Why do you think Cameo was inclined to date two of her friends?"

Cameo tensed as if poised to strike. "That's not true."

Hera flinched.

Lazarus schooled his features to reveal nothing but mild contempt. "No, it's not true. The self-proclaimed champion of women is trying to tear down another female. I guess hate knows no prejudice as it grows. And understand me now. Cameo was created to be my perfect mate, just as I was created to be hers."

Hera's eyes—those hated eyes that reflected the aerial view of Earth—filled with regret, sorrow…relief? She shook her head a second time, shouting, "No one has a perfect mate. Men have obsessions, at least for a little while. Cameo should not have aligned with one such as you, Lazarus. Now, enough chatter. I will have the box. I must."

Must. A very telling word. Why *must* she?

The answer didn't matter, really. He would not be

giving it to her. Ever. The box could be used to slay Cameo.

"I'm the only one who knows where it is, and with my illusion in place, you will never find it," Lazarus said. "Send Cameo home, and we'll talk."

She glared at him. "Your father wasn't as protective of your mother. Do you think he knew how badly Echidna wanted to die? How she begged me to punish him with her murder?"

The words shook him. "You lie."

"No, but I do kill." Hera pressed the sword in a little deeper, drawing a bead of blood from Cameo's vulnerable pulse. "Give me. The box."

Cameo's lips parted, a soft sound leaving her.

His rage continued to build, scorching the reins of his control, soon growing into a wildfire. He forgot about the crystals as his muscles and bones expanded, as fangs sharpened from his gums and claws extended from his fingertips.

The monster was back.

As he took a step forward, Hera screeched, "Do not move!"

An animalistic roar echoed through the entire chamber, and Lazarus almost smiled. Rathbone was back, as well. The leopard—no longer a stuffed animal but the real deal—leaped into action, locking his teeth around Lazarus's wrist and then flinging him across the room. He slammed into Hera, knocking her down, and the sword skittered from her grip.

Cameo sprinted across the open floor and claimed the weapon.

Lazarus jumped up to push his boot into the goddess's throat, trapping her on the dirty floor as Rathbone's image shifted into that of a leather-clad male.

He grinned at Lazarus. "Having a friend is better than having an enemy. Admit it."

"A true friend would have gone for the bad guy instead of launching me across the room," he replied drily.

Panicked, Hera struggled against his hold. "Let me go!"

"You threatened my woman. You die one way or another this day." He peered down at her. "How you do so is your only choice. Tell me where my father is, and I'll end you quick and easy."

Despite the raggedness of her inhalations, she uttered a small laugh. "Like all your kind, you are a fool. You never see what's right in front of you."

What did that mean? Had Lazarus seen his father, but failed to recognize him?

"You are also easily distracted," she said, grinning now, no hint of panic. Her skin darkened, quickly turning to mist, until a small tornado had taken her place.

He punched his claws at her, intending to rip out her trachea if any part of her remained inside the wind, but she whisked away, and he cut through the marble.

The tornado slammed into Rathbone, pitching him across the temple. The warrior crashed into the floor face-first. Then the tornado executed a sharp turn and slammed into Cameo. Lazarus shouted a denial as he stood. He expected his sunshine to fly backward, but the closer the winds came to her, the weaker they blew.

Something had impeded Hera's power. Cameo's demon?

No, the queen wasn't sobbing. Pandora's box? No, she wasn't demon possessed.

The way she'd shaken her head…

Was she possessed?

The tornado died, and Hera appeared once more. Cameo was ready. She planted a foot in Hera's midsection, using the goddess as a stepping-stone to wind her other leg around the bitch's neck and take her down. As they fell, Cameo swung around to ensure she landed on top. Without pause, she shoved a dagger into Hera's chest.

Hera grunted with surprise. Lazarus gaped, awed. *That's my woman.*

The wound wouldn't kill the goddess, but it would definitely weaken her. Blood pooled around her; any move she made to free herself would only send the blade deeper.

Recovering quickly, Rathbone crouched beside the pair and savagely snapped the bones in both of the goddess's wrists. Hera screamed, the cries clearly rousing no compassion in Rathbone as he did the same to her ankles.

"There." The king wiped his hands together in a job well done. "She won't be punching or kicking for a while. I wonder if breaking her jaw would shut her up? Never heard noises quite like the ones she's making. Sounds like hell." He rubbed his jaw with two fingers. "Yes, I think I will."

Hera quieted.

"Or not. Good girl."

Lazarus dug through the go bags and withdrew the Paring Rod, as well as the piece of pipe that had been taken from the Cage of Compulsion. His fangs and claws retracted, his adrenaline crashing. The crystals burned, growing closer to his heart.

Finish this. Before it's too late. "Do you know where the portal is?" he asked Rathbone.

"I do." He scooped up a handful of dirt from the floor and flung it at the right side of the temple. There was no wall, only a mile-long free fall to land, and yet the grains got caught in a large section of air, forming a doorway.

Finally. Something worked in his favor.

His gaze sought and found Cameo. Beautiful Cameo. "I love you. I will always love you."

"Lazarus." Sadness radiated from her. She reached for him. "Don't say goodbye. Not yet. I'll stay here with you. We can—"

He blocked out the raspy timbre of her voice as he faced Rathbone. "Get her home safely." Lazarus would stay here…forever. He would kill Hera, once and for all. He would watch as her corpse rotted, content to know her spirit had entered the spirit realm. He would use the Paring Rod and pipe to make sure of it.

If his suspicions were correct and Hera actually housed a demon, she would end up in the prison realm.

Either way, she died.

As for Typhon, Lazarus would have hunted him down if he had more days. With Hera out of the picture, his father would be easier to kill. But Lazarus didn't have more days, and had to resign himself to the knowledge that the bastard still lived. Knowing Typhon was trapped inside a crystal prison of his own softened the blow.

Rathbone scooped Cameo into his arms and headed for the portal.

"I'm not leaving." She fought the warrior—fought

dirty and didn't pull her punches—but he never lost his hold on her.

Even without her memory, she wanted to help Lazarus.

His chest burned as he stalked to the goddess, doing everything in his power to mask his pain, intending to end her once and for all.

"I don't know why, but I can't get through." Rathbone banged his fists into an invisible wall.

They were trapped? Had to be Hera's fault. "Take down the wall," he commanded her.

Panting, Hera yanked the blade from her chest and pointed the crimson-soaked tip in his direction. Her grip shook, but it was clear her bones had already begun to heal. Such swift regeneration, even for a goddess, was unnatural. "Give me...the box..."

"This isn't a negotiation any longer. Take down the wall."

With a screech, she jumped to her feet, and yes, her bones had healed. She launched into a full-on attack and swung the sword at him. He sidestepped her. Barely. Weakened, he tripped. As he stumbled, she changed her focus, attacking Cameo and Rathbone.

Lazarus roared a denial, but he needn't have bothered. Rathbone blocked. Cameo pulled a sword from the sheath at his back and joined the fray. She thrust. Hera parried. *Clang. Clang.*

Lazarus jumped in the middle, blocking the next blow before delivering one of his own. The pipe met Hera's skull. She careened to the side, but she wasn't out any more than she was down for the count.

She rallied quickly and resumed the fight. She knew when to duck, jump and dodge. She knew when to spin and when to maintain her position, and what was worse, she delivered more injuries than she received. *Lazarus* was the recipient of most, his reflexes nearly completely shot. At least she was tiring, her motions slowing. Every time she breathed, she wheezed.

When Cameo landed a massive blow to her midsection, slicing through her stomach, Hera attempted to leave the temple. Any other day, in any other place, Lazarus could have flashed or dived in front of Hera to stop her. Today, he could only cast an illusion, the ability as strong as ever despite his physical limitations.

He conjured the worst of the worst. The monstrous form of Typhon in his prime.

Typhon had dark hair and dark eyes, like Lazarus, and his ears pointed at both ends, the tops so high and thick they appeared to be horns. Red flames crackled inside his nostrils and mouth. He had a barrel chest, with an image of Lazarus's mother branded in the center, snakes curling from her scalp rather than hair.

From Typhon's back stretched three sets of wings. One extended from the tops of his shoulders, the other from between his shoulders, and the last from his hip bones. The first two projected backward while the third wrapped forward, offering protection to his midsection and groin.

His legs were as thick as tree trunks and covered in scales veined with molten fire—with a single cut, the fire would spill out, burning to ash everyone who came into contact with the embers. His hands and feet were clawed.

Hera screamed and darted back. "You can't…you can't be here. Not like this. Your chrysalis…"

Chrysalis. The word rattled around in Lazarus's

brain. Like a butterfly's chrysalis, made of pupa and silk, not crystal?

Lazarus…king…butterflies.

"He isn't real," she said. "He can't be real."

The last time Hera had faced Lazarus's father, he'd been weakened, barely able to move. In the illusion, he was at full strength. A male she could not hope to best.

Phantom Typhon breathed a stream of fire at her, hitting the floor just in front of her. The flames ricocheted upward, several landing on her boots. She struggled to remove the footwear but ultimately succeeded. Blisters appeared all over her hands.

"You were saying?" Lazarus smiled. "If Typhon isn't real, why are you burned?"

Hera's mouth floundered open and closed. If she had been born with the ability to cast illusions, she would know the mind had the power to inflict the expected injury.

As Rathbone returned his attention to the invisible wall, Cameo focused on the goddess, a weapon in hand, her brow furrowed with confusion as she watched the monster.

Lazarus stepped toward Hera and winced. The crystals—pupa? Or perhaps a mix of both in his case?—were spreading even now, rising up his neck, over his cheeks and clogging his ears. Dead silence overtook him. He heard nothing, not even a tremulous ring. The substance filled his lungs. Breathing became more difficult.

He had mere minutes left.

Though he wanted to go to Cameo, to stare into her exquisite face as he met his end, he lumbered toward Hera. The goddess had no place to go. Typhon's fire surrounded her. She narrowed her eyes, lifted her chin. Ever rebellious against the inevitable.

Kill the threat to my woman, welcome eternity. He swung.

A look of horror contorted Cameo's features. She screamed and lunged in front of Hera. No time to pull his arm back or angle the direction of the weapon. The Paring Rod pierced her chest. She gasped and shook. He roared.

No! What had she done? What had *he* done?

He'd hurt the woman he loved. He might have killed—

No, no, no. "Why? Why did you do this?" He attempted to yank the Paring Rod out of her. Any moment now, the artifact would suck her spirit through a portal…but the tip of the weapon remained caught in her sternum. To remove it, he would have to remove her entire rib cage. Her lungs would collapse, and her already damaged heart would stop.

The injuries would agonize her, but they would heal.

First…he shoved the pipe over the Rod, sheathing it. "Live forever," he commanded. "I demand the demon leave you. Demand your spirit remains inside your body. Do you hear me? I own the pipe and therefore the compulsion. It was a gift. I demand that you live. Obey me!"

Blood poured from the corners of her mouth as she tried to speak.

She was still dying.

No! He gave a final yank, the Paring Rod at last pulling free. It took only half of her rib cage with it. Hardly a silver lining. Her back bowed as her legs and chest collapsed. She released another scream as her knees gave out, and he tossed the artifacts aside. Beneath her skin, veins of black appeared, tentacles seeming to writhe inside them. Her entire body seized.

The demon was leaving her?

Black soon turned to gray and gray to blue, until the tracery of veins beneath her skin appeared normal, healthy. Then a black mist rose from her shirt—no, not her shirt but the pendant underneath her shirt.

Yes! Her demon.

The mist hovered over her, neon eyes glowing from within. Those eyes locked on Lazarus. Fangs snapped at him before the mist darted out of the temple, unencumbered by the invisible wall.

Had his Cami survived?

Lazarus dropped to his knees, knew he would be frozen in this humbled position for the rest of his life, but didn't care. He had to touch Cameo, had to learn her fate. Trembling, he smoothed his fingertips over the softness of her cheek.

The healthy color had vanished, leaving her chalk white. She panted and wheezed. But she hadn't entered the spirit realm. Why?

"He's…gone," she said. "Misery…gone…cleansed…happiness…remember…"

She remembered…Lazarus?

He wanted to shout with joy. He wanted to sob. What would happen next? She couldn't die. She couldn't!

"My apple!" Hera, who stood on Cameo's other side, reached for the pendant.

Rathbone caught her wrist and wrestled her away. Leaving Lazarus to his goodbye.

No! Hell, no. This would not be Cameo's end. Only his.

"Why?" he demanded.

"She was…about to…stab you…"

Hera had cast an illusion, then. And Cameo had thought she was saving him. Him, a man she hadn't even remembered at the time.

How could he let her go?

Lazarus…king…butterflies.

Butterflies had always been drawn to him. Why? Because like was drawn to like? Was he… Could he be…

Caterpillars transformed into butterflies when they entered a chrysalis.

Hydra, his ancestor, could not be killed. Typhon could not be killed. *Chrysalis…* As a spirit, Lazarus had passed through a portal meant for mortals. Because of the pupa—or forming chrysalis? Because it had caused his physical body to change…to regenerate?

Because it strengthened him rather than weakened?

Chrysalis… The butterfly could not escape without fighting free. Could he fight his way free? Would he be stronger if—when—he emerged?

His father hadn't fought his way out of his chrysalis. But then, his father had hated his μονομανία. He'd had no reason to fight. Lazarus loved his sunshine. And love trumped hate every time.

Lazarus…king…butterflies.

What if he could help Cameo with the pupa?

What if he doomed her?

No time to debate. Her breaths were coming faster now, were only growing shallower. Neither of them had any other options. Hera looked to be strengthening, the color returning to her cheeks. At the same time, the illusion of Typhon began to fade, just like the illusion around the apple had faded.

With a grunt, Lazarus used the last of his strength

to unsheathe a dagger and slice his wrist. He placed the wound over Cameo's, letting his pupa and blood pour into her.

His gaze remained locked on her—no movement, no pulse—as the pupa continued to grow and spread through him…no! Not yet! He had to know if she survived. Had to see her smile one last time. But the substance stabbed through his eyes, blinding him…then finally entered the chambers of his heart, leaving him aware of the world, but completely incapacitated.

30

"Every end heralds a new beginning. Never waste yours."

~~*How Boys Become Men*~~
—*The Darkest Promise*
Subtitle: The Story of Lazarus and His Cameo

Memories deluged Cameo, overtaking her completely. She lived in those memories, the rest of the world forgotten. She remembered every time she'd ever smiled or laughed.

The time Torin told her, "If Disease spread Ebola rather than the dreaded man-cold, people would have a chance at survival!"

When Maddox said, "You hit like a bitch. If bitches hit like Mack trucks."

When Kane had teasingly said, "The fact that Misery and Disaster couldn't make a relationship work? One of life's greatest mysteries."

She remembered the times she'd felt valued. When Sabin and Strider presented her with the heads of her torturers. When Amun took a bullet meant for her. When Lucien, Gideon and Reyes cooked a Thanksgiving meal, just because she'd mentioned wanting to spend the holiday like a normal person. When Paris and Aeron showed up at an immortal bar after she'd agreed to meet a shifter for a "night of fun you'll never forget." The shifter had run away after only ten minutes in her company, but her boys had stayed behind to dance with her. And later kicked the shifter's ass, of course.

Those warriors loved her without exception. And yet she'd allowed Misery to wipe her mind of each and every instance. Again and again he'd preyed on her fear of knowing—and losing—true happiness. He'd tricked her. Actually, she'd tricked herself. She hadn't let herself believe good things could happen to her. She'd expected the worst, and she'd gotten it.

She had created her own misery. Had welcomed her own destruction. Had cast her own emotional illusions, believing in them until they became her reality.

Worst of all, she'd given up her memories of Lazarus because she hadn't believed a happily-ever-after was possible.

Lazarus! He'd played in the mud with her. Teased her, and protected her. He'd given her orgasm after orgasm, held her close and loved her when she was unlovable.

He'd…stabbed her.

Yes. Yes, he had. But only because Cameo had leaped between him and Hera. Hera, who'd nearly stabbed *him*.

Though Cameo had had no memory of Lazarus at the time, she'd remained highly attuned to him, aware of his every movement. Her body had ached, as if recalling his touch and only wanting more. The desire to stay with him had plagued her. He'd looked to be in great pain with every move he made, but even still, he'd kept moving through the temple, had kept fighting the goddess. Cameo had desperately wanted to ease him, to help and protect him.

Had she retained her memory, she would have wanted the same things, only at a much more intense level.

Oh, yes. She had created her own misery.

Now Lazarus was…she frowned. Where was he? Last thing she remembered, he'd been crouched beside her. He'd slashed his wrist and—

He'd slashed his wrist! Her stomach twisted into a thousand knots. He'd slashed his wrist as crystals grew over his flesh, no longer content to stay underneath the surface of his skin.

What if he was dead? What if *she* was dead and he lived, trapped? What if—

Nope. No more depressing thoughts without any gleam of hope. Whatever the circumstances, there was a solution.

"—hell happened?"

The voice cut into her awareness. Hades. Had she traveled to the underworld?

"Hera can siphon abilities. She stole from Typhon and then Lazarus and used his power to cast an illusion." Rathbone's voice now. "Made Cameo think Lazarus was about to take a blow."

Another illusion. Well, Cameo couldn't bring herself to regret her actions. The Paring Rod had done as its name implied, paring the demon from her spirit. The cut had been clean, and the spiritual wound cauterized by Lazarus. By her love for him, and his love for her.

Misery hadn't entered the box, however. The box had tried to suck him inside—they'd both felt its pull—but the demon had met with a block and bounced free.

Now he roamed Hera's realm. Unless he'd found a way out?

"Where is Hera now?" William the Ever Randy demanded.

"She escaped upon your arrival," Rathbone grated.

"So she lives." Relief vibrated from Hades. "She is possessed by hundreds of demons. The moment she dies, they'll be released. We must proceed with caution or Lucifer will use her and her fiends to his advantage."

Enough chitchat about Hera. Tell me about Lazarus!

He'd given Cameo some of his blood. Her body had begun to heal. She owed him her life.

Cameo fought her way through the mire of her thoughts. Consciousness beckoned…she fought harder… there!

With a gasp, she sat up and blinked. Her gaze found the man she loved, and alarm choked her. He crouched beside her, his hand outstretched. Pupa mixed with crystals covered him from head to toe, molding to his body. Two butterflies perched on his head.

"Lazarus." She scrambled to her knees and frantically patted his cheek. "I'm alive, not dead. Come back to me. Please."

No reaction. Underneath the glistening crystals, she could see the outline of his beautiful face. His eyes stared at nothing. His chest never rose or lowered with breath.

Unacceptable!

A strong, comforting hand squeezed her shoulder. "I'm sorry, sweet. Let's get you home."

"No." She batted William away. She could feel the lure of true happiness for the first time in centuries, but a familiar grief tried to lock her in a bear trap, clamping metal spikes around her heart. Again—unacceptable. "I'm not leaving without Lazarus."

She would cut and hack at the crystal tomb until she reached him!

"Listen to her." Rathbone rubbed his healing jaw. Cameo had accidentally broken it while fighting to escape. "She means what she says."

"Lazarus…or what remains of him…can go with us," William said. Pity coated every word.

"Yes," she said, and nodded. "Yes." Her friends would help her. "Take us home."

Days passed. Lazarus remained trapped inside the chrysalis, in a crouched position on the floor of her bedroom, and Cameo remained nearby. Always nearby. She'd left her room only once and only to give Torin the apple—box—for safekeeping.

"I need you, Lazarus." She paced in front of him. "Break free."

The day of his arrival, she'd grabbed an ice pick, intending to chisel him out, but Keeley had burst into the room, shouting, "Don't you dare! Cut a butterfly from his chrysalis, and he'll be forever weakened. Lazarus will not thank you for weakness. Make him work for it, and he will be stronger."

The Red Queen merely confirmed what Lazarus had once told her.

Even still, she'd replied, "He's not a butterfly." Her mind had continued to race as butterflies had swarmed the fortress, perching on Lazarus, nearly covering him completely, as if to protect him.

"He is," Keeley had said. "Guess what? I found his info on my corkboard." Corkboard—what she called her millennia-old brain. "He's the son of Typhon, the last living king of butterflies. Meaning he is the king of butterflies."

"Uh, there's no way that's true." Cameo had received her first look at the Monster inside Hera's temple. To be honest, "monster" was an insult to monsters. "Typhon wasn't delicate. Or tiny. Or winged. Nor was—is—Lazarus."

Keeley had shaken her fists at the sky. "Why does everyone only rely on their own experiences and not believe my firsthand account? Look. I knew Typhon. He was a horrid male. His great-however-many-other-greats grandmother was Hydra, and Hydra had a secret affair with the king of the Lepidoptera—warriors without equal. They branded every soldier, weapon and piece of armor with the mark of the butterfly. A symbol of rebirth, since they always came back from the dead."

But... "If they're able to come back from the dead, where are they now?"

"Perhaps they weren't strong enough to break free of the chrysalis? Typhon wasn't. I mean, he isn't. He's still trapped. And if he hated his mate, well, hate is a drain, not a strength. True strength comes from love."

Good point.

And she wasn't done. "I questioned William and Hades about Hera's secret realm, and discovered the Monster is there. His chrysalis is infected, probably because of the hatred in his heart. It oozes poison."

Oozes. Something in the realm had oozed all right.

The tar-covered tree thing that had helped Lazarus escape the homicidal vines. Was the tree his father, the chrysalis hidden underneath the ooze? Perhaps his dad wasn't all bad?

Never mind. Rapist. All bad.

"A chrysalis isn't made of crystal," Cameo had said.

"No. Not for insects. For immortals like Lazarus, they are made of pupa *and* crystal. Anyway, gotta jet. There's a *Psych* marathon I'm *not* missing. I'm learning to be a detective. Gonna solve me some mysteries." Keeley had skipped toward the bedroom door before pausing and glancing over her shoulder. "Parting advice from the Red Queen. You need to give Lazarus a reason to fight his way free. Well, a reason to fight harder." She wiggled her brows. "Harder. Get it?" Then she was gone.

Cameo made a pallet on the floor, directly in front of Lazarus, and through her shirt she rubbed the spot on her chest—the place the Paring Rod had pierced her. A thin line marked the center of her sternum. A scar... what looked to be wings branching from both sides.

Another butterfly, she thought with a smile. An actual smile she wouldn't be made to regret.

"Zeus and the rest of the Greeks escaped Tartarus," she told Lazarus. "They've joined Lucifer in the war with Hades and their forces grow stronger by the day. Hera has been spotted in the third heaven, hiding among the Sent Ones. I need you here, fighting by my side. Lucien nearly died in the last battle, and Maddox has yet to recover from his newest set of wounds."

Nothing. No reaction.

"Did you ever meet Atlas and Nike? They're the Greek and Titan god and goddess of Strength. They're married now, and they've allied with Hades. They convinced him to agree to the mother of all battles, set to take place in one week. I'm going to be there, in the midst of the fray. Do you really want me going without you?"

Still nothing.

Her nails dug into her upper thighs. Not giving up. *Never* giving up.

"I've stolen the devotion of your pets. They fly outside my balcony, and I give them reports about your condition. You never told me the little buggers could speak eleven different languages but had chosen to speak Typhonish, the only one I didn't know, simply to irritate me."

Annnd nothing.

All right. Time to play hardball. Literally.

Keeley thought he needed to fight harder. Or maybe Cameo needed to make *him* harder. Love wasn't just stronger than hate; it was stronger than *anything*. And Lazarus's desire for her was an extension of his love.

"The butterfly tattoo on my back is gone. But I have a scar in need of kissing." Cameo tore her shirt over her head, ripped the center clasp of her bra and shimmied out of her pants and underwear, leaving her totally and completely bare. Cool air wafted over her as she leaned back, anchoring her weight on her elbows, and offered Lazarus a full frontal view.

"See?" She traced her fingertips over her sternum. "What do you think?"

Her heart raced as she waited. Hoped, prayed. But one minute bled into another and nothing happened.

She stretched out atop the pallet. The covers smelled of Lazarus, of sweet chocolate and heady champagne.

"This is what you're missing." A husky note had entered her voice. "Every part of me misses every part of you. I need your kiss…your touch…your hard and fast possession." She cupped her breasts, plucked at her nipples. Pleasure burned through her, making her shiver. "Bet I can make myself come without you…but it won't be nearly as fun."

She spread her legs, giving him a look at the heart of her desire. How swollen with need she was. How wet. "I need a man. How long should I wait for you before I turn to another, hmm? Maybe I'll—"

The chrysalis shattered, shards of crystallized pupa flying in every direction. Lazarus remained crouched. A faint outline of wings rose above his shoulders, and seemed to be made entirely of…lightning?

Were they an illusion? Or real?

She gasped, her gaze welded to his. His eyes were… changed. They were dark, but now his irises appeared to be rimmed by the pupa he'd shed, and his skin glistened as if he'd been dipped in diamond dust. Or played motorboat with a stripper.

"You did it!" she cried. "You broke free!"

His hands were balled, his chest rising and falling quickly. "So I did. And just so you know, you will *never* turn to another."

At the sound of his low, sexy timbre—nothing but a predatory growl—undiluted joy burst inside Cameo. "I should have gotten naked and threatened to seduce someone else days ago." A laugh escaped her then.

He sucked in a breath. "That is the laugh I've dreamed of hearing, but it's better in reality, *far better* than anything I'd imagined. Your laughter is magic. A spell of enchantment. An incantation meant to entice, lure and seduce, and if I hadn't loved you already, I would have fallen right then."

She quieted, suddenly caught up in a maelstrom of sensations. Tingling, heat, aches and needs, so many needs. He crawled across the pallet and hovered over her, his palms braced at her temples. They stared at each other for a long while, soaking up the moment.

They had a future.

He lowered his head and kissed her. His soft lips tasted her—and then they devoured her. She traced her hands over his back, and though she didn't feel the wings, she knew they were there. Electric currents rushed up her arms.

By the time he lifted his head, they were both out of breath and panting.

"I love you more than I can ever articulate, sunshine. You are my light on the darkest of days. To me, you are first. You will always be first. Nothing and no one will ever come before you."

"I love you, too. You are first…though in the spirit of full disclosure, you are tied with your penis."

He barked out a laugh. "Is this my sweet Cameo without a hint of misery?"

"It is indeed. But you may call me Queen Cameo," she corrected with a smile. "Apparently you are king of the butterflies, and as your woman, I claim half of your possessions. Starting with this…" She cupped his shaft, and he hissed in a breath. "Mmm, your love for me is growing."

He nipped at her bottom lip. "We are going to have a glorious life together. That is a command…and a promise."

"We'll be happy," she said, and nipped his lip right back.

"Happy," he confirmed. "And, sunshine? I have a feeling my love for you will grow every morning, afternoon and evening."

She chuckled. "Yay, me!"

He swooped down to claim another kiss and Cameo lost herself in the promise of an eternity ever after.

* * * * *

Lords of the Underworld

INSIDER'S GUIDE

Lords of the Underworld

TIMELINE

THE DARKEST FIRE,
ebook prequel

*   When the goddess of Oppression dies, Hera, the queen of the Greeks, uses her bones to create dimOuniak, a small box she fills with demons. Also trapped inside is a being known as the Morning Star.

*   Zeus, king of the Greeks and husband to Hera, steals dimOuniak and orders an immortal soldier named Pandora to guard it.

*   dimOuniak becomes known as Pandora's box, and it is stolen by thirteen immortal warriors—Sabin, Lucien, Maddox, Baden, Strider, Torin, Gideon, Kane, Reyes, Aeron, Paris, Amun and Cameo. They are betrayed by their friend Galen, who tells Zeus of their plans. Before they can be stopped, the box is opened and the demons are unleashed. No one knows what happens to the Morning Star.

* As punishment, the warriors responsible are paired with the demons. Maddox, new keeper of Violence, becomes crazed and slays Pandora. In turn, he is cursed to die every night only to awaken the next morning knowing he has to die again.

* The warriors are kicked out of Mount Olympus and forced to live among mortals, where they become known as the Lords of the Underworld. They settle in ancient Greece.

* Rhea, queen of the Titans and new keeper of Strife, escapes Tartarus—a prison for immortals. She allies with Galen, new keeper of False Hope and Jealousy. They recruit an army of human soldiers known as Hunters and task them with killing the Lords.

* Baden, new keeper of Distrust, is beheaded. In their grief, the Lords split into two factions, one moving to Budapest, the other traveling the world to destroy Hunters.

* Torin, new keeper of Disease, accidentally unleashes the Black Plague in ancient Greece.

THE DARKEST NIGHT,
story of Maddox

*   Centuries ago, twelve immortal warriors stole and opened Pandora's box. Those warriors eventually split into two groups: the Budapest faction and the New York faction. The group in Budapest wants peace. The group in New York continues to war with Hunters, a cult of humans determined to slaughter all immortals.

*   Meanwhile, Titan gods escape Tartarus and take over Mount Olympus, imprisoning the Greek gods.

*   In the human world, Maddox, keeper of Violence, is part of the Budapest faction. He has been cursed to die every night, only to awaken the next morning knowing he has to die again.

*   He meets a human named Ashlyn Darrow. She possesses the ability to hear any conversa-

tion that has ever taken place in any location she's standing.

*   As Maddox battles his attraction to the girl, Aeron, the keeper of Wrath and also a member of the Budapest faction, is ordered by Cronus, king of the Titans, to kill a human named Danika Ford and all her family. He isn't told why.

*   Through love and sacrifice, Ashlyn breaks Maddox's curse. She becomes pregnant with twins.

*   Aeron descends into madness as he's overcome by a mystical desire to kill Danika. His friends are forced to lock him in the dungeon.

*   The New York faction follows Hunters to Budapest, and the twelve demon-possessed warriors are reunited at long last.

THE DARKEST KISS,
story of Lucien

* Lucien, keeper of Death, meets Anya, goddess of Anarchy, at a nightclub. They are total opposites. He is by the book. She is chaos. He is scarred. She is flawless. Though they crave each other more than breath, Cronus orders Lucien to kill Anya, or suffer. The chase begins.

* Paris, keeper of Promiscuity, is captured by Hunters. He meets Sienna Blackstone, a Hunter spy and the only woman he can bed more than once. He doesn't know why. Determined to win her over, Paris escapes with her—but along the way she is killed by her own people. Paris is devastated.

* Aeron breaks free of the dungeon, determined to slay Danika.

*   The Lords learn about four ancient artifacts with the power to lead them to Pandora's box. They've been told the box is a weapon capable of killing them all in one fell swoop—but it might also be the only key to their salvation.

*   The Cage of Compulsion, one of the four artifacts, is found, guarded by William the Ever Randy, the greatest warrior of all time—just ask him.

*   Working together, Lucien and Anya manage to defeat him and steal the cage. They fall in lust…and in love. The greatest love story of all time—just ask *her*. Lucien knows he cannot kill his woman. He would rather die.

*   To free Lucien from Cronus's command, Anya gives the king of Titans her most prized possession. An object known as the All-Key.

*   Aeron ends up in hell, where he meets a demon girl named Legion.

THE DARKEST PLEASURE,
story of Reyes

*   Reyes, keeper of Pain, searches for human Danika Ford, desperate to protect her from Aeron's bloodlust. From the moment Reyes first spotted her, he's been attracted to her.

*   His desperation only grows when Aeron and Legion are rescued from hell and brought back to the Lords' home in Budapest.

*   The Lords learn that Galen, keeper of Jealousy and False Hope—the male who betrayed them in the heavens, who suggested they steal Pandora's box, only to inform Cronus of their plans—is the leader of the Hunters.

*   Paris receives a boon from Cronus and, rather than bring Sienna back to life, he uses it to free Aeron from his bloodlust.

*   Hunters want to use Danika to destroy the Lords. But she is falling in love with Reyes, same as he's falling in love with her. When he saves her life, he discovers she is the second artifact needed to find the box. She is the All-Seeing Eye.

*   Danika's friend Gillian Shaw—also known as Gilly Bradshaw—is a homeless teenager who moves to Budapest and strikes up a friendship with William.

THE DARKEST WHISPER,
story of Sabin

*   The Lords free an immortal Harpy named Gwendolyn Skyhawk—aka Gwen the Timid—from a Hunter prison.

*   Sabin, keeper of Doubt, is fascinated by Gwen, but places battle before desire, and he decides to use her against his enemies.

*   Aeron discovers an invisible being is spying on him.

*   Paris thinks he sees Sienna—who is dead.

*   Hunters capture Gideon, keeper of Lies, and cut off his hands.

*   Gwen learns that Galen is her father and, when the time comes, she frees him rather than kills him.

*   Sabin, who has always abhorred weakness of any kind, lets Galen go, his love for Gwen greater than anything else.

THE DARKEST PASSION,
story of Aeron

* Olivia, a Sent One—also known as demon assassins—is ordered to kill Aeron for crimes of evil he committed. Thinking she might love him, she chooses to give up her wings for a chance to save him instead.

* Galen successfully places the demon of Distrust in the body of his right-hand woman, Fox.

* Legion makes a deal with Lucifer to become human, hoping to win Aeron's heart.

* Aeron rejects her gently, for he is falling in love with Olivia.

* The Lords capture an immortal named Scarlet, the keeper of Nightmares. She has a secret agenda toward Gideon.

*   Olivia steals the third artifact—the Cloak of Invisibility—from Galen.

*   In an effort to help Aeron, Legion decides to kill Galen. She gives the leader of the Hunters her virginity and strikes—only to fail. She escapes.

*   Aeron is beheaded and freed from Wrath. Thanks to the leader of the Sent Ones, he is given a new body, so he and Olivia can be together forever.

*   Cronus successfully bonds the demon Wrath to the spirit of Sienna, making her immortal and tangible to the rest of the world.

THE DARKEST LIE,
story of Gideon

* Scarlet believes she shares a secret past with Gideon. She thinks they got married while she was imprisoned in Tartarus and that they had a child together—a child they named Steal, who later died. Gideon remembers none of this and wonders if someone stole his memories.

* Amun, the keeper of Secrets, Aeron and William journey to hell to save Legion, who has been captured. She is being tortured in the worst of ways.

* The rest of the Lords take the three artifacts they've acquired and split up, hoping to prevent other immortals from stealing their property.

* Strider, keeper of Defeat, kidnaps Haidee, an immortal Hunter who helped kill Baden. He hates

her and wants to kill her, but can't bring himself to render the final strike.

*   Legion is rescued from hell, and in the process Amun is infected by a horde of new demons.

*   Gideon and Scarlet work together and learn the truth about their past, but in the end, they decide the past doesn't matter. Only the future. They have fallen in love.

THE DARKEST SECRET,
story of Amun

* Amun and Haidee enter hell to rid Amun of the horde of new demons now living inside him. He is intrigued by this woman who should be his enemy; somehow, she is the only one who can quiet the evil whispers in his head.

* Strider, William and Paris go on vacation. Kaia, a Harpy as well as Gwen's sister, joins them, hoping to seduce Strider. She has realized he is her fated consort, meant to be hers forever.

* Amun meets the Four Horsemen of the Apocalypse, William's children.

* Amun finds himself falling for Haidee, despite her past actions against Baden. Haidee, too, finds herself falling for Amun, a warrior she should despise.

* Haidee is killed, but she reanimates because she is possessed by the demon of Hate. A fact no one knew.

* Only when Haidee and Amun give in to their feelings for each other is Love able to overcome Hate, allowing the pair to live happily-ever-after.

THE DARKEST SURRENDER,
story of Strider

*   A new Harpy Games kicks off, a type of Olympics for immortals. Kaia the Disappointment forms a team with her sisters, determined to win. The prize is the fourth and final artifact needed to find Pandora's box: the Paring Rod.

*   The Moirai, keepers of Fate, tell Kane, the keeper of Disaster, that he will start an apocalypse.

*   William kills Gilly's parents as punishment for abusing her.

*   Kane is captured and transported to hell, where he is tortured by demons.

*   Despite his determination to resist Kaia, Strider falls for the feisty Harpy and agrees to be her consort during the games.

* Strider kills Lazarus the Cruel and Unusual, the consort of Juliette the Eradicator, to gain possession of the fourth artifact, the Paring Rod.

THE DARKEST SEDUCTION,
story of Paris

* Paris hunts for Sienna, desperate to save the only woman he can bed more than once.

* Viola, goddess of the Afterlife and keeper of Narcissism, is taken to Budapest to help the Lords.

* William and Paris find Sienna, the new keeper of Wrath. Cronus has locked her away.

* Galen kidnaps a pregnant Ashlyn in order to trade her for the artifacts.

* Kane is captured and tortured by the Four Horsemen.

* Legion, who has not recovered from her trauma in hell, gives herself to Galen in order to save Ashlyn.

* Ashlyn gives birth to twins, Urban and Ever.

* Sienna kills Cronus and becomes queen of the Titans.

* Josephina, a blood slave to the Fae royal family, rescues Kane from torture.

* Paris falls in love—and in like—with Sienna, just as she falls in love and like with him.

THE DARKEST CRAVING,
story of Kane

*   Cameo and Viola vanish after touching the Paring Rod.

*   Cameo meets Lazarus in a spirit realm. She is intrigued—and irritated—by him.

*   Kane is supposed to marry Josephina's sister, a woman who has abused Josephina all her life, but he can't do it. He's too attracted to Josephina and insists on wedding her instead.

*   Torin inadvertently infects a human girl named Mari before the two are imprisoned in another realm.

*   Josephina defeats her father and becomes queen of the Fae.

*   William's daughter White is beheaded.
*   Josephina is killed in her husband's place, but thanks to her child, she is brought back to life.

THE DARKEST TOUCH,
story of Torin

* Torin is locked up in an immortal prison. He accidentally kills Mari, the only friend of Keeley the Red Queen, and Keeley vows to punish him.

* When Torin accidentally touches Keeley, she sickens like the humans and everyone else he's ever touched. However, unlike the others, she heals. He is overjoyed—and so attracted to her, he can't get her out of his mind.

* Cameo and Lazarus arrive in Lazarus's spirit-kingdom, though Lazarus manages to convince her they are in enemy territory and she must rely on him to save her.

* Lucifer the Destroyer kidnaps Cameo, Baden, Cronus and Rhea.

* Keeley shows the Lords how to use the four artifacts.

* Baden and Pandora are given serpentine wreaths, making them tangible once again but also slaves to Hades, one of the nine kings of the underworld.

* Keeley and Torin rescue Baden and Cameo from Lucifer, and the two agree to help Hades win his war with Lucifer.

* Torin proposes to Keeley, and she accepts.

THE DARKEST TORMENT,
story of Baden

* Baden learns he's bound to Hades and, to survive, he must do as the king of the underworld orders.

* Following those orders, Baden kidnaps Katarina Joelle, a famed dog trainer, from her wedding in order to force her new husband to part with a golden coin. The former keeper of Distrust is drawn to the human woman and begins to crave her touch, even though skin-to-skin contact pains him.

* Katarina is drawn to Baden, as well. She hates her husband. He threatened to kill her beloved dogs if she refused him.

* During this time, Gillian Shaw sickens, and

William the Ever Randy whisks her away to a secret location.

* Lucifer—son to Hades, and enemy number one—sends an assassin to destroy the Lords' Budapest fortress, hoping to kill the warriors before they can help Hades destroy *him*.

* To save her life, Gillian marries an immortal prince named Puck, the keeper of Indifference, and she herself becomes immortal.

* As Katarina learns to trust and love Baden, she is inadvertently bound to a pack of hellhounds—immortal dogs.

* Hades adopts Baden as his son, meaning Baden is no longer a slave. Katarina marries Baden and becomes Hades's daughter-in-law.

* They all live happily-ever-after...until the next book...

GLOSSARY OF TERMS
AND PLAYERS

Aeron—Lord of the Underworld; former keeper of Wrath; husband to Olivia.

Alexander—aka Alex; Cameo's former boyfriend.

All-Seeing Eye—Godly artifact with the power to see into heaven and hell; aka Danika Ford.

Amun—Lord of the Underworld; keeper of Secrets; husband to Haidee.

Anya—(minor) goddess of Anarchy; engaged to Lucien.

Ashlyn Darrow—human female with supernatural ability to listen to past conversations; wife to Maddox; mother of Urban and Ever.

Axel—Sent One with a secret; resembles William the Ever Randy.

Baden—Lord of the Underworld; former keeper of Distrust; husband to Katarina.

Bianka Skyhawk—Harpy; sister of Gwen, Kaia and Taliyah.

Bjorn—Sent One.

Brochan—fallen Sent One; brother of McCadden.

Cage of Compulsion—Godly artifact with the power to enslave anyone trapped inside.

Cameo—Lord of the Underworld; keeper of the demon Misery.

Cameron—keeper of Obsession; brother to Winter.

Cloak of Invisibility—Godly artifact with the power to shield its wearer from prying eyes.

Cronus—former king of the Titans; former keeper of Greed; husband to Rhea.

Danika Ford—human female; wife to Reyes; known as the All-Seeing Eye.

dimOuniak—Pandora's box.

Downfall—nightclub for immortals owned by Thane, Bjorn and Xerxes.

Echidna—most feared Gorgon ever to live; mother of Lazarus.

Elin—Phoenix/human hybrid; mate to Thane.

Ever—daughter to Maddox and Ashlyn; sister to Urban.

Fae—race of immortals descended from Titans.

Flashing—transporting oneself with just a thought.

Galen—Lord of the Underworld; keeper of Jealousy and False Hope.

Gideon—Lord of the Underworld; keeper of Lies.

Gillian Shaw—aka Gilly Bradshaw; human female recently made immortal; wife to Puck.

Greeks—former rulers of Olympus.

Gwen Skyhawk—Harpy; consort of Sabin; daughter of Galen; sister to Kaia, Bianka and Taliyah.

Hades—one of the nine kings of the underworld.

Haidee Alexander—former Hunter; keeper of Love; mated to Amun.

Hera—queen of the Greeks; wife to Zeus.

Hilda—Sphinx; guard of the Realm of the Skulls.

Hunters—mortal enemies of the Lords of the Underworld; disbanded.

Josephina Aisling—queen of the Fae; wife to Kane.

Juliette Eagleshield—aka the Eradicator; Harpy; self-appointed consort of Lazarus.

Kadence—the goddess of Oppression; deceased yet in spirit form.

Kaia Skyhawk—part Harpy, part Phoenix; sister of Gwen, Taliyah and Bianka; consort of Strider.

Kane—Lord of the Underworld; keeper of Disaster; husband to Josephina.

Katarina Joelle—formerly human; alpha of the hellhounds; consort of Baden.

Keeleycael—a Curator; the Red Queen; engaged to Torin.

Lazarus (the Cruel and Unusual)—an immortal warrior; only son of Typhon and Echidna.

Legion—demon minion in a human body; adopted daughter of Aeron and Olivia; aka Honey.

Lords of the Underworld—exiled immortal warriors now hosting the demons once locked inside Pandora's box.

Lucien—coleader of the Lords of the Underworld; keeper of Death; engaged to Anya.

Lucifer—one of the nine kings of the underworld; son to Hades; brother to William.

Lysander—Elite Sent One; consort to Bianka.

Maddox—Lord of the Underworld; keeper of Violence; father to Urban and Ever; husband to Ashlyn.

McCadden—fallen Sent One; brother to Brochan.

Morning Star—thought to be hidden in Pandora's box; with it anything is possible.

Olivia—Sent One; mated to Aeron.

Pandora—immortal warrior; once guardian of dimOuniak (newly resurrected).

Pandora's box—aka dimOuniak; made of bones from the goddess of Oppression; now shaped as a small apple charm; once housed demon high lords.

Paring Rod—Godly artifact with ability to rend soul from body.

Paris—Lord of the Underworld; keeper of Promiscuity; husband to Sienna.

Phoenix—fire-thriving immortals descended from Greeks.

Puck the Undefeated—full name Púkinn Neale Brion Connacht the 4th; keeper of Indifference; prince of the Connacht clan in the desert realm of Amaranthia; husband to Gillian Shaw.

Rathbone—one of the kings of the underworld.

Reyes—Lord of the Underworld; keeper of Pain; husband to Danika.

Sabin—coleader of the Lords of the Underworld; keeper of Doubt; consort of Gwen.

Scarlet—keeper of Nightmares; wife of Gideon.

Sent Ones—winged warriors; demon assassins.

Sienna Blackstone—former Hunter; current keeper of Wrath; current ruler of Olympus; beloved of Paris.

Siobhan—goddess of Many Futures; cursed to live inside a magic mirror.

Strider—Lord of the Underworld; keeper of Defeat.

Taliyah Skyhawk—Harpy; sister of Gwen, Bianka and Kaia.

Tartarus—Greek god of Confinement; also the immortal prison on Mount Olympus.

Titans—rulers of Titania; children of fallen angels and humans.

Thane—Sent One; mate to Elin.

Torin—Lord of the Underworld; keeper of Disease; engaged to Keeleycael.

Typhon—father of Lazarus.

Urban—son of Maddox and Ashlyn; brother of Ever.

Viola—goddess of the Afterlife; keeper of Narcissism.

Winter—keeper of Selfishness; sister to Cameron.

William the Ever Randy—immortal warrior of questionable origins; aka the Panty Melter and William of the Dark.

Xerxes—Sent One.

Zeus—king of the Greeks; husband to Hera.

A CONVERSATION WITH GENA ABOUT THE DARKEST PROMISE

Q: Cameo plays host to Misery and yet she somehow manages to showcase a great sense of humor. (Good job!) She even made me laugh a time or twelve. How in the world were you able to do the impossible and make people smile while reading about Misery?

Gena: You just nailed my biggest challenge while writing this book. Not only did I have to overcome everything I'd set up in previous books—how Cameo was constantly flooded with sorrow thanks to her inner demon, how she couldn't smile or laugh, how she made others cry every time she spoke—I had to do it without creating the most depressing book of all time. Thankfully, I'd also established a pattern in those pre-

vious books. Each Lord of the Underworld has had to fight his inner demon, as well—with the help of his heroine. That meant I could use Lazarus to combat Cameo's misery and actually hit her with other emotions. Anger...lust. Even happiness. As soon as Lazarus realizes the power he has over his woman's emotions—shiver! Lazarus considers Cameo's happiness his job. Well, her happiness and her orgasms. And he's very good at his job.

Q: Cameo hates making people cry when she speaks. Why doesn't she rely on ASL like Amun, the keeper of Secrets? I know she mentions that she has a voice and she wants to use it, but why put herself through such misery—well, besides the demon?

Gena: Because Cameo is careful about when and where she speaks, she's able to use her words as a weapon. As a warrior through and through, she's all about weapons.

Q: Even though Misery wiped away Cameo's happy memories, readers know all about her past, having read scenes in previous Lords of the Underworld books. How were you able to balance what Cameo didn't know versus what other characters in the series remembered about her?

Gena: I had to figure out what Cameo's friends had seen/witnessed and how much they would be willing to tell her after her memory got wiped—they wouldn't want her to make the same mistakes, but they also wouldn't want to make her more miserable, remembering some of the trials she'd faced in order to get happy, even temporarily. I also had to figure out what information the demon would use to taunt her—what would make her the most miserable. Demons suck.

Q. Lazarus first appeared in Strider's book, *The Darkest Surrender*. Let's face it. He was villain-ish. What was it like taking a former villain and turning him into a hero?

Gena: I loved it! And what's really funny is the fact that yes, Lazarus was a bit of a villain in another book, but even though he's now a hero, he's darker and more menacing. Of course, he's had to build a new life for himself, forge a new path in the afterlife realms, kill or be killed (again), and he's realized what is most important to him: strength.

Q: Readers got to see Urban and Ever born into the Lords of the Underworld world. Now they are growing up right before our eyes. Is this fun for you as a writer or difficult?

Gena: Very fun! It's like watching my own children grow up. New milestones every day. In fact, I smiled every time the children stepped onto the pages. (Especially because I got to watch savage, brutal immortal warriors turn to mush in the presence of the children.)

Q: Let's talk research. How deeply do you study the different but connected mythologies in this series?

Gena: I like to read several versions of a particular myth, use the basics as a foundation, take a little of this, a little of that, then twist everything else to suit my particular needs. With Pandora's box, I decided to take the idea of a box filled with evil, and built my own mythology from there—blaming MEN for all the world's misery. (You're welcome.)

Q: The Lords of the Underworld series has a long cast of characters. How do you keep track of who's who in the immortal underworld?

Gena: Used to be, I simply remembered. Then, with more books under my belt, edits, revisions and more edits, I realized I'd forgotten key elements. You know, like killing off a certain character and then using him again. Oops! But my readers are awesome, and they let me know when I've contradicted a plotline, allowing me to fix the mistakes in upcoming books.

Q. With so many delicious heroes and heroines to choose from, we've got to know: who's next?

Gena: I originally planned to write Viola's story. I had an opportunity to sit down and brainstorm some amazing ideas with fellow authors Jill Monroe and Kresley Cole. (Those ladies crack me up!) But. After speaking with my amazing editor, we decided it was time to give readers closure for the Gillian/William/Puck story line. The book is titled The Darkest Warrior, *and it is one of the most emotionally gut-wrenching books I've ever written. With Gillian's past...and William's desire for her...and Puck—the keeper of Indifference—able to feel for the first time in centuries... Yeah. The story line got me right in the feels.*

*This conversation was inspired by an interview Gena did with *RT Book Reviews*.

Bonus Scene

This snippet takes place before
THE DARKEST TORMENT.

Hades had been called the Keeper of Flames, the Monster Other Monsters Feared, the Lord of Death, the Heartless Foe and many other things. He was all those things, and more. He didn't care about anything or anyone…except his children.

He threw open his bedroom door, nearly ripping the solid gold hinges from the frame. He stomped down the hall, his boots leaving cracks in the marble. Any soldier foolish enough to remain in the area would soon find the heart ripped out of his chest. Too bad, not sad.

Mystical blue fires blazed here and there with no distinguishable pattern; they were simply warnings for spirits and humans alike. *Approach my quarters without my permission and die horribly.* He stepped through each of the flames, welcoming the heat. While the infernos would agonize others, they only strengthened him.

When he reached the throne room, he dismissed the surrounding guards with a roared "Go! Now. While you still have legs."

The men scrambled out as fast as their feet would carry them. Those who had witnessed the repercussions of his temper would do anything to avoid his notice. Wise. Most days he could control the all-consuming rage that was so much a part of him. On very rare occasions, he…couldn't. Today was one of those rare occasions.

The only way to regain control was to purge. Meaning, he had to remove his own heart—or other people's heads. *Many* other people.

Care to guess which way I'm leaning?

Though a door never opened, he suddenly sensed another presence in the room. Someone had flashed here, moving from one place to another in only a blink, and that someone was behind him.

Someone. His son. William the Ever Randy. Also known as William of the Dark and the Panty Melter.

Lately William had radiated all kinds of crazy. He wanted a woman who wasn't destined to be with him.

No, she belonged with another man. Soon, William would learn the truth of this.

Hades turned. William reclined on Hades's throne, a deceptively casual pose.

"What are you doing here?" Hades asked. "Besides pouting."

"Needed a distraction. Came to see if you wanted help with Lucifer."

Lucifer, William's brother. The worst of the worst.

The slayer of innocents, and the father of lies. Pride and greed, the most dangerous commodities in this world or any other, drove him to do despicable things. His soul was now so black it was nothing but an abyss. The original Bermuda Triangle, where happiness vanished, never to be seen or heard from again.

The day Hades adopted him was the day his own life—a life forged in the gutters of inhumanity—had truly taken a turn for the worse. But he'd done it for his own pride and greed. Because he'd wanted a family. Sons to stand with him against any threat. Instead he'd helped create a *new* threat.

"I don't need your help," Hades said. "I don't need anything. But I'll accept your help. Lucifer has declared war against me."

"This isn't the first time," William reminded him.

"I know. But this time, we will war to the death."

"So? Kill him and be done with it."

There was no love lost between the brothers, and with good reason. Lucifer had often tortured the once-vulnerable William just for grins and giggles.

"There are…complications." Only the Morning Star could kill him, but it was supposedly locked inside Pandora's box, and Hades wasn't in possession of it. Wasn't even sure where to search. Every time he found it, it was somehow flashed to a new location.

"If you're going to help, you're going to have to snap out of this…" Hades waved a hand through the air. "This. Whatever this is. Stop thinking about the human girl. You need a beautiful, smart, bloodthirsty woman. Such a rarity these days, when so many feel they deserve a participation medal just for showing up, and

everyone cries about their overly sensitive feelings."
Shudder.

Taliyah, a Harpy Hades had thought he wanted, until
she'd stolen from him, had never cried about anything.
In fact, she had challenged him about *everything*.

"Someone you don't care about," he added. He'd had
to dismiss Taliyah before he actually wanted to dismiss her.

In past wars, his women had been used against him.
Either they had been captured and tortured for information, killed just to hurt him or paid to turn against him.

He was better off alone.

"Boo-hoo. My heart bleeds for your travesty. I weep
for your pain, blah, blah, blah. When the time comes,
you'll find a new woman. Multiple women."

Hades arched a brow in a show of derision. "*This*
from the male who's been waiting for the human for
two years." As William sucked in a breath, he nodded.
"You've been waiting—drooling—for her to turn eigh-
teen so you could pounce."

Those crystalline eyes narrowed to tiny slits, black
lashes fusing together. "That's different."

"How?"

"She's mine." William beat at his chest with a tightly
clenched fist. "Mine."

"And yet you haven't kept little Willy in your pants."

"Big Willy, thank you very much."

"So, what does that tell you?" Hades insisted.

"Tells me I'm a man with very particular needs."

"Or that you can, in fact, live without her."

Propelled by a blast of his own rage—rage so similar to Hades's own—William jumped to his feet, his

hands fisted. "You're one to talk, old man. You've never waited for anyone. You even have a harem!"

The harem. Right. He stroked his chin. Perhaps he should free the females he'd collected over the centuries. They had willingly signed on for active duty in his bed, happy to do whatever he desired whenever he desired, and he'd made sure to accept only the applicants he could easily dismiss, but he would hate to see one or all of them targeted.

On the other hand, he needed an outlet for his passions. The less sex he had, the more his rages won, and wars like this could last decades, even centuries.

Well. Sacrifices had to be made. He'd keep the harem in place.

I am such *a giver.*

"I'm not here to gossip about our romantic relationships," William announced, cutting into his thoughts. "I'm here to discuss Baden."

Baden. The former keeper of the demon of Distrust. Former, because he'd been beheaded, his spirit sent to another realm. But Hades had given him a pair of serpentine wreaths, making his body tangible once again…and unbeknownst to Baden, also making Hades his master.

Lost a lover, gained a soldier. Well. Life wasn't as bad as he'd assumed.

He buffed his nails against his shoulder. "I'm keeping him. End of discussion."

"He's changing," William said. "And not for the better."

"So?" he replied, mocking his son for the earlier dismissal of his problems.

Straight white teeth flashed in a scowl. "Either free

him before it's too late or use him. Just do *something* with him!"

Again Hades stroked his chin. He'd given Baden the wreaths as a favor to William. He'd owed the boy, and he always ~~sometimes~~ paid his debts. But Baden *couldn't* be freed without returning to the spirit realm. And with the war…

Now was the time to stockpile allies. Now *wasn't* the time to give someone the chance to align against him. And if Baden worked for him, all the other Lords of the Underworld would work for him. Including their very powerful mates.

Well. Decision made. "I'll use him."

William pushed out a heavy sigh. "That's exactly what I thought you'd say."

"Prepare him," he said. "I'll give you two days." Just enough time to figure out what, exactly, he would have Baden do for him. Pad his arsenal, perhaps, acquiring weapons used throughout the ages. Persuade others to aid him. Other royals, even. Slay the humans and immortals Lucifer would one day attempt to use to his advantage.

So many options!

Who knew? Maybe the war would be fought and won within a matter of weeks. *If* miracles really happened.

"I stopped having to obey your orders centuries ago, you know," William said.

Hades closed the distance, peering pointedly at his son. "You and I both know what will happen if Lucifer wins. The reign of chaos. Unimaginable atrocities committed. You and yours will never again be safe." And, because Hades was who he was, willing to manipulate *anyone* to get what he wanted, he added, "Gillian will never again be safe."

William glared at him, even while nodding. "I will prepare him."

"Exactly what I thought you'd say."

They clasped hands to shake goodbye, but William used the contact to yank him against the hard line of his body and pat him on the back. "If anything happens to Baden, I will hold you responsible. Because others will hold *me* responsible. Tit for tat."

Hades could carry the blame. Why not? He carried so many other things. The fate of the underworld. A past steeped in so much violence there was no part of him unscarred. Still, he said, "I will protect him. You have my word."

What William hadn't yet learned: ensure your opponent spelled out every aspect of his promise, otherwise there would be loopholes...loopholes that could be exploited. Not that Hades would ever exploit his son, but like anyone who'd suffered a wealth of betrayals over the centuries, he liked to keep his options open.

"Then I will help you destroy Lucifer," William said.

He nodded, even while thinking, *You would have, anyway, my son.*

They might argue and fight—with swords, daggers, whips and guns of every make and model—but at the end of the day, they had each other's back.

He hoped.

Bottom line. He had trust issues. He'd always had trust issues, and he always would. That violent past hadn't just shaped him—it had hardened him. There would be no changing him.

"Go now," he said, and severed contact.

Hades walked away before he broke one of his cardinal rules. No allowing emotion to lead decisions. Ever. But only then, as he passed through the door and the guards waiting for reentry into the throne room breathed a sigh of relief, did he realize the worst of his rage had abated. Because of a conversation.

Well, hell. Miracles really did happen.

He'd find out if this one stayed the course...

If you enjoyed Cameo and Lazarus's story,
don't miss the next sizzling tale in the
LORDS OF THE UNDERWORLD *series,*
featuring Gilly and Puck, keeper of Indifference!

THE DARKEST WARRIOR,
available soon from HQN Books.

Turn the page for a sneak peek!

Puck entered the first hotel he encountered. The employees gave him twice-overs as he purchased a room, and a few guests gave him the side-eye, but no one asked any questions. He dismissed the bellhop and took the stairs, stopping on every floor to ensure no exits were blocked.

In his room, he found a king-size bed with a white comforter, a desk, dresser, television and coffee table. He moved everything to a single corner and waited.

He didn't have to wait long.

Boom!

The hinges on the front door shattered, wood splintering. In the center of the chaos stood William of the Dark. Puck did a quick visual survey. William held a small gold band but had no discernible weapons. Of course, if he was anything like Puck, he didn't need them. His body was weapon enough.

Silence stretched between them as they took each other's measure. The red had faded from William's irises, and the blue returned, like a morning sky set aflame.

Did eye color matter to Gillian? Did she prefer—

Stop. Her preferences had no bearing on the situation.

"Tell me where Gillian is or I'll turn your testicles into tiny disco balls." William spoke at a normal volume, but menace laced every word.

Still cares for her, as I knew he would. Ice threatened to crack as resentment flared, and Indifference dug sharp claws into his mind. "She is safe. That is all you need to know right now."

One step, two, closing in… With a low, menacing war cry, William launched at Puck.

As they plummeted to the floor, William grabbed hold of Puck's wrist and anchored the gold band around it. Not a piece of jewelry, but not a shackle, either. Whatever it was, magic pulsed from it.

Impact. Air gusted from Puck's lungs as he absorbed the collision with the floor and the warrior.

Fast as lightning, William rose to his knees and whaled. Punch, punch, punch. Puck's brain rattled against skull, sharp pains shooting through his temples. As rage began to burn through him, Indifference clawing his mind harder, faster, he blocked the next blow.

Steady. Exercise strict control. Though the demon no longer had the power to weaken him, emotion could prove a deadly distraction.

Of course, William didn't hesitate to throw a punch with his free hand.

Puck caught this fist, too, and said, "Think this through. You can't hurt me without hurting Gillian."

"Wrong." William smiled for the first time, a cold,

calculating smile without any hint of amusement. "Did you think I'd do nothing but twiddle my thumbs after you bonded to her? Oh, no. I learned everything I could about you, *as well as* bonds. You were betrayed by your brother, your kingdom stolen. Ringing any bells? Oh, and I made you a gift." He motioned to the gold wrist cuff with a tilt of his chin.

Symbols had been carved into the metal. "Magic?" Puck asked.

"What you call magic, I call power. As the son of Hades, I have power—in spades. Now your pain will remain your own. And I know what you're thinking. *Wow, that Willy sure is the total package.* Well, you're right, but you're still going to die." Punch, punch. "I cannot be beaten."

Puck caught his fists once again and offered a cold smile of his own. "Despite your power, you cannot sever my bond to Gillian. It's alive and well, deep inside me, still tying my life to hers, and there's nothing you can do about it."

Fury exploded inside those ocean-water blues. "Don't worry." Wrenching free of Puck's hold, William punch, punch, punched again. "I'm not going to kill you, Pucker. Oh, no. You're going to suffer for *centuries*."

Puck withstood the newest round of hammering fists in order to work his legs between their bodies, grab the male by the waist and toss him overhead. Man met plaster. The entire wall cracked from ceiling to floor, bits and pieces raining down. Dust plumed the air.

Jumping to his feet, Puck felt warm blood dripping from his mouth. "Here's what is going to happen. You're going to raise an army and help me dethrone my brother and reclaim my kingdom. Afterward, I will use the shears of Ananke to sever my bond to Gillian. She will be free of me, once and for all." *And I will not miss her every day of my life.*

"I don't need an army. I *am* an army." Teeth bared, William stood and popped the bones in his neck. "Where is she? Did you bed her?"

"I have not." He told himself to shut up and say no more. But his lips parted and a single word escaped. "Yet."

William took another menacing step forward.

"Once we've dethroned my brother," Puck said, "I'll use the shears. *Then* Gillian will be yours." The promise tasted foul, but he refused to negate it. "Agree. Now."

"How about this? I'll steal the shears and sever the bond myself. Then I'll sever your twig and berries, and stuff the little trio down your throat. As an appetizer. Then, after all those centuries of suffering I mentioned, where I feed you different parts of yourself, I might grow sick and tired of hearing you scream and beg for mercy, so finally I'll consider killing you. *Then* I'll conquer your kingdom, just for grins and giggles."

Yawn. "Trust me when I say you won't find the shears without me." He'd taken extreme precautions in order to hide them. "So how about this? You agree to help me within the next five seconds, or I'll return to her and bed her for the first time. And second... third." A frisson of anticipation heated the very twig and berries William had mentioned. "Do you like the idea of her splayed over my bed, naked, her dark hair spilling over my pillow, her legs spread wide for me, and me alone?" *Because I do.*

He expected another explosion from William.

Instead, the male arched a dark brow and raked his

gaze over Puck from head to toe. "Are you sure she'll welcome you? Nice legs. Shave much?"

A growl rumbled low in his chest. "Why would I shave, when my wife loves to rub against me and use me for warmth? Four seconds."

Nostrils flared, William circled him. "Do you have a pedigree? Nah. You're a mutt, guaranteed. Do you keep your hooves off the bed or do you not care about dirtying the sheets?"

Head high. Shoulders back. "Sheets can be cleaned. My mind cannot. Oh, the things I want to do to my wife… Three."

Stiff as a board, William said, "Shall I turn around and let you sniff my ass?" He tsk-tsked. "If the bed is a rockin', don't come a knockin'—because you're probably under it, chewing on a shoe, *amirite*."

"Or giving my wife her next dozen orgasms. Two."

Though his nostrils flared, and a muscle jumped beneath William's eye, his tone remained casual as he said, "Be honest. Is that a furbaby in your pants, or are you just happy to see me?"

"That is all me, and I'll be giving every throbbing inch to my wife. One."

William huffed and puffed in time to the chirp of a cricket.

"Very well. I'll mark this first plan as unsuccessful and move on," Puck said. He would return to Amaranthia and proceed without William.

With Gillian at his side, Indifference would be unable to weaken him—maybe. Probably. He hadn't tested the theory yet. Either way, Puck might be able to pull this off. He had his outcast clan as backup, and especially Cameron and Winter.

The siblings were warriors to the core and had killed some of the biggest baddies in "mythology." But unless and until Cameron became obsessed with a mission, he was too easily distracted by his other obsessions. And Winter would betray *anyone* to appease her selfish nature.

They might do his cause more harm than good.

And these are the ones you left in charge of Gillian's care?

The sense of urgency returned and redoubled. Pressing his tongue to the roof of his mouth, he ignored the demon's newest roars. He moved toward the door, steps harried.

"What? No goodbye?" William asked, stepping into his path. "Perhaps I'll raise an army and help your *brother* defeat *you*."

Puck's body acted of its own accord, not waiting to receive permission from his mind. One second he intended to leave, the next he had William pressed against the wall, his fingers wrapped around the warrior's neck. The remaining plaster crumbled.

"Perhaps I'll kill you," he stated. Gillian would cry, but tears could be dried. Broken hearts could be comforted, even mended.

William kicked his outside leg up, up and hooked his ankle over Puck's wrist. Then he brought his leg down, hard. It happened in less than a blink, but Puck's thoughts rolled through his mind *faster*. He knew he had a choice. Release his opponent and emerge unscathed, or hold on and deal with a broken arm. Because of the wrist cuff, Gillian would not be hurt.

Finally. An easy decision to make. *I'll take option B.* Puck had to kneel, but so did William. The bone in his forearm snapped, and pain seared him. He welcomed it, even as he maintained his iron grip. Without pause, he used his free hand to grab a hunk of hair and press multiple razor blades against William's throat.

William laughed, the sound half-wild. "You want her, don't you, and think she wants you back? Well, too bad. You'll never have her. Bonds make couples think they desire each other, but *you* will always know her desire is forced. After all, what woman in her right mind would ever desire someone like you? Those horns..." He shuddered.

"Your mother *loved* my horns last night. Polished them up real nice."

Another wild laugh from William before he sobered and glared. "You think I wouldn't find out about your Oracles during my search for information? For some reason, I'm the key to your success. I don't know why, i don't know how, I only know you can't dethrone Sin without me. So, if you want your brother out of the way, you will swear an unbreakable blood oath to cut your tie to Gillian the moment I present you with the Connacht crown."

This was it. The moment Puck had been waiting for. The moment he'd schemed and fought for. He had only to agree.

He opened his mouth and, with a surprising amount of bite, said, "I'll agree to your terms, if you'll agree to mine. While we are in my home-realm, you will not touch Gillian." The statement registered in his mind, and he jolted. What he didn't do? Negate his demand.

"I'll touch her when and where I please," William snapped.

Puck unveiled another cold smile—a promise of pain. "Then we do not have a deal."

"Please. You won't walk away from vengeance against Sin. You won't abandon your people to a life of fear and torment."

"I can. I will. You forget who I am." He turned on his heel with every intention of walking away. Sometimes he despised Indifference; other times, he reveled in his ability to simply stop caring.

Today, he reveled. *Ice, ice, baby.*

"Fine," William snapped. "I've waited this long, and I can wait a little longer. I won't attempt to seduce her. If she attempts to seduce me, however…"

Teeth, grinding. Hands, fisting.

Feel nothing, want nothing.

Sirens sounded in the distance. Someone had heard the commotion and called the cops.

If he stuck around much longer, he and William would face arrest.

Puck raised his chin. "I accept your terms."

"When this is done," William continued, "you will use those shears." He reached out, plucked a razor from Puck's hair and made an incision in his own wrist. "I'll have your blood oath."

As soon as their blood mixed, as soon as the oath left his mouth, Puck would be forever bound, physically unable to renege.

No other way.

Using the same razor, Puck mimicked the warrior. Blood welled inside the wound as he clasped the other male's hand. "The day we defeat Sin…the day you give the Connacht crown to me and leave Amaranthia, never to return, never to strike out at me or my realm or my people in retaliation for deeds I committed…that is the day I use the shears of Ananke to sever my bond with Gillian Connacht—Shaw. This I vow."

There. It was done. His course had been set, his future decided.

Any other man would have experienced triumph. Puck nodded, confused by the hollow sensation in his chest.

William stared at him, silent, before nodding. "The deal is set," he grated. Growled, really. "Now let's go dethrone Sin and win back your kingdom."

THE DARKEST WARRIOR—
available soon wherever books are sold.

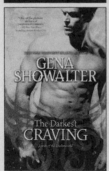